Edmund White teaches writing at C[...] the executive director for the New Y[...] Humanities. He is a frequent contrib[...] the *New York Times* Book Review, the [...] World and the *Village Voice*; and has w[...] non-fiction work, *States of Desire*. His l[...]st novel, *A Boy's Own Story*, is also published in Picador.

Also by Edmund White in Picador
A Boy's Own Story

Edmund White

Forgetting Elena
and
Nocturnes for the
King of Naples

 published by Pan Books

The author gratefully acknowledges the support of the Ingram Merrill Foundation during the writing of *Nocturnes for the King of Naples*, and parts of the book have appeared in the *Chicago Review*, *Christopher Street Magazine*, and *Shenandoah*.

Forgetting Elena first published 1973
© Edmund White 1973

Nocturnes for the King of Naples first published in Great Britain 1979 by André Deutsch Ltd
© Edmund White 1978

This Picador one-volume edition published 1984 by Pan Books Ltd,
Cavaye Place, London SW10 9PG
9 8 7 6 5 4 3 2 1
ISBN 0 330 28374 X
Photoset by Parker Typesetting Service, Leicester
Printed in Great Britain by Cox & Wyman Ltd, Reading

Contents

Forgetting Elena

To Ann and Alfred

1

I am the first person in the house to awaken, but I am unsure of the implications. I can't be absolutely certain, of course, whether everyone else is still sleeping, but the other two men in the room are breathing heavily and their hands are stretched out, curled or closed in positions that seem at once natural and improbable—in short, I doubt whether anyone would be clever enough to improvise such convincing gestures of repose. Moreover, their closed eyes are ringed with puffy circles and their lips are softly parted.

As for the occupants of the other rooms, I have no way of knowing whether they're asleep or even inside the house at all. No one is moving about, however; of that I can be quite confident, since the walls are thin and don't run all the way up to the ceiling and the cottage is so small that no part of it is more than thirty feet away from my bed.

I wonder what sort of impression I might make if I should go to the bathroom now? Perhaps no one would notice or care that I was the first to use it; perhaps people here are quite "natural" about bodily functions and find them humorous or, alternatively, too trivial to mention. On the other hand, a carefully regulated procedure may govern the whole matter, and the men of the house may take turns in the order of their height, popularity or seniority.

I simply must use the bathroom, no matter what the consequences may be. If I'm making a mistake, I strongly doubt whether anyone will reproach me directly. An air of permissiveness seems to be the rule, despite the fact that any impropriety is observed on all sides and endlessly joked about—lightly, casually and insistently. Last night, when Bob stood up after dinner, he walked around the room and, I imagine, felt uneasy about what he should do next. Summoning up his nerve, he said, to nobody in particular, "I guess I'll stroll down to the hotel and dance for a while." His statement drew no comments. He walked around the room once more and yawned in a distinctly forced way—not a real yawn at all but a rather poor copy. Then he left.

As soon as his footsteps could be heard no longer, the men still at table burst into laughter. "Dance? How absurd! No one ever goes to the hotel until the stroke of midnight. But Bob's always out of phase. For instance, I've told him again and again that the good people leave the hotel about two in the morning and return home. But he's so literal-minded that he now leaves *precisely* at two, regardless of the conditions, regardless of the social nuances. Naturally, he's been left out in the cold more than once, and then he becomes petulant and says to me, 'But you *told* me two.' I try to point out to him that he must scrutinize the mood of the crowd, keep his eye on important people, observe when *they* appear to be restless and likely to leave."

"That will never happen," said Herbert, who, though often silent, unmistakably rules the cottage and may quite possibly be an important official. He, more than any of the other men in the cottage, has mastered the casual, permissive air; when I asked him last night if I should clear the table, he put an unfriendly, utterly cheerless hand on my shoulder and said, "But my dear fellow, do as you like. Who keeps track of these things? Everyone follows his own impulse and, amazingly, the house runs along all by itself."

"That will never happen," Herbert was saying, "because Bob is quite lacking in the social instincts. But who needs them?" he asked, glancing at me. "He has other, more important qualities. I even find his ineptitude charming. Today I isolated a new mannerism in Bob: shall I call it the 'yawning syndrome'?"

Everyone urged Herbert to describe the syndrome. As the group leaned closer to the table (Herbert had judiciously lowered his voice), I served another round of coffee as silently as I could.

"The 'yawning syndrome' occurs whenever Bob feels ill-at-ease, uncertain about going or coming, or when he's aware of some tension he may have provoked in the company. At such times he *ululates*—no, perhaps that's an unkind word. His voice heavily aspirant, his jaw dropped, his eyes averted, he sounds one high note and then slides down a 'fifth,' if you will forgive the technicality of my expression. I recognized the syndrome this morning and have been amused exactly six times since to see—or rather, hear—it in action."

Billy, Herbert's houseboy, or perhaps secretary, valet or younger brother—I'm uncertain of his exact position and am careful to treat him respectfully, lest he turn out to be a person of some, even extraordinary, importance—Billy laughed convulsively and said, "You have swept that boy *back*."

Someone asked about this curious usage, and Billy explained quite cheerfully that "back" was the latest way of saying "thoroughly" at the hotel. "For instance, you might say, 'I'm going to clean this house *back*,' or, if you're dressing up, 'Tonight I'll give you fashion *back*.'"

I made a mental note of "back" and "give you fashion" and resolved to try them out when I'd be chatting with another newcomer (if that's what I am); once the expressions fitted easily into my conversation, I would employ them with the other people, all the while remembering to emphasize the words slightly, ironically, since I suspected that hotel slang was considered amusing only so long as its impurity was acknowledged.

I wasted little time over the words, however, before turning my attention to a more pressing question: was Billy's remark ("I'm going to clean this house *back*") a subtle hint sent indirectly from Herbert, or the group, to me, informing me of duties I had unwittingly neglected to perform? I dared not ask them point-blank, since I would only be told once again, "But my dear fellow, do as you like."

"Why do we put up with Bob?" someone asked Herbert laughingly. "He's so ridiculous—dancing at eleven and yawning. And have you noticed the clever way he imagines he's by-passed all the intricacies of fashion? Last night he announced that he intended to wear a green shirt and blue jeans all summer—that was to be his 'trademark' he told me with evident satisfaction. Not only is that a misguided and primitive notion of dress, a sort of packaging the product for easy recognition, but it also ignores any sort of a *look* we might want to achieve as a group. Not that I'm proposing we contrive little uniforms or anything, but there are times when one should accommodate one's companions, and give them at least a little sartorial nod. If he were to wear all blue, for instance, I might choose a blue scarf as an allusion to his costume."

"More importantly," Herbert said, "for Bob to persevere in green and blue shows no awareness of the change of weather or seasons. God knows I don't demand conformity in clothes, but an eccentricity, to be noticeable at all, must be a rare and calculated exception. Of course, he has a perfect right to wear whatever he chooses. We mustn't be petty." Then he looked at all of us and slowly pushed his chin forward, like a pianist embarking on a new phrase. "As to your question, 'Why do we put up with Bob?,' I should have thought that nothing would be easier to do. He's a charming young man. We are all equals now."

Herbert's closing words, delivered almost inaudibly, arose as unexpectedly out of the drift of his argument as a human arm out of the waves at night. The room was filled with the sound of scraping chairs as the men rose. Herbert crossed the room and ascended the three steps that led to the cottage's higher level, turned right and switched on a dim lamp behind the bamboo blinds. He sat on the edge of his cot and read a book.

The man who asked "Why do we put up with Bob?" was in disgrace; he left the house immediately but, I noticed, neglected to pull the door all the way shut behind him. Had the others seen this new impropriety, I wondered.

Someone put a record of Mozart's "Dissonant" string quartet and this comment on the state of affairs in our house was not wasted on me. I cleared the table and did the dishes. One of the older men volunteered to dry for me, but I assured him that I loved to do dishes because I found it so restful. I'm hoping he believed me. How I would enjoy having my own chore, a definite assignment—but I doubt if they'll give me one. As I slid the dishes into the suds, wiped them with a cloth, rinsed them and then examined them to make sure they were really clean before transferring them to the draining rack, my hands were shaking so much I was afraid of dropping something. Would they then ask me why I was so nervous? What would I say? Fortunately I completed the task without mishap. As I hung the towel beside the stove to dry, I hummed a song—the same song Herbert had hummed when he had done the dishes after lunch. I didn't know its title; I certainly hope it was as appropriate to eleven in the evening as it must have been to two-thirty in the afternoon!

"Why so cheerful?" one of the men asked me, touching my shoulder.

"It's so pleasant being here," I said, "away from everything. I don't know. There's just a nice atmosphere in the house right now, don't you think?"

I was apprehensive that he might misconstrue my remark to mean that at other times the atmosphere was less than pleasant, but he only nodded, smiled and glanced at the other men who were sitting on the long narrow sofa. They were all reading what appeared to be copies of the same book. At least the covers were identical: purple cloth with gold lettering on the binding. From the top of each volume dangled what I took to be a bookmark—a single strand of carved wooden beads attached to a red silk tassel.

The reading period continued for half an hour. I was quite at a loss as to how to occupy myself. Was I expected to read something as well, and if so, what? I didn't see an extra purple book lying around, and if I had I wouldn't by any means have assumed automatically that it had been provided for my study. As the minutes passed by, I sat on a high stool in the kitchen, sipped a cup of coffee and studied the white whorls ingrained in the pink plastic top of the counter, hoping by my reticence and downcast eyes to set whirling like a top the dizzying and powerful contradiction of being at one and the same time both the bored modern young man vacantly sipping his coffee *and* the earnest acolyte humbly waiting for admission at the gates of the temple. I think my ruse worked well.

Through the screen I saw Herbert lay his book aside and rise from his cot. He came to the head of the stairs and said, "Shouldn't we be getting ready for the hotel?"

"Really, so soon?" I asked, risking all. "What time is it?"

"Eleven-thirty," Herbert said, "and we all have to shower and shave still."

"Eleven-thirty!" I exclaimed. "The time really flies here."

Herbert smiled. "It does, doesn't it? I'm going to take my shower first, if nobody objects."

As he closed the bathroom door behind him, I gave a sigh of relief, reassured that I had won a smile from Herbert. My luck with him eased for a moment the tension in my shoulders. I saw that by lying low and observing closely and acting with tact and occasional verve, one could advance on the island—but I feared my energy would give out at any second now. I was very, very tired.

Herbert had left his book on the kitchen counter. I opened it and read: "When the prince descends from the boat, shining in white, everyone kneels. From then until dark the Old Code is in effect. All traditional forms are observed." In the margin Herbert had written, "Tedious but shrewd."

After all the other men in the house had finished using the bathroom, I took my turn. No sooner had I sat on the toilet, however, than someone knocked on the door and asked me if I would be long. "A while," I said. "Is it an emergency?"

"Oh, no. Take your time. I left a scarf in there, but I can get it later."

Despite his reassurances, my bowels froze, and I was unable to perform, if that is the word. The door to the bathroom was quite thin and couldn't be locked, and although the walls did run all the way to the ceiling in this one room, I felt exposed. Every cough, every footstep sounded like my own. I rose from my thankless task, tore off a sheet of toilet paper, crumpled it and flushed it. Completing the mock ceremony—sitting, straining, wiping—fitted in perfectly with my

15

resolve to go through all the proper motions, even if they were done in private and in vain. I wondered how many days it had been since my bowels had moved. Only one? Two? Three? I had no way of knowing.

After I had transferred my host of toilet things from my case to the washstand and to a table beside the sink, I became vaguely uneasy about having my own property scattered around in this room we all shared. What if I forgot something? Even as I applied lather to my face and changed razor blades, even as I was shaving, I kept repeating to myself, "Don't forget to put the deodorant back into the case, don't forget the hand-mirror, the blue and brown bottles, the pumice stone, the nail clipper, the cotton, the toothpaste and the toothbrush, or the cologne." After I named each article, my free hand (the left) flew out to touch it, to draw it a fraction of an inch closer to me and to the case where it must soon return. My eyes darted to my reflection. I shaved a stroke, then a floorboard squeaked outside the door and I reached out to the hand-mirror which was lying flat on the table beside me, a circle holding the reflection of a bare lightbulb. I pulled the mirror closer; the lightbulb slipped out of the circle and a plaster crack on the ceiling slipped in to take its place. I was quite relieved when I had finally finished my toilette and could herd my straying charges back into the fold. I wiped the bowl, the toilet seat and floor with several sheets of toilet paper, which I then flushed (would the others wonder why I had flushed the toilet twice? Would they either silently or vocally, privately or openly, speculate on the meaning of the second flush?).

"Sorry to be so long," I said to the man who had knocked earlier.

"Yeah," he said jocularly, "what took you so long?"

"Oh, you know me."

But I couldn't be certain that he did know me. If he replied, "Yeah, you always do take your time in there," I would have ascertained both that we had known each other for a while and that I was usually slow in getting out of the bathroom; I would have a bit of a past and one characteristic. If, on the other hand, he had said, "You're not usually so slow" or "Herbert's told me you're a dawdler," I would have new clues to build on. Unfortunately he said nothing but only smiled.

At the stroke of midnight our group, freshly groomed and faultlessly dressed, left the cottage and proceeded to the hotel, thrilled yet pretending to be reserved, like legacy hunters attending a deathbed. My white shirt and white pants fitted so perfectly that I could only assume that they belonged to me. In selecting clothes after my shower I had been forced to decide which of the cabinet drawers in the bedroom contained my belongings. One of my roommates was extremely tall, and I had seen at a glance that the top drawer must be his: the shirts were marked L for "large" (I'm only guessing that's what L means—it could be an initial, of course) and the underwear was marked 35, presumably the number of inches around the man's waist. The middle drawer, I had reason to believe, was my other roommate's; I saw in it the two bracelets he had worn during dinner and the "devotional" reading period. That left the bottom drawer.

I opened it with eagerness and amusement, since I hoped that its contents would reveal something about my own taste. If luck was on my side, I might even find a memento of some trip I had taken or historic occasion I had witnessed. I was bitterly disappointed when I saw nothing but a blaze of anonymous white. White slacks, white shirts, a black comb, white socks, white underwear and a pair of comical wire spectacles framing yellow glass circles. I held the glasses to my eyes. They did nothing to improve my vision, and I concluded they were merely an eccentric prop. For an instant an image, or perhaps a memory, flashed through my mind of me, a laugh a minute, convulsing a crowd on the palace steps, peering over my spectacles with mock-reproach and then pulling them off, suddenly serious, no, romantic, lacing arms with a silent woman, yes, hurrying her away, looking back at the others from the corner, flashing them a last elusive grin, the glasses now dangling from my belt and forming shiny amber drops against the chalky fabric of my pants as I vanished with the woman, the two of us as white and glamorous as gardenias.

But I dropped them back in the drawer—I wasn't ready to deal with all the remarks the spectacles might invite.

As we continued walking, we could hear the relentless duet of the singers at the hotel across the harbor. As the voices climbed higher, they became louder and sharper. The hollow sound of our footfalls on the boardwalk was nearly drowned out by the clear, impassioned boy sopranos. The chimes and drums—performing older, more decorous music in the dimly lit palace, which was in fact quite a bit closer to us—could scarcely be heard. After we had walked about another block, the boys' voices had become so distinct that I could pick out words, or almost. "Blood" and a soft falling away on "seizing . . ." and something like "Return now, it's night." But I couldn't be certain of the words because by now the boys were shouting at the top of their register and

17

the dialect they sang was hard for me to understand.

The hotel deck was brightly lit and swarming with people. One man was wearing a gauze gown printed with blown-up photographs of black insects; a centipede crawled up his chest, its mandibles under his chin, and a fly was draped over either shoulder. Two women had shared their costumes; each wore the halter that matched the other's skirt. A boy was leaning against the rail, his back to us, with three dark plumes stuck into his hair. Six or seven men were dressed in white, like me. What does that signify, I wondered. Is white an indication of age or position or bachelorhood, or what? Fortunately there were enough of us in white to keep me from drawing any special notice and yet not so many that I needed to feel common.

Before we reached the hotel, we had passed the palace. I permitted myself only one glance at the low, rambling edifice. Candles glowed behind bamboo shades, glinting on what seemed to be brass or silver instruments (surely those long, short and shorter metal bars were part of a gamelan or a standing xylophone). No one was moving about inside. The solemn, dull music had stopped. Books with purple bindings and gold lettering lined five shelves of a little porch just outside the gate.

Leaving behind the oppressive palace, we turned the corner, and as the hotel came into view again and was now only a few feet away, a new song began. I spotted the boy singers standing on a platform on the other side of a half-opened sliding glass door. They were wearing rough country clothes, heavily embroidered (perhaps wedding costumes of some sort); their long black hair was so wet from perspiration that it had curled into tight, unruly knots. As they waited for the three old musicians to finish playing the introduction, they stared out over the heads of the dancing crowd, their eyes betraying exhaustion or fear. Once they started singing, however, they were transformed. It was a love duet, and these children, no more than ten years old, bored, tired or frightened as they might have been, slid with no discernible preparation or hesitation into their parts: the boy on the left was a sly rogue, smoothly seducing the boy on the right, who was cast as the timid girl. Like puppets the twins executed broad, unambiguous gestures that had been reduced to the expressive minimum, and like puppets their faces never changed but rather stiffened into a leer and a look of virginal modesty. True, their words were slurred and their dialect unfamiliar, but nonetheless I gathered that the lyric concerned a request for a kiss which, once granted, became a plea for an embrace and so on. At each step the

18

rogue invented some innocent reason or other that would excuse the new intimacy he was seeking. In the end, after the virgin had given all her favors, the rogue ran off. The stage lights dimmed on the villain and brightened on the wronged girl. A minor chord was struck, and she launched into a long lament. Despite the absurd plot and dialogue that had gone before, the solo was quite moving.

Herbert and all the other members of my cottage stopped talking with friends and acquaintances and clustered near the singers' podium to hear what I later learned was called in hotel slang the "*fatalia*." The boy was obviously blinded by the poetry of this particular *fatalia*, for he took no notice of the powerful men gathered at his feet. His heavily made-up eyes glistened as though wet with tears; his high voice—that boy's voice which sounds mysterious because it's so matter-of-fact, divine because human—expressed all the despair of a broken heart. Indeed, his impersonation of adult (and feminine) grief was so convincing that it was with a momentary shock that I saw his hand, glittering with rubies though small and dirty, yank at his embroidered collar the way boys do, tug it open and scratch, unconcernedly, the smooth skin stretched over his clavicle. This unplanned, childish movement belied the sorrow in his voice and eyes and yet made it all the more specific, as though the singer were a medium, possessed by a tragedy queen.

I had no idea whether it was good form or bad to speak to Herbert in this assemblage, but after the *fatalia* and the applause had ended I approached Herbert and said, "Did you see that? Did you notice, when he was comparing his unhappiness to—"

"Oh," Herbert said, placing a hand on mine, "so you saw it too: shall I call it 'the clavicle'?"

"Yes!" I exclaimed, nodding and probably smiling too broadly, "precisely: 'the clavicle.' "

"A delightful moment. Shall I call for paper and ink?"

"Well, yes," I said, not knowing what was in store for me but eager to oblige.

If Herbert gave someone a signal then, it was virtually imperceptible, or was the sort of movement or sound one doesn't usually consider a signal. Nevertheless, by the time we had reached the far table under the awning on the deck, a small leather case lay open in front of two canvas chairs and in it was paper of every color, size and texture as well as several writing instruments. "We must dash off our poems without delay," Herbert whispered, "or else everyone will have forgotten 'the clavicle' and our words will seem obscure and ridiculous."

"My mind's a blank," I said. "I would be very grateful if you did something first and let me see it."

Herbert nodded, never guessing that what I wanted from him was a lesson in the most basic conventions: the number of syllables, rhymes and so on.

As Herbert thought out his verse, I watched the boy sopranos share a cigarette. They were on a break and had been invited aboard a white yacht that was moored to the dock not more than twenty feet away from where we were sitting. Two uniformed crew members were passing trays of food to the boys and to an older woman and man; none of them was talking. All they did was glance periodically at the night sky, at the water (as black and faceted as coal) and, superciliously, at the ordinary people strolling down the boardwalk. The boat was named *The Doris*.

Seized suddenly by a thought, Herbert tore a page from the leather case—a pale yellow sheet so thin it was translucent—and scrawled across it in violent strokes of the blackest ink. Contemptuously he pushed it toward me:

Rubies shiver and a child's impassioned hand
Rises, touches skin the color of a wedding band,
But those eyes were born to weep or give command.

"What perfect taste!" I exclaimed. "How delicately handled—and yet, at the same time, how strong!" Herbert smiled at my praise, a quicker and more heartfelt smile than he may have intended; I had won my second smile from him in a day. Delicacy and strength, delicacy and strength . . . that must be the combination he's striving for. He summoned a messenger to the table, who stood silently by, waiting for my poem. I was alarmed to see that like me he was dressed in white—were he and I, then, on the same footing?—until I noticed a black pin, a maple leaf, clipped to his sleeve. My own sleeve, I observed, was innocent of all badges.

I took another look at Herbert's poem. Not terrible, I thought, but strained and unmusical, the work of a well-educated man devoid of talent. The only good thing in it is the wedding band, and that obviously was suggested by the rhyme (though "the color of the land" would have been a more likely, if less happy, choice). I felt under great pressure to better it, but in such a way as would be apparent only to another poet, a poem that would strike Herbert as actually inferior to his own offering.

Each line trochaic pentameter with a masculine ending; a rhymed triplet; why must there be a messenger standing here? Or is he a messenger? Perhaps a friend. I must empty my mind of all distractions and concentrate on my poem (vain resolution, the mind will not be emptied). And I suppose I must compose the verses in my mind, since, for all I know, custom demands that the first draft be the last.

Can I do anything with the boy-as-a-medium idea? Clavicle—a play on words? On what: clavichord? Not good enough, not on center. Too pedantic. And *clavichord* is so unusual a word for such a short form that it could only be sustained in the closing line, where it would derail the train of thought. Can the medium then be implied without stating it? Make it a metaphor rather than a simile.

The messenger worked a plain green band down one finger until it passed both knuckles and was resting on his nail; then he worked it back in place. What if the boy's skin was the color of *that* wedding band, I thought, and laughed inwardly. One of the sopranos had risen and walked to the prow of the yacht. I feared that the boys would return to the podium before they had received our tributes.

The obvious climax to the poem is to put the boy's scratching at the end. But Herbert avoided that solution, and I suppose I'd be considered crude if I grabbed for it now that he's passed it by. What I must do is prove, to any connoisseur who might read my work, that my poem is more direct, modest and original than Herbert's (I presume the poems will be passed around among the good people; sending them to the singers must be only a formality. They probably can't read. They'll hand the poems over to their hosts on *The Doris*, who will recognize Herbert's distinctive hand and style and immediately start showing our verses to everyone. Yes, that must be Herbert's plan; he's counting on the fact that the boys can't read).

Tentatively I pull a sheet of heavy red paper from the leather case. I haven't the faintest idea what I mean by my red paper, but I can't weigh every decision at this point; I'll invent an explanation later. I choose ink and a writing point of the most ordinary sort, which should contrast favorably with Herbert's irritable eccentricities. Herbert has motioned the messenger to sit down. That's as much pressure on me as he, dedicated as he is to appearing casual and permissive, dare permit himself.

Notice the boy tug at his shirt and scratch

is the first line I dash off, fearing that it's all wrong, fearing that I won't find two rhymes for "scratch," knowing I've mixed trochees with iambs, resolving to plunge on anyway.

Young boy, old shirt, dirty hand—yes, but watch
The eyes (a tragedy queen) (a burning match).

Without checking out the meter (which I can do only on my fingers—surely a grave solecism), I hand the poem over to Herbert. He reads it expressionlessly, and I read it upside down, regretting the false rhyme, regarding "burning match" as an absurdity, a dull-witted reach for a rhyme masquerading as a metaphor, loathing the whole enterprise, dry, dry as dust.

Herbert said, "It will do," and after folding it picturesquely, dispatched our missiles to the yacht. No sooner had the messenger delivered them (Herbert and I having meanwhile withdrawn to a discreet distance so that we wouldn't seem to be waiting for congratulatory nods or replies), than someone shouted "Fire! Fire!" Not more than two or three people responded to the cry at first. The bulk of the crowd was on the dance floor, watching the girls who had shared costumes doing a mirror dance, every movement made by the one perfectly imitated by the other. But now other voices had taken up the call. The boys on the yacht, their hosts and, in a neighboring boat, a heavy blond woman dressed in a knee-length coat, her hair brushed, I supposed, with a chemical that caused it to glow and dim in slow pulsations—all stood, paced their decks and searched the sky for the sign of flames.

"Fire! Fire!" shouted a voice from the top of the hotel. I looked up and saw on the highest balcony the man in the insect robe, his skirts flowing, the line of the backswept cloth balanced by his outstretched hand (now I realize he must have been pointing frantically toward the fire, yet this realization does not detract from the interest I had originally found in his pose but simply reassigns its beauty from art to necessity).

"Fire! Fire!" called a corps of messengers from the dance floor. But they, somewhat childishly, were repeating the cry only because they must have imagined it was the latest catchword. Never thinking for a moment that there might actually be a fire on the island, the messengers formed a semicircle around the girls performing the mirror dance, clapped and, their backs turned to the rouging sky, called out in a singsong fashion on every third and fourth beat, "Fire fire," their voices dropping a fifth each time exactly as Bob's had during his now famous "yawning syndrome" described earlier by Herbert.

"Fire! Fire!" exclaimed five men and one woman dressed in matching purple Byzantine pants, purple but streaked with white iris roots twining asymmetrically into knots over the knees before unraveling into crisp points above the feet, like so many witnesses identifying a wanted person. The six people in puple fanned out through the hotel crowd, angrily trying to silence the music and chatter, trying to make everyone see the sky, which was now glowing scarlet, trying to shake some sense into this stupid, frivolous assemblage.

Although a few merrymakers finally realized what was happening, the corps of messengers had lost itself in a new dance and could not be drawn out of it. Grinning and keeping up the slightly bored, certainly stylized chant of "Fire fire," the dancers stepped forward with the right foot on the first "Fire" and simultaneously pushed the right hand, palm up, into the air (like waiters lifting trays); on the second "fire" they repeated the motion but with the left foot and hand. The remaining two beats to the measure they filled in by crouching and slowly rising while swinging their arms forward from their sides in arcs (like children pushing swings), all the while saying "who?" like owls (although I think they were imitating the sound of flames rather than owls). In an instant the boy sopranos, ever alert to a dance or song innovation, had abandoned *The Doris* (in the confusion I had neglected to notice whether they had read our poems) and had joined, or rather had decided to lead, the chorus line of white-uniformed messengers boldly strutting across the floor singing "Fire fire who? Fire fire who?" Predictably enough, the boy sopranos had not only mastered the step by watching it once or twice, but were now executing it with the same blasé look they put on while doing even the most intricate or suggestive dances. By the time they had crossed the room once and were leading the line back in the opposite direction, they were already adding decorative flourishes, turns and rapid half and quarter beats and were splitting *fire* into two and even three syllables, pronouncing the *r* so far back in their throats that the word had become countrified and virtually unrecognizable.

Herbert touched my sleeve and whispered, with a wan smile, "The poems will be forgotten now. Well ... Shall we go up to the hotel balcony for the fire-viewing?" I nodded, proud possessor of yet another of Herbert's smiles, and a touch as well; moreover, I sensed that what had happened to our poems would form a bond between Herbert and

23

me far more useful than the vogue we might have enjoyed had our verses been circulated.

From the balcony I saw the fire, a red in constant motion beyond the stationary silhouettes of black treetops. The flames seemed to be miles away. They weren't making any sound, unless that soft roar was the sound of fire. The bellies of low clouds were incandescent.

At a glance I realized that the men around me on the balcony were important. They moved so gravely, they spoke in such low voices, they seemed so concerned—they *had* to be important, and I was grateful to Herbert for bringing me here with him. I observed the way the men beside me leaned slightly over the rail, held a hand above their eyes as though shielding them from sunlight, and then drew back and turned to one another and conferred. The only element of their behavior that could be criticized was the unnecessary shielding of their eyes, but on second thought I supposed it, too, could be forgiven, since it was probably an automatic accompaniment to viewing or, what's more likely, a dramatization of their anxiety and thus a mild reproof to the dancers in the hotel who were still chanting "Fire fire who?" Among some of the dancers the phrase had already degenerated into "Far far you." The blond hair of the woman on the yacht below continued to brighten and darken, but more slowly and dimly, as though in deference to the seriousness of the moment.

Then Herbert and I were invited by several of the men on the balcony to accompany them to the actual site of the fire (which later last night came to be known as "The Closer Look" as opposed to this earlier occasion on the balcony, called, simply, "The Fire Viewing").

All of these older men and I hurried toward the fire. They were chattering away about the look of the flames. The man in the centipede costume said, "Pity there isn't a touch more blue in the flames. Blue, being a recessive color, would give more depth, more plasticity to the whole *swirl* and make it much more impressive, I think." Suddenly a woman in a nightgown emerged out of the shadows and shouted at us all, "You damn fools! This fire is no accident! Go home!" and she started trying to shove the man in the insect robe back toward the hotel. Before he could recover his poise and speak to her, her energy gave out and she ran away, sobbing.

"The poor woman," Herbert murmured.

"Yes," another man sighed, "so sad. Maybe that was her house.

Or maybe she knows the people. You can understand her grief easily enough."

"There is nothing so, well, so noble as that sort of grief," Herbert added.

"Very stirring and very noble," the insect man hastened to concede. "Very stirring and very noble. But the fire *is* an accident."

"Yes," Herbert said, "an accident, Jason."

They resumed the discussion of the lamentable lack of blue in the flames.

The fire turned out to be much farther away than anyone had at first suspected. When at last we drew near it, the boardwalk, fortunately, was higher above the ground than ordinary. It rose at this point in order to negotiate a hill that lay just ahead. From the elevated platform, approximately ten and a half feet high, we had a good view of the ornate burning house and the toiling fire-fighters. ("We might join them!" Jason cried out airily.) A broad river of orange sparks shot over our heads and rained soot and flaming splinters on us and the marsh grasses below.

The heat and the light created an acre of daylight in the vast plantation of the night. One whole wall collapsed and gave us a doll's-house view of the interior. A falling painting, framed in a fiery oval, branded its way right through a striped silk love seat. Garden furniture in the solarium was melting into puddles of white iron. Upstairs a bedroom mirror boiled reflections of a chandelier, then went black and cracked. The weathervane spun merrily in the strong updraught.

Observers were sweating and opening their shirts. A sudden movement of people who wanted to leave set off rumors, "The walk is collapsing . . . The walkway is on fire." Someone said, "Who would have guessed he was still living in such luxury? There should be a law." "There is," someone else said, chuckling, and added, "This is the last of the great houses; now they've all gone up in smoke."

The crashing timbers were making so much noise that we could scarcely hear what the fire-fighters were shouting as they wrestled with the writhing hoses in their arms. The strong men in their glittering slickers struggled and fell away from those thick serpents. Herbert whispered to me, "I wish I'd brought my writing case."

And then I remembered the wording of my poem to the boy soprano and was seized by fear.

Hadn't I, yes, I had compared him to a "burning match." The comparison was so unlikely, so uncalled for, that mightn't the islanders, yes, they might, conclude that I had started the fire? Of course I could explain that the rhyme demanded, or at least suggested "match" but they could just as reasonably argue that "match" had generated the rest of the poem, at least unwittingly. And then what would I say? Herbert and Jason knew the fire was no accident. People might speculate (or know) that I was an enemy of the owner of the house, or of his luxurious way of living, or in the employ of such an enemy.

I slipped away from the group and went back to our deserted cottage, anxiously awaiting a mob, or, what seemed more likely, a polite poem from perhaps the palace, delicately but unmistakably ringing changes on my disastrous choice of words.

2

When I come out of the bathroom, I find Herbert sitting on the porch, reading a book. Although he is wearing only a pair of shorts and sneakers, his body is so trim and his hair so carefully combed that he gives the impression of being fully clothed, as though his bare skin were a sort of sporting costume.

"Good morning," he says.

"Have you been up long?" I ask.

"For hours," he replies with evident satisfaction. "I've already been to the store and bought things for breakfast—nothing fancy, just eggs and sausage and milk and coffee and bread for toast. Did everyone come back last night in your room?"

"Yes," I say.

"Then Bob's the only one missing. I didn't see him last night at the hotel either, did you?"

"No. I didn't." I can't decide whether Herbert's eager to get back to his book or whether he wants to chat. I decide to sit down in the canvas chair beside him, and staring at the rough wood planks of the dock, pretend to be still dazed with sleep. If he's in a mood to talk, he'll take my continuing presence as encouragement to do so; if he wants to read, he can interpret my stupor as permission to leave me to my thoughts.

Unfortunately he's as unsure of himself as I am. I can sense it. From the corner of my eye, I watch him studying me surreptitiously. He fidgets in his chair. His hand tenses on the armrest—and then he picks up his book and whistles. He gets through the opening bar of the song he was humming yesterday while washing the dishes, and breaks off. A moment later he resumes the melody, but not, I notice, several measures further along, as he would if he were genuinely lost in his reverie, but rather precisely at the point where he lapsed into silence: a clear indication that he's whistling for my benefit. As ridiculous and self-conscious as Bob's yawning syndrome. Or so, at least, it would seem to someone interested in finding fault.

I can't find fault with Herbert this morning. The sun's already warm on my shoulders and two sparrows are chattering on the burnt-out limb of a tall tree nearby. The birds alight on the branch, a massive charred horizontal almost as thick as the trunk; they emit a few calls and then flutter for a few moments in the air before landing again. They rotate around the branch in constant, restless volleys as though they can't find a proper grip on anything so alien to them, on anything so dead. The tree is a relic of an old fire; perhaps one of the vanished great houses once stood nearby.

No, I can't find fault with Herbert. He turns a page in his book, peers at a sentence, rereads it, furrows his brow in consternation, which slowly gives way to a smile of enlightenment and little nods—a complete illustrated lecture on the thinking process, the sort of display that never occurs when one is actually absorbed in thought.

Surely he would welcome any attempt on my part to start a conversation, but I don't know what to say and besides I prefer staring at the foliage that has nearly engulfed our cottage. Although my stomach has already tightened, my well-rested arms and neck and shoulders haven't received the news of panic yet; perhaps I can prolong their calm. One bush, or tree, particularly interests me because it has three different leaf shapes, one that looks like an elm's, another with three lobes and a third that resembles a mitten. This plant has arched over to touch a holly bush, creating a dark tunnel of waxy greenery and a grill of shadows. Our house, like all the others I've seen, stands on stilts above marshy ground. The decks and the walks, built of rough-cut weathered planks, are also raised. Long strands of grass have grown up between the slats. Constantly bruised by passing feet, the strands have withered, turned brown and now lie listlessly across the wood, like tiny whips in tatters. The immediate vicinity is hillier than the area around the harbor and in one direction I see a black cottage, timidly ostentatious, perched high above us, flying four purple pennants.

Suddenly Herbert slams his book down on the table between us and says, "I think we have a little work to do today, don't you?" He says the first few words too loudly and immediately lowers his voice. He's staring at me with determination, or is it anger, as though he's let things get out of hand and must now, belatedly, buckle down. No, maybe he's received orders from above and is so embarrassed about transmitting them to me that he's hiding his embarrassment behind gruffness.

But what sort of work? I haven't seen anyone working on the island except messengers in the hotel and the firemen. And the messengers may have been friends, and Jason had offered to relieve the firemen.

"Yes of course," I say cheerfully. "That's an excellent idea."

"Well, should we go there now? I can show you what has to be done."

"Lead on," I tell him, wondering whether I'm offending him by seeming so jaunty rather than by saluting or standing at attention. Yet if I saluted, I might be making a terrible mistake. He has consistently indicated that whatever our relationship might be in fact, we are to treat each other casually and permissively. It's not for me to change the tone.

He stands and I do the same, though, somewhat clownishly, I pause for an instant, pretending laziness or reluctance, before levering myself out of the chair in a burst by grabbing the armrests with my hands and pushing down; a slight joke, registered by my body alone and not by anything so controversial as a smile. Even so, I mustn't lend so much character to my actions until I discover what sort of person I'm generally considered to be.

"I wouldn't go like that," Herbert says, pointing at my swimsuit. "There's a lot of underbrush around that house and you might scratch your legs. You'd better wear long pants—I'm not telling you what to do, but—"

"I don't care if I do get scratched."

I run into the bathroom to comb my hair, and see in the mirror a friendly face, deep lines around my eyes and on either side of my mouth. I smile, and realize that the lines have come from frequent smiling; yes, a friendly, disarming person, no furrows in the forehead, not used to frowning. How old? Late twenties if poorly preserved, early thirties if well. Not handsome but not ugly (I think; perhaps these large nostrils, down-turned eyebrows and small chin are considered hideous). My head starts bobbing. A short jerk every few moments, like a curt nod. My neck becomes so tight that I half fear my head will lose its mobility. Nodding reassures me I still have control over it.

As soon as Herbert hears me walking up behind him he leads me, without looking around, down the path under the heavy arch formed by the holly on the one side and, on the other, by the versatile bush with the three different leaf patterns.

I load the wheelbarrow with brown, aromatic pine needles once again. The hill, which is very steep, leads from what Herbert called, I think, the "Detached Residence" down to the dunes and the ocean.

I've made a pile of needles with my rake. Now, using the rake as a sort of shovel, I scoop up part of the mound, and keeping the needles in place with my free hand (the right), transfer the burden, which is bulky but light, to the wheelbarrow. As I extract the rake, its tines scrape against the sides of the wheelbarrow. A drop of sweat stings my eye. I try to wipe it away with the back of my right forearm, since my hands are black and I'm afraid of streaking my face with dirt. The attempt fails. Slowly the sting dulls.

For the hundredth time I survey the hill and calculate how long I'll need to clear it. I expend more energy on these estimations than on actually working, as though I hope to will all the needles away with one powerful thought. Or is it that I'm still childishly planning to seize upon a brilliant plan for cutting my work in half, even though I know full well that no such plan can possibly be devised?

I must get back to the job.

Closing my eyes, I determine the shape, position and extension of my body by noticing: the pain in my stiff, steadily bobbing neck; the faint pressure of collecting sweat above my left eyebrow; the slow throbbing between my shoulders and at the base of my spine; the smooth roundness of the rake in my closed palm; the binding of the swimsuit across my hips; and the solidity of the earth under my feet, a force exerted more powerfully on my toes than on my heels, since I'm facing downhill. Aside from these few sensations, I feel nothing, either internally or externally, except the flow of breath escaping through my nostrils. If I were blind and beginning consciousness this instant, would I be able to start from these few points of sensation and sketch in a fully accurate picture of my body? Since I feel nothing below my shoulders and above the slight cinching of my drawstring, would I imagine that I came in two separate sections, one floating above the other on a cushion of air? Ah, but now a drop of sweat courses from my armpit down my side, drawing in a connecting line. Yet, if I stood absolutely still and didn't flex my solar plexus or chest or bend my arms, I might still labor under the delusion that the perspiration marked only a thin stem of flesh growing between the upper and lower decks of my body; similarly, I might believe that my rake-holding hand was an appendage not of my shoulder but of my waist.

I must stop drifting off into these reveries. What if Herbert's watching me?

Slowly and, I suppose, sadly, yes, sadly, forlornly, I push the wheelbarrow up the hill, avoiding a long root growing above ground, steering clear of that declivity, wondering whether the ground I'm crossing is sufficiently clear of needles to meet Herbert's approval or whether I should get down on my hands and knees and pick it clean; no, I won't do that.

I tip the wheelbarrow forward on its wheel and watch the contents resist and then suddenly slide in one matted tangle onto the dump that Herbert pointed out when he gave me my instructions; or were they instructions? Could it possibly be that this Detached Residence or whatever it is belongs to us and that he was only reminding me of a task and a way to execute it that we had agreed upon a few days ago? But if we discussed the entire venture before, then why did he give me such detailed orders? Unless, of course, he doubts my memory. I may be considered a forgetful person. Or maybe this is a ritual task, seldom performed.

A few needles, twigs, leaves and pebbles huddle in the depression at the far end of the wheelbarrow. I brush them out; is that a cut on my palm? No, only a needle stuck to my skin.

The wheelbarrow is light and capricious as I push it back down the hill. For an instant I playfully guide it with only one hand until it begins to veer to one side and I right it. I want to do as little work as possible, since I can't see any sense in it and regard it as beneath my dignity. Nevertheless, I certainly don't want to give Herbert or any of my superiors grounds for complaint. My ridiculous compromise is to do my job conscientiously but cheat the authorities by taking a short, scarcely noticeable pause between raking and loading, or between loading and conveying, or between conveying and emptying. Or by indulging in such stunts as one-handed guiding; tiny acts of sabotage. In the strictest sense, of course—and I have no notion how strictly such things are judged—wiping away sweat from my forehead or stretching to ease the cramp in my back could all be deemed presumptuous, punishable.

How I long to be on the beach or on the deck of a beautiful house with a smart crowd of people. Everyone in my house has long since finished breakfast and is probably swimming or drinking by now or dancing at the hotel. Even cleaning up our cottage, even something as taxing as painting the whole thing, would be far preferable to working on this desolate hill, not knowing for how long or to what purpose, hungry. Yesterday I was wishing they'd give me a definite assignment rather than make me guess what was expected of me, but I hadn't foreseen an assignment to this hill, alone. The sunlight scarcely filters through the branches of the old pines, and tonight, at the hotel, I'll be noticeably paler than everyone else, which will lead to questions. If I do tan by some miracle, only my shoulders and the back of my neck and possibly my forehead will get dark, and people will ask me if I was working, and I'll not dare to lie because I know too little about them, myself, everything, to lie intelligently.

I've tackled this section of ground because the needles are scattered more thinly here than over there, and in the same time and with the same amount of effort I can clear a larger piece of terrain. Eventually I'll have to rake up the thicker parts as well, but if Herbert should come in a few minutes to take me away I'd make a better impression by following my current strategy.

There's no sense in neatening this pile any more. I'll inevitably scatter it in transferring the needles to the wheelbarrow, no matter how carefully I work.

Voices, laughing; where are they coming from? Are they laughing at me? No, people on the beach; they don't see me; they're on the other side of the dunes; have they forgotten me? When shall I go back to the cottage? Would Herbert be angry if I returned now? The worst thing is that this is all so humiliating that I won't be able to look anyone in the eye tonight at the hotel.

I push my freight of needles up the hill, knowing now to avoid that steep path where I lost my footing the time before, giving wide berth to the above-ground root and the shallow declivity, ascending on an angle, wondering if there is anyone who is my protector, anyone who cares about me, anyone who realizes I'm here, if I could move to another cottage and escape Herbert's tyranny; wondering how I offended him or whom I offended if I offended anyone at all; wondering if I will be permitted to go to the hotel tonight and the beach tomorrow, or if I am to work here from now on, perhaps sleep here, too; wondering if I am even an islander; wondering whether I could gain a protector by begging for help from someone, by throwing myself on his mercy, but that's too risky, much too risky, he might pretend to honor my plea but then secretly notify Herbert and return me to him; wondering if I could do something dramatic, recite a long, brilliant poem on the beach or execute a startling dance at the hotel, fling myself into the harbor—anything that would win favor or prove despair.

The needles slide in a mass onto the damp pile, and only a residue of gray sand remains at the far end of the wheelbarrow; I'll empty it after the next trip. A bird is singing now, and . . . now! And now. My spirits pick up as I descend the hill and as every shock registers a muted jolt in my hands. The hard part of the job depresses me and the easy elates. If my mood's as mechanically determined as that, then why can't I discount the fluctuations? It would be absurd to say these shifts of mood don't matter, for what could matter more to me? Yet, granting their supreme importance, can't I average out the extremes and enjoy a mildly pleasant, or at least comfortable, mean? Can't I gather enough momentum from the gay periods to carry me through the grim?

Look at it this way: there's a job to be done, and I'll be doing it no matter what I feel. By tomorrow I doubt if I'll even be able to recall exactly what I was feeling today. Since all these little pleasures and pains are so irrelevant, so unmemorable, wouldn't it be best not to feel them at all, or if I must, and I suppose I must, then shouldn't I view them from a great distance, force them to filter their way through a hundred purifying ironies until, when they finally submit to introspection, they're abstract and odorless? Or, if my emotions refuse to be generalized, can't I generalize myself, that is, view myself as a laborer, a stick figure conveying pine needles—and dissociate my thoughts from that figure? Can I make myself a mind witnessing action, and whose action never wonder? Naturally, part of my brain must continue to concern itself with lifting the needles to the wheelbarrow, guiding the wheelbarrow between the exposed root and the declivity, with tipping the needles onto the dump; yet I can surely distance these concerns.

Do I want to cry? If not, then why this tightening of my chest, this swelling in my throat? A mosquito haunts my ear.

Why have they left me here alone? The work itself is not so terrible, except insofar as I believe it's a form of punishment. It's the punishment that weighs so heavily on me, the punishment and the loneliness and the uncertainty that it will ever end.

How could Mind find a way to like all this? Fancy could see it as a lark, a privilege granted by the palace only to the lucky few, a magic raking of a sacred precinct. Detached Residence (if I heard correctly), but detached from what? Is it a sort of summer palace or temple? Surely these stones seem, or almost seem, to be consciously arranged and the moss trained to carpet them. Am I, then, the Master of the Grove, and did Herbert only intend for me to rake the ground once or twice, symbolically, and leave the actual work to the staff of gardeners? Is he waiting for me even now at the wicker gate, puzzled because I'm taking so long but too discreet to return lest he interrupt my meditations or overhear an invocation he's forbidden to know? Yet must the Master of the Grove be alone, so lonely, laughter, voices, people on the beach beyond the dunes . . .?

Could it be that I'm missing the point with all my questions? Perhaps, just as I hope to escape my lot by astracting my moods, by averaging them out or by making even myself an abstraction (a stick figure raking pine needles), in the same way the good people of the island may have placed this hill and its sole inhabitant, me, under a fine gauze of abstractions until, at least to their mind's eye, the hill has vanished, a pure subject devoid of all attributes and hence of any palpable existence. I look up and the sky, seen through the branches, appears gauzy—the gauze, the very gauze that is hiding me from the other islanders. If the gauze were to float down, of course, it would catch on the branches at first; but who knows when it might drift silently to earth and smother me in its intricate mesh.

Wondering what's on the far side of the hill, I walk to the crest and see, enclosed within a rim of inland dunes, a desolate plain, flat and sandy, planted with scrub bushes, marsh grasses and leafless trees (to be more exact, only the taller trees are dead; the second growth sprouting up around the denuded trunks is scraggly but green)—a plain that would be desolate except it's crowded with people.

A procession of some twenty or thirty men is approaching. They are coming across the sand toward a small inclined path near me that probably connects with the wooden walk leading back to the harbor and the houses surrounding it. Keeping no sort of orderly formation, they walk in twos and threes, not talking, their long robes—some dyed blue, others red, one a faded patchwork of many colors in diamond shapes—swinging freely with their steps, the hems swirling around bare feet. A black man, completely naked, is running from a great distance to catch up with them. His long, skinny arms flop wildly and his head lists from side to side; even his legs seem too relaxed and out of control. None of the others sees him, or at least no one slackens his pace. Their lack of attention can partly be blamed on the pursuer himself, who hasn't alerted them by hallooing. He isn't even running very fast, although now he could overtake the group in a moment if he increased his speed. Perhaps he isn't one of the party, in fact he must not be; he's heading off at an angle, his black body creating a long shadow on the gray sand, gray but marbled with bands that look as damp and brown as fresh bruises. The men in robes, led by Herbert, notice the runner with no more interest than they would pay a passing bird.

I crouch behind a hillock so that they won't spot me. Herbert may collect me on his way back; I'd better return to my job. Where are they coming from?

The men are filing up the path to the walkway. One of them—Jason—is wearing a necklace of rubies and holding a transistor to his ear. Are those the same rubies one of the boy singers had on last night? Herbert has peeled a banana; he's throwing the peel into a bush. Split but still joined at one end, the three strips of the peel catch on a cluster of twigs which bounce for a moment under the sudden weight. Herbert and two other men are holding silver spades; they've been digging something.

From my hideout I watch Herbert's party passing behind a stand of trees, the robes flickering in and out of columns of sunlight. Music from the transistor reaches me in fitful bursts of sound. Herbert has set a brisk pace. The men are talking, but "Poor thing, poor thing" are the only words I catch.

They're gone. Is the black man the "Poor thing, poor thing," or am I? Or someone else? What were they digging? I go back to the dump and feel so alone that I get an erection as I press the rusted metal underside of the wheelbarrow against my legs, trying to tip it so far over that all the sand will slide out. After righting my now completely empty wheelbarrow, I leave it and adjust myself. As I rub my hand across the front of my swimsuit, the erection moves from one side to the other. Removing my hand, I notice that if allowed to assume its natural position, the bulge remains just to the left of the drawstring. I pull my swimsuit down. I shouldn't sit, but I do, right beside the dump. The earth feels cool and damp on my buttocks and the scent of pine needles has become sharper; a vague smell of stale sweat rises from between my legs. Propping myself up with my left hand, I examine the erection with the right. A bird sings now. And now. An ant struggles to carry, no, to get out from under a pine needle—and succeeds. A heavy blue artery runs up the extraordinarily white cylinder and branches into two lateral tributaries. So many of the black hairs catch the sunlight that for a moment I imagine they're white. Others glint blue and look so glossy that when I touch them I'm surprised to discover how coarse and wiry they are. I pull the cylinder out, away from my body, then release it; it snaps back against my stomach, thud of flesh on flesh.

The hairs on my chest leap ecstatically out from the skin and then crest, but between my nipples they curl so far back upon themselves that they form little ringlets, curving in much the same way as a hand, reaching to greet a friend, retracts when the friend turns out to be a stranger, and touches the head or heart.

3

I quickly rise and pull up my swimsuit. A woman is descending the hill, a boy beside her. The boy, yes, the boy is Billy. Herbert's valet or nephew or perhaps lieutenant—the boy who taught me, without intending to teach me anything, possibly without even noticing my existence, the hotel expressions "give them fashion" and "back," meaning "thoroughly."

The woman is murmuring to Billy quite softly, and I'm unable to hear what she's saying, but I do catch a charming inflection in her voice, the sort of story-book tone adopted when addressing children. Yet there is nothing condescending or false in the voice. It's simply the way a mature woman speaks to an adolescent when she feels comfortable with him and realizes that for her comfort to continue she must go on insisting, in every intonation, that she is much older, he much younger. An amorous boy, or a proud one, might resent such a firm, though delicate positioning, but Billy doesn't seem to mind. In fact, he seems indifferent to her charm but nonetheless attentive, curious, cautious. He leans closer to her when her voice subsides, he prefers to clamber over exposed tree roots rather than follow her on the path and miss a precious word, and his face so perfectly registers every shift in her conversation that I can almost guess what she must be saying. She's obviously quite important (if women can be important), for why else would Billy, who enjoys Herbert's protection, dance attendance on her? In her right hand she holds a parasol of varnished paper and as she sways it back and forth its umber shadow swims over their faces and bodies and then tilts out and elongates upon the slanting ground beside them.

"Don't be," I hear her saying, then she adds, "quite foolish." "Absurd?" she asks a bit later. As they draw closer she confides, "I couldn't care less" and laughs with so much force, though quietly, that she is soon gasping for breath and must lean on Billy's arm. With a long white handkerchief she dabs at her eyes.

"I'm sure Herbert will codify *that*, too," Billy says, quite distinctly, studying her face to see if his remark will renew her laughter, which it does. She buries her head on his shoulder and sobs with merriment. Looking irritated, Billy stares at the stone step and paws it with his left foot once, twice, as the smile vanishes from his lips. Only the sound of her irregular gasps fills the clear summer air now. The parasol has fallen from her hand and lies on the earth, upside down and on an angle, its brown handle pressing against her bare legs. Her hand closes around the handle intuitively, lifts it and sets the dark circle flying once again over the ground.

They're coming closer and at any moment they will notice me. I can't help being pleased as I start raking the ground already raked clean and quickly construct an agreeable expression for them to observe. I turn one corner of my mouth down in a bored, or rather wry, smile to show the amused resignation with which I am performing my menial job. Lest amusement seem out of place in a servant (if that is what I am), I temper it with a frown of concentration. Now I am covered on both sides. Should the woman appear amazed at my doing such work, I can deepen the sardonic smile and erase the frown; if, on the other hand, she is the mistress of the Detached Residence come to give me further instructions, I can drop the smile and intensify the frown.

She catches sight of me, smiles and without taking her eyes off mine, hands the parasol to Billy and walks briskly to my side, pushing her hair back behind her ear in a nonchalant, perhaps by now an unconscious gesture, but one that is surely too beautiful not to have been practiced at one time or another in front of a mirror. "Darling," she says, making the word into a statement, as simple and matter-of-fact as if she had just turned to a companion and said "Nice day" or "Let's turn here" and not expected an answer. And yet, when a word like *darling* is uttered, a word which carries so much warmth and tenderness in its two syllables, the first decisive and deep, the second falling away and trembling with music—when such a word is spoken, it gains through an easy, even prosaic delivery, for if the tone is so at variance with the meaning, the listener is confused for a moment, wonders whether he had heard it correctly, then, slowly growing more and more certain that his ears have not tricked him, rejoices inwardly while betraying none of his joy to the speaker and, as a last test to make absolutely sure, mentally repeats the word to himself, or rather plays back the remembered, still vivid sounds, and once again, what was a mere wave in the air, a mere noise, becomes a meaning powerful enough to elicit tears (if tears could be elicited from such a guarded listener), thus showing the economy and foresight of the original delivery which was able to arouse in the poor, hopeful, relieved listener such studious attention, my darling, my darling! She kisses my cheek, not puckering her lips but just slowly brushing her mouth against my skin; when I steal a glance at her I see that her eyes are turned upward to a tree on my left. She looks preoccupied, naïve and serious. I put a hand lightly around her waist and am almost shocked to discover such a solid body. Her face is so radiant that for a moment I must have imagined it contained all her being.

"We looked everywhere for you," she says, not reproachfully but again with the same matter-of-fact tone.

"And you found me here," I reply with a slight smile.

"Everyone's on the beach today. I suppose that's why you're here."

"And because Herbert reminded me of my duties."

"Of course." Herbert's name has embarrassed her. "Do you think he'd mind—could you sneak away for a moment?"

"What do you think, Billy?" The boy has drawn closer to us. "What would Herbert do if I left and ran away with you two?"

Billy shrugs. Usually he has a ready answer; he must be confused—or cautious.

"Hell with it," I say, without rancor or even much conviction. I throw the rake aside and take the woman's arm. Billy follows us down the steps, holding the parasol above the woman's head.

We cross the dunes on a narrow path, stepping over the wooden pickets of a low, rambling fence which may have been put up to retain sand against the ravages of the tide. The stakes, once red, now a softer hue, stand erect only in a few places. Most of them are half buried in the dunes; they are lavender eyelashes lowered against white cheeks.

"Do you like my bracelet?" the woman asks, holding up her arm and looking at it, not me. Two leathery black spirals, grained with thousands of small lateral lines and joined into a thick muscular band which circles her wrist, shine malevolently. The bracelet slips down an inch toward her hand and reveals, I notice, no pale circles on her sun-browned skin.

"New?" I ask.

"Yes. Is it too ghoulish?"

"Something grotesque on your arm only makes you appear all the more gentle."

"Gentle," Billy drawls. The woman stops and turns to the boy with a look of merry expectation. He casts his eyes to the sky and recites:

"Though grisly, loathsome, what you will,
A spider's lips—"

"Oh," the woman interrupts, touching Billy's shoulder, "don't struggle so much, Billy. You know how I hate these horrible, puffing 'spontaneous' poems everyone feels obliged to recite nowadays. In fact . . ." she whispers, turning to me with a smile, "we'll each polish, very carefully, a whole set of 'spontaneous' poems at the end of the day, commit them to memory and repeat them to the *others*. I mean, before rejoining Herbert, *et al.*, we'll spend half an hour winnowing the poetic grain for the day, working deliberately, cynically. But aside from that half hour, we'll cut out versifying completely from our precious time together. That way, we'll never be *straining* around each other. Agreed?"

"Agreed," I say, taking her hand and nibbling on the back of her ring finger, not voraciously but rather coolly, with the same faraway abstracted look she wore when kissing my cheek.

Billy says nothing. He is watching us.

"Ridiculous custom, anyway," she announces, striding ahead down the beach as Billy and I follow her. Suddenly she stops, sights an impish idea in a low bank of clouds massed over the ocean horizon, and whispers, "Aren't we powerful enough, the three of us, to put an end to the whole thing? What if we started laughing uproariously every time someone embarked on a 'spontaneous' couplet? Loud, I mean *rude*. Wouldn't the whole custom die a quick death then? It's true Herbert and his ilk are always sending for that blasted paper and ink, and *he* is a formidable power—but could even he stand up to our ridicule?"

"Perhaps he could," Billy says, as neutrally as possible.

"Who cares, anyway?" I ask, walking ahead of them, appearing to be bored with the question. "Let's run!"

"Great!" Billy calls back. He closes the parasol. The three of us take off down the beach. In the distance people are promenading back and forth from their towels to the water's edge, or visiting from towel to towel, or leaping and dodging at a volleyball net, like so many digits shifting from one column to another. Haze had risen from the water and floated over the white sand. We run and run.

Gilt clouds tumble like dwarfs along the horizon. Ahead of us sandpipers evade the surf and then, as the water retreats and the glossy sand goes matte, scuttle back to peck for plankton. The next wave— and our flying feet—drives them away again on stiff little legs and white-edged wings. In a shallow tide-pool, a very high wave has left behind billows of dirty foam. Evaporating and contracting, the foam shifts soundlessly in its gutter; in a few moments it will vanish. Bubbles topping one shred of foam glower red and green in the late afternoon sunlight and then break, one after another, like small eyes winking shut.

"Let's walk," the woman shouts. I break pace; she jogs to my side and puts an arm around my waist. Billy comes up on the other side (my left) and he, too, puts his arm around me. I lace my arms around both of them, as though it were the most natural thing in the world, and continue walking, not looking at them. Billy's hand grips my side firmly; the woman's rests delicately against my ribs, its weight supported by Billy's arm. Their bare, flushed shoulders brush against mine. I can smell the sweet cocoanut oil they're both wearing. Their ribs rapidly rise and fall, slippery under my palms. Gradually their breathing evens out.

We draw near a cluster of men lounging on the sand, some crouching beside the towels of others, pairs strolling down to the sea, others emerging from the waves, tugging at their trunks or slicking their hair back out of their eyes. My companions automatically pull away from me and arrange *their* hair and swimsuits. They slow down and let their glance graze lightly over the different men, never staring at any one group for long, always maintaining cool, expressionless masks as though they're certain of their superiority and want to impress it upon all observers.

"Those idiotic tank suits," the woman mutters out of the corner of her mouth without disturbing the indifference of her face or halting the steady scanning of her eyes. "Why must every old man resort to that particular look?"

"Rather than the tank suits, why don't they just go ahead and wear those creations their designers make for them?" Billy asks. "At least those have the virtue of being original *and* ugly, not just ugly."

"Don't look now," she replies, "but the old Minister of the Left is waving at us from that striped tent."

"I suppose we must avoid him," Billy says with conviction.

"At all costs," I assure him. I know Billy is repeating Herbert's orders. The woman has ridiculed "Herbert and his ilk," but I cannot afford to take such liberties.

"At all costs," the woman repeats bitterly, a slight smile on her lips, her eyebrows raised superbly. I've disappointed her.

Three men issue out of the striped tent and intersect our path. "The Minister would appreciate a little visit from the three of you," one of them whispers. "He was quite charmed by the sight of your approach and said, 'Here come the three most attractive people on the island, and the cleverest.' "

"Attractive?" Billy asks, winking at the woman.

"Did he say attractive?" I repeat.

"That's a word we find absurd," the woman insists. "It's come to mean 'our sort' or 'rich' or 'aristocratic,' and the other day I actually heard one woman ask another if so-and-so was attractive. 'Why, yes,' was the answer, 'he's terribly well-bred and attractive.' 'No, you don't understand,' returned the first woman. 'Is he attractive-*looking?*' Now, really, could the Minister have called us attractive? If he did, assure him that we are at a loss to understand him."

"You really want us to tell him that?"

"Why of course," I assure the messengers. They lower their heads in unison and hurry back to the tent.

"Do you think we overstepped ourselves?" Billy asks rhetorically.

"Possibly," the woman replies, facing out to sea. "But if we have a reputation for being original, perhaps we can get away with it? In any event, you needn't worry, Billy. You always have Herbert to wrap his arm about you."

"His cold arm . . ." I mumble.

Billy stares at me.

"He's coming in person to see us," the woman whispers with suppressed glee. "Is everyone watching, Billy?"

"Yes."

"Good."

A handsome old man in khaki pants and shirt approaches us but stops several yards up the beach and sends one of his attendants on ahead.

"The Minister would like you to accompany him to his house. He would like to discuss the subtleties of language with you over drinks; he finds it very encouraging to discover an interest in words in people so young."

"*Drinks!?*" the woman exclaims rudely, loud enough to be overheard by the Minister. "But we don't want drinks. We were just going on a little stroll down the beach. Invite him to come along if he likes."

The messenger returns to the Minister and repeats our invitation. In an undertone the woman confides to us, "If we've gone this far we mustn't capitulate; he must come all the way to us. We won't join him. What a triumph if we succeed!" She hurls a look of hysterical excitement at me, underlined by such sadness that I feel she'd rather not be here, acting this way.

Nodding genially, the Minister brushes aside his attendants and walks up to the woman and kisses her hand.

"Hi," she says breezily, "come along, but not with your gang. It will just be the four of us. We can stop by my house if you really want a drink, or I can fix us a snack."

"A snack? You yourself would prepare it?" the Minister asks.

"Of course," the woman replies, heading down the beach, saying over her shoulder, "I told you I wasn't the *attractive* sort who keeps a retinue or whatever you call it."

"Attraction," the Minister chants in that special tone I've come to recognize as the signal of approaching poetry. "Attraction—"

"Sir," I interrupt, laying a hand on his arm as we catch up with the woman, "We've put a ban on poetry for the rest of the afternoon."

"Please don't call me Sir," the Minister requests with so much force, even alarm, that I can only wonder whether the word isn't reserved for someone of even higher rank. Since everyone seems so determined to appear casual, perhaps all titles are eschewed and simple, innocent words like *Sir* have gained, as substitutes, heraldic significance.

The woman takes the Minister's hand, pulls him along at a brisker pace and says, with a blinding smile, "You were wrong to think of us as clever. I promise you, you won't hear a single clever word for the rest of the afternoon."

In only a few minutes about twenty young men have joined our promenade, and every time we pass another cluster of sunbathers someone new leaps up to fall into the procession. One young man, rather pale and covered with black hair from his neck down, asks me timidly if he may walk with us. "Of course," I tell him politely, though I'm so exhilarated at the thought of being a leader, or at least an original member of this triumphal march, that I'm half tempted to ignore him.

The Pale Stranger, I quickly realize, must be either extremely important or extremely unimportant, for everyone in the party, including the woman, is stealing nervous glances at him and falling silent, whether from awe or aversion I have no way of knowing. Then the woman, regaining her poise, resumes, quite loudly, her conversation about words with the Minister. "Have you noticed," she asks, "how the good people persist in saying you look very *well* in that coat when they mean *good?* Now I don't know much about grammar, but isn't *good* the more natural expression? Or do they mean that the coat has improved the wearer's vision, or his general health? Only yesterday I told a woman, 'Why, thank you, but my health, strangely enough, seems to be excellent even when I'm not wearing my coat.' "

"She's always very clever, isn't she?" the Pale Stranger remarks to me. "How I'd like to speak to her."

"Wouldn't we all?" I reply. "But she's apparently quite engrossed in her linguistic studies with the Minister."

"Is the Minister a member of this smart crowd? I had no idea."

Billy comes deftly to my aid. "It's not a crowd. We're just taking a little stroll."

Herbert! Herbert's watching us. Billy completes a beautifully meaningless speech to the Pale Stranger, something to the effect that if we had become a crowd, it was only because so many people, quite spontaneously, had been kind enough to swell our ranks—and in a few neat phrases indicates exactly which of us originated the Little Stroll, as I can see it's going to be called from now on. I can think of nothing but Herbert, who is propped up on a gleaming arm above an orange-striped towel. The reflected color from the towel glows like bands of iodine on his oiled side and cheek.

My terror, however, is quickly allayed. Herbert looks so flabbergasted at seeing me in such distinguished company that he must be revising rapidly his opinion of my worth. Now, at last, he can't help but sense that he was wrong to bully me, I who have the ear of the old Minister of the

Left and the Pale Stranger. Now at last Herbert realizes that I have only been masquerading as his subordinate, not out of a desire to deceive him but merely because I'm too nonchalant, too agreeable to quibble over anything as silly as rank.

If the woman, Billy and I had come down the beach alone, Herbert might have attempted a test of wills and ordered Billy back to the house and me to my lonely hill. But in one glance he has surmised that our trio has become a movement, and a movement that he must join. Join he does, as he steps into place beside the Pale Stranger. Herbert's clipped nod, his polite smile and his crisp, unsensual way of walking have turned his body into a uniform. He might as well be wearing epaulettes and white gloves, so contained and hygienic are the hairs on his chest, the navel in his belly, the feet on his legs.

Our slow progress beside the scalloping waves is now the only event worth studying on the entire beach, and the unfortunates who have neither the nerve nor the right to join us study us seriously, as though we were a new, particularly baffling and dangerous force to contend with, as indeed perhaps we are.

A smiling olive-skinned little bystander—a playful monkey, rolling his eyes and baring his teeth in nervous spasms—blows a yellow plastic whistle hanging from his neck on a cord. We all stop. He kneels in front of us. He is taking our picture.

Herbert is suddenly photogenic. He has slipped into the front row beside the woman and is kneeling at her feet, looking up at her adoringly. I stamp my foot, gently, with rage at his presumption. People will see the snapshot and assume that he was an original member, possibly the leader, of the Little Stroll. They'll forget that I was even present. I will only be hair glimpsed behind someone's head, a black aureole crowning a bright face on that carefree day when the Minister's fortunes took a turn for the better, when the Pale Stranger, by his mere presence, raised to the height of fashion a group that five minutes earlier had not been a group at all. If the good people recall that on that summer day a new clique rose to power, they will praise Herbert for his perspicacity in picking a winner. If the new clique will seem a year from now to have always existed, or at least to have been only a slight realignment of much older elements, then, once again, Herbert's sense of subtle transitions will be credited with the very ease of this particular transition. In either case he comes out looking good.

Unless I stop him. If I could only speak up, protest, or, better yet, draw

Billy, the Minister, the woman and the Pale Stranger away into a smaller nucleus, all done effortlessly, in the woman's style ("Oh, we're going to stop for a snack; 'bye, everybody").

The olive-skinned gremlin blows his whistle a second time, and again we freeze for our picture. Somehow Herbert has tricked the woman into returning his adoring look, perhaps because he's handsome (or "attractive," as some fools say). Or because she fears him.

For some reason I turn my head toward the dunes on my right and see, fifty yards away, a gate fitted into the side of one sand hill. The gate's thrown open to reveal a passageway so low that an adult would have to stoop to enter it. Framed in the doorway, but some ten feet down the passage, stands a workman hunched over a pneumatic drill. Dressed in black boots and gray coveralls, his face encased in a gas mask and goggles, a white handkerchief tied over his hair like a bandana, he leans over the stuttering machine, which is throwing up clouds of white dust. The man's mask, chest and particularly the front of his legs are blanching visibly moment by moment as the dust, radiating upward from the floor in strong, straight shafts, settles on his body.

Behind him I can distinguish a low-ceilinged vault, its back wall a gray concrete stained grayer by patches of moisture or fungus exposed by the harsh blue light of a caged work-lamp which dangles above the man and extrudes a heavy black cord from its base. The man looks out at me. Sunlight ignites his mica goggles. Beside his feet is the first step leading down.

Could there be a whole city under the sand? Or might it be that the pines, the marsh grasses, the rough-hewn walkways, the rambling little cottages are only deceptively primitive, that beneath them, as beneath the casual manners, a sophisticated machinery is governing every detail? Just as every word or movement takes on overtones and produces ripples that work through the entire society, so every object must be wired to every other and I was not misguided in finding order in the rocks strewn about the Detached Residence, rocks which might well correspond to, and communicate with, the four purple pennants flying from the black cottage that towers above ours. Or the rocks might repeat as a group the shape of a single leaf of trampled grass on our dock, a repetition effected on a vast scale and in a different medium, perhaps, but all the more satisfying for the transposition. Yes, even the most innocent and insignificant thing, like a particular leaf of grass, may serve as a template for all natural and human configurations and events, and if I could only pick out which leaf, which pebble, which shadow cast at what hour, which lowering of bamboo blinds, which combination of colors, exactly which crossing and uncrossing of whose legs was the ruling impulse, then, magically, all else would fall into place.

The whistle blows. We are released and continue the Little Stroll. No sooner have we taken twenty steps, however, than the woman works her way back through the others to me, who am now, ironically, the last in the procession. "I've got a splitting headache, darling. Want to stop by my place? It will just be us—the Minister, Billy, you and me and"—she touches the Pale Stranger on the shoulder—"and you, too, if you'd like."

4

The sunlight sparkles on the ocean and bounces up through venetian blinds into the room. An extremely tall Negress slouches beside the window, her back to the light, her features thrown into doubt. She's painted a blue emulsion around her eyes, and it picks up the brightness of the white, sun-drenched ceiling and holds the sheen on her smooth cheekbones. Her sloping shoulders, tiny breasts and cello hips stand out clearly under her dress. Her left arm, so long and subtle that it seems to be bending at some extra joint between the elbow and wrist, runs like a black river across her torso. She has buck teeth.

She coughs, giggles behind a cupped hand, then relapses into stately impassivity.

"Shall I read?" the woman asks, standing behind the kitchen counter, lifting plates. She's shut her parasol and laid it on a chair beside her.

"Do," says the Minister.

"Do," echoes the Pale Stranger.

"And you?" she asks me. "What do you think? It's about us."

"Do."

"Maria has heard it all," the woman says, setting each plate on a little tray. The Negress shrugs.

I must practice a shrug in the mirror, must study the expressiveness of my entire range of tics, frowns, postures and grimaces. I may be dropping involuntarily all sorts of misleading or indiscreet hints. On the other hand, my inexperienced face may be earning me credit for a sensitivity or compassion I don't actually possess. For surely there's something about me the woman likes. I mustn't change too much, or she'll stop liking me.

"When you're left alone for a moment," she says to me, softly, from across the room, "you go so far into yourself."

"Do I? I do. You're quite right."

"You're so pensive today. So distant. Is there anything wrong?"

The Negress has stopped chewing her gum to await my reply, stopped not with her teeth together but with her jaw dropped and pointed. As she holds her face in that position, her features seem to grow longer and thinner.

"Nothing's wrong," I assure everyone. The Minister and the Pale Stranger, both sitting on kitchen stools beside the woman, study me with some embarrassment. They're embarrassed, I'm certain, because they have to look at me, since she's drawn attention to my mood, and yet they don't know how to appraise me or it. My mood isn't visible (at least I trust it's not); my presence is simply an indecipherable sign marking the frontier of a new country. Billy is playing with a toy poodle beside the half-opened door. The Negress begins to chew again.

"I don't know if you'll like what I've written about us," the woman continues, pouring hot broth out of a white enamel kettle into six bowls decorated with blue peonies.

The Negress stops chewing.

"Two people execute a thousand little steps with one another—"

Munch, munch. The Negress is chewing.

"—assuming all the while that they're in total agreement about what it all means and where it's all leading."

Munch. Stop.

"And then," the Minister interjects, "one day they're disabused—"

"No," says the woman, "they can go on that way for years, making delicate allusions to their shared understanding without ever guessing that they're in complete disagreement about the main issue. If each—"

Munch, munch.

"—*fantasy*, if you'll forgive, and I don't, that abzurd expression—"

The woman has so enjoyed pronouncing the word as "ab-zurd" (on the beach she said it the other way, with the ess sibilant) that her eyes flick up to the ceiling and search for a way to repeat it.

"—in fact, I find *fantasy* a total ab-zurdity, but if each, if you will, *fantasy* is a perfect formal counterpart to the other, while differing from

46

it entirely in content, then all references to the two fantasies, if tactful and unspecific enough, will synchronize quite well and the disparity will never show up. *Until*, well, *until* a fool like me, darling"— she looks at me tenderly and her shrill voice softens and lowers— "gets it into her head to *write* about—"

Munch.

"—it."

"Do you follow her?" the Pale Stranger asks the Minister so accusingly that the Minister can't fathom what his answer should be.

"Yes . . . I believe so."

"So do I!" the Pale Stranger declares by fiat, slamming a manful fist through the air but braking it just before it touches the counter. "Utterly lucid." He drops his opened palm onto the formica.

"If poems are banned in conversation," the Minister asks the woman with a sly smile, "is a sincere admirer also forbidden to send into this house a *written* poetic tribute to your lucidity?"

"I've heard," the woman replies, "that your sincerity will know no bounds."

Munch.

"We find," Billy pipes up, rolling on his back and holding the poodle up at arm's length, "the word *sincerity* absurd."

"Ab-zurd!" the woman corrects him mechanically before correcting herself. "No, not ab-zurd. *Sincerity* is merely too important a word to be squandered on someone who merits it less than you, my dear Minister." She smiles, very much the great lady.

The Pale Stranger lifts his hand. It's covered with blood.

"Look," I exclaim, though I'm so lethargic from the sun that for a second I flirt with the idea of not saying anything more, of just lazily contemplating the catastrophe, "you're bleeding."

"It's nothing, nothing. A nosebleed. I'm frightfully sorry. Perhaps a napkin, nothing good, paper's the best thing. How silly. Seldom happens. How embarrassing."

Two scarlet bands flow from his right nostril. One collects above his thick upper lip and forms a shiny mustache. The other pools in the dimple at the corner of his mouth and then seeps past down his dead-white skin and into the black stubble along his jaw.

"I'll get paper. Billy, help me," the woman commands.

"No, stay, uh, Billy," the Stranger insists, uncomfortable with the nickname and the attention.

"Shall I call your doctor? Is he waiting outside?" Billy asks, the poodle yapping at his feet, one loop of its blue bow undone and flicking in and out between its legs.

The Negress leans on an arched hand against a small table by the window, the sunlight from the distant water yellowing as it passes through one of her long fingernails.

"No, not the doctor. He'll make me leave—oh, I've dropped some blood on the floor, so sorry—and I don't want to leave. I can't bear to end our charming 'snack.' This, believe it or not, is my first 'snack.' "

The woman returns from the toilet with a handful of paper tissue in her hand, arranged with such exuberance that she must have taken an instant to compose it. The Pale Stranger starts to grab for the paper when he notices its beauty and ends up by tearing off only a scrap from a swatch at the bottom. But the woman tosses the whole bouquet carelessly on the counter.

"This is terribly awkward, ab-zurd as you would say, but could I—"

"Yes?" asks the woman.

"Could I, uh, stretch *out* on the counter?"

"Of course. You're upset. The fire last night, your house . . ."

I see. The Pale Stranger is that luxury-loving man; his was the last of the great houses to be destroyed. No wonder people treat him with respect or deference. They know of his tragedy.

The Pale Stranger hoists himself clumsily, his chin a clot of browning blood, onto the counter and lies down, then throws his head back over the side until his face is upside down. Working deftly, his hands crumple paper into pellets and force them into his nostril. The Pale Stranger's eyes, upside down, follow me as I walk to the table and kneel beside my tray.

Five pink shrimps rest in one section of the white dish beside a dab of dark sauce. In a smaller section is a cold compote of vegetables. The bowl of broth nestles in the third section, beside a thin band of blue ribbon, an inch long, pressed flat against the porcelain, an allusion to the poodle's bow.

The woman sits beside Maria on an oversized cushion covered in candy-stripe silk. The Negress, never taking her eyes off me, reclines and props her head up against the woman's knee.

"This soup has a very delicate flavor," the Minister tells the woman from his mat on the other side of the table.

"I would tell you its odd ingredients," the woman replies, slipping a hand under Maria's dress and fondling her small breast, "but you'd

48

think I was being pretentious. I suppose it's good we all avoid ostentation—"

Maria licks the woman's forearm with her delicate pink tongue.

"—because if we didn't, many people would be too poor to keep up, and *think* of the rich bores we'd be reduced to eating with."

"How true," the Minister says, sounding unconvinced.

"Here, just slip your dress down to your waist, Maria." Sitting forward, the Negress lazily complies and pulls the straps off both her shoulders. Lying back again, she permits the woman to put a pink shrimp on her brown belly. They both contemplate the shrimp and then slowly their studiousness turns into laughter. Cultivated and soft, their voices overlap, and as one rises, the other falls in a breathy rondino, while the shrimp jogs merrily up and down on the taut skin drum. Maria finds a round hand-mirror under the table and, suddenly serious, studies the shrimp's reflection. In a fever of inspiration the Minister pulls a paper doily out from under the dishes on his tray, turns it over, dips his index finger in the dark sauce and sketches the Negress. In a moment he's finished. We gather around him to see the drawing. He's shown Maria's shoulder straps twisting like snakes at her waist, bounding elastically into the air. Her mouth hangs open in fascination—a childish, sensual, perhaps cruel fascination—and her eyes start from her head too much. He's also shown too much of the whites; she looks like a startled horse. The shrimp is shown from one angle on her stomach and from another in the mirror.

"Of course, I regret the absence of a color contrast."

"Not at all," the woman tells him firmly. "That would have been vulgar. Color isn't vulgar in life, because everything happens so quickly in life, but in a picture it—"

"Let me see," the Pale Stranger, no longer so pale, implores from the kitchen counter. On the linoleum below him the poodle is softly clattering.

"Of course," the woman murmurs, hurrying to him and turning the picture upside down.

"Adorable," he pronounces, and I have the distinct impression that the Pale Stranger's pronouncement will make the rounds and that for a few weeks it will become the vogue word on everyone's lips.

The Minister has returned to his soup and sips it quietly, looking older and smaller after his exertions, his dare. How easy (and also how difficult) it is to remain mute while everyone else chatters so brilliantly, to permit their colored wings to glide over your shadows, to grow darker and clumsier by the moment. An effort of the will is required to enter the commotion. Your heart is in your mouth as you turn your phrase. Anything could go wrong, you could follow, at least technically, any word with any other, and possible ridicule greets you at every juncture. You find it more and more difficult to venture even a "yes" or a "no"; silence enfolds you. Yet the absence of your comments grows increasingly conspicuous, and even if you had decided that your strength lay precisely in your taciturnity, a casual remark would still be needed from time to time to point it up, to demonstrate that you are quiet because you choose to be, not because you're afraid to speak.

"Not adorable," I call out in a ringing voice. "Not adorable," I repeat.

The woman flinches at my remark, my heavy demolition of the little moment she had achieved, my boorish rejoinder to the Stranger's cherished pronouncement, flinches again at my dull repetition of the offending words, and yet, so totally does she believe in me, so convinced is she that I would not risk destroying a balance without planning to regain it on some higher, more precarious perch, that, breathing excitedly, she feeds me the question: "If not adorable, then what is it?"

The room is quite still. Billy looks delighted.

A dozen words flash through my mind, none of them right or even sensible, and I repeat, huskily, appalled at myself, "Not adorable."

We've moved to the Minister's cottage on the bayside for the Sunset. This is a strange time to be out and about. Most of the islanders are at home, taking after-beach naps or beginning to prepare supper or quietly having a drink with a neighbor or two on their decks. Coldness, like a calculated change of affections, has followed the heat of the day. I'm shivering in my swimsuit, even though the woman has lent me a terry-cloth shirt that ties in front with a heavy sash. The woman has put on a long pink pullover, but it couldn't be too warm; it's so sheer I can see her two-piece blue swimsuit through it. Silver birds, each with a short chain dangling from its mouth, fasten the red-embroidered neck. They must be like points of ice on her skin. The Minister has been wearing his khakis all along. While we were on the walkway an attendant handed the Pale Stranger a long robe with a hood. The transaction was effected without the two men exchanging a word. The Stranger has drawn the hood over his head and now, as he sits beside me, his face—and his swollen nose—are cowled in darkness. Aside from the

Stranger's attendant, the only other people we ran into on the walkway as we came here were solitary men scurrying past, eyes downcast. The woman laughed each time we encountered someone. "Oh, these afternoon assignations . . ." she drawled.

"One could write the comprehensive social history of the island," the Minister said, "by simply standing at a crossroads in the evening and figuring out who was coming from whose house."

"I hate love after the beach," the woman commented. "Sand and oil."

"If not in the afternoon, then when do you think of country matters?" asked the Minister hesitantly, wanting to be forward enough to seem modern but fearful of offending the lady.

" 'Country matters?' " Billy echoed skeptically, but he was ignored. Whispering to me, Billy added, "He uses his vocabulary *back!*"

The woman was not to be offended, not after an afternoon when the talk had flowed so freely and she had so completely had her way. "Frankly, I prefer used men."

"Used?" Billy asked. He, still wearing only his swimsuit, had laced his arm around the woman for warmth. As they walked slowly along, their heads close together, their voices subdued, they seemed as sad as an unrenewable friendship. Her hand rested on his waist, a hand curiously white against the boy's tanned skin, which in the dusky light looked even darker than it had before. They had known each other for years, I thought; they were not to know each other now; circumstance alone had thrown them together. Old habits of intimacy were resumed against a backdrop of recent enmity or reticence.

"Yes, used," she said. "Nothing's more delightful than seeing a man in the early morning on his way home from a night of love, unshaven, relaxed, smelling of the other woman, enjoying the songs of the birds and the dawn light, composing the poem he must send her, but really too relaxed to think of anything much at all. I stand by my window and he sees me and waves; I wave for him to come up. I offer him a cup of coffee. Then I kiss him on the neck; he laughs and apologizes and says he's very tired. He suggests meeting me some other time, maybe that evening. Oh no, I tell him, now or never. I may not even speak to you in the evening. Now or never. He laughs again, rises from his chair, and I lead him into my bedroom. An hour later, slightly bewildered, he's on his way home again. It's now almost scandalously late for his Return Home. People are watering flowers, making breakfast, and speedboats can already be heard on the bay and the smell of coffee sweetens the air.

51

The poor man's composing two poems now instead of one as he hurries toward his cottage, and the poem for me is giving him some trouble, since he must make at least a nod toward the unusual circumstances under which we met, but none of the poetic conventions quite fits, and he doesn't know what to say."

"But why," asked the Minister, "why do you like your men used?"

"Oh, please," the woman said wildly, looking at me. The Negress was attempting without success to stop giggling. "Are we expected to know why? Isn't it enough to have determined *what* we can like?"

"Amen," intoned the Pale Stranger so wearily that we all (or at least I) doubted that he had discovered his own propensities yet.

The woman opens her manuscript. She's seated on the step above me, Billy two steps below—in a sense the Minister's cottage is nothing but flights of steps and large landings in between. The lowest flight, as wide as the house, rises from a shored-up square of beach which has been meticulously patterned by rakes with tines set farther apart than ordinary, so far apart, in fact, that they must be quite useless for collecting debris, unless it's of some unimaginably large variety. The first landing is the high-ceilinged living room, almost devoid of furniture except for the three low couches reclining around the fireplace and a mist of electric lights glowing in one corner, wires as thin and transparent as strings of saliva, bulbs as tiny as captured, phosphorescing bugs.

The second flight of stairs modulates into pairs of stuffy bedrooms, windowless, damp, smelling of tangled bedclothes, graced with paintings by ungifted relatives and senior officials—views of the bay and the palace through branches snowy or blossoming, or mountains rendered by men who have never seen mountains and whose sole interest is to win acclaim by rejuggling in novel ways the five brushstrokes used to do rock: the Sheer, the Veined, the Pebbled, the Beautiful and the Cold.

A final flight, short and narrow, as though it were the last resistance to gravity the structure could come up with, passes through glass doors to an open balcony overlooking a charming old garden of chinaberries and variegated mosses and birches peeling in papery white tatters around a pool that undoubtedly spells out a word like *heart* or *mind* but has been allowed to revert so thoroughly to nature that its letters, like the snow-weathered features of a marble bust, have lapsed into incoherence.

The path that leads to the bottom of all these stairs is the red path of the sinking sun across the bay, smooth when not scutched by slashes of wind. We are all as lifeless as though the water had borrowed our blood for the moment as we hug our knees on the steps above the engraved sand.

A curious horror overtakes me. It's a form of elation, appropriate to nothing but attaching itself readily to everything. Like a page where the commonest words are inexplicably thrown into italics, my mind is investing objects and sounds with a significance devoid of meaning. A deck chair, turned away from us and toward the house, is *excluding*, a pure attitude of exclusion, not a chair; an attitude made intricate by rattan weaving and jaunty, impertinent armrests. The woman's way of shuffling and evening up the pages of her manuscript has borrowed an excitement from—from what? I look around and see the two thinning, dying brown pines beside a neighbor's house, and wish I hadn't looked; the pines are full of reproach. I'm like someone who has just heard overwhelming news, and to still a beating heart, has plunged himself into household chores. After half an hour of puttering around he's succeeded in forgetting the news but the excitement remains, disjunct, sparkling devilishly in the aluminum curves of the coffee pot he's scouring, lurking behind the bit of cooked egg in the frying pan, spilling acute accent marks over the furniture and over a voice beyond the window. I try to narrow my eyes and stop my ears to inhibit the field of significance that is rapidly expanding around me.

I await the woman's reading with the hope that it will deliver me from the landscape. These books and poems have a way of fighting off the world. Terrible new things are happening all around us, but people write about only a few old things. Even their "suffering" has a familiar ring. Books overexplain and at a rate slower than the understanding requires—in fact, too slowly to be understood.

She has said her book is about "us." As she glances quickly through the pages, smiling over a passage, skipping a whole chapter she knows by heart, pausing at another point and mouthing words, as though she's trying to phrase them differently, I feel as impatient as a man watching a gypsy deal out cards. She already knows everything, sees it as Mozart saw his symphony, in a single instant; I know nothing, and must wait to hear it told in time.

"This is a . . . sort of . . . history of the Valentines. Are you sure you want to hear it? I feel foolish all of a sudden."

"Don't do that," the Minister says. "Just read."

"Yes, read us this 'history of the Valentines,' " I tell her sarcastically. She looks at me.

I want to assure her that I'm not really sarcastic, that I won't question her work, that I want it to be good. I was sarcastic simply because I wanted to hear those words coming from my own lips—"history of the Valentines." I wanted to repeat them myself, but then, at the last moment, I said them mockingly. How else could I justify lingering over what must be a perfectly common phrase?

"At sixteen I was suddenly, improbably introduced into island society," she reads, a bit dubiously, as though she were reading from someone else's book. "If I had stepped out of a medieval book of hours I couldn't have seemed odder to the islanders or they to me. Doris had brought me up very strictly and in total isolation. From my earliest years, however, I had nursed longings for glory, and as I made my debut I took mental note of everything, and decided then and there to imitate—and eventually dominate—it all."

The Minister catches the Pale Stranger's eye; they smile nervously, the Stranger's lips curling down like the ends of a snippet of ribbon that's been spooled too long. Maria catches me looking at her. She's sitting two steps below the Minister and is hugging herself with her arms; she wants to be as inconspicuous as possible, all ears.

That sound! Ah, a sea bird.

"What I comprehended quickly was that alone I would have neither the stamina nor the resourcefulness to rise far, but that—well, I'd have to have an ally."

The Minister is smiling faintly, as is Billy. Am I the ally she found?

"I had a lot of money and, believe me, I wasn't ignored on the island." Billy yawns conspicuously.

"But of course there were snickers about my hair, my dresses, my hats, my ideas, my speech. I decided to save some ·of my Old Code eccentricities, to become 'an original.' In a society mad for novelty, I knew I could become something of a fad by clinging to bits of the past, but I also recognized that the strange is acceptable only if it fits people's familiar notions of it. An oddity that suits everyone's preconceptions must be nothing more than a slight variation on the ordinary. If a dancer turns left instead of right, or shrugs after the fourth beat instead of the third, then her daring will be endlessly discussed; but if she insists that dancing itself is absurd, forget it."

I can scarcely breathe. It's as though small hands were holding my chest, forbidding it to expand. I can't bear listening to her, can't bear being a captive. I lean slightly backward, away from her. Ordinarily, despite the fact that people watch their words as closely as possible, conversation dips and flows, presses in one direction like ectoplasm, retreats, seeps onward: inexact, experimental, an amoeba possessing mobility but sluggish and perfectly adjustable to the lay of the land. That must be why it's so agonizing watching her lips forming shiny sentence after sentence, every phrase unyielding to the touch. She doesn't like it either. Her eyes keep roaming over us. She spots every sign of boredom, every smile, every trace of indignation, and she'd like to respond, go into that point a bit more, shape it and serve it up in the most attractive way, but she can't. She's chained to that text, which was composed long ago, in solitude, for a different audience or, if for the same, one in a different mood. Why does she persist? Could it be that she hopes to woo us with the cumulative force of her writing, draw us into the tale, and lull us into dropping our objections?

When is she going to mention me (she said the book was "about us")?

"Accordingly, I tailored my differences in thought and dress so that they would ring subtle changes on prevailing themes and I even went so far as to create out of thin air a few charming 'barbarous' customs with which to regale the good people. I insisted that I always swam in the nude, that all the Old Code Valentines did it for 'hygienic reasons.' But I threw away all my old clothes, believing, I think wisely, that our ideas of beauty can expand to admit some new trimmings but no big changes. After all, our most 'shocking' designers lower a hem an inch but never propose that we wear bread-and-butter epaulettes or shadows of clothes rather than clothes themselves.

"And then, as all the world knows, I attached myself to the perfect man. If I did so then out of the most childish sort of ambition, I quickly learned that, miraculously, the man who suited my shallowest aspirations also satisfied my deepest needs, that the arm that would lead me to an envied place in society would bear me on past pride of place into an intimacy more rewarding than any of the absurd privileges I had once coveted so greedily. We, he and I, are not so close now as we once were—but that is another story."

Yes, indeed, and precisely the one I'd like to hear. I suppose I couldn't be the "perfect man"—could it be Herbert? Or the Pale Stranger? But I don't think she's risen that high, or why would she be courting the Minister, himself someone out of favor, or only now, this evening, reascending into it? Even the Pale Stranger is in disgrace. He broke the sumptuary laws and his house, accordingly, was burned.

The sun, which appears flattened slightly on its top and bottom, is about a quarter of an inch high and is falling perceptibly, black smoke gushing out of a fissure in its side. Now it is half sunk; it's growing smaller; and now it is gone. A pale band in the west turns momentarily paler. It's striated as meticulously as the beach. But after an instant of afterglow the band also dims into darkness and a higher, more distant cloud bank, pinker than flesh, takes the light. Blowing across the sky away from us is a cloud resembling a black wing, torn from the shoulder, pulling along behind it an immense dark pubic fleece. Miraculously, the wing, as it nears the point where the sun has set, catches fire and calmly disintegrates and the fleece in turn reddens and pauses. Now nothing drifts in the entire sky. Looking behind me, I see that the east has assumed a blue as blue as grapes.

Do these men think that the woman is beautiful? Her eyebrows are curved and thin; that must be desirable, for surely she's plucked them to look that way. Her mouth is small. Should it be large? Do they adore her for her wit, in spite of her looks? I like her looks. A man in white comes out from under the staircase we're sitting on and walks across the beach with a torch in his hand. He plants it in the sand beside the sea wall, then cuts back by a slightly different path, never glancing up or down. A door slams below us.

"Before I met my friend, the only man I had ever known so well was my brother."

Am I her brother? Could my name be Valentine? Something Valentine? I wish she'd tell us more about me, her brother.

"My brother was a flaccid, friendly boy, lazy and affable, a damp log capable of crackling when kindled but liable, as soon as no external flame was applied, to grow cold. He could reflect other people's excitement, but when he was alone he was no one at all. My new friend, the perfect man, was not nearly so easygoing and pleasant. He was reserved and a little cruel, not above encouraging the pompous to display their vanity and the silly their ignorance. But for all that, he set himself an independent course and seldom tacked."

And which am I? She's commented today on my remoteness, but that could be an attribute of either character.

"The customs were as easy to master as the styles. I only had trouble learning to speak correctly. Perhaps Herbert's islanders have no

56

conception of what a peculiar, unfathomable dialect they've worked out for themselves, but any outsider, if he's honest, can testify how hard the language is to pick up. Stark simplicity alternates with the most extreme indirection; bathroom humor unexpectedly gives way to supersubtle, virtually invisible wit. Worst of all, as with any inbred group left idle for a long time, an immense lore of gossip and history has built up, which for insiders can be invoked with a word.

"Early on I saw that if I waited until I had unraveled every mystery before entering into conversation, I would wait for years and bore everyone with my questions. I boldly decided to speak anyway, but to veil my meaning in clouds of imprecision, never to complete a sentence and to pronounce every syllable with a certain irony that could be diverted in mid-sentence into whatever attitude I might discover was appropriate. If I heard more than five words in a row that were thoroughly incomprehensible, I'd lower my eyes, since I knew that the eyes are so perverse they always betray a lack of understanding, no matter how artfully they're adjusted to signify intelligence.

"Because I listened more than I talked, people began to confide in me. So well did I listen that I was astonished to hear the most discrepant types of people declare that I was precisely like them; never had they met anyone so similar and sympathetic. I was fascinated to study the opposing urges that battled in every breast. Among the Valentines a proud reticence would have checked the need to confess, but among my new friends I witnessed a different sort of struggle, one waged between candor and the desire to appear original and complex and elusive: *not quite human*. We all know that human emotions are banal, that only a handful of motives exist (lust and greed and particularly vanity); and even fewer sentiments—notably love, fear and hate—which form, at that, an extremely unstable triad in which any element may transmute in an instant into any other. But the islanders are not reconciled to this parsimony of human nature. They crave a whole host of new sensations and reflexes. As soon as one of my new friends would grow truly passionate in the expression of an enthusiasm or antipathy, he'd suddenly remember to be—not more discreet, but more puzzling. With some amusement I'd watch him check the flow of his feelings and painfully backtrack and fabricate, without having his heart in it, a wry cluster of delicate, chiming emotions. For instance, Flavia came running to me one day in a fury at her mother, who had canceled her party, but no sooner had she overflowed with the first rush of her resentment than she stopped in mid-sentence and reconsidered. What will she do now, I wondered. She's already spilled too much bile. How will she make such a petty, age-old reaction seem august and never-before-felt? 'What really annoys me, of course,' the girl said at length, setting her jaw with a determination that indicated she would brook no contradictions, 'is that now I won't have a chance to be truly bored and disenchanted. As long as my mother keeps me from plunging headlong into society, I still regard parties and such things as tantalizing. But if I could drink my fill of it, I'd quickly come to hate it, since at heart I'm a very retiring, religious person. My mother knows this and fears it, and is determined to frustrate my religious vocation.'

"Now, no one ever *felt* that way, least of all an adolescent girl, and only an extraordinary sort of community ever could have convinced a child to reason in that fashion. But I said nothing. I simply chided her for referring to herself as a 'religious person'; no one said 'person' that season, nor used 'individual' or 'human' as a noun.

"Although I had little understanding of half the allusions people made and only half grasped, at first, their characteristic ways of distorting their thoughts, nonetheless I developed an oddly abstract feel for the *shapes* of conversation. I could tell when someone was ready to be reproved, not because he had said something *I* disagreed with but because I could sense *he* didn't believe what he was saying and would welcome a question or a doubt on my part. In the same way I learned to sense when people felt they were being boring and needed little nods and smiles of encouragement, and I also knew when they wanted to be drawn out or left alone, or when, despite their rueful self-deprecation, they wanted wholehearted approval, or when they hoped to be teased or flattered. I came to see myself as someone who was playing an organ whose music I couldn't hear; the sound was coming out of pipes in a distant room in another building. I knew nothing about performing on this instrument or any other, but I had been ordered to play for my life, and so I played, by intuition, seeing a likely combination of keys to strike and striking it. I'd wait and someone would rush in from the other building and exclaim, 'Oh, what beautiful music!' I quickly gained confidence and let each impulse growing within me translate itself into action, and never was I wrong. Of course I realized that my concertizing was only the blindest sort of speculation and that at any moment if I attempted to execute a new fancy, I might produce a disastrous sound. But I never did. The messengers always came in saying it was beautiful—and I never heard a note of it. In just that way, Herbert's islanders acclaimed me as the most accomplished conversationalist they knew, but I never understood a word of what we were saying.

"The Valentines are feudal and cruel. I seldom saw them then; now, never. I have no idea of what they think of me. At one time I'm certain they imagined I was infiltrating the enemy ranks. But when I made it very clear to them that I was not their agent, Doris was momentarily angry. Yet her sense of family is so strong that she soon came to think that if she must have an enemy, that enemy should at least be her relative. 'We've weathered the centuries,' she liked to say. 'For two centuries, long ago, we dropped out of history before and went underground, remember.' She said to me once, 'You *are* clever, mastering Herbert's rules, playing the egalitarian, putting off airs.' She liked that phrase, 'putting off airs,' and laughed.

"The truth is that I liked neither her rules nor Herbert's. Herbert had kept everyone amused and had once seemed sincere about wanting to simplify things. We could wear what we wanted (within limits), come and go as we pleased (more or less), make friends where we found them—or so people liked to think. Of course, my friendship was not an ordinary one, and Herbert kept his eye on it. Not knowing how circumscribed our freedom was, the perfect man and I planned a trip we never made, kept to ourselves for days at a time, turned skeptical. We asked a lot of questions, at first because we had fun teasing Herbert, soon because our silly questions had led to serious doubts. Surely Herbert had known that by changing the Old Code to the New he had introduced the dangerous notion of change itself. Surely he had guessed that his reform might lead to others. Yes, he had known, he had guessed. He took steps."

Billy is standing beside me. He's young and inexperienced, he has some lingering fondness for the woman, but he is ready to intervene.

He doesn't need to. The woman says, "But I've read enough. Here, I'll let you take the manuscript and parse it in private—if you want to. There's more in it about us. In fact, I hardly got to *us*, did I?"

The woman hands me the loose pages of the book and a box to put them in made out of hard shiny milk-white substance that looks like bone or horn. I smile at her and say, "It was quite illuminating."

"Do you hate me for it?"

"Not at all. I said illuminating, not shocking."

I have no idea whether my judgment pleases her or not. Composing the impassive expression she wore on the beach this afternoon, she takes Maria by the hand, pulls her to her feet and heads toward the walkway. At the gate she hesitates, turns and calls back to me, "Come by my house on your way home; I'll be alone." And then she and the Negress disappear.

"She always could make an impressive departure," the Pale Stranger says, pushing back the hood of his robe, as though he no longer needed its protection. His distended nose looks even larger when seen in profile, bulging out from his long, narrow skull.

"Too bad her prose is not as grand," the Minister says.

"I quite agree," Billy pipes up, obviously relieved that someone has started dissecting the book.

Simultaneously they all look in my direction to see if I'll go along with them. I'll go along. "I wish I could put my finger on exactly what was wrong with it," I say. "All of the obvious things were more or less right, or almost right, but surely . . ."

"I'm sorry," Billy says, "but I felt it was too organized. I like ellipses and teeny jottings and spontaneous poems and particularly all those devices like long lists of melancholy things."

"Let's be merciful and not dwell on her style," the Minister says. "Should we go in? It's getting chilly."

We re-form our circle in the living room on the three low couches beside the fireplace. The same attendant who planted the torch in the sand lights the fire and serves sherry to Billy and me. He sighs heavily, I could even say angrily, when Billy hesitates to take his drink, but no one else seems to notice the man's impatience. I take my drink very promptly, but instead of the smile I expected to elicit, all I get is downcast eyes and a sigh louder than the first. Somewhat impishly I sigh back. I suppose I shouldn't call it impish, since I did it involuntarily, perhaps imitatively, though I did have the good sense to tilt it, just at the end, toward teasing. When I turn to my left I see the exchange of sighs has not escaped the Minister, who is sitting beside me. The servant's face flushes. The dry wood pops softly and constantly, sounding like a bird dropping seeds on the floor of its cage. The servant pauses beside a mahogany drop-leaf table and leans on it for an instant, as though he felt faint and was trying to steady himself. Through a window next to the front door I can see a single streetlamp, as tall as the trees, made of thick poured concrete, its bulb heavy like the belly of an insect, the light it casts a strong, unpleasant orange like the smell of iron. Pop, pop, the bird drops two more seeds out of its overflowing feeder.

Light flashes in the Stranger's cupped hand as he moves it and for an instant I imagine he's holding a flame; no, the metal top of a beer can. He seems quite unaware of his nose. All through the reading, though he followed the text closely, he kept lowering his head or drawing it back like a tortoise into his hood. Now, unhooded, he sizes us all up in rapid, penetrating looks as one hand makes a fist in his lap and the other clenches his drink. During the reading I was able to decipher in his face the lineaments of the boy he once was; now I can predict the grizzled, strong-willed old man he'll soon become. "Let's be honest," he announces brusquely, "I'm as glad as you are that women believe all these fads and styles are so desperately important; it keeps them busy and makes them feel they count. But we know it's money and power that keep the first families first; she was a Valentine and she would have risen to the top no matter how she dressed her hair, even if she had shaved and shellacked her skull. So, I submit, what can we learn about the world from her?"

"She's swallowed our lies. I see your point," the Minister says. His servant is standing beside him and creates a minor explosion as he pops off the flip top of another beer can. He begins to walk away when the Minister catches him by the coattails and drags him back. "I want you to see something. The most extraordinary rash. I can't quite decide how to treat it." As he speaks to the Stranger, the Minister unzips the servant's fly and tugs his pants halfway down. A large purple blotch stains the inside of the man's right thigh; the blotch is rather long and narrow but fans out at one end—exactly as I've imagined a map of the island must look. The servant's eyes are lowered.

"Let *me* see," Billy insists. The Minister and the Stranger laugh heartily at Billy's expense; the Minister slaps the servant jovially on the hip and the man pulls up his trousers and stumbles off to the kitchen. Just as the laughter is finally subsiding, Billy says angrily, "You know you're not supposed to keep him on; we do our own work, why shouldn't you? For instance, Bob used to be a servant, but now he works no harder than the rest of us, than Herbert or you." He looks at me. I produce what I believe is called a pained smile. Precisely such outbursts—whether sudden laughter, anger or amazement—catch me unawares, and eventually someone is bound to notice and wonder. If only I could tense my body with an excess of energy that could be triggered instantaneously into guffaws or snarls or gasps, then I'd be safe.

Billy is standing now, an indignant angel, his back to the fire. "Both of you"—he looks at the Minister and the Stranger—"pretended to go along with the New Code, but you didn't fool Herbert for an instant. It's disgusting the way you blandly assume that the New Code is nothing but lies, that Herbert still intends for the 'first' families to be first."

"You've misunderstood us," the Minister says. "I've always gone along with Herbert."

"Oh?" Billy asks. "It seems to me you go along with this and then that and then this again."

The Minister yawns nervously and pulls off his hair—a wig. He tosses it on the floor, a small skinned hide.

"And would you say that *I'm* too flexible?" the Pale Stranger asks. "Is that why Herbert had my house burned down?"

"I adore flexibility," Billy replies. "Are you going to rebuild your house?"

"No," the Stranger says.

"It was so large, so formal, you're well rid of it."

Pop, pop; the fire is talking to itself.

"Why has Herbert turned on us?" the Stranger asks. "First he dismissed the Minister, now me. But we both served him well."

"And served yourselves well, and Doris—"

"Not Doris," the Stranger interrupts. "We never see her."

The Minister sips his beer in resignation.

Perversely, I suppose, I choose this moment to get up and leave. Composing my face, I realize that by leaving now, without a comment, I'll give Billy and possibly the others a little scare. "Good-bye," I say very simply and walk toward the door, wondering if they'll call me back. I may have just broken a hundred rules, and each infraction may be reported to Herbert—yet, even as I feel their fear or derision or whatever it may be stretching like rubber from them to me, growing ever tauter, I also experience the excitement of being on my own for the first time; that is, for the first time today, drawing me toward the door and the Mercurochrome glow of the concrete streetlamp beyond.

It can't be this easy to leave, but it is. I close the door behind me. Someone glides into the shadows of an overgrown path near me. On a balcony of a house just this side of the dunes someone is silhouetted in a doorway. The horn case containing the manuscript is under my arm. Someone whistles.

5

I walk past the woman's seaside cottage. Simply knowing that it's my next destination permits me to amble aimlessly for a while. I feel my way down a wooden stairway onto the dark beach. A discarded pair of sunglasses warps the moonlight. My foot sinks into a rut I hadn't seen and I almost lose my balance. Shivering slightly, I tie my terry-cloth robe more tightly around me.

Long furrows in the sand; perhaps a jeep's tire tracks. A recording of a woman's voice floats on a soft breeze from a one-story frame house cupped between two nearby hillocks.

Scuffing my bare feet across the sand, I scatter showers of fool's gold. Plankton. Experimenting, I jump in place and awaken a circle of light around me, a gilded lotus supporting a Bodhisattva. Then I jog for a moment, digging my heels in deep, and observe over my shoulder fading footprints, the farthest already subsiding into darkness. I swoop down and hurl clumps of cold, wet sand in front of me, minuscule meteors flaming apart and landing silently on this imperturbable planet of moonlight and shadows.

The ocean thuds and fizzes behind me. I feel like a fish flung on land, a square-faced fish breathing the scorching air and flexing my whiskers spasmodically.

Emerging out of the dark, surprising me, a man and a woman walk past. They speak softly. A blue cashmere sweater draped over the woman's shoulders dangles empty sleeves behind her. The people are holding hands. A small dog, panting happily, trots ahead of them, closes its mouth and points into the wind; discovering nothing, the dog looks around to see if the man and woman are still following, begins to pant innocently again and scampers on ahead, the silky hair on its shanks matted with sand. They don't see me. I would like to join them or be him or her.

Someone's standing by the window, tall and operatic. Could it be the woman, wearing a robe of some sort? Is she grinning? Is she dead?

No, it's only a bird cage, covered with a long trailing cloth.

The door at the other end of the porch opens, a head emerges, a white hand rests on the white doorjamb. "Why are you standing there? I thought you'd never come," the woman says raucously, her voice overly distinct and the emotion too pat, as though she were playing the scene for someone else's benefit. And indeed I can hear shaking, hissing laughter coming from inside the house: Maria.

As I brush past the woman, she flattens herself against the door and salutes, which elicits more hissing from the Negress. As my eyes adjust to the darkness, I pick out the white rectangle of the mattress on the floor; the flowered sheets—is there someone in the bed?—no, the sheets are simply tangled; a sudden glint of light—another room? Brilliants in Maria's hair? No, a mirror on the wall. A heavy perfume rises from the furs on the floor, a scent laden with associations. Our mother may have worn it when we were children; it's barbarous and musky enough to suit the Valentines. Or does the woman always sprinkle it about when she expects the perfect man? Am I her brother or her lover?

She stands in front of me, her face lifted toward mine, her eyes closed. I don't know what she expects. I put a hand on her shoulder. She draws the fingers to her mouth and licks each one, then forces two between her lips, then three and then, my knuckles touching the roof of her mouth, she licks my palm. Her tongue is sandy. Her eyes never open. Removing my hand from her mouth, she guides it under her robe and places it upon her right breast. I suppose I should rub it. Should I wet *her* hand as well and put it under my shirt?

The only thing for me to do is experiment. I only want to please. And yet, her pleasure may depend on mine; we may turn out to be one mirror reflecting another, two mirrors bandying absence back and forth.

I put my hands around her waist and lock them. She presses her pelvis against mine and arches her back, tossing her head so that her hair flicks over her shoulder. She's behaving so queerly I can only presume the occasion dictates sudden movements, heavy breathing and long, silent glances. Ordinarily she carries herself in a quite natural, unobtrusive way, but now she's smiling and now she's nuzzling her lips against my neck. What is she—she's biting me!

This sharp sting on my neck seems familiar.

"So you're here," she whispers. I nod. Her voice sounds unexpectedly normal. It reminds me of our walk on the beach, where everything was so sane and purposeful.

Now I am her purpose, I or my body, and her legs, her lips, her breasts are mine to do with as I wish. Where is Maria? I don't see her anywhere around. Perhaps she scurried out of the room as soon as I came in, or perhaps she's watching us from behind the mirror on the wall.

As though she were blind, the woman closes her eyes and traces my features lightly with her fingertips. "I can't believe you're here."

"But I am," I say, gentle, compassionate, maybe bemused.

"Put your hand on my breast," she orders me solemnly. "There. It's yours. My body is yours. You can kill me if you like. I belong to you. Do you know what that means? I mean it. I belong to you."

I don't know what to say. Apparently her declaration excites her; I realize that I'm in the presence of a fantasy I don't understand, and that she's rehearsed this last little speech so often that the words amaze her now that her mouth has finally formed them. She trembles from head to foot when I touch her hair, as though I had just flooded her body with energy.

She pulls away from me. Turning to her bedside table, she putters aimlessly with the objects on it—a bracelet? a comb? No, a necklace that she slips over her hair. Humming a little song, she dances. She shakes her head from side to side and lowers her eyes. Very nonchalant. She fears her declaration has embarrassed me and she's marking time. What she wants is to seem at once occupied and free, absorbed with her dancing (not expecting a thing), but available to any whim I might chance upon. If I touch her, she'll awaken, open her eyes, come back into my arms. As she said, she belongs to me.

Her hands circulate, she feints and fades, her head double-times the beat, and yet there's something tentative and sketchy about what she's doing. She may be self-enclosed, but if so, she's a package with ribbons half untied.

Someone, I suppose Maria, starts strumming the guitar in the next room, or the room beyond, and its chords, interrupted by long silence, destroy the woman's dance. The woman stops where she's standing and fidgets with her hair. Marooned, uncertain, caught between emotions, she looks at me blankly. I notice a dressmaker's dummy by the window. "What's that?"

"My dress for the royal arrival," she says. "I'm afraid it's as complicated as I am."

She's so little and lonely. I put my arms around her. She's a very fragile creature. I'm much bigger than she, much stronger. I adore her. If anyone tried to hurt her—ah! I'm feeling what people must experience when they pant or stare at each other or bite. They are feeling so many things, feeling and dreaming. Ordinary conversation is so mannered and constrained that little is expressed and that little in contorted forms, like plants stunted and shaped by wires. Only in dark bedrooms can the foliage rush free and loud. If people looked so tragically at one another on the beach, everyone would burst out laughing; but at night, in private, they no longer have to be nonchalant or original. When they make love they're like singers in an opera. The woman is a prima donna, rising quickly at the hero's arrival, drinking in his presence, embracing him passionately, and launching into her aria, "O safely returned!"— except no sound is uttered. Some convention or other permits islanders to indulge in histrionics in the dark.

I pull her blouse open and for a moment I think I've made a mistake because she covers both breasts with her hands. But then she kisses me briskly and lies down on the bed, her hands by her sides, her eyes open and glimmering. I kneel above her on the mattress and decide—how odd!—to let her *worship* me.

And she does. Her hands travel up my sides, explore my skin under my robe, and seek to pull me down to her level, but I resist. I do more than resist, I frown at her. My contempt either excites her or alarms her, I don't care which. Her breathing quickens. She rises to her knees and pulls off my robe, feverishly kissing my hands, my neck and my shoulders.

Very deliberately I get up and slip my swimsuit off. She never takes her eyes off me but her hands fumble with her own clothes as she raises her hips off the mattress and works her panties down her legs.

Now we are both naked.

I debate for a moment what I should do next, I puzzle over what's correct. I could cross the room, squat on my haunches, my chin in my hand, and stare at her impassively. Or I could pace restlessly from the head of the bed to the foot, lost in thought, my head dropped as she struggles to gain my attention. By walking back and forth, so close, yet my thoughts so far away, I'd become more and more worthy of worship, untouchable. But if I'm right, if people take off their clothes in their rooms in order to pantomime their fantasies ("an ab-zurd expression"), then what is my fantasy? How can I translate what I've been going through today and yesterday into an action, or a series of actions, that will tell my little tale? The exhaustion pressing strong fingers into my neck and shoulders, powdering the base of my backbone into dust and slowing my feet—surely this exhaustion is a sign I'm not living right. Not everyone could be this tired, day in and day out. The correct way of thinking, talking, moving, second-guessing—if there is a correct way— must be much easier.

Then if my way is too strenuous to be right, I should be able to dramatize my errors, convert my mistakes into a charade or hieroglyph. And if I were successful in doing that? She might in turn devise her own dumbshow. That's what I must do, give a show.

My bowels roll over. I glance at my stomach to see if the skin of my stomach is rippling, is giving me away. No. I'm safe.

The woman puts her hands behind her head and her small breasts rise and flatten, no longer oranges but pears. Then she nervously lowers a hand—one orange, one pear—and rests it next to the cleft between her legs where I can only faintly distinguish her long fingers now, nesting like a soft waterfowl beyond the sprouting of her hair. "If you're not willing. . ." she says, slightly irritated.

"What do you want me to do?"

"Let me at least hold you?"

I begin to smile, I don't know whether from embarrassment or as a way of eliciting a smile from her, a sort of safe conduct into intimacy— but I banish it from my lips at once and make my face a blank. The whole secret in making love seems to be to skip the polite transitions, the haze of words and smiles and shrugs that in ordinary society dull the outlines of each new event. I must decide what to do and then do it, without apologizing or preparing her. This is not an exchange, but a perpet- ration.

I lie beside her and kiss her lips and plan to smear the kiss the length of her body, to the cleft, the knee, the sole of her foot. But I become involved with her hair and want it cascading around me. I roll her over on top of me and the hair drizzles on either side of my face, whether I look to the right or the left.

She shakes her head slowly, back and forth, trailing hair over first one of my cheeks, then the other. Now she is working her way down my body, but like a pilgrim making her progress toward a shrine, she stops to rest at every wayside shelter, forgetting none, giving each its due. Taking my limp penis in hand, she puts it in her mouth and oscillates around the tip of it. She licks it, she tries to swallow it—if this is *her* dumbshow, what's she saying by it? Perhaps she saw me inspecting my erection by the Detached Residence and she wants to show me that she knows it was the instrument of my loneliness. By joining her mouth to it, she may be telling me I'm no longer alone. We are together.

Or then again, for her its head may represent the Residence itself and the supporting column may stand for the grounds and the motions of her tongue may be mocking me, each lick may be a subtle remonstration, pointing out, on this tubular map, places I neglected to rake clean. Or she may be silently giving me instructions for my work tomorrow, saying, in effect, go here first and Herbert will tell you what must be done, and then rake . . .

Is it becoming harder? Yes, and she seems to find its extension more exciting (its growth aggrandizing the grounds of the Residence?). She says, "Oh, my darling," and renews her exertions. It may please her because I have a penis and she doesn't. By reciprocal reasoning, what she has and I lack I should find especially delightful. Her breasts, in fact, and her cleft.

I take her breasts into my hands and massage them. She moans so loudly, she says again, "Oh, my darling." Perhaps what we're seeking is pain, or at least an intense sensation halfway between pain and pleasure, for, truth to tell, I would be hard put to describe the feeling crowding my erection. Similarity of position would suggest that her cleft was the counterpart to my penis, but if so, then what in me corresponds to her breasts? Or could it be that, greedy for sensation, she has swallowed or injected a chemical to swell and sensitize her breasts?

When will this end? Shall we continue to lick and massage each other all night until exhaustion puts a stop to our work, or does something happen to signal the end? Maria may grow bored and interrupt us, but at least for now, her guitar sounds so self-centered it could go on playing forever. Or it may be that daylight when it comes will be inimical to such posturing, or perhaps the woman will become more and more tragic until she's had her fill or has completed a predetermined cycle at a predetermined point.

She slips off me, rolls on her back and adjusts a pillow under her buttocks. With great finesse and delicacy she extracts a hair—mine, I suppose—from between her teeth. Her legs open. I understand at last what she expects of me and make the insertion. It feels warm. Does she want something more, some movement? Yes, she has begun to move her pelvis back and forth.

I take up the rhythm and raise my hips and then lower myself into her, posting to a stately measure as her hands flutter, tentative and unconscious, around my face, brushing my cheek, grazing my chin, pressing firmly against my chest in a sudden spasm, finally collapsing and loudly slapping the mattress, once, twice. "My darl, my darling," she whispers, never once, not once, calling me by my name.

A terrifying pressure is mounting within me. I have no idea what it is, I wonder if I should stop, but I don't, I can't, I move faster and faster. A drop, two, three drops of sweat from my clavicle clavichord fall onto her neck, but she doesn't seem to mind, her hand gathers the drops, the triplet, to her mouth and she tastes it greedily. A high, gravelly noise rises in the back of her throat as her head twists from side to side. Then the sound breaks off, her body tightens only to go soft a moment later and her lips form a perfect circle. She stops breathing. She pronounces a single astonished "Oh."

I fear that she's secreted a burning liquid onto me, or possibly the fluids of her body are hostile to mine; whatever the cause, I know that something's seriously wrong; so much pain, if only I could inspect myself I'm certain I'd find blood. Perhaps her satisfaction requires my suffering. An offensive smell rises off our bodies—offensive but interesting. Am I really swelling, growing still larger, or is it only my imagination? I wish this would stop. I don't like it at all. Even if what we're doing is quite customary, I'm certain I'm not pursuing it in the right way. I'm wrong, it's wrong, this will come out badly. My heart is beating wildly and a vein pulses along my arm. My breath dries the moisture on her face. I much prefer the ordinary feelings. Is she killing me? Am I dying? So much pain. I'll shriek if it doesn't—

I explode and sob on her breast, no longer able to keep up this pretense, weary of not knowing anything, finally realizing that what she and everyone else expects of me is unbearable. "Why do you want so much?" I ask her—I shouldn't have said that. "I can't give you any more." I shouldn't have said that.

We turn on our sides and uncouple. My legs and arms tremble spasmodically. Curling up and resting her head on her hand, she surveys me coolly and smiles. "I would have thought you had just given me all I might have asked for." She laughs and hops out of bed, slim and energetic. After she finds a towel, she hurries back to me, perches lightly on the edge of the bed and slowly, thoughtfully wipes the sweat from my body. Although she touches me very softly between the legs I pull away in pain—even greater than before.

"Tell me, who am I? Who are you?"

She laughs. "Don't tease me," she says.

"No, I have to know. Who am I?"

"Darling," she replies, shaking her head, hurt for some reason, "my darling, you have the oddest sense of humor."

6

I recognize my crosswalk by the black house flying purple pennants.

"Hello, there," someone calls from the balcony. "We're having a drink. Care to join us?"

"No thanks. I'm on my way home."

"*What* are you wearing?" a theatrical voice asks out of the depths of a chair, his mouth a thin ring around the planet of a brightening cigarette.

"What?"

The red glow, dimmed now, travels to the balcony rail: powerful legs engorging leather pants, a leather jacket flung open to expose a muscular chest, crew-cut white hair fringing a bald dome. The dangling buckle of his jacket strikes a post. "It's Jimmy. I'm Jimmy."

"Hi, Jimmy."

"What *are* you wearing?"

"A swimsuit and a robe."

"Been swimming?"

"Come on."

"Don't tease him," admonishes a thinner male voice from another chair.

Jimmy runs a hand over his chest and the dangling belt buckle touches the post again. Spreading his legs slowly, settling into a solid stance, he cocks his head to one side and asks, "Just one drink?"

"All right," I tell him, unable to resist his calm baritone but afraid that I'm missing dinner at home, afraid that I still smell of the woman. As I head up the slanting walk to the gate, his "Just one drink?" vibrates in my ear, as though he had activated the lobe by pitching his words at exactly the right timbre. "Just one drink?" I feel for the latch inside the gate, find it and lift it. "Just one drink?"

Jimmy is propped against the rail. Closer to me, a hand, emerging out of the recesses of a covered chair, holds a wineglass by its stem. Inside, a middle-aged woman sits at a massive desk doing crosswords under a lamp held by a servant in livery. Behind the servant an open doorway reveals a still larger room. Three more men in livery dart past the open door and disappear. They return in an instant and set a folding screen in place—smoke-darkened brocade veined with lines of green gilt. Beside the woman a young man is thumbing through a pocket dictionary.

"What'll you have?" asks the Hand.

"Campari?" Jimmy suggests. "We're drinking Campari."

"Fine."

Jimmy lifts a bell from the table and rings it. A Russian wolfhound at the other end of the balcony peers intently out of the shadows at a wind chime above him, its colorless rectangles of glass turning lazily and throwing the lights from the living room over the porch walls and straw floor. Everything smells of straw and Braggi.

"What's a verb, six letters, meaning 'to brutalize'?" shouts the boy from the living room.

"*Savage*," says the Hand. "To *savage*."

The Hand sits forward so that his face comes into view: a simple mouth that lacks a line to mark off the upper lip, like a man's mouth in a fashion illustration; a bump in the nose, a flexed knuckle, paler than the surrounding skin; and ears swept aerodynamically close to the skull. "We're quite interested in your house," he says. "I can see your bathroom window from my bedroom. I'd prefer a view into your living room, or bedrooms, any place in fact where several people congregate at once. We have so much to learn about how things are to be done, Doris and I, and to watch a dinner or a conversation is so much more informative than spying on a private toilette, but even glimpses into a room that is steamy or partially shaded can be telling, tell *me* a great deal. Perhaps it's even *purer* to have so little data."

A servant slips up beside me, a tray in his hand.

"Your Campari," Jimmy mutters, handing me a small glass.

Jimmy's hand drifts vaguely toward a plant in the corner under a grow light. The servant goes over to it, picks up an atomizer and sprays a mist over the blossoms. Flowers and pets, I'm certain, are interdicted.

"Thank you." I sip the bitter red liquid and smile; perhaps it's unusually good and I should exclaim over it. Then again, perhaps Campari's Campari and any comment would seem silly. When I smile I'm careful not to show my teeth. No one does. Nor does anyone snap a smile on or abruptly switch it off. The smile starts as a slight pursing of the lips, the corners turned down in mock disapproval, and the eyes wide open and sharp as tacks: a skeptical *French* smile. But then the lips relax, going neutral for one disconcerting moment, before they begin their slow ascent toward happiness, an orchid opening in mist. The bright, sensible look in the eyes also clouds over and the entire face floats behind a veil of serenity. Just at the point when the mouth would seem about to burst open, to *grin*, the entire head tilts suddenly to one side like a punctured balloon, the eyelids click shut, the smile vanishes and the brow crinkles as though it were in fact shriveling rubber. Another breath can inspire the face again, open eyes, widen the mouth, but the renewed animation is only temporary; leakage will occur. Alternately full and deflating, the changing expressions keep the viewer off balance and attest to the smiler's volatile sentiments. But I may be doing it all wrong. I haven't practiced my smiles. I must find a mirror.

"What constructions have you put upon your data?" I ask the Hand. He looks directly at me for the first time and his far ear becomes visible. There's something tan on the lobe that looks exactly like a Rice Krispie.

"Nothing conclusive of course," the Hand says. "Herbert's always the quickest at the mirror, very brusque with himself, I'd say; brusque, hygienic. He's quite dashing, don't you agree? But apparently he doesn't think so. Though you will be amused to learn that he does the most absurd isometric—"

"Ab-zurd!" I exclaim, correcting him.

"As you will . . . The most, say, *ridiculous* isometric exercise for the 'character' lines below his nose. Like this." He hooks an index finger into each corner of his mouth and stretches the skin out toward his ears until he's formed a black, lipless horizontal line. "Yuh puh awt like this. Then yuh trah to clothes yuh noush." Tension hardens his cheeks as the mouth pushes shut against the tug of the fingers.

"But that's his only vanity?" Jimmy asks as a wind chime slice of light glides over his glass of Campari and glistens on the Hand's wet fingers, now returned to his lap.

"The only one," the Hand asserts. "But despite Herbert's speed at the mirror, he takes an unconscionably long time on the toilet."

"What's an eight-letter word meaning 'sterile' and beginning with A?"

"Sterile?" the Hand asks.

"Yes, beginning with A." The boy squints as he looks out at us. Perhaps there's too much glare on the living-room window for him to be able to see the porch clearly. The older woman at the desk is massaging her temples.

"Sterile?" the Hand repeats. "Don't know. Now, Bob," he continues, addressing me, "is really such a beguilingly simple young man. We keep wondering how he fits in at all in your house now that his position has changed so radically. He's worried about his thining hair and keeps *tossing* it with his fingers, like a salad, trying to make those few wilted lettuce leaves appear to be a *garden*. He's quite frighteningly quick on the toilet, a perfectly natural animal, and though he always sits down with a magazine, he couldn't possibly have time to read more than half a column. Apparently he's become vain only quite recently, since he doesn't know what to *do* about his looks. He can only peer wistfully at himself in the mirror, *toss* his hair and pose for the glass, sucking in his stomach, swelling his chest, smiling boyishly, arranging himself for a photograph, as though the mirror were the one and only arbiter, as though, once he had contrived a satisfactory reflection, he had achieved an image that would serve him faithfully wherever he went. What's touching is the way, when he's at the hotel, he suddenly remembers to employ the boyish grin or to retract his gut—but the effort is never natural and never as successful as it is during his toilette, partly because he's usually in motion and hasn't practiced *moving* in front of the mirror, and partly because no other person's eye ever gives him quite the loving encouragement, the intimate attention that his own so lavishly bestows upon his person. Do you keep him around for laughs?"

"Not at all," I reply, lifting my head slightly and studying the living-room lights through the brilliant red liquid in my glass. "I would have thought that nothing would be easier to do than to put up with Bob. I find his ineptitude charming."

"Quite," the Hand mutters, his face invisible.

"But go on," I insist. "You've done Herbert and Bob. But what of the others? What of myself? Your descriptions are so vivid."

"Are you cold?" Jimmy asks me, his voice rising too abruptly on the last word.

"No, I have my robe." Is that the correct term? "That is, my what-do-you-call-it, my this. And I must be going soon."

"Won't you stay?" the Hand asks. "I think I recognize that robe. It's not yours, is it? No, of course not." He sits forward again, smiling slyly. "You'll stay, won't you." A statement, not a question. "Yes, I recognize the robe."

"More Campari?" Jimmy asks, as he reaches for my glass, a spell broken, a threat dispelled.

"Why not?" I reply so faintly that I fear he hasn't heard me. I clear my throat and state clearly, "Yes. One more."

"Oh, good," the Hand says airily. "Now, on to the others. If Bob has come to vanity only lately, your room-mates Tod and Hunter have long been adepts of the mirror. They are seldom apart in the world, and even in the bathroom they frequently assist one another. How doubly charming Bob's ineptitude seems in contrast to their savvy. No wan, immobile mooning in the mirror for them! No, quite the contrary, each has become the other's esthetic conscience, and a harsh, realistic conscience at that. Tod will button every button; Hunter will unbutton half for him. Hunter will spray a curl in place; Tod will free the captive lock. One tucks a shirttail in, only to have the other pull it out. Scarves, headbands, rings and feathers pass from hand to hand. The two compose themselves by trial and error. Neither has a chance to fly high, to dress for the part he would like to play, to become the person he wants to be but isn't; no, Tod is always there to reconcile Hunter to the possible, Hunter forces Tod to hide his defects, accentuate his assets and don the costume that suits the self he goes by."

The wolfhound has stretched out and rested his lean face upon one long leg, just below the orbit of the revolving lights. Moving fast, then slow, turning in one direction and then in the other, sometimes turning not at all, the wind chimes cast their faint reflections across the dog's raised, bony shoulder and upon the black, slatted porch wall. Is it wrong to be here? The living room looks so luxurious—velvets, dark woods, bits of brass, pink flowers with red centers on a table—so unlike our cottage; this place is too cluttered and comfortable to be correct. The young man is assisting the older woman by writing in a word. She disagrees and shakes her head.

"And me? How do you characterize my toilette?" I ask the Hand. "I expect you to be as objective with me as you have been with the others."

"Objective!" Jimmy exclaims.

He could be questioning the philosophical possibility of ever being "objective," or he could be criticizing my use of the word—I may have made an error in diction.

"Tsss!" the Hand hisses, putting his glass down and settling back into the chasm of his chair, exasperated.

Jimmy strokes the tight, gleaming dome of his head, an act of symbolic submission, and his jacket creaks in pain. Preparing to dive into an apology, he brings his boots together and crouches slightly, but then, just as he's about to take the plunge, he reconsiders and straightens up, says coldly, "Shall we listen?"

"Why not?" I reply.

Jimmy strides into the living room, his leathers taking the lights. His hands—positive, prominently veined, beautifully cared for—sort through a rack of records. The Hand stands. Much shorter than I would have guessed, barely coming to my shoulder. He offers me his arm and I take it. Outside, on the walkway, someone walks past; it's Billy, heading home, looking at me.

As the Hand guides me inside, I'm struck by how thin his arm is, a bone beneath a yard of cloth, or possibly two yards, for I notice the linen slides easily over what must be an undersleeve of silk.

Jimmy looks up from the records. "Doris, Daryl, we have a visitor." I grow tense—will he give my name?

"Daryl, meet our neighbor."

Daryl bounds across the room toward me, shy in such a buoyant, convincing way that I can only conclude he's "indicating" shyness, as actors say. "Hi there." I put the woman's manuscript down. His hand pumps mine, his a meaty, insensitive hand, the exact opposite of the Hand's phthisic arm which only now releases me.

So. I'm a neighbor, a permanent neighbor, and not Herbert's guest, not a newcomer. Daryl was introduced to me, and not I to him; I'm more important than he. Or merely older. I've learned nothing, then. But I'd hazard Daryl's nobody. He's too earnest. Certainly the Pale Stranger was also earnest, but in a dim, ineffectual way that seems truer to the seigneurial style. Yes, Daryl's earnest and so conscious of his charm and animality that someone must have praised them—namely, Jimmy, Doris and the Hand, who're keeping him here precisely for, and only so long as he continues to display, those admirable qualities.

The music begins. Daryl takes a seat beside Doris on the couch. Jimmy sits on a tabouret beside the fireplace, his veined hands dangling between his legs, and the Hand slumps to the floor and crosses his legs. I suspect that the best seat, the couch, has gone to the most insignificant person here, Daryl; and the worst to the best, for the Hand is on the floor. Despite the implied impertinence, I would take the lowest position of all, if there were one below the floor, for that would indicate, by an excess of modesty, my superiority to everyone else here. But that option isn't open to me and I try to evade taking a position at all by leaning against the window sill.

A violin calls out orders in a deceptively sweet voice, and the commands are loudly repeated by a sycophantic orchestra. Then, just to confuse the rank and file, the violin prances off boldly in one direction, the first drill squad follows, repeating the movement exactly, then the second, then the third—but, unbeknownst to these absurd imitators, their leader has ducked out of the procession and run back behind them. The orchestra suddenly and unanimously senses it's been duped and comes to a dead halt. In the ensuing silence the violin sings sadly, hypocritically.

Several men are shouting outside on the walkway, calling in to us: "We want to see you. We've got to see you now." Doris clucks in disapproval. "Go see who those men are," she orders me. "Who could be addressing us in such an outrageous way?"

The simple, natural manner in which she instructs me to do her bidding rearranges all of the putative relationships I had worked out, like extended hands holding a web of string in the "Chrysanthemum" pattern and then, with a few deft plucks, transforming it into the asymmetrical "Horse and Rider."

"Who's there?" I call from the porch.

Billy, flanked by two boys I don't recognize, says in a hoarse voice, "I told Herbert your remark of this afternoon—when you declared the Minister's painting 'not adorable.' He was terribly amused and now the word's spreading like wildfire across the island. It's the best laugh we've had in months. Herbert's amazed at your erudition and your powers of instant recall. He had no idea that you ever knew that old poem."

"That poem?" I ask, hugging my robe to my chest, my teeth chattering. "But I had no idea I was quoting a poem."

"Stop putting us on," Billy calls back. His companions are grinning. "You swept the Minister *back!* Here, I have a note for you from Herbert."

I walk to the little gate and meet him halfway. "Can't you come in?"

"In there? You must be joking. What *are* you wearing?"

"I've decided to be eccentric."

"Here." He hands me a pale-green sheet of paper folded neatly into a triangle, a single pine needle pierced through the apex. I open it: no words, only a red circle. If I were to ask Billy what it meant, he'd only laugh. I, the clever scholar of poetry, the ready wit, not knowing! A single needle. A red circle . . . Perhaps Herbert's telling me to start raking the grounds of the Detached Residence at sunrise tomorrow. Or the needle could be a phonograph stylus and the circle the label of a particular record, and the message is excerpted from the words of that song. Or the needle suggests sewing, to sew, possibly "So" and the disc is red, which rhymes with bed: "And so to bed"—I must retire, this is the hour to come home and sleep. Or the needle stands for "pine" and red for my name, which rhymes, "Valentine," and my heart; he's telling me that he pines for me. Or all of these things. He loves me, his love is enduring, evergreen, but singular, only a needle, a sharp, stinging needle in his heart; and I must meet him at dawn beside the Detached Residence. That's it. Graciously I break an entire bough of pine hanging by the gate and give it to Billy, who is waiting for my reply. "Tell Herbert I'll come." Billy nods discreetly.

Rejoining the others, I become ever more conscious of my naked legs as I approach Doris, still seated on the couch; her face is clear and fresh, the dyed blond wisps of hair in front of her ears fanning out and curving like the shattered filaments of a bird's nest.

I examine my palm under the lamp; pinpoints of sweat sparkle on the skin as though I had brushed my hand through broken glass.

"What did they want?" Doris asks.

"They came to praise me, or rather to convey Herbert's compliments on my *mot* of the afternoon; I called the Minister's painting 'not adorable.'"

"You see? You exert such a benign influence on this household," Doris says complacently, folding her hands in her lap. "We've been so removed, have pursued our private interests so blindly that were it not for *your* visit, we might be tempted to underestimate the advantages of polite conversation . . . But perhaps you think my whole style of address old-fashioned and tiresome."

"If you regard *old-fashioned* as a derogatory word, then I will forbid you the description, since"—I pause, thunderstruck, waiting to hear what words of mine will flow into the trench I've dug with that connective, that *since*— "since your style of address must remain, in my eyes, unexceptionable."

Doris and I breathe heavily as we eye each other across the arena where our words continue to posture and spin, mimes seized by the last spasms of their fugitive energy.

"Now we have to go to the hotel to dance," the Hand announces, getting to his feet. "It's time. *L'heure solenelle*. You'll come with us."

"But I'm not dressed properly!" I exclaim.

"A bit casually perhaps," Jimmy says, standing, stretching, his bones cracking.

I yawn. The sound disturbs me. It is the gasp of someone in pain. "No," I say thickly, "I must change. My house is so close. We'll be able to stop there for an instant on the way."

Doris, apparently despising discussions on the business of leaving, walks quite briskly across the arena between us, treading on the transparent shells of our formal language, her feet crunching the brittle chrysalis of each turn of phrase. "Well?" she asks over her shoulder as she stands in the doorway.

We walk quickly down the ramp leading to my house. Another party draws up behind us, and we move Indian file so that the others can pass. It's too dark to see who they are. Someone murmurs "Thanks." Two dead trees stand out against clouds in the night sky. I pass a lamp and my shadow grows, curving out in front of me, until it dives into the next pool of light and disappears. Then I pass under that lamp and another shadow leaves my side and lengthens into a black direction for me to follow: I am a dial traveling past stationary suns, telling a daytime every twenty paces.

"Here?" someone asks.

"Yes," I say. I turn right onto our narrow dock and push apart the over-arching branches: wet. The yellow porch light glimmers feebly behind a small mitten cutout . . . ah, yes, the versatile bush with the three shapes of leaf. My feet attain the smoother wood of the deck. I peer through the plate-glass window. A half-drawn burlap curtain filters the glow of a single light, the lamp at one end of the couch. I try the door. A cold metal knob. "The door's locked."

"Locked?" Doris asks.

"No one's at home," I say. "Now what am I going to do?"

"Are you terribly cold?" the Hand wants to know. "Jimmy could run back and get something *leather* for you, perhaps . . ."

"I'll just stay here."

"Here!" Doris exclaims.

"They'll be back, I'm sure. I'll just stay here."

"Here! Of course not. You'll catch your death. Only *Herbert*, if you don't mind my saying so, would *lock* his cottage. Is there a key under the mat? He must leave a key under the mat."

"You'll come with us to the hotel," the Hand says. "You're dressed fine, in that robe I recognized so readily. No one will notice your costume. They're all self-absorbed. Say you've been swimming. That will impress them."

The breeze slides past my face as we rush down the boardwalk; I am a cutter, slicing into the air, my hands the foils, the prow my nose. A moonscape of sand unscrolls below us on the left, always different, always similar, for no gleaming mountain, scuffed plateau or tight-lipped sea resembles another, yet a moment after passing into one phase I cannot recall the last: pores, warts, stubble—the microscope travels over the skin, all varied, all the same, the color of old parchment. Vertigo tosses me toward the sand, but the ship regains its course and the wind sluices past so smoothly that I would wonder whether *it* were moving or only *I* unless I saw the scumbled waves on my right. Raised on my platform like a proud somnambulist, I march with strangers into the brilliant lights projected from the palace roof, as important as though I were on the stage. Flashlights on tributary walkways flash through pine boughs.

"Excuse me," murmurs someone behind me. We let three men pass, the palace lights gleaming on the mellow uppers of their loafers, on their nails, teeth and the white of an eye turned back to examine us. The smell of wet wool interfuses with the briny air. Their voices rise and fall intimately without releasing a single intelligible word. Six brass-bound pilings in the bay put their heads together: stalks of asparagus in a steamer. Daryl, Doris's plaything, pulls up beside me and makes a remark; I don't catch a word but I don't bother to ask him to repeat it. I simply smile, since I know that's the proper reply. He steps ahead of me, his hair flaming in the spotlight. We all take a detour down a ramp and peer into a yacht—*The Doris*. The cracked cushions exhale the burnt-rubber smell of patent leather. A clock sunk into the control panel ticks under a dim light, which is a German "scientific" green. Stainless-steel fittings circle the gauges. Oiled mahogany doors fold over the hatch.

Trapped waves slap against the dockside of the hull. Compared to the improvised, matchbox character of the island's houses, the yacht seems expensive, enduring, impressive, as though a rich child, joining a band of ragamuffins dueling with sticks, had pulled out a real sword.

As we walk up the three steps leading to the hotel deck, all my apprehensions mass themselves in front of me, urging me to turn back. But I push through them without hesitation, the very nonchalance of my entrance exhilarating me. I know that my companions are Herbert's enemies and my costume is a scandal. The deck forms an L on two sides of the glass-enclosed dancing floor. On the shorter leg of the L, orange and pink lights focus on round tables under a blue canvas awning, the colored effulgence restoring the bloom to the Minister's cheeks and even adding a blush to the Pale Stranger's faded skin as they talk and nod behind a boy in white pants, no shirt and an unzipped windbreaker, its plastic folds faceting the light like a piece of quartz. The barechested boy threads his way past a young man and woman (tall, blond twins wearing steel collars), then dips to whisper something to a girl who is seated in a red canvas chair; the boy laughs, leans back into Herbert's drink, turns to apologize, catches sight of a couple leaving the dance floor, flies to their side, his jacket disorganizing the brilliant air, walks them to a table, sits glumly for a second, hails Billy, who is slumped in darkness against a railing, the yachts rolling slowly behind him, crosses to him, offers Billy a sip of his Scotch, laughs, thumps Billy on the back, lapses abruptly into silence, his face aging.

Loudspeakers crackle. The song, "Hunted Hinds," begins to play. Daryl and Doris sidle up to the blond twins. Doris fingers the blond man's steel collar, her lips parted. They dance, or rather move their hands and shift their weight from foot to foot.

"Get us drinks," the Hand tells Jimmy.

"Sure. What will you have?"

"Campari?" I ask.

"Make it two," the Hand says. "Now," he adds in a louder voice, "I have some people for you to meet." He steers me toward the twins.

"I have no objection to *talking* to anyone," I whisper, "but I don't want to be introduced." Herbert is watching me; I mustn't meet the friends of his enemy, Doris.

"Will you take their hands?"

"No," I say as firmly as possible. "But I will be as courteous as you might have wanted me to be." He looks troubled, and I reassure him by pointing out, "Anyone looking on would assume the twins and I had been introduced, or at least had held hands. You must understand my position."

"Which is?"

I hadn't expected to be pressed for a further explanation. "Well, not the position I'm taking, but rather the one I'm *in*. There are so many pressures on me. Perhaps they're beneath notice, but nonetheless I feel them. But you mustn't imagine I'm simply trying to skirt all possible objections. I'm not just adjusting. I do exactly what I want to do."

The Hand says, "I see."

"Hello," the blond man calls down to me from his great height. "I'm Kaj. This is my sister, Sys."

The Hand coughs and studies his shoes.

I extend my arm, avoid Kaj's outstretched hand and take my Campari from Jimmy, who's rejoined us. "Thanks," I tell him.

"Oh sure. You're welcome."

"We had a chance to look into that yacht," I announce, nodding toward the one I mean.

"Oh?" Kaj asks. Doris sinks into a chair beside him and shades her eyes from the glare of the lights, executing exactly the same gesture made by the men during "The Fire Viewing." She must be hinting that I should mention the fire.

"Say, were you here for the excitement last night?" I ask.

"The fire?" Kaj nods.

"It was terrible," Sys says, undoing the scarf at her elbow and tying it around her left thigh, which is so fleshless I wonder how she will keep the tourniquet from slipping off. "Let's not—how do you say?—*dwell* on it. I am too sensitive."

The Hand glances in Herbert's direction to see if he and the Pale Stranger have registered the fact of this interesting conjunction, have witnessed my intercourse with the twins, so animated and so public.

The Negress Maria is standing on the second balcony of the hotel, attired in boots, chaps and Stetson. My roommates, Tod and Hunter, are behind her, looking through an open door into a dark bedroom, their faces streaked by shifting white lights: television.

"We *won't* dwell on it," I say to Sys.

"Thank you." She sighs and raises a friendly hand toward my shoulder. I back away just in time. "Of course, the fire was an accident," she hastens to add.

"Excuse me. I must say a word to Herbert." Not waiting for a response, I depart, hurry to his side. "Forgive me for not coming back to dinner. I was sidetracked."

"Are you cold?" he asks me.

"No. I'm going swimming later."

"Don't people usually wait till August?"

The two *fatalia* singers, sloppy in shirttails, their night off, join the girls who did the mirror dance last night; as before, one is wearing the halter that matches the other's skirt.

"Let's sit down," Herbert suggests. "It's dull tonight, isn't it?"

"Yes. Very." Dull? How can he tell? The judgment presupposes a measure of calm independence, a connoisseurship of evenings, a recollection of other, better evenings. "Very dull," I repeat. "I may take a long walk."

"Yes, well, of course," Herbert says, searching my face, "it *is* a long walk . . . Or have you forgotten already?"

He's referring to our assignation at dawn beside the Detached Residence. "Forget!" I exclaim indignantly.

"Walking . . . Yes, walking." He laughs. "The wind is always around us when we're out walking, even in the shrubbery. No protection. There's a symbol there."

"There and everywhere," I say.

"Everywhere," he affirms. "Oh, I'm being lugubrious. I notice you're *with* Doris tonight. What could be your interest in *them*, I wondered; I won't ask. I won't pry . . . The wind, always invisible, always stirring, this restlessness—you'll accuse me of philosophizing in a minute. Yes, I've been drinking, and then, the day *has* been eventful, for you possibly more than me; after all, you've been to see Doris and however else that might be construed, it must be accounted as an *event*. The wolfhound, the music—and see, you're drinking Campari! You might as well be wearing her colors as drinking that. But I don't suspect you of defection. You answered my message, perhaps ambiguously, but we live by ambiguities, spiders balancing in midair on threads of our spit and casting still further threads, hoping they'll catch on something but content, should they not, to blow about on those fragile hawsers and *take our chances*. But I'm only a boring aspect of an evening that is already dull by your own admission; if I keep this talk up I run the risk of becoming indistinguishable from it, from *Doris*, from *The Doris* you inspected. Notice the way all these people are standing still but seem to be moving.

It's the wind in their hair, their draperies; they appear to move like buoys in turbulent water. The wind disturbs me so much tonight!"

He gets up, moves away. I smell food. The people at the table on the bayside are eating. I've had nothing since the "snack." I study the people at the table surrounding the cupped candlelight which ignores their shoulders and hands but cuts arcs across their necks and illuminates their flushed faces. A woman in gray sits with her back to me; on her right is Doris chewing thoroughly, the muscles just below her shiny, knobby-knee temples sliding with each bite. Facing me is Jimmy, who keeps assessing his wine as though it were a professional chore, his face as nerveless as wet clay except for the disdainful, opening lips. The fourth at table is the Hand. He is dabbling good-naturedly at a kitten with a heavy damask napkin, and as he gets into the game and teases the animal in earnest, his face slips below the candle's beams. But now he bobs back into the light. Says something. The others laugh. The cat quizzically cuffs the dangling cloth, runs around in circles below it, inspects it from another angle, then crouches beneath the chair and springs an attack upon this outsize mouse, this mercator projection of a mouse.

A breeze brings me the smell of the barbecued meat, and involuntarily I take a few steps toward the table, salivating. Perhaps the cat also smells the meat, isn't playing a game but wants to lick the grease fingerprinted on the damask. If I wait for my opportunity, they may retire to the dance floor and leave some scraps on their plates which I could snatch, or the cat might clamber up and run away to a corner with a piece of meat that I could wrest away. Now I'm so close to the table I can see its spread: silver trays burdened with black roasts. Scattered across the top of the burnt, corrugated meat are thin sheets of edible silver leaf. As Doris lifts a bite with her right hand to her mouth, only the fastidious tips of her fingers touching the food, she inclines her head slightly forward. The teeth close and the silver crumbles to powder (some of the bright dust settling on her sleeve). Such manners and the gross, ostentatious food itself seem quite in contrast to the "snack" at the woman's cottage, so elegant and undernourishing.

"All the same," Doris says to the woman in gray, "it was a smart move, taking him on a stroll."

"And his visit to *us* has set everyone talking," the Hand says.

"Why his sudden turnabout? That's what I want to know," Doris asks.

The smell of the roast and the glistening of grease on their fingers draws me still closer to the diners. The silvered meat, its conspicuous consumption, the talk—everything repels me, but simple hunger overcomes all delicacy.

"Perhaps there's no turnabout," the woman in gray says softly. "A whim. Perhaps he's indulging a whim."

The Hand has stopped playing with the cat. Sitting under the chair, the animal pays no attention, beyond a quick deviation of the eyes, to the passing of each huge shoe or bare foot outside its lair; a much smaller movement, however, like the rattling progress of a cellophane cigarette wrapper across the deck or the jiggling of the tablecloth's hem causes it to crouch. Movements must be small and inhuman and nervous to awaken a cat's interest, or mine. We're both poets of phantom inconsequence.

"A whim?" the Hand remarks. "I think not. Herbert may have moved a bit too fast. The fire last night . . . Such sudden realignments puzzle people, offend others. Of course, you may be right—a whim. You know your man better than we. He responds to the latest stimulus, the nearest voice; now that your voice can be heard again, the Valentines may witness a turn for the better in their fortunes."

The lady in gray stands—it's the woman! My woman, my sister, my Valentine, my love. "Why do you say such vulgar, commonplace things?" she sobs. "I shouldn't have come."

"But my dear," Doris protests, "he meant no harm, I'm sure he—"

But my Valentine doesn't stand to hear apologies. She gathers up her full skirts and pushes her way through the throng, arrives at the steps, descends and hurries off into the night. Maria, still standing on the second balcony, leans over and calls to her, but fails to catch her attention. Uncertain as to what she should do, Maria tightens the drawstring under her chin and snaps the brim of her Stetson. Doris, Jimmy and the Hand slam their chairs back (the cat nimbly hopping over the moving rungs and running to a safe corner) and rush after the woman. The boy in the open plastic jacket steps back to make way for them. In the melee, I slide up to the abandoned table and rapidly fill my pockets with burnt meat.

Jumping off the dock, I land in cold sand dredged with bent grass. I hide in the shadow of a side flap depending from the canopy, put the woman's manuscript down and start to devour the meat. No sooner have I swallowed three big, scarcely chewed bites than I begin to hiccup, but the sudden gasps, the spasms working up from my stomach do nothing to impede my frantic gnawings on the meat.

I steal a glance at the table through the laced space where the canvas flap joins the blue metal standard. The damask sparkles, no people surround it, no Doris, no Jimmy, no Hand, only empty chairs thrust at angles. In the heightened glare of the centerpiece candle, its flame rising for the occasion like wrath, the kitten tentatively dips its paw into a silver platter, shakes a drop of sauce from its padded foot with exquisite, trembling grace, then prods at a chunk of half-carved roast. The meat whizzes across the oiled surface, caroming off the platter's embossed border.

"Uh . . ."

There's someone standing beside me.

"Uh . . . Prometheus—"

It's Billy! Reciting a poem.

"—stole heaven's flame one night.
And brought it home to revel in its light."

Must stall for time. Must respond with a verse of my own. I'll scrawl it with my finger in the sand. Crouching, I write in a trapezoid of light released upon the ground by an interstice in the canvas flap: "But I—" Yes, that's right, I must dissociate myself from Prometheus, his downfall. "—the robber's lesson duly learned—" Perfect! *Burned* will rhyme with *learned*. What verb? *Pilfer?* No. I've got it, a pun, inspired—*eschewed*. "Eschewed the flame but took—" Took what? I took the meat, but that's too many syllables, I've got to end on *burned*. "—what fire had burned." Squatting beside me, Billy reads the couplet with difficulty, then looks me in the eye and smiles. He stands up.

I also rise, in awe of my words. Two terns are dozing on adjacent stumps beside the harbor: feather and bone, father and son. Terns, turns of phrase, turn by day, turn off by night. Extricating myself from my thoughts, I whisper, with a trace of anxious amusement, "Billy, isn't it enchanting, meeting like this, exchanging verses?"

"Enchanting."

"But I'm embarrassed."

"Why?"

"Because you caught me."

"Caught you eating? We had no idea where you had gone."

Billy has changed clothes again. His white silk hose shine like birch logs on the forest floor. Against his tanned neck and hands are points of lace suspended on net. A bouquet of three marigolds and a single wild rose hangs upside down from his dark lapel. I touch his velvet coat. He smells of daytime and sunlight, like linen left out to dry in grass.

"Would you like some?" I offer him a handful of meat.

"Of course not. It's been *served*. How can you touch something that's been *served* to others, particularly *those* others? You're very strange recently. I rather like it. Do you imagine it's always been like this?"

"Like what?"

"That no one has ever followed the rules. Perhaps all those noble people in history had no sense of propriety and did just as they pleased." Suspended beneath Billy's grass scent is the smell of matted fur.

I shrug.

His warm brown hand clasps mine. "Ick. You're greasy." He rubs his palm against his velvet trousers. "I hope you don't get sick from all that meat. Don't think about it, please. Don't think about flesh, about fat. Pretend it came out of a package, or off a tree. *Picture* the tree. You'd better wash up."

Billy guides me by the elbow around a dark corner of the hotel and up a small path past a plate-glass window: inside, dancers are turning beside an open fire in the center of the room. The flames fly up the mouth of a metal chimney that hangs expectantly over the bed of hot stones. The moon's reflection floats on the window as well. When one dancer stops, the moon rests upon his shoulders, becomes his head. The moon-head holds pale and cold on the glass.

We continue our ascent, turn left and come to the back door of the hotel; as we enter, the crickets trapped within the bowl on the lintel chirp a warning din. Two, three, four paces down the hall, past a pastille burner, and Billy steers me to the left into a blue-tiled bathroom.

A full-length mirror hangs on the far wall and I watch my reflection approach me—no, it's Herbert, it's not a mirror. I had forgotten what I look like.

"There you are," Herbert comments as he brushes by and hurries back to the dance floor.

The warm water flows over my hands. I look up and catch myself (yes ... that's really me) in the small glass offered by the white towel dispenser. My mouth's working. The lines incised in my palm—do they mean anything? A small blister is rising on the side of my right index finger, where I put pressure on the rake. Raking couldn't be my ordinary occupation; I wouldn't have such soft hands.

"You haven't danced with us all evening," Jimmy exclaims as he enters the lavatory. He unzips his fly as he stands at a urinal beside me. He pulls out his penis. It looks small and blue emerging out of so much shiny black leather.

"I meant to get back to you," I say. Billy chuckles behind me. In the small mirror I can only see one of Billy's shoulders leaning against the wall, dark-blue velvet on pale-blue tile.

Jimmy addresses the wall in front of him: "Well, when you get a chance join our circle."

Billy laughs out loud. His shoulder shakes against the tile. He's moved slightly, so that the marigold in his boutonniere has entered the mirror. The yellow water has stopped coming out of Jimmy. He shakes himself. A small trickle dribbles under low pressure. The marigold, pinned on upside down, splattering into petals, comments on the urine, as does Billy's chuckle on Jimmy's words, flower to water as laughter to language, Billy taking the superior option in each case.

Jimmy leaves us.

Marooned and desperate, that's the way I feel, as though the urinals and sinks and the two toilets lurking behind their half-closed doors were blanched, vitrified persons—humbled persons bred stunted for their specialized functions. I turn toward Billy and my heel rasps on the sand someone must have shaken out of a sneaker.

Billy smiles at me. This moment means nothing in particular to him. But his very youth; the pea-sized indentation on his cheek, like a drop of paraffin on an apricot; the jauntiness of his stance; even the wrinkles spiraling down his stockings like hardened candle-drippings— everything marks him as unobtainable in a space made deep only by artifice, and I won't be able to reach him, draw words from him meant for me. The sink's dripping at one-second intervals. I'm a patient in an operating room, standing instead of lying down for some reason, the urinals are nurses, the faucet, an anesthetician counting out the ether.

"His circle!" Billy exclaims. "'When you get a chance join our *circle!*' Well, you see what lofty ideas you've put in their heads by simply visiting them. Come on." And before I know how, we're leaving the glare of the operating room, walking down the hall, and the dance floor opens up before us. The mirror dancers open their hands and reach for me. Billy nods and takes the horn case. I float toward them and grasp their hot, soft hands, both girls smile radiantly at me, their faces flushed from exertion, wisps of hair falling out of their *brioches* and curling in the heat of the open fire blazing behind them. A new song starts up and everyone does the "Fire fire who." I, too, crouch and lift my arms as I advance between the girls across the room. The flames waver above their bed of white stones in the night breeze infiltrating the room, trying to remind us of something. The embodiment of that search to recollect, Herbert stands in the glass doorway, his full sleeves billowing, his collar lifting and falling in the live wind. He stares me down; the movements of his clothes become ripples in his will. And insofar as the luffing of his shirt can suggest a ship, he sails toward me, his body dimming, his face sharpening until, like an object dialed into focus by binoculars, then brought in still closer, his features blur into something huge and vague. I am dancing for him.

Kaj and Sys are three couples away from me, and I see an opportunity for touching them lightly, for garnering their smiles and nods without actually having to stop to talk to them. I need their support, all the support I can get, but I don't want to be stuck with them. Nor do I want to return to "our circle"—Doris is at the far end of the room, she's no longer associated in people's minds with the Swedish twins. Billy hands me a drink. I sip it through a straw, grateful it's not Campari. One of the couples dancing between me and the Swedes is leaving the floor. I dart around the remaining boy and girl and say, "Hi!"

"Hello," Kaj responds. Sys's hands rise on "who." She's singing along, her lips are rounded. She blows me a little kiss from her rounded lips.

The Hand, standing beside Doris, spots my greeting to members of his circle and tries to catch my eye. He smiles, waves, nods, tells Doris of the happy occurrence; she involuntarily claps her hands in delight, but then, embarrassed, feigns indifference, shrugs, returns to her conversation with Jimmy. Poor Jimmy! If only I could invite him to join us, without getting involved with Doris and the Hand. But that's impossible. Or is it? Here he comes. Doris has probably sent him off for another drink. I'll grab him. I do grab him by the hand.

"What!" he exclaims. "Oh. It's you."

I don't say a word, simply pull him toward me.

"You want me to dance?"

I nod, smiling, not missing a step.

"Doris wants me—"

He starts to pull away but, still smiling, I tug him back onto the floor. Looking around, he sees that Billy and the mirror girls are the other members of my party.

"But Doris—"

"Fire fire who!" I announce, my head metronoming too rapidly for him to read my expression. A quick scan informs me that Doris and the Hand are taking it all in. They're alarmed, insulted—perfect! They're coming this way. No, now it dawns on them that that would be folly, they've stopped, retreated. Herbert, on the other side of the room, comprehends everything. He's smiling faintly. Jimmy rocks adequately from side to side.

The music stops. Doris and the Hand, armed with some new strategy, are approaching, ready to suborn us into their "circle," or whatever it is. I deftly steer Billy and the mirror girls toward the fire in the center of the room. Jimmy's left behind without a word of explanation. Maria and the Minister are toying with their drinks, the air filaments trapped within the ice cubes looking like fossils. "Won't you dance with us?" I ask them.

The Minister's eyes widen. "We'd be charmed." He looks to Maria for confirmation. Perhaps they weren't having a friendly chat after all; despite their smiles and lowered voices, they might have been engaged in a fierce argument. I've forced a false amiability upon them. Behind me I can hear Doris shouting at Jimmy. A new song submerges all voices.

Maria pushes her cowboy hat back off her head. It dangles behind her shoulders on a cord circling her neck. A row of mother-of-pearl snaps outlines each cuff, another row travels down the front of the shirt and single snaps fasten each pocket shut, white nipples tipping full breasts.

A bell tinkles above the slow, unpitched rumblings of gongs—palace music. Strange that they should play that here. "It's not up-to-date," Billy remarks, as though he were reading my mind. "Of course *you*"—he stares at me—"loving history as you do, would like it, but I find anything that's not up-to-date preposterous."

"I'm with Billy," Maria announces. "Oh, the old songs are all right, but not for dancing. At home, fine. I play this one on the guitar as a matter of course. But for dancing?"

"It's a real *down*," Billy complains.

"I'll dance alone then," I tell them. For some reason all my fears have dropped away, as though I had seen in the lavatory the very creatures that fear breeds (urinals, toilets, sinks) and by leaving them had left fear behind. Great powers are surging through me. I must express them or burst. Everyone in the room, or at least a face in every group, is familiar, has been propitiated. Doris, Daryl, Jimmy and the Hand lie vanquished. The *fatalia* singers? Placated with poems. The woman has fled the hotel. Tentative lines of good will have been cast to Kaj and Sys; I suspect they'd be reluctant to sever ties. Herbert's smiling. He's in love with me. Billy, the mirror girls, the Minister and Maria are my own dancing partners; they have to stand behind me. Tod and Hunter, chatting with a stranger next to the bar—they're my roommates, after all! And there's Bob by the passageway to the lavatory, we've found him at last, a servant taking *two* nights off, still in his green shirt and blue pants, harmless, uncritical.

No one else is dancing. I don't know the proper steps. At one time, however, I must have known them. They're still within me, stored within my muscles.

"You'll do what!" Billy shouts.

"Dance," I reply offhandedly. "Alone."

"But you can't do that!"

"No?"

Maria's started giggling, her lips parting to reveal her buck teeth. Her long-fingered paw flies to her mouth.

I slowly lift my right arm above my head, a swimmer's backstroke, wrist limp. My head bows to the left. My left arm straightens out at shoulder height, horizontal to the floor. My left foot steps forward. My pelvis tenses. Shoulders square.

The gong strikes.

Like water thundering off the surfacing dome of a bathyscope, the crowd drains away from me and forms a silent circle.

The circle, imperfect as it is, I regard as charmed space, myself the geometer.

Taking infinite pains, I lift my left knee to waist height and slowly point my toe, a trembling compass finding North (Herbert, alarmed, frowning, pale, about to intervene). To compensate for my shift in balance, my left hand folds demurely toward my chest and the right descends in a slow arc behind me, stopping just above my tensed buttock. The negative spaces held within my crooked left elbow and between my right arm and stiff right leg are emblematic, each a V for Valentine, the name I press to my heart, the woman's name that upholds me, my solace. The pointing left leg, the compass, wavers, is drawn to another spectator: the Hand. *J'accuse!* My pointed toe continues to single him out, unmistakably, yet I pivot on my right foot completely around so that I end up giving him my back. Yes, my left leg, stretched out behind me, still identifies the center of evil, but now I appear to be running away from the Hand since my right arm is reaching forward and my left stretches out behind me in arabesque. Tremors in the accusatory leg force it to fall, for who can designate evil for long? Courage shrinks, the witness tires.

Four notes rise, stop, repeat the ascent, rise again. I have firmed up my circle, confirmed suspicions, found due Herbert, rendered him his due. "What. Do. You. Want?" ask the four rising notes. "What. Do. You. Want." Each note's equally spaced, similarly sounded, neither louder nor faster than the rest, the entire interrogation uninsistent. "What. Do. You. Want?"

Yes, indeed, what *do* I want? Order. The Hand and Doris figure as old dangers reasserting themselves. The old Minister of the Left has no counterpart, no one on the Right as young as he's old, as candid as he's crafty. And then the fire last night, the childish, indecorous reactions of the dancers, their blindness to danger, their levity once they saw it—askew! The ground swell of a new clique gathering weight and momentum during the Little Stroll, suggestive of revolving, collapsing forms.

But I am here now, a circle has been drawn and I am *occupying the center*. How can fires break out, impropriety prosper once someone occupies the center and makes motions of order? With one hand I pull in the invisible mainsheet of my world, cranking it taut with the other. Then I step forward, as sticks rattle on cymbals, and mime the "Fire fire who" (a secular quotation cited in sacred text), only to hold the flames at their peaks—orange, lengthening blades, points riveting my palms like needles, jabbing, pricking, but me hanging on—hold the flames, though they sear my hands, leap higher, I'm standing on tiptoe!

Subsiding, the cymbals quiver into silence. The fire dips, banks, spurts, drops, glows, flickers and dies. I'm crouching on my knees, my bare chest silvered with sweat, the robe undone, my hands quieting the *essential* embers, while the merely apparent fire, the hotel's, crackles irrelevantly behind me on its bed of white stones. I stand and compose myself.

Now for Doris and the Hand . . . I sit on air, then hunker, then cross my legs on the floor, lightly sketching in the black house with purple pennants and its occupants: Doris and Daryl on the couch, Jimmy on the tabouret, the Hand on the floor. Purely by accident I look up and see Doris on the periphery of the crowd, an intersecting tangent; her face is struck with horror, terrified the denunciation to come. But I'm not an avenger, Doris. I don't want to destroy you, only lift you up and set your black house in order.

Suiting the solemnity of my intentions, the echoing drums take up a march, majestic, unhurried, as confident but as economical as Herbert's self-presentation, and I gather my dignity, assume Herbert's rational, upright pose, the lines of force spilling off my body as symmetrical as I am.

But how to act out my admonitions to Doris?

Ah! Of course. By not *acting* at all. Yes, for I'm not an *agent* of order, but its source. No need for me to mend the design when I am generating it from the center. My usefulness to all the elements of the island (the cottages, their denizens, the bay and ocean, the woman and her manuscript) is not as exemplar. What I'm doing is far more generic. I occupy the center. Knowing that, I stop all movement, banish even the twitchings from my fingers, stand tall, my robe shed, head up, my chest argent in sweat, and lest I seem to be favoring the direction I happen to be facing, sprout three other faces, each contemplating a cardinal point.

The music ends. Faint applause.

"Well," Maria drawls, "it's not my cup of tea but you've got to admit, Billy, it's up-to-date—so up it's off the calendar." Loud laughter.

Billy takes my hand. My epiphenomenal faces retract, and no longer a metal dancer at the hub of a wheel, I take a step, diminish in size, stumble, stoop, fumble on the floor for my robe, laugh a silly laugh, thoroughly untranced.

"Jesus!" Billy whispers. "What got into you?"

"Didn't you understand?"

"No, frankly."

"Oh, I'm so disappointed. It was—" How can I explain it to Billy, tell him how much I hoped to accomplish? "It was—"

"You'd better get going. Herbert's already left." Billy hands me the woman's manuscript.

92

"He has? Is it that late? All right."

I hurry toward the glass door. A perfect stranger, an old man with a flesh-colored hearing aid, looms up in my path, croaks, "Charming. *Most* original."

"Yes," his companion faintly echoes, an equally old woman with plucked eyebrows, wearing a shiny tuxedo. "Yes." She struggles to say yet another word, which turns out to be: "Yes."

"Thank you. I'm sorry. Forgive me. I must be going. I mustn't be detained."

"*Most* original," the old man repeats.

"Yes," the tuxedo lady echoes, the word jiggled in several syllables out of her like coins from a piggy bank.

A black cloud stains the moon. Crawling out of the west, other clouds form an army of crustaceans, claws catching white mucus floating by. The surf pounds beside me, collapsing on a low note, then ascending the shore, ascending the scale. On scallops of sheen the moon glows, banking its cold fires.

Water, moon and sand: varieties of transparence, filterings. The water unflagging, hurling itself like an exhausted but persevering lover on the sand. Pointless energy. The moon reflects, quizzically, on the ocean's labors. Three sides in a love triangle: moon, water, sand. Each in love with the other, all frustrated, all unsatisfied. The ocean possesses the beach, but never quite, losing ground as fast as it's gained. The moon, pretending to be above it all, bestows disinterested affection on the other two, her darlings, draws them toward her, but so much radiance is somewhat suspect. She's radiant, yes, but melancholy in spite of herself; she *says* she wants them all to be friends, but it's love, not friendship, that torments all three. And the sand hopes to please everyone, offend neither water nor moon, by being sublimely inert, laid open to any attack. But such passivity in the last analysis is a stratagem like any other.

The wind must be the animating soul of the world. That's what Herbert was trying to tell me. Its cool dilutions of memory seep out of the ground, lift off the water, corkscrew down tree trunks, turning us around, riffling hair, awakening old hopes or troubling their sleep. I remember nothing. Nothing clearly, nothing precise: nothing. In that way I differ from everyone else. I have only fleeting glimpses of other times, other places, quicksilver traces like the shivering beams cast by that moving lantern up ahead on my left, bobbing across the dunes and revealing now a black line of seaweed deposited by the evening tide halfway up the bone-white sand, now dipping to spotlight brown shoes walking, now streaking up the trunk of a distant, wind-trained pine and for a second opalescing a bird's sleepless eye, then dropping out of sight. The light refuses to concentrate on any object.

I feel there's something familiar about these wastes of water, sand and sky. Nothing recollected or well known. Not familiar in that way. But similar. They resemble me, we're all dispersed. I'm a carousel of possibilities turning on emptiness. But someone might say something to me. I might answer. My answer exists. One remark produces another. Now we have something to go on. Statements to reconcile, consistency to maintain, inventions to elaborate. Features emerge, waves gather, a dune dries, crumbles and slides.

It's so cold. The sand explores the cracks between my toes. I feel sorry for my legs, for the bowed shanks and their drawstrings of muscle, old weapons advancing on the night. They're not very pretty, my legs, hairy, strong, large legs, rather embarrassing, they're my animal arms, not supple and thin like the arms on top.

Nothing familiar about the beach; it's as cold as I am. And yet, distributed across the sand, across everything surrounding me, might be elements that could be assembled into something familiar. These black shells on the tideline, an undulating boa draped across white shoulders; and the grit between my toes, like a man's five-o'clock shadow scraping a lady's cheek; and the fishy smell, unpleasant surely, but the base for an intoxicating scent, yes, like civet before it's mixed with flowers; and that disgusting, upturned shell with its jointed tail and four empty gauntlets in which the legs have rotted away, the armor of a horseshoe crab, but if it were small, were gold? Everything reminds me of the woman, of a man and a woman, of a woman's brooch, perfume, boa, of lovers in a triangle (Herbert, the woman and me). Then the contours of the beach become hers, the moon's radiance hers, the sea her desire; all the elements for making a woman are here. I alone can fuse them.

Yes. There she is. Standing on the dune up ahead. She's still wearing gray, a gray cloak over a *feuille-morte* dress, a dress the color of dead leaves.

Her small hands are encased in gray gloves seamed in welts of a darker gray. She doesn't see me, or if she has she doesn't acknowledge my presence now. Her eyes are lowered. Her hands hang at her sides

94

with the impressive naturalness of a singer who has finally learned not to act, who comes center stage and simply sings.

I struggle up the dune toward her, making slow headway. Each step precipitates a minor sandslide. Now I'm reaching the top. The woman looks at me for an instant, steps forward, about to say something.

"Did you know I'd be here?" I ask her, my voice too light for what I feel.

She shakes her head.

"I saw you at the hotel with those terrible people," I tell her.

I tell her, "I overheard the conversation. I admired your outrage."

"I wanted to step forward to defend you," I tell her.

I tell her, "Your dress is the color of dead leaves—most appropriate for—"

But she stops me, pressing her opened fingers to my mouth. Then she lifts her skirt slightly with one hand and descends the narrow path on the forest side of the dune. She's picking her way cautiously over a natural bridge that separates two stagnant pools. Her pale hand releases her skirt, now gathers it up again over the swamp, dulled by slime, pocked by mating insects, a mourner's hand gliding past the silver fittings on the coffin. She stops under a tree, turns and faces me. If I didn't know she was there, I'd never be able to find her in the shadows.

What do you want me to do?

Is that your hand or an aspen leaf blown back? Is that your face there, or there, farther to the right?

A mosquito bites my bare leg. She must have noticed her manuscript under my arm. Surely that pleased her. Or perhaps she was distressed, fancied that I was planning to pore over it with Herbert and ridicule her confessions, grammar, epigrams. Her precise, sensible voice, her merry impudence when we met the Minister on the beach, her restless, lively motions as she flitted about her cottage preparing the "snack"—all those qualities seem so hard to reconcile with that dim garden goddess under the tree.

She's nearby, cool, gray and green and I want to run to her.

There she is! She moved.

Herbert sits cross-legged under an umbrella pine, a bow and violin on the ground beside him. Moisture sparkles on the varnished sherry-colored wood between the bridge and neck rest, and also to one side of the A-string. Moisture shines in Herbert's hair. The rumor of daybreak spreads across the sky. The Detached Residence sprawls asleep behind Herbert.

He's putting something on the ground—transferring a white stone from the small mound beside him to the circle he's already started to build around himself. Minute wrinkles stream from his eyes like wind across his cheekbones.

The wind, aging us, reminding us of something still unclear, hinting at a turbulence within us, sifts through the treetops.

Herbert's hands return to his lap. Birds call to one another from unseen perches. A five-note whistle breaks off abruptly. There's such a strong odor of resin that I'm beginning to get a headache.

Herbert's sitting perfectly still, cross-legged, but his chin and the bridge of his nose are pale and shiny, as though the wind were pressing the skin back from his bones. Lanes of sunlight are forming on the forest floor.

"Sit down beside me," Herbert says. "We must write dawn poems." He offers me his hand. I squeeze it. He studies the small black mole beside my thumbnail and sniffs a laugh in two quick wheezes through his nose. "When I was young, women put beauty patches right there, only beside the left thumb, not the right. What did they call them? *Tornerò*. That's right. *Tornerò*. There were names for everything then. And the patches weren't simply coquettish; they often had a political significance. And the language of fans, of cards . . . Rouge above the cheekbone was called, for some reason, *Aurora;* perfect little circles of paint below the cheekbones were called *Il Dottore*. I don't know why. The Old Code . . . The gate to this house has been black for as long as I can remember, but of course it's the So-Called Red Door. So-Called . . . Just a lot of nonsense! Come, sit down."

He draws his writing case out of his sleeve and lays it on the ground before us. I cross my legs and sink to the ground and as I do my bones crack—did they have names for the different sounds of cracking bones?

The sky's much brighter now. I look back over my shoulder and notice that the windows of the Residence have turned to gray rectangles. A breeze has come up. I pick a long, flat blade of marsh grass sprouting up out of the soil beside me. The bottom third of the leaf is purple, but the rest green. The veins, unlike those in my wrist, run longitudinally from the base to the tip.

"If I brought up the detritus of the past," Herbert says, "it was merely to remind us both of exactly what a dawn poem is *not* about."

A pine cone falls beside my abandoned, overturned wheelbarrow.

"Forgive my reminiscing. I'm certain I'm not guilty of nostalgia. Choose your papers," he instructs me, waving his hand nonchalantly over the open case.

I select a sheet of watered gray vellum and a stubby, unsharpened pencil. Herbert sniffs inscrutably. He's removing identical materials from the leather pocket.

A bird is fathoming another depth of the forest with its song. I could transcribe its song—what better hymn to dawn? But Herbert's so conventional, he might be indignant. " 'Zeet? Zeet? Zeet?' " he'd ask. "What could that mean?" If only he'd show me his poem first.

The thought of competing with Herbert again tightens a valve within me.

Then I'll abstain from writing anything that conceivably could be compared to his effort. I'll put down a nonsense syllable, a "Zeet" after all, but not even something that clear. Something as incomprehensible as possible. A single word. I mustn't arrive at any word through any logical process or ordinary stream of associations. It will be so irrelevant that it won't even point the way back to a significant starting point. All right. *Zeet*. And what rhymes with it? *Sweet*. Spelled backward that's *teews*. Or then, *twos*. If *twos*, why not *threes*? Two threes make *six*. *Six* suggests *sex*. And *sex*, by a bit of legerdemain, becomes *love*. That's it! The single word: *love*. I scrawl it across the gray paper in a childish hand, fold the sheet in a crisp, businesslike manner and place it on the ground before me.

Herbert's having some difficulty composing his lines. He sighs and nibbles on the eraser, or rather, on the brass calyx containing the dirty, worn-down rubber pistil. Earlier musings have squeezed the metal circle into a tooth-marked ellipse. He looks at me uneasily. I lower my eyes and then look up into the red light of the rapidly rising sun, the rumor that's turned out to be true.

With a final sigh Herbert hands me his poem, folded exactly like mine. Out of the dancing sea of possibilities, what words will surface? I open it and for a second imagine it *is* mine. "Love," it says. That's all. Were it not for Herbert's darker, neater letters, the two compositions would be identical.

He opens mine. I study my hands. He sniffs. From the corner of my eye I can see him put the paper in his case. He snaps the case shut, extinguishing its ray of pink silk, and secretes it again in his sleeve. Now he's turning slowly toward me. I mirror his motion. He's crying.

"I suppose—" He clears his throat. "I suppose we had to write it, we couldn't say it. I know you think of me as someone who's always in control of my emotions. I hope I'm not embarrassing you by this *display*. Curious, isn't it? The same . . . Remarkable!" He groans. "Why did I say that? 'Remarkable.' Yes, it *is*, but not because it's a coincidence—"

The woman is coming up the embankment.

"—but because we have both finally found a way, found the same way, the same word . . ." Herbert nervously lifts another white stone from the pyramid and adds it to the crescent around him.

She's coming closer, a moonrise by day.

"We should be congratulated on our simplicity, I suppose. Of all the words and ways we might have—what could be more direct? Not the verb or the gerund came to mind, simply the noun, an existent—Oh, help me out, say something!"

"We have a visitor."

"What?"

"There." Her shoulders, her arms, her hands swing into view, and unlike the sun, as she rises she becomes larger, closer.

"Perfect!" Herbert exclaims bitterly. "Are you staying?" He stands. The dew has evaporated off the silent violin. With one fastidious toe he topples the mound of unplaced stones.

"Yes."

He stoops and picks up the instrument and the bow. "Very well." He nods coldly at the woman, who is now only a few yards away and has halted, as though she were waiting for him to leave. He plucks a single buzzing sound out of the violin. For an instant it reverberates until his thumb dampens the note and a faint overtone trails behind him. His hem catches on a clump of whitening wild grass and then pulls free of the darkening, straightening leaves, crosses through a wide shadow and swirls in a pool of sunlight before he begins his descent down a gradual knoll and onto a trail back toward the harbor.

I glance up at the woman. The day has filled out her face again, restoring depths and highlights to last night's flat anemone. I run to her, seize her hands. As I fold her in my arms my astral self, trembling with joy, covers her with kisses in the gold light clashing like gold just above our heads, kissing and weeping in that gold splendor where gold plumage and rolling eyes turn in baroque confusion, in expanding gold.

In the morning's strong crosslight leaves ring like bells without clappers. A jangle of bird calls attempts, ineffectually, to mimic the silent cacophony of pealing foliage and to transpose the ultrasonic music into songs within the range of merely human ears.

7

All day long the woman and I have made love and slept and made love. We turned like hours on the bed. She lay with her back to me and I held her in my arms, her body against mine, then she rolled over, as I did, and she held me. Her fingers, touching my leg, one by one pressed me, as though I were her keyboard.

Slowly her body uncoiled and dropped a foot deeper into sleep. My own thoughts turned to Herbert, the burning house and the illuminated faces of the crowd, to the moment when Billy and the woman came down the steps under a swaying parasol, to the Campari and the wolfhound—but I never lingered over any thought. I have no heart to pursue a memory; in fact, I feel even these few memories slipping away from me, and I don't try to hug them to me. Let them go. When I danced at the hotel I suppose I was trying to reconcile irreconcilable energies. I tried all afternoon to synchronize my breathing with the woman's. I was hers, her breath was animating me. But when I'm with Herbert again, I'll attune my harmonies to his. I'll forget the woman; perhaps not. No, I will forget her. An hour or two ago an attack of impatience overcame me, annoyance at being touched. *Mauled* is the word that sprang to mind, although she did nothing more than rest candidly by my side.

Maria's monotonous guitar continued its musing as we descended into twilight; as I dozed off, the music became a carved wooden face, an ancestor, kind yet half-savage. Peace filled the closed room.

I feel that I am innocent.

Of course I am an innocent. I don't remember anything.

Finally Maria came into the bedroom with a tray. We ate and then we dressed. The woman presented the idea of going to the party and the costume she had sewn for me as surprises, things I had no way of knowing about, and I was careful to register the surprise I usually work so hard to conceal.

The night is airy and expectant as I step out onto the porch in my toga. Even in the dark the soft white fabric glows.

"You don't mind going to this party, do you?"

"Not particularly," I tell her. "What is it again?"

"A sort of Greek or Roman love feast. God knows. I hate parties with *themes*. Perhaps they're indulging in *historics* so as to be ready for the Arrival tomorrow."

"And the host?"

"Jason. Really grotesque, isn't it, only two days after the fire. But now that he's received the appointment, now that the post has been vacated and he's 'agreed' to fill it, why, naturally," she says sarcastically, "Herbert must feel a victory celebration is in order. A *love* feast, if you will."

I see. Herbert burned the Pale Stranger's house, dismissed him from his post, and now has replaced him with this Jason.

"The fire was no accident," I tell her.

"Of course it wasn't," she says impatiently. She looks at me suspiciously and then decides to be glittery and gay. "Oh, the party's going to be awful. I can tell in advance. Jason's so old that he's determined to be modern in spite of the classical *theme*. He's called in an orchestra that plays only the most *advanced* music; of course, it's impossible to dance to. And then, I don't know exactly why, his house has a horrible ambiance. Worst of all, he serves nothing but dreadful punch. All his friends got together recently and criticized him for it, but he pretended he didn't hear us and a week later he drew up a list of rules for giving a great party, exactly as though he were a famous host, and sent us all a copy. Rule number one was: 'Don't waste money on liquor. Everyone prefers a delicious punch.' "

Crickets discuss the night on one side of the boardwalk.

A cigarette and a laugh pass us—I strain to see whom they belong to, but it's no use, it's too dark.

We take a turn toward the bay and a house on top of a hill. A neon arrow, orange, zigzags above the roof like a bolt of lightning. Music— electronic beeps fighting through a cloud cover of organ pedal points— hurls itself down the hill and over the marshes, over the cricket chirps that sound, by contrast, disappointingly natural.

We're turning onto the path leading to the neon arrow. The woman lifts her loose blue robe as she goes up a step. An unimpressive rock garden lurks behind the weeds on our left, and a stone lantern, not at all old or worn, casts a dull glow on the second landing of the stairs. We pass a bamboo gate and the woman hisses, "Isn't it ridiculous? I hate this house. I hate exotica. I love you." She grabs my hand and kisses the place on my neck where she bit me yesterday. When she bit me she already knew the design of the costume I'd be wearing later (since she made it), knew that the other guests would see the wound, knew they'd infer it was she who inflicted it.

A middle-aged man with gold-sprayed hair and a mini-toga clinging to his heavy gold thighs stumbles past us drunkenly, wanders off the path, shouts in pain and runs down the rest of the stairs. A low bush, its burrs gilded, trembles into immobility. "Jack," someone calls from above. "Where'd Jack go? Jack! Where'd that Jack go off to?"

At the next landing we turn, pass a giant carved frog and cross a damp plateau marked with flagstones shaped and placed so irregularly that they impede our progress, and for no purpose, since there is nothing here worth looking at. Icy slivers of broken glass shatter over a relentless roll of snare-drums. "Charming," the woman says. "They're playing our song."

The "ab-zurd" fakery of the tea-garden peters out at the foot of broad concrete steps, sparkling with too much mica, wide enough to accommodate an army, and quite devoid of character, as though the terrain, finally freed of so much sinuous and coy *japonerie*, had turned sober and functional. A decrepit old man, his knees as round and dark as empty eyesockets, stands at the head of the stairs, his train borne by two naked baby boys. He descends slowly, the boys, no more than five years old and almost perfectly matched, cautiously following on pudgy legs. It's the man who wore the insect robe and watched the fire with Herbert and me.

"Welcome," the man proclaims grandly and clasps my elbow with his hand. He's been drinking gin. His frail legs take a wide stance and the boys on cue flank him, draw the folds of his cloak around their shoulders, stoop to place the hem symmetrically at their toes and then lean against his withered thighs and stare at us impudently. Blond curls bounce in the faint breeze.

"How grand you are, Jason," the woman says in a flat, nasal voice, though she places an arm around my waist for protection.

Fugitive teeth chatter baroque triplets on the right, the left, above us, below: we've entered a grove of concealed speakers amplifying the tense figures of old music but through hollow, electronic sonorities, on no instruments I could name, and out of sequence. Devoid of connective passagework, divorced from their familiar settings, the traditional questions and answers, the themes and inversions, the false resolutions giving way to the true, the interlocking voices—all stutter and break off, then rush hysterically into a dense fog of noise, slow to a hypnotic grind, finally bark at each other in tiny, stifled yaps. Just as though a pedant had reduced the balanced periods of the literature of the day into a calculus of opposed words, a minimal gestuary, and having found the madness in the language of utter clarity, had jumbled snippets from Dryden and Bossuet, shrieked apostrophes to nymphs and satyrs, raced incoherently through alexandrines on Man or Nature—the same way the speakers are scrambling Vivaldi and Scarlatti into fever dreams. Now the very earth under my feet is throbbing on a bass note, already held too long to be a meaningful quantity, but ominous because at any moment it's likely to splinter into more breaking glass. No glass. Silence. Silence.

Silence.

The blond boys continue to peer at us fixedly; the one on the right scratches his button nose. Now the glass breaks all around us, the thin crystal atmosphere finds a fault and falls.

"Come," Jason intones. "Follow."

The babies emerge simultaneously from the folds of his robe and draw its length out behind him as he ascends, heroic, tipsy, up the glittering mica-laden steps. One of the boys falls on the penultimate step and nicks his knee. Bursting into tears, he rubs his hands into his eyes and wails. The other boy crosses his arms and stares impatiently at his companion. But Jason takes pity on him, lifts the chubby creature into his arms and soothes him. Sensing that compassion is more in order than impatience, the other child is suddenly fawning on his brother, kissing the scratched knee, burbling in baby talk, "Poor widdle thing."

As I look up from the scratched knee I see a crowd pouring off the dance floor and collecting on the terrace. An ear elongated and pointed at the top: a satyr. Twisting ram's horns sprouting out of curly black hair—Moses? A cuckold? No, it's Alexander the Great; the profile perfectly resembles the portrait on the coins. The mirror girls are flagellants tonight, tiny whips in their hands, lipsticked "wounds" on their bare shoulders, their hair tangled and stiff ("We washed it but didn't rinse the soap out," one of them explains to a boy who keeps blowing a gold whistle hanging from his neck on a leather thong. The whistle falls from his lips and thumps his shaved chest; it's a gold phallus).

Beside the swimming pool ("Champagne?" someone asks Jason, pointing to the pool. "Probably punch," the woman whispers to me) stands a towering black statue, the face an enlargement of Maria's. Sequins star its upper lids. The body is naked and as shiny as ebony.

"No wonder you didn't invite Maria," the woman says to Jason.

"The hair is made of Brillo pads," he replies, obviously quite pleased with himself. He pulls back the sleeve of his robe and checks his watch. "Stand back, everyone. Get away from the statue."

The statue's glass eyes light up, its mouth drops open an inch, revealing pink gums and hinged jaws, and the band stops playing. A giggle spills out of the statue's mouth. It sounds exactly like Maria.

Issuing out of all the speakers around us, the statue's giggling grows so loud my ears hurt and I notice Jason alternates between wincing in pain at the screeching noise and stupidly smiling in sympathy with the canned merriment.

Bare feet, slave bells jangling on one ankle, run past us. One of Jason's baby attendants, the one who wasn't crying, trots up to the barefooted person and tugs at his hem. The figure stoops: it's the young man with the phallus whistle around his neck. Smiling shyly, the baby reaches out for the phallus and the young man edges closer so that the child can blow it. Peep. Peep. They both laugh and the young man tosses the baby up into the air and then nuzzles the tot's tiny penis and intones in a low, comical voice, "Peep. Peep."

"It tickles," the baby squeals. As soon as he's lowered to the ground he scampers off into the crowd of swirling white cloaks, dotted and crossed with gilt fingernails and small black whips and ornamented with clusters of swollen grapes and boughs of laminated ivy leaves.

"Stand back! Stand back from the statue!" Jason shouts, his eyes on his watch. The young man, just about to loop around the neck of the black effigy his phallus whistle, makes a sour expression and walks away without presenting his offering.

"Fire fire who? Fire fire who?" chants a chorus line as it slinks across the terrace. It's the messengers in white from the hotel, dressed tonight in leopard-skin breech-clouts, led by the *fatalia* singers attired in full leopard skins. The front paws dangle freely over

103

the singers' bare chests; the jaws of each leopard are sprung open to frame the human face.

A sudden explosion. The black statue lies in rubble, springs and wires falling out of its broken head, a black hand, still miraculously intact, bobbing in the swimming pool. The smoke from the explosion envelops me with its acrid stench, but quickly blows away. The chorus line has come to a dead halt; most of its members are nervously applauding the demolition of the statue. Now their nervousness is fading and the applause gathers conviction and becomes a jubilant cacophony.

"Well?" Jason asks us.

"I hadn't realized the ancient bacchantes were quite so partial to blowing up Negroes," the woman says loudly.

Jason frowns.

"Although perhaps my reading in the period," she continues ruthlessly, "is not as extensive as yours." She steals a look at me, unsure of her effect. She's very tired.

At her initiative, we walk away from Jason toward the dance floor, past the dancers in the chorus line who have staged a raid on the broken statue and are dancing the "Fire fire who" with bits black rubble in their hands, a black toe projecting out of one boy's leopard-skin loincloth, a hollow breast serving another as a cloche cap. The woman asks, "Why didn't you take my part in that?"

"What would you have me do? You ridiculed him, I'd say, adequately." I add, "Besides, you're with me. I'm with you. Give me your hand. There. That should count for something."

She smiles, sighs heavily and her hand comes to life in mine. "Yes," she says hoarsely. She clears her throat. "That counts for something."

I hold her tightly with my right hand and carry the horn case containing her memoirs in the left and realize that I'm completely surrounded by the woman: I have her living, opaque presence on one side and her clarified past on the other.

No one's paying any attention to us as we cross the dance floor under purple lights reflected from the tinfoil ceiling: the lights have found the white hems basting the casual folds of her costume and made them shine.

The musicians are seated at a lavishly laid supper table and every time they move a fork, lift a cover from a casserole, fold a napkin or pour wine, electronic rumbles and wails trace the aural shape of the action. Upon closer examination I'm able to distinguish the thousands of colored filaments wiring every diner and dish to every other, connecting the entire table to a blinking transformer on a small balcony nearby.

At the other end of the room is Bacchus himself. He's about nineteen or twenty, with long straight hair falling over his eyes, ears and neck. A red heart, broken in half, is tattooed on his arm. Reclining on a flowery couch, drilled by red and amber spotlights, he's nude except for a large bunch of purple grapes resting on his crotch and an armband of woven daisies. As people hold their paper cups up to him, he tilts an ewer and fills them with, I suppose, Jason's ridiculous punch.

"Shall I get you a drink?"

"Thanks," the young woman murmurs. Her eyes linger on me. She seems full of emotion, but she quickly masters it. "If I'm not here when you return, wait for me. I'll be circulating." She catches someone's eye, lights up with a false smile and plunges into the throng of dancers.

I approach the throne of Bacchus and watch my toga metamorphose in the colored air from dry ice into chamois. My amber hand casts a red shadow on the floor. The heat and brilliance of the spots excite me; the other people around me are gleaming so brightly that I have to squint to see them. Black hair passes in front of an amber gel and stray wisps glow like sun flares. A diamond earplug facets scarlet and orange, then moves and projects blues and greens. A tall girl gives Bacchus an unrecognizable fragment of the exploded statue.

He turns the bit of black shrapnel over, studying it, and then throws it, without looking, over his shoulder. He sees me holding two paper cups. He fills them.

"Who's the other drink for?" he asks me.

"Who? What do you mean?"

"Come on," he says. "You can admit it. It's for Elena. I saw you come in with her."

Elena . . . Elena Valentine. Now that I know her name, I feel I've gained a new purchase on her, new rights, a lien on my Elena. I'm so excited I can't wait to get back to her, like a painter eager to check a title he's conceived during a walk against the canvas drying in his studio.

"Yes, it's for her."

"No wonder you look sheepish," he says. A ripple of curiosity and embarrassment passes through the bystanders. The rapid crossfire of exchanged glances grooves the illumined air.

"Sheepish?" I ask. "Why should I feel sheepish?"

Two of the devotees start a vague dance that quickens into a mechanical chugging; they disappear into the crowd. Another boy pretends to catch sight of a friend and hurries off.

"No reason," Bacchus says very deliberately, the red and golden spokes in his irises seeming to revolve. "No reason at all." A bead of sweat trails down his broad hairless chest—a wax crayon marking a lithograph stone.

A paper cup in either hand, I wander off, so lost in thought that I scarcely notice the color rioting around me as a band of entertainers, dressed in sleazy gauze, races past me onto the dance floor. The painted stick, the chains the arms and neck rush past into place under the follow spot, a roar of feigned surprise issues out of the spectators, castanets click. The sounds and sights fail to attract my attention.

Sheepish? Had I rejected Elena? Is there something wrong with my knowing her?

"I'd like to write my own sexual meta-etiquette," Herbert's telling the mirror girls. I hold the paper cups at my sides. "When you're carried away by ecstasy, you let your eyes sink slowly shut. Which *feels* right, but looks terrible to the other person. For a sickening moment all she can see are the whites of your eyes, horrible crescents of white."

"What's wrong with you?" Billy asks me.

"Everything's very complicated tonight." I rejoice over my happy choice of words, the general "everything" and the concrete "tonight," composing a phrase too vague to question but too specific to doubt.

"And then the hairs that cling to your lips?" Herbert says. "Since the dawn of time people must have been plagued by those hairs, but everyone acts as though it were dreadfully embarrassing to remove them. Removing hairs should become part of the *douceur*. It should be done slowly, meditatively. There should be a whole chapter on it in the meta-etiquette. It should be done *en douceur*, should be a way *de dire des douceurs à* whomsoever."

"How fascinating," the mirror girls say in unison. "Tell me," one of them pursues, "how do you handle the *tristesse?* Men are always so glum afterward."

"It depends," Herbert replies. "Some women insist on fondling a man 'down there,' as we said as children. Nothing's more annoying, indeed painful. If he's feeling guilty, put on a fast record and start dancing by yourself in the dark. Or turn on a dim light, be very matter-of-fact ('Do you want some water? An aspirin? What time should I set the alarm for?'). That will show him you expect no more sweet nothings. Or if he's feeling too crowded and possessed, too married, then tell him you need your sleep, would he please leave, you've got a rendezvous with another man tomorrow at lunch. Or if the *tristesse* is simply what *every animal feels*, then there's always scrabble, or a rubber of bridge."

Where's Elena?

"Where's Elena?" Herbert asks me. "Oh, that drink must be for her. Why are you dawdling here with me, with us? Won't she be peeved? Well? Why don't you say something?"

"More! Tell us more!" the mirror girls exclaim. One of them has grabbed Herbert's shoulder; he looks at her hand disdainfully, as though it were an unfamiliar microbe of huge proportions. She releases him.

"Well, I've made a few notes, but I can't recall them now . . . Oh! Here's one!" Herbert shouts. "It works very well with lovers, even with friends. Suggest that there are a thousand steps leading toward full intimacy with you. After two years tell someone, 'But we really don't know each other *that* well yet.' "

"I've got another question for you," the more talkative mirror girl says. "How do you correct a mistake made by your lover? *That's* a terrible problem, I feel."

"Sometimes you simply find a new lover," Herbert says softly.

The performers have finished whatever they were doing. They run out of the room through a light shower of applause, carrying their apparatus. A pink sequin shimmies into motionlessness beside my foot.

"Be serious!" the girl demands.

"I am," Herbert replies.

Where's Elena?

"Where's Elena?" Herbert asks me.

"But can you find a new lover that easily?"

"Actually," Herbert tells the mirror girl, "you become less interested in love after a great disappointment. Your desire to control him or her remains, but you no longer expect or even want affection, you wouldn't even accept affection, you just want control."

"Who's the other drink for?" Billy asks me. He and Herbert are dressed in matching tunics of the chastest design, the smallest possible concession to the "theme" of the party.

"Elena."

"Oh? You two are suddenly quite thick again, aren't you?"

"Are we?"

"If I didn't know you so well, I'd say you were torturing a fly."

"But then," Herbert tells the girl, "perhaps you aren't in a position to control your lover. You may simply have to retire, even gracelessly. What's painful, of course, is to have known someone so long, to have trusted him or her, and then to have that trust betrayed. Especially painful when what should be merely a private matter must by its very nature become public."

"Question! Question!" the talkative mirror girl calls out, coyly waving a finger under Herbert's nose. "This is all so fascinating."

"Please . . ." Billy groans.

"Am I being a bore?" the mirror girl asks Billy.

"Of course not," Herbert says. "*When* an alliance is public, it takes on a very different aspect, or should. A certain stoicism is called for—on both parts. A royal alliance can't be undone by a whim. Now, I know you're suprised to hear me say a word like *stoicism*. I've rejected the past, I've helped us all free ourselves from that burden, but I secretly admire some of the old virtues. I think we were hasty to spurn them. I think we must reconsider the best part of the Old Code."

This afternoon, after we woke up and made love, Elena and I looked at the latticed sunlight on the floor, like sand near the shore. I hid in her hair, a big fish under seaweed. Two children were playing right outside the window, bouncing a beachball on the service porch with delicious tedium. "We could, we could . . ." one of them said, letting her little voice trail off dreamily. Thud. Thud. Thid thid thid. Thud. "What?" the other one asked. And then they started whispering with that sort of exaggerated excitement children pick up from the way adults read fairy tales. "Okay?" one child asked out loud. The other swore solemnly, "Okay," and they ran off.

At dawn, at the Detached Residence, Elena had seemed so forceful that I was jarred to discover later how small she actually was as she lay beside me. The effort of will that had drawn her features together into an expression this morning had relaxed and the lines of her face had fallen into disarray.

Although the sheet followed the contours of her body, it had compositional intricacies of its own. Her raised knee was a mound as round and snowy as a scoop of lemon ice, but the formal pleats falling away from that summit extended out and away into a tent of linen, as though she were a statue emerging from marble.

"I love it when we don't say anything," she murmured.

"Why?"

"Then I can imagine what you must be thinking." She turned on her side, a Winged Victory gyrating, a new fold stretched taut from her elbow to her heel. The sunlight filtered through the space between her legs under the sheet. "I can invent your thoughts, invent all sorts of wonderful thoughts for you."

"Like what?"

"I can imagine our going away. Or even staying here, but staying together. Becoming different people. Forgetting all codes, old and new. Walking out of a room in a simple, natural fashion instead of *recessing*. No more arch comments. No more mystification. We all pass judgments on one another. We have to. It's the easiest way to be witty. But if we didn't? I don't trust you, darling. Are you laughing at me now? How can I know? We're so ironic, we never know when we're serious."

I stroked her hair tenderly, but I don't think she trusted me. I didn't trust her.

Someone's tugging my sleeve—it's Doris. But so tall! "You're so tall, Doris."

"I'm wearing cothurni. Buskins. Greek shoes, like ancient Greek actors."

Her chin's above me, and as I look up into it, I notice a pouch of fat I hadn't seen before. "Oh."

"Can I speak to you for a moment? Privately?"

"Of course."

Herbert and Billy are conspicuously ignoring our departure. My white paper cups gleam in the purple light as we cross to an empty corner of the room, Doris clumping slowly and noisily beside me on her tall shoes.

She lays a majestic hand on my shoulder. "My friend, have you gone out of your mind?"

"Perhaps. I don't know."

"Why are you spending time with Elena again? Of course, when you stopped by the house last night, I recognized the robe you were wearing. I knew it was hers, but I told Jimmy I was certain there must be an explanation."

Looking out the window I see the performers on the gravel path down below packing up their chains, coiling them and placing them in a badly scarred wooden box.

"If it were any other time, I'd say it was simply an aberration. Or nostalgia on your part. I'm a woman. I understand how you might miss her. The *heart*, after all . . . The *heart*. But now? With what's facing you tomorrow? The Royal Arrival is a solemn event. No one's saying a word, but you can be certain they're concerned. Herbert's terribly upset. He doesn't understand it at all.'

I look up and see a wet gold filling in her open mouth.

"Will you speak to her? She must understand there are *claims* on us we can't ignore. Daryl and I have been frantic. And then your dance or whatever it was at the hotel. We've been frantic all day. Tongues are wagging. I won't say another word. It's painful for me to take this tone with you."

"I'll speak to her."

"That's all I wanted to hear. There she is. See?"

"I thought you and all the Valentines would be delighted about the reconciliation between Elena and me."

"And so we were—at first. But Elena is not one of us. She's a bewitching woman, fascinating, quite fascinating of course. Who should know that better than I? But she is not a realist. This is not the best of all possible worlds, but we must live in it. Herbert came to me today. For lunch. When you rejected him this morning for Elena you hurt him very deeply. He and I have had a reconciliation, a meeting of minds. He changed things too quickly, he admitted. But then we Valentines were at fault, too. We clung too tenaciously to our privileges, servants, out-moded points of distinction. Ridiculous pride."

"So you will be changing, or adjusting, to the New Code?"

"I don't like that word. It's silly. A New Order is what we have in mind, Herbert and I."

I smile up at her.

"But Elena's a troublemaker. 'I'll speak to her.' That's what you said. Now I will hold you to your word."

Elena's beside the band table. She takes her paper cup of punch and the two of us silently observe the musical diners. One lifts a gravy boat, which dangles its phonic wire, and the action traces a crooked aural scratch. The fall of the gravy, however, evokes a long, lovely trill, loud at first but trickling away into a diminuendo. An innuendo of thunder rumbles from the speakers on the balcony when a sleeve grazes the tablecloth. A couple of musicians are arguing and emphatically jabbing at the air with knives; the lifted knives register an uncomfortably close dyad, relieved only when one knife or the other rises or falls an inch and a tone sharps, or flats. At last their melancholy duet ends as both knives fall and start slicing the steaks, evoking a turgid bass tremelo.

"Elena?"

"Yes?"

"I'm afraid I'm not very good company tonight."

"But you are!"

"Would you mind terribly . . ."

"If we left?"

"No, don't leave. And neither shall I, at least not right away. But perhaps we could circulate—"

"Yes?"

"—independently."

"Oh. By all means. It is tiresome to be *attached* to someone at a party. God knows I have my own calls to pay. A party is fun only when it's a sea of infinite horizons; even one small island of certainty—oh, forgive the expression, forgive the ugliness of the phrase—'geometrizes the flux.' What a scandal!" she shrieks with laughter, her hands rigid as they grip two folds in her skirt. "What a scandal to talk that way, yes, *don't you think?*" Her question, intended as a mere rhetorical fillip, gets out of control and presses me with her real terror.

"I'm not familiar with that expression, 'geometrizes the flux.' Good night, Elena."

"Darling," she asks, "what have I done?"

"I beg your pardon," I say, bending closer to her, speaking clearly and slowly, "I didn't catch your question."

Her fingers toy with a wisp of hair. She's trembling. "Must you humiliate me in front of all these people?"

"I've only asked permission to—"

"To desert me."

"As you wish." I nod and withdraw to a corner. She wanders onto the dance floor in a daze and hesitates, displays confusion, freezes. The chorus line in the leopard skins sweeps past her, shouting the "Fire fire who?" Couples jostle her. Someone approaches her, talks to her, but she pays him no heed. She's looking from door to door, planning an exit.

Alone in her dress, her blue eyes squinting, her hands rhythmically stroking her skirt, she takes a step in one direction, only to retract it. Her eyes pass over me as though she didn't see me, and locate the door to the balcony where the speakers are blasting out the dinner music. Her hand rises and rubs her neck. Someone jostles her elbow and she jumps back. That small alarm at being touched overcomes her bewilderment and provides her with the momentum to reach the veranda. She strides past the pool, hurries through the crowd loitering on the lower deck and disappears into the tea-garden.

I move from the third step to the second. The mica chips sparkle, but not randomly, I notice; they're secretly in session under the presidency of an idea lurking within the stone frog.

I descend from the third step to the second. I really must get home. It's not safe to be out and about. What if I stumbled into the ocean, became fascinated with the mathematics of the waves and wanted to factor into it? Stop it. You can control your thoughts. Get home. Just get home. The horn case containing Elena's memoirs is in my hand. My appearance is in order. I am on my way home.

I descend from the third step to the second. The lights fail to throw my shadow. A presence behind me is angry! I can feel eyes on my neck, angry eyes . . . What was that about waves? Was it that waves were like *numbers?* Or *food?* Which was it? One: food. Two: numbers. Three: numbers. Three? But how many items are there? Surely only two—food and numbers. Food: one. Numbers: two. That makes two.

I descend from the third step to the second. The sound of my foot crushing the concrete shatters my leg and I crack.

A high kilocycle wail pulses through me: eighty thousand feet. The mica—under the *presidency* of the stone frog or the *residency*, which did I say? President: one. Resident: two. There are two possibilities. I just thought of another twosome—what were they? Food and waves? No. That didn't happen. I didn't think that. I don't remember. I'm innocent. My heart is pounding faster and faster. The kilocycle dips from eighty thousand to seventy thousand feet. Good. I must stay below the eighty-thousand-foot barrier. Safer to fly low.

I prepare to descend from the second step to the first. Mica chips in the concrete surround a black something and I stoop to see it more clearly. This chip is a parallelepiped, so shiny it seems to be resting on top of the concrete and not to be affixed to it. I touch it to see if it will move. No, it's firmly imbedded in the step. An adjoining chip is a very regular square but its energy is being funneled off into a mere sliver of mica, a dart; the dart's distressing the square, poking fun at it. Has anyone else gotten the joke, seen the humor in it? I completely sympathize with the dart, and adore the way it's threatening the square. Without the dart the square would be a perfect burgomaster, belching happily, humming polkas, dozing after dinner. Food?

Food and waves? Food and numbers? Waves and numbers?

I've got to get home. In my interlude with the mica dart and square the kilocycle has dropped to twenty thousand feet, but that's *too* low, surely that's too low. There's the path. The rock garden. The gate. I must get from here to there—and then what? Where will I go then? Which way is home? The kilocycle soars dangerously upward: calm down! Think of something else.

I'm suddenly beside the gate. How did I get from the steps to the gate so quickly? I don't recall passing the rock garden. But I'm here now. It all happened while I wasn't noticing.

What is this in my hand, this milk-white case? I may have stolen it from someone. The angry eyes on my neck belong to the rightful owner of the horn case, perhaps. I'd return it but I'm afraid of the punishment in store for me.

The gate will be a witness at my trial. The gate: an old weathered shepherd speaking Basque (who's the translator?) telling the judge with the wart on his chin (the frog), "It was two in the morning when the culprit stole past." I'm innocent. The gate creaks as I push it open. I'm innocent.

I prepare to descend from the second step to the first. The lights fail to throw my shadow. A presence behind me is angry; I can feel eyes on my neck, angry eyes. The kilocycle nips playfully at the eighty-thousand-foot barrier; eighty-one thousand? it asks, smiling, knowing better. How many times must I tell you it's eighty thousand feet and that's that.

A cool wind stirs my toga as I step barefoot through the cold sand.

The presence flies behind that half-burned tree and watches. Collecting evidence, that's all I'm doing, it says. Just collecting evidence. If you're innocent you needn't worry.

I'm gliding at a comfortable forty thousand feet.

I reach the Detached Residence and proceed beyond it, across the plain of marbled black sand and scrub foliage. The angry presence flies ten thousand feet below me, but its flight is not smooth and even like my own. It slows, then sticks, finally jumps to catch up: slows, sticks, jumps. My feet trail behind me in collusion with the erratic presence, and when it stops, they stop. Although my feet are held back, my shoulders continue flowing smoothly forward and my legs, as a consequence, stretch into long taffy pulls. Only when the presence catches up with me do my feet rebound like rubber bands.

A scene other than the one I face (marbled sand, a distant rim of dunes, scabrous underbrush) unfolds in a space I couldn't identify, space separate from but penetrating into the black earth and air around me. I see: a cool reception room with dark-green walls dadoed in aquamarine tile. It's afternoon. Someone is playing a drowsy piano down the hall. Winter sunlight slants into the room, glistens on the tile floors. A bell rings. The sound of scraping chairs and girls' clear laughter. Someone walks briskly toward me, shoes sounding the tile. She approaches. She smiles. It's Elena.

A piano plays scales five or six rooms away. The scales break off, unfinished. Sunlight brightens and dims on green tiles. Frost flowers cloud the leaded windowpanes. Green plants climb out of massive ceramic jars, pale-green celadon, shiny smooth but crackled below the glaze. The piano undertakes a melody. Bell. Scraping chairs. Laughter and steps. It's Elena.

When I squint, the dashes of sunlight on the tile floor form an unbroken line. The plant beside me is rigid with life in a warm room stirring with warm smells. The bell rings. Nothing moves in the room except my hand, relaxing a cigarette to my lap. I walk toward the door and notice, in passing, that the frost flowers disperse the sunlight into points of red and blue and winking green. Elena smiles and takes my hand.

Flowing steadily onward, I approach the rim of the dunes, accompanied by the presence. From the dunes, and from whatever lies beyond them, issued Herbert's band of tatterdemalion priests carrying silver spades and, behind them, the solitary Negro runner running naked, arms flopping wildly, across the deserted land.

Elena leads me by the hand down echoing green corridors. A bell rings and everything is silent except our feet. Up two steps, down two steps, everything is silent except our feet. The red border of tiles racing along above the aquamarine dado portrays in separate squares girls playing tennis, girls reading books, girls diving into a pool, girls on horseback, girls playing tennis, girls reading books, diving, and on horseback. She glances at me and smiles.

I sit down on the ground and hear piano music. The aquamarine dado to my right mirrors in its glassy tiles the slowly throbbing sunlight on the conservatory floor and reveals, behind a spidery shrub in a ceramic planter, the figure of a man, brightness glancing off his canescent shirt collar and cuff and the hand raising a cigarette to his lips. Echoing steps approach down a long corridor.

Sifting handfuls of cold sand, I feel goose bumps rising on my naked calf. Men step out of shadows, or seem to, for truth to tell I only sense, rather than clearly see, an activity. Yet surely that flash is the gleam of goggles belonging to the man who was working the pneumatic drill on the beach. And that smile, that dim sliver of brilliance, is Herbert's. Billy's whispering something to him. Pressed against a tree is the black body of the Negro runner. Or is it? The shadows of men—is that the Minister's bald head?—collect and disperse in vague, fitful gusts, whispering, or is it only the sound of wind in their robes, or is it only the sound of wind?

A pensive melody, drawn out on a late winter afternoon from a distant piano, enters the green room and grows and fades in imperfect harmony with the slower rise and fall of sunlight on the tiled floor. A bell rings. I inhale the cigarette, then crush it out impatiently and stand up. I say her name and hear one of the shadowy men ask, "What did he say?" and hear another whisper, "Elena. He said Elena."

The moon is suddenly snapped off. Everything is black. I have the sense that I'm sinking, that the sand I'm sitting on is descending, but I can't see anything against which I could check whether I'm moving and if so in what direction. But my instincts tell me I'm going down and the damp, close air, smelling of salt and soil, also suggests that I'm being lowered below ground.

Some thing or person to my right is breathing—no, it's two people, at least two, since one's breath is higher and more rapid than the other's. On my left, sounding as though it were so close I could touch it if I stretched out a hand, a wheel (or several) is revolving rapidly and at odd intervals snapping a thin conveyor belt. The space in front of me remains mysterious, without depth or denizens. For all I know I could be facing a solid wall or a wide valley. I cough. No echo. The area remains unmapped. The breathing pair on my right are rustling with clothes or a sail or flag; I fancy they're staggering under folds of canvas, trying to find corners so they can fold it.

A blaze of light sweeps over the snowy mound and the valley of blue shadows beyond a tan curve: my nose against my pillow. The width of the room fills in and, with another glance, I wrench my bed around so that the

115

bureau is to the right instead of the left, where I had for some reason at first felt it should be. The sloping ceiling and exposed beams slide into place. I move a toe and discover the shape and disposition of my body. I sit up. My roommates, Tod and Hunter, are still asleep. No one is moving about in the adjoining rooms and all I can hear is the refrigerator humming and a squirrel scrabbling on hard, flinty claws across the tar-paper roof. All I have on is my underwear.

Getting out of bed I notice a yellow stain like a yellow moth, one wing unfurled, the other crimped, on the bottom sheet. I quickly draw the covers over it. I must have urinated in my sleep. If I poke around the house at odd moments during the day I may find the linen closet and then, when everyone's out, I can change my bed in secret. But what will I do with the stained sheet? I could hide it under the house, or better, leave it out beyond the rim of dunes.

Herbert.

He's probably already awake, reading his newspaper on the deck. I move a step and stagger against my bed, run a hand through my hair as I right myself and survey my sleeping roommates. They must have gone swimming yesterday; their nylon suits are hung up on the window sill, and they must have gone dancing, not at Jason's but probably at the hotel, for their silk shirts, feathers, bells, boots, headbands, bellbottoms are all piled in a heap in the armchair, as though shed in drunken confusion.

The horn case containing the woman's—Elena's—manuscript lies on top of the bureau.

Descending the steps that separate the bedrooms from the rest of the house I catch sight of Bob in his green T-shirt and blue jeans—his absurd "trademark"—slumbering on the couch, a green pillow pressed over his eyes and held under his huge, hairless arm, white as fresh ham. His palm, slightly cupped, lies exposed to the ceiling as though he were prepared to catch a visiting mosquito. When in motion, he looks rather trim, but sleep uncorsets him, releasing rolls of flesh. On the coffee table beside him are: a half-filled glass with a slice of lemon floating in it, the swollen pulp fibrous and disintegrating; a tin box containing pills; and a purple-jacketed book, a rosary of wooden beads marking the place.

After tiptoeing over to the table I pick the book up and turn to the table of contents. "Chapter One: Meta-etiquette. Chapter Two: Women, Sex and Wit. Chapter Three: The Royal Arrival. Chapter Four: Aesthetics as Ethics. Epilogue: In Search of Experience." The

116

beads mark the chapter on the Royal Arrival, where I read: ". . . have allowed so many other celebrations to lapse into disuse, the Arrival, the sole remaining holiday of importance, has gained . . ." My eye skips down the page. "The Prince is the one who 'arrives,' the people 'welcome' him and their obesiance (the only public display of palace etiquette still permitted under the New Code) symbolizes submission to his rule."

I turn to an earlier page in the same chapter. "Two days before the Royal Arrival, a party of gentlemen visit the ancient burial grounds beyond the dunes. They carry silver spades and dig a fresh grave in accordance with the superstitious customs of the past. Here, on the evening of the Arrival, the Prince buries a memory of the year that has just concluded—perhaps a poem, perhaps an article of winter clothing, perhaps a ring or a book.

"In no way does the New Code approve of the continuation of the Old Code barbarisms. The Regent has inaugurated an enlightened era in which egalitarianism rules and reason is revered, in which elegance has superseded clumsy pomp.

"During the Arrival, however, old forms are revived, but only so that they can be filled with new content. For instance, young victims were once buried alive during the Arrival in order to propitiate the spirits of dead monarchs; now only a symbol of what the Prince might regret or wish to forget is dropped into the grave. Similarly, the Arrival once recalled the royal family's conquest of the indigenous black population; now the holiday merely acknowledges the end to all such gross pride and the beginning of serene humility."

Herbert is watching me through the window. His newspaper is spread open on his lap and he's pretending to read it, but he keeps glancing up and studying me. There's nothing to do except stroll out there and talk to him as casually as possible.

I wander out onto the deck, letting the screen door slam behind me.

He puts his paper aside. "Good morning."

"Good morning. It sure is overcast. Not a very good beach day, is it?"

"No, no it's not. Uh, sit down."

I do.

"I have some news that may shock you. I can't say, of course, but it may. That's why I think *I* should tell you rather than letting you hear it from a stranger, or overhear it—that might be unpleasant."

"I appreciate your consideration. What's the news?"

"Elena killed herself last night."

"Oh."

"After that dismal bacchanalia. I wonder if Jason knows? I don't know the details. She, uh, she did it at home, which seems sensible. In private. With pills. She didn't leave a note. Maria sent someone to tell us this morning. I don't think arrangements have been made yet for the funeral. I suppose the task will fall to Maria, though who's to tell? Not I, surely."

"No," I repeat, "not you."

My eye falls on the burned tree stump and then shifts to a bruised leaf of grass sticking up between two planks of the walkway and trampled flat against the wood. Brown and desiccated, it's frayed at the tip, as I noticed yesterday, like the loose leather strips on the working end of a whip.

Herbert leans forward, his blue eyes clear and vivid. "Shall I bring you paper and ink?"

"Why would you do that?" I inquire.

"So you can record your first impressions of the news. A poem, you see; people may expect a poem."

"No, don't bring paper and ink." I can't think what to say next; Herbert politely returns to his newspaper. "A poem," I say at last, "would be inappropriate. Elena hated them, as you may recall. What I'll do is devote the morning to reading her memoirs; she gave them to me. Reading her book would be the right sort of commemoration, don't you imagine?"

"Yes," Herbert replies, brightening, "inspired. Don't worry; I'll tell everyone about your decision. I'll explain why not doing a poem was, given the context, quite correct, and let everyone know of your private hours devoted to the manuscript. In fact, I fancy that your reading of the memoirs will come to be known as 'The Absent Poem.'"

Passing through the living room, I spot my bacchanalia toga thrown over the back of a chair. I pick it up and hold it to my shoulders. A shower of sand patters to the floor. Bob's hand, pressed palm upward to his forehead, seems now to be saying, "Oh my God! Can it be true?" and I resent it. I roll my costume into a ball and hurl it passionately into the seat of the chair beside me. On contact, the ball falls half open and one sleeve dangles free and swings anemically for a moment or two, possibly three. Bob's ring finger, as though it were tied to the empty sleeve, twitches. I hate the way these phantom things are starting to play around with the grief in the air. They should contain themselves and let the man

118

who's grieved feel the grief, should he know what he's feeling and should that happen to be grief.

What I'm feeling is unclear, and I almost wish now I had written that poem and been done with it. It's too hard to invent sincerity at times like these, if "times like these" are in fact as momentous as my clenched stomach would seem to indicate. How many days is it since my bowels have moved? Can constipation be dangerous? I don't trust my body. I'm not at all sure that left to its own devices it would ever function properly. Pills and poems are called for; a purge for the bowels; a poem to facilitate the search for experience. Left to its own devices the body won't come through. I don't even trust this gripping fist in my stomach, and far from finding it reassuring, a proof that I'm responding to the news about Elena appropriately, I can't help sneering at the visceral alarmist inside me. But then, I'm an islander, and as Elena said in her book, Herbert's islanders can't accept the paucity of the possible emotions. They're always trying to work up some exquisitely novel shade of feeling in themselves; they want to appear *not quite human*.

I walk into my room, find the horn case and take it to my bed. Of course I open it diligently and begin to examine the contents, but the islander in me resents the facile piety of the act. It's all too predictable, the obligatory scene. I announced I would read the book and here I am, sure enough, reading it. What the islander despises isn't the bogus sentiment, for the sadness of studying a dead woman's writing is real enough, I suppose. No, what the islander hates is being bound by contract to any emotion at all. We're endlessly tantalized by the allure of the uncatalogued.

I look at the last sentence on the last page: "If that should ever happen, I don't think I could go on living."

Flipping to the middle of the book, I read: "He hated the island and constantly made fun of the lame little verses, the fancy clothes, the mechanical production of 'shocking' remarks. We even toyed with the idea of leaving the island. We resented the way Herbert and the others were meddling in our lives. Sometimes I felt they didn't even notice our friendship and that we were being absurd to fear them, but then, just as I would start to breathe more easily, convinced that we were safe, something would happen to revive our apprehensions. Herbert was invariably polite but he *was* watching.

"If we couldn't leave the island (where would we go?), we decided that at least we could make ourselves over. We saw how the island's cult of

119

beauty was at the heart of its vapidity, and we tried to be as blunt and awkward as possible. We may have been a little ridiculous in our efforts to be common and unaffected; after all, we had been trained to thread subtleties and spout verses and deflate enemies, and on some days both of us were irritable from our struggle to speak plainly and ignore double meanings.

"Under the New Code the islanders, forbidden to ridicule people for their low birth or humble position, have resorted to rejecting their inferiors for some supposed insensitivity to beauty or for some social blunder. But it all amounts to the same thing. The good people are automatically considered creative and tactful, no matter how gross they may actually be; the wrong sort, try as they might, are always found to be bores.

"We were different. Neither of us was keeping score or collecting grievances. We weren't parading delicate perceptions. In the evening we spent hours confessing the secrets we had hidden an entire lifetime, and we weren't ashamed to be only human.

"I was perfectly happy. But our idyll didn't last long. Herbert began to spend every day with us. We stopped talking. Soon we stopped seeing one another. Herbert had been his guardian for so many years, and I suppose Herbert loved him. Despite his great show of egalitarianism, Herbert would never have considered conferring his love on anyone less distinguished.

"But how did Herbert do it, regain control? It wasn't very difficult. Herbert had created him after all, had trained him to catch allusions, invent poems, adjust to whims, smile, bow, conform. The odd thing was that Herbert had never converted to the New Code he had himself invented. Herbert is a realist, as I am not, as his creature could not be. For the perfect man, who was Herbert's creature, our adventure in sincerity must have been only one more novel sensation, a delicious *frisson*. When he tired of me, or when what I demanded of him became too much of a strain, he put me out of his mind. He forgot me. He became more and more eccentric, crafty and at the same time more innocent; he met my eyes with enormous innocence; he was a child, born again, all memories erased.

"Maria—my servant, my companion—and I found a little house together, but we had few visitors. Herbert saw to that. My lover, who no longer seemed to love me, would nod in my direction at parties but seldom speak. I'd observe him from my porch as he strolled down the beach with Herbert and the men from his house, gossiping, laughing. Their lives—and my own—seemed once again so delicate and so brutal.

"Some mornings I wake up thinking you'll come see me today. I remind myself that our months together were not just a dream, that you loved me then and it could all happen again. Perhaps you're only waiting until you've won a decisive victory over Herbert. Perhaps our new life was too difficult, and you recoiled from it, but only temporarily.

"If only I didn't see you so often. Do you remember that night at the hotel? I bumped into someone and then turned and saw it was you. I'd see you wearing those silly yellow sunglasses by the quay, talking to your admirers, smirking; Maria and I would hurry past like shadows or servants.

"I tried staying home. But I'd go crazy listening for your step on the deck. Maria and I analyzed every tiny thing we heard you say or saw you do—and they weren't many—hoping, I suppose, to detect signs that you were about to come back to me. Then I'd be so ashamed of myself— reduced to this!—and I'd get very angry at you and storm about the house shouting, 'You can't do this to me. You're not going to get away with this.'

"In the morning as soon as I was awake I'd vomit. I was so afraid. Maria played her guitar and changed clothes and created new perfumes and changed clothes and played her guitar. I'd take long baths and stare at the water dripping from the faucet and hate the ring of dirt slowly forming on the porcelain. I'd sigh, say, 'Well, time to pull myself together,' but I'd continue sitting in the cold water. I examined every inch of my body and found it wanting. Maria and I got drunk one night and went to bed and made love, but my mind wandered and it never came to an end. The next day I couldn't speak to her. Then we finally talked—about you. I'd hear your step on the deck. I've been humbled by waiting. So much waiting, like water dissolving soap. The soap becomes white on the underside, then it's coated in white slush. Soon it's slush all the way through, it's lost its shape and scent, and if someone tried to pick it up he'd have only a handful of soft grease.

"Perhaps you will come back—but then I imagine that all my waiting may have disfigured me and you'll not like me and you'll return only for a night or two or three and then leave me again. If that should happen, I don't think I could go on living."

"It's time for us to get ready," Herbert announces, standing in the doorway. "We're wearing white, of course. How's the book?"

"I just finished it this very moment."

"And how was it? Did she speak badly of me? I don't want to pry, naturally, but I am curious."

"Well, she may have thought you came between us."

"I see. And do you think that?"

"I don't know what to think."

"I see. We must get ready now."

Low swells of water heave and sink and travel, like knuckles gliding under a blanket. A band of sunlight glances off the plastic visor of a speedboat that has just raced up to our barge and cut its motors; its wake swamps our low gunwales. The air is cold and salty, recommending escape. But I don't pay it any attention. I'm trembling slightly. Darting breezes grave thousands of fine lines across the swollen seas.

We're entering the harbor. The other men and I are dressed in the simplest white shirts and pants without pockets or cuffs or ornaments. We're standing at the bow. No one is talking. The Pale Stranger is leaning on Herbert's arm. They're in the center of our group, which has formed a deferential half-circle around them. The Pale Stranger's nose is still a bit puffy, his clean hair fanning in every gust, the whites of his eyes yellowish.

A sudden shift of wind carries the faint noise of trumpets from the shore and then angles it out of hearing. Tall marble columns (probably made for the occasion out of painted cloth stretched over wood) line the breakwater; on top of each capital is a heroic statue of stucco so gritty that I can see the rough mix even from this distance. Curving catenaries of roses and pink carnations link the columns and live birds bob on little coloured ribbons tied to the outstretched hands of the chalky white figures.

Now that we're past the breakwater, the music surges loudly around us, and simultaneously I spot the musicians on the hotel steps. Four heralds in purple plush tunics, their legs straddled (one leg in yellow hose, the other in kelly green) blow long C-trumpets.

Weaving unsteadily through the crowd, a three-tiered gold standard soars over the heads of women, who have woven strings of pearls into their coiffed hair, and passes under two mustachioed men on stilts. The banners dip in mock reverence toward the hotel balcony where Jason, clad as Mars, holds hands with a bare-bosomed Venus; Jason's two baby attendants are balancing on his shoulders and gripping his hair with their pudgy hands. Blue wings strapped to their backs pivot ineffectually in the wind.

On a distant hill I can just catch a glimpse of the house where Elena and Maria lived.

Then I look back at Jason. His face is quite old and sad. Venus appears to be bored. Everything seems as static as a tapestry that keeps becoming abstract. So much movement, and yet everything seems still. So much color, brilliant color, but it seems to be fading.

On the landing men and women, wrapped in silk heliotrope mantles that billow like spinnakers, raise a toast and a shout, but the noise is muffled. Behind them, beside an open door to the palace, two cooks in aprons and toques smoke and chat, one of them sitting on stacked wicker cages filled with white rabbits.

At the main gate to the palace, a gilded papier-mâché baldachino, decked with hundreds of votive candles flickering whitely in the day-light, serves as an archway for the greeting committee which is just coming out. The thick blue velvet of their sleeves is divided into successive puffs by crimson strings, and their collars rise in stiff ruffles to their chins.

Our barge touches the dock. Three lean dogs strain toward us on their leashes, but Doris, sporting a single pearl on a chain between her breasts, reins them in with a firm hand and laughs. Some of the men in our party leap to shore with ropes and secure them to iron cleats. Should I be helping them? I have no idea what my responsibilities are supposed to be.

The crowd has become absolutely silent and attentive. The trumpets have stopped playing. The only sound is of the distant surf and of the approaching footsteps of the greeting committee. The only things visibly moving are the banners, the rippling heliotrope cloaks and the pink ears of the rabbits behind their wooden bars.

Herbert places an arm around the Pale Stranger, surveys us all with a sober glance, breathes deeply and disembarks. The lean dogs have lost interest in us; two of them are reclining and one sitting, sniffing the sea breeze. The Pale Stranger steps off the barge. The members of the greeting committee are watching us solemnly. Falling in behind all the other men, I follow them down the short, slightly canted gangplank.

A distant clacking can be heard. I look up: a brown helicopter, a drab Army-brown. The blades spin vague silver haloes over the cockpit and tail. Now the sound is becoming deafening as the plane hovers over us and slowly descends, throwing a larger and larger shadow over the barking dogs and the upturned faces of the spectators. The constant ack-ack racket of the churning helicals hurts my ears. The large brown hull is so close and huge that I can see every bolt distinct and hexagonal. Blown by steady volumes of roaring wind, everyone's hair is riffled and tangled and leaping in antic wisps, and the helitrope robes bulk like tumors but flip up in sudden swoops. Because of its terrifying noise and the torrential gale, the plane seems to take up much more space than it actually occupies, and everyone squints and cringes a bit, as though we were about to be crushed and diced. A newsreel photographer leans out of the helicopter window and aims his big black camera at us.

I step off the barge. All the other men in my party back away from me, their shirts fluttering in the giant centrifuge. And then, in a single motion, as though responding to a signal, the entire population of the island sinks slowly to its knees, facing me, yes, I see, facing me, a prince, *the* prince.

I go into the palace with just Herbert and Doris. Blind musicians—yes, Gilles and Vinnie and . . . Shunkin—are seated cross-legged on the polished floor in front of the enclosed garden. Their old hands strike the little drums in their laps or the gongs and chimes beside them without ruffling the starched immobility of their full sleeves. In the gloss of their cylindrical hats our reflections move and warp.

How I used to study that garden and lose myself in its shallow, infinite perspectives! No more than three yards deep, I suppose, but so cleverly scaled down, so devoid of any reminders of true dimension that after only a few moments a bored child, propped up on one elbow, could be flying over the mountains, or wandering through a forest, or standing beside a stream.

Nanda (how *old* she looks) hobbles toward me on the tiny feet she once took such pride in, opens a napkin, smiling, shows me a hot cake, which is so glutted with butter it's about to fall apart. It does as she tries to feed it to me with her own hands, and we both start laughing. That I'm here with Herbert and Doris doesn't surprise her, of course; she hasn't kept track of events, and it seems only natural to her that they're beside me as they so often were years and years ago, taking me from or bringing me back to the nursery. Herbert slips me a little package, which I, in turn, present to Nanda. She kisses my hand and tries to kneel, but I start laughing again for some reason and pull her into my arms and kiss her.

Lily of the valley: first her maiden then her maiden-lady scent.

One of the coarse grains of Nanda's cake has lodged between my teeth and I worry it with my tongue as the crowd follows me into the precincts of the Detached Residence. Like light passing through a prism, the procession, which was all jumbled outside, goes through the wicker gate single file and then fans out into solemn ranks, each family in a line. The Master of the Grove, I tie a new silk band around the trunk of the sacred pine. Everyone applauds: a summer shower on a tin roof.

The large boulder beside the tree, the one they call Moonlight, has always depressed me, ever since I learned that a man was crushed under it when it was brought here from the harbor site of Doris's former mansion. The islanders congratulate themselves on the "simplicity" of our gardens, but I'd have been happier with a yard full of plaster flamingos, happier with less taste and more humanity.

All alone, I walk into the Residence.

In this very room, in this carved chair, my father died, or so they tell me. Toppled over. In his sleep. I never had a face to go with his name, but the name itself became as disturbing as a face you can't quite see in the dark but which you know is there because you can hear someone talking to you.

What was he saying? I'll never be certain. Herbert put posthumous words in his mouth ("Your father wouldn't have wanted you to . . ." "Your father disliked that family . . ." "When your father appointed me regent he suggested that you and I . . .").

As I walk barefoot down the dark corridor my muscles remember to sidestep a loose strip of parquet that's needed mending for thirty years at least.

Rich, hasty, sexual—that tangle of sensations confronts me as I go into my old bedroom. It's all coming from the smell of eucalyptus leaves, there, brown in a vase by the shuttered window. Of course, the room may *look* like childhood (the glass bird with the chipped tail on the sill, the night lamp I could dial down until its glow just touched my pillowslip), but childhood things are now becoming vacant, entranced observers of later mysteries, of a young man and woman locking the door behind them. Then Elena's hands on my back, pulling me into her, then both of us sitting up, startled ("Oh. It's just a squirrel on the roof"), then we relax and recline and my hand resumes its exploration of the long landscape of her body.

I suppose we quickly become indifferent to a person's real beauty,

125

that love can find any face or body beautiful; nonetheless, I'm grateful that my love had so little work, so much idle admiring, to do. She puts my fingers in her mouth (she knows how that excites me) and then puts them on her breast. She lifts my head away from her breast, all red from my beard; I look up and catch her eye, neither of us smiles, she presses me back to her pain, her pleasure, and she's so entirely within my compass that I can continue to kiss her nipple and still reach down and grab the smooth bottom of her foot. Her toes curl round my index finger.

After we make love she gets up and finds an old panama hat in the closet, much too large for her, and puts it on. We sit naked and cross-legged on the bare mattress and smoke cigarettes (a seashell she brought along just for this purpose is our ashtray). We should be as quiet as possible, but she sings me my favorite song, a turn-of-the-century Italian café song, and she sounds the low notes but whispers the high. The straw hat with the soiled band, the secrecy, the nearly motionless cloud of smoke collecting like intimacy above our heads, the litter of our clothes by the door, the voiced and unvoiced refrain ("*Pioveva, piangevo*")—all combine to still my fears. I could live forever with that song, this woman, through this afternoon. I close my eyes.

When I open them, there's Herbert, looking perplexed. "Custom doesn't demand—"

"A visit to *this* room?" I ask him. "You're quite right. It doesn't. I suppose you're eager to finish the Arrival before sunset."

Pioveva, piangevo. That song always seemed so glamorous to me.

Herbert and I rejoin the waiting crowd outside the Residence.

It was about a man who'd loved a girl years ago but they'd parted ("*Non mi ricordo perché*"), then he finds himself one day standing beside her under an awning. They're both waiting for the rain to stop. At first he doesn't recognize her, but after only a moment he remembers the dear face, only now she's wearing a smart hat, a veil, a diamond bracelet. He tries to be casual, he offers her his umbrella, but she says her husband is coming to pick her up any moment now in his car or carriage, whichever it was.

Herbert and I go out through the wicker gate. The rest follow.

The man recalls how happy they were for two years in their little room, though it was always raining outside. He left her one day, he doesn't remember why. Now they say good-bye to each other rather formally; the rain is letting up. He leaves her waiting under the awning and returns to his house. Just as he's about to go up the stairs he feels a little hand on his sleeve. She's returned! "You have such sappy taste in music," Elena said, putting the straw hat away. We pull our clothes on and sneak out of the house.

Twisting trees scatter shadows over us until we get beyond the last house, the last boardwalk; I brush off an annoying cobweb, or perhaps it's just one free-floating, unspun filament—and we step down into the full realism of sunlight. Out of sight, on the other side of the dunes, the ocean detonates depth charges, wave after slow wave going off, it seems, *under* the beach. We walk over marbled black sand, past scrub foliage. The leaves of one plant shine like wax or sincerity. Four marigolds some good soul planted way out here God alone knows why have distilled all the yellow out of the day. Herbert has taken a step ahead of me and come into my peripheral vision.

We enter the ancient burial grounds. A black native is running away from us across the plain, his hands flopping at his side. Past crouching stone animals we make our way. Here's the new grave Herbert and his gentlemen dug.

A circle of people forms around the hole and the adjacent mounds of sand mixed with black earth. We are in a sort of basin protected by the dunes from the cold wind flowing off the ocean. Doris joins hands with Herbert. They look at each other mournfully. The single pearl on her exposed breast rises with a sigh; he squeezes her hand. Next to him is Jon (how it amuses me to call him the Pale Stranger), equally solemn but coming off as wispy Melancholy beside the Minister's more stolid Dolor. Across from me, on the other side of the grave, is Maria. She won't look at me.

Four pallbearers led by Billy bring the coffin on their shoulders to the site. They lower it into the hole. Silver spades start to scoop up the dislodged earth, but stop when Herbert raises his hand.

"Do you want to say a little something about Elena?" he asks me.

I look around at this ring of strangers and wonder what this man expects from me. Is there a dead person in that box? Am I a newcomer to the island? I remember nothing. Who is Elena?

Nocturnes
for the
King of Naples

To David Kalstone

> The abstract joy,
> The half-read wisdom of daemonic images.
> Suffice the ageing man as once the growing boy.

W. B. Yeats, "Meditations In Time Of Civil War"

1

A young man leans with one shoulder against the wall, and his slender body remains motionless against the huge open slab of night sky and night water behind him. He is facing the river. Little waves scuttling shoreward from a passing, passed scow slap against boards: perfunctory applause. On the other side of the water, lights trace senseless paths up across hills, lash-marks left by an amateur whip. He turns toward me a look of hope tempered by discretion, eyes dilated by a longing too large—as large as this briny night panel behind him—to focus in on any single human being.

I have failed to interest him. He turns back to his river as though it were the masterpiece and I the retreating guard.

For me there was the deeper vastness of the enclosed, ruined cathedral I was entering. Soaring above me hung the pitched roof, wings on the downstroke, its windows broken and lying at my feet.

A wind said incantations and hypnotized a match flame up and out of someone's cupped hands. Now the flame went out and only the cigarette pulsed, each draw molding gold leaf to cheekbones.

There are qualities of darkness, the darkness of gray silk stretched taut to form the sky, watered by city lights, the darkness of black quartz boiling to make a river, and the penciled figures of men in the distance, minute figures on—is that a second story? What are they doing up there? A cigarette rhymes its glow with my own across the huge expanse that has shattered its crystal lining to the ground.

I told myself to stand still in the shadow of an immobile crane, its teeth rusted shut, to stand still and watch. What I was looking for were the other men secreted in corners, or posted on dilapidated stairs, or only half-visible behind tarred bollards. The wind died and in my hiding place a bowl of fragrances was lifted like a potpourri culled from leaves, cloves, tar, burned rubber—droll hobby. I could scarcely get past the preserving odor of brine. But just beneath it hovered the smell of trapped sweat on bodies. Beneath everything else I smelled (or rather heard) the melancholy of an old, waterlogged industrial building, a sound as virile but at the same time as sexless as a Russian basso descending liturgically from low G to F to E, on and on down on narrow steps below the stave into a resonant deep C.

The men I was searching for now became palpable. They leaned out of the low shelf of night. They whispered, if they were in twos, or shifted their weight from foot to tentative foot if alone. At the far end of the vaulted room in a second-story window, one gnat-sized man knelt before another.

I had moved out from under the crane to walk the length of the pier, intrigued by the symmetrical placement of people on the far-away landing deck. They stood at attention, motionless—ah! posts. They were posts, but the sound beside my right hand was human breathing. Through the glassless window of an office I saw a man sitting on the floor, breathing. I didn't speak but rather rested my hand on the sill, which was grained as fur. He plopped his hand over mine: not dry, not clean. Beneath the concealing ridge of his brow his eyes could have been staring up at me.

Congeries of bodies; the slow, blind tread on sloped steps; the faces floating up like thoughts out of ink, then trailing away like thoughts out of memory; entrances and exits; the dignified advance and retreat as an approaching car on the highway outside casts headlights through the window and plants a faint square on the wall. The square brightens till it blazes, then rotates into a trapezoid narrowing to the point of extinction, its last spark igniting a hand raised to hit a face. A new square grows on the wall but when it veers off it reveals not the stunned face, nor the punishing hand—ooze on old boards, nothing else.

Down the steps, past the polite, embarrassed face of someone I know. I mount a loading ramp onto a platform where an insubstantial shack, doorless and windowless, shelters another cigarette. I stop at the doorway. He turns to the wall, causing me to retreat. There is another dubious figure, tall, face visored. I won't risk encountering him now. He can wait—that he *will* wait is the bet I'm willing to place. A shed at the extreme end of the platform glistens and sweats with water; running water can be heard, muted, sloshing through moss-slick pilings. Into that wet vault I take a step. A hand; a bearded face; the smell of whiskey; another hand. My motionless shoes turn cold—no, wet. A vagrant wave wallops against the pier like a blanket someone shakes out during spring cleaning. A boy with pale arms bruised by shadow is caught in the cross-currents of fear and curiosity. Something behind me is ticking, an electrical timer in good running order within a building I had assumed was long ago defunct.

Retracing my steps, I notice that the sentinel I'd left posted by the door to the shack has been relieved but not replaced. Down a ramp I go into the central hall, which not only reports but also magnifies the waves drumming the dock in triplets of dotted eighths over the sustained crescendo-diminuendo of a passing barge. As it passes, the barge pivots its spotlight into our immense darkness; two voices, male, call back and forth to one another from bow to stern over tons of clean gravel. Instructions. Orders.

Our orders, scattered by the prying beam, emerge out of hiding places. A hand-rail, wrenched away from the stairs it was designed to guard, stencils opposed pairs of black S's on absorbent gray air. A protective sheathing of corrugated tin, torn free from the clerestory, rattles stage thunder above us.

Yes—us. A moment before the barge's beam invaded the cathedral we were isolated men at prayer, that man by the font (rainwater stagnant in the lid of a barrel), and this one in a side chapel (the damp vault), that pair of celebrants holding up a flame near the dome, those communicants telling beads or buttons pierced through denim, the greater number shuffling through, ignoring everything in their search for the god among us.

This glorious image I've made, sustained like a baldachino on points of shadow above the glass mosaic on the floor, gently folds under the sun. The sun is rising. It recalls us to work, play, reputation, plans, to guilt, and sends everyone away until only I remain, hugging my knees, my eyes unfocused into the refracted dazzle of water. The red line painted on a boat's hull rises and dips, its reflections flaring on the waves like flames from the sun's corona, scorching the mystic vacuum.

On my way home I see one last man pressed against the wall, gathering about him the last tatters of darkness to be had. He is very rough with me.

"Do you want to go to my place?" he asks.

"Yes."

"Promise you won't change your mind when you see me in the light?"

"Do I know you?"

"Promise?"

I nod.

And then, once we're in the light, I see he's one of your old admirers, the crazy one who gave you the dog. We smile and begin to talk about you.

In that lady's house we were all standing in the July heat. Encased in my white suit, tie, shirt, I stood very still and felt the sweat explore my body. That afternoon I was handsome and drunk. The glare on the water outside projected a rippling shoal on the ceiling of her salon. Motorboats just outside the open windows plunged noisily by.

I stood there intrigued by the sweat secretly bathing my chest, as though the thinnest, purest stream of silver, poured over its living model, were hardening into flexible armor against—against doing anything. I nodded to the woman who had found me and asked her another question about—well, her jewelry, why not her jewelry, that antique jewelry? Behind me stood my father. He did not recognize me and I kept hesitating to introduce myself.

He did not seem to know the language of this place, and the girl with him had to translate everything. She did it charmingly, interpolating compliments.

Our shoulders touched. While listening to the woman with the old necklace, I had shifted my stance ever so slightly until I brushed against my father. Naturally he drew away—he was here to talk to everyone simply and openly, but not to touch them.

Where had he just come from? And who was the girl? Returning from the bar I slumped into a white cane-bottomed chair and ran the fingers of my left hand over the bulges calculated to simulate joints of bamboo. Like the clearest French olive oil, the sunlight fried on the dark water. The plant beside me had been stretched taut on strings as though it were a vine, or would be, and I fingered one of its cool, heart-shaped leaves and hairless stems.

No one was bothered by my retreat into the chair. People were content, I suppose, to have seen another young man, his face handsome enough to explain why he might have been invited.

My father didn't recognize me. That made me become all the more a white suit and tanned hands and face. Once, when I was a child, I had seen him consult a list of six points to cover during lunch and only after coffee did I realize, with a chill, that he had indeed touched, or led others to touch, all six points. Not even his stammer could be trusted since it was only a ruse he had devised to force other men to finish his ambiguous sentences for him. His decision to ignore an adult son might easily have been just such a stratagem, a sacrifice to vanity, to his own ageless face.

There are qualities of light: the light heightened by the sheer curtains, made as pure as the napkin over the host by these folds in the tablecloth, or the light freshly revived in the ruche of that blouse or caught in the gray, splintered fern in my ice cube. The bands of silk and velvet striping

138

that S-shaped couch they call a *causerie* lit and extinguished the light in rapid succession, the velvet grained like fur, the silk as wind.

The girl with my father, yes, reminded me of myself. She was one more functionary he had drummed up, a pretty face, as pretty as Linda's or mine might have been when I was sixteen and he leaned over the table and said softly, "A boy your age could be a girl." Later he said, "You have your mother's eyes."

As I looked around the room I prized the blown glass figures behind the vitrine, our hostess's folly, things she would never have commissioned while her husband was still her husband, but which now, between solitude and senility, she had succumbed to because the blue objects were . . . "pretty." As indeed they and we and, now, I were, the unrecognizable face above the white shirt front that disguised the rivulets of sweat collecting at the clavicle and then coursing down my body. He was capable of ignoring me if it suited his purposes.

He'd always had purposes: his own amusement, or failing that, relief from boredom. And like a child staring through the back window of a family car at the last lights of the party where for the first time he has seen two men hold hands a second too long—like that child I returned to the open door.

Standing, I hold myself in tight reserve. If his talent let him cover all points, then mine instructed me to wait, not see the meanings exposed in broad gesturing, nor did I take the slightest pains to make *me* evident in gestures big or small. I find and light an old, bent, damp Pall Mall—till now I was keeping it in reserve. A bare-legged boy lifts a guitar to make a sound that draws attention from all points and silences the crowd. Then, gesturing, he halloos a friend back from the sea. He strikes a flat A first, now sharp C, now F. I let myself forget it all, good times, good sex, good food; gesturing farewell, I spend my past without reserve, a pauper king, whom every subject points to—but that's a fantasy I make in idle moments, and I'm sure to make them each as idle as the evening sea's become beyond the masts, beyond the points of architectural lace, under the small but rising wind. "They're about to serve," our hostess tells everyone, gesturing.

"Look at the poor old thing there, gesturing at all these perfect strangers. What can make her do it night after night? What reserves of habit is she drawing on that see her through another dull party at all?"

"Entertaining's not one of her strong points."

Useless as a sundial in shade that points gray on gray, I keep from gesturing (or am kept) by luxurious if small delights in poverty from wanting to make the signs that others would be sure to see as telling. Hold yourself in deep reserve. At so many points I wanted to serve myself up and then, gesturing, to call out. But I don't, I make them wait and see.

During dinner a carafe slips from the butler's hand—wine and glass on the floor.

My father's one of the first to leave. He has a plane to catch to—I don't hear the name of his next resort. A month later he was dead in Majorca. During the farewells the girl's face is as veiled as mine—so similar, in fact, that he might notice the resemblance, which would never do, not now. Turning away, returning to my open door, I examine the jumble shop the water's become.

Just across the water you and I stayed. There. On the second floor. The room at the far end on the right. How we laughed when we ordered ham and eggs and got thin pink slices of meat on a bed of ice and egg salad. You're the only thing I ever saved. If a lady were to ask me I'd say love dwells in memory, moves in memory, is formed by memory, just as the evening light was formed in the curtains that screened it—but no lady asks.

2

Can't sleep tonight. I was lying in bed reading the biography of a great man whose genius deserted him. Then I switched off the light and tried to sleep, but I was afraid of something. I got up and made scrambled eggs in the dark, standing there naked and cold, watching the slime from the bowl churn up into gray curds in the pan. They looked like brains on the plate. I ate them and they were delicious, perfumed with tarragon. I poured myself a glass of milk and felt like a good little boy, though the glare from the refrigerator revealed that my body's no longer boyish— odd, troubling reminder. Good boy in a man's body.

I sat by the window on a cold metal chair and looked out at a black building across the way pressing its bulk against the wintry haze, which was bright enough to suggest dawn, though surely that's at least an hour away. The genius who deserted me was you.

A psychiatrist I once knew told me that the unconscious, that irritating retard, can't distinguish between abandoning someone and being abandoned by him. I guess he meant that even though I left you, it's come to seem as though you left me. That rings true. He also said that I was making myself into a "quiet disaster" in order to force you into returning to save me—once again a dimwit stratagem hatched by the unconscious, which doesn't recognize any of the ordinary dimensions such as time, distance, causality or your indifference.

I never kept a diary. I never save up witty things people told me. I never even bothered to remember my own past, the events that mattered most to me. Nor have I tried to piece things together. I'm a master of the art of pruning, you might say, as though I'd heard that plants should be cut back to make them flourish—except I keep hacking them down to the roots and wonder why they die.

Not all of them do. You're tenacious. Like a tree in paradise heavy with birds.

The leaves hang against the summer sky, real, not stirring, transected by the evening sun; the birds circle and light on its branches weightlessly. You know not to touch me, though I can sense you want to. We're both in jackets and ties, feeling formal after so many days on the beach in swimsuits. I can't be more than . . . twenty, but I look younger. Everyone says I do except you. You've learned to avoid describing me to myself, since everything you say provides me with another excuse to be vexed. It's a holiday and we've strung lanterns and put out flags along the walkway in honor of the occasion. The decorations, too, lend formality to the evening.

Belle comes toward us across the lawn, smiling, her nose and temples red with today's sunburn. Now she's dressed and has a cardigan over her shoulders. She kisses my cheek, as she did the first time we met, though this evening I catch her darting a glance in your direction the moment she pulls away. Have you told her we're having one of our little disagreements?

Over supper the Captain, the only man who looks natural wearing an ascot (his is yellow with age and the ends hang straight down in crumpled afterthought), neglects my glass and my remarks, which is not like him. And he brings up names I don't know but that you and Belle do. He's excluding me from your old circle, reminding me that there are dozens of people who have admired you for years—tribute-bearers assembled before the throne in their native regalia (gauze leggings over

141

gold pants, woven-feather bodice above a hairless stomach, a short military skirt), their origins so exotic and the precise degree of their vassalage so old and various that only a historian could explain it—but the Captain explains nothing and you're invisible behind the incense rising from the bronze tripod.

All during the festival and the fireworks after supper I avoid you and stay with the Portuguese family who take care of your house. When you catch up with me and ask me where I've been, I say, "It's impolite for couples to stick together."

"Are we still a couple?" you ask.

"Maybe. You should know. You've known so many people whose names I can't even recognize—"

"I don't know *why* the Captain—"

"Why shouldn't he talk about anyone he wants to? Isn't it a little artificial to pretend I'm part of your old gang?"

As we walk out to the end of the dock, our feet sounding a different note on each slat of this crooked xylophone, your hands sketch out several possible replies, none to your satisfaction. From a distance we might look like a patriarch and his heir in our nice summer jackets, out for a stroll on a resort island. That's what a stranger would think. Your friends might say, "They've reconciled. Thank God we didn't let slip anything nasty about the boy while they were quarreling." We stare across the bay toward the lights of a town that rise in a curved band like the crown of a child coming toward us, candles in her hair to celebrate the festival.

The gleam of that bright town in the distance, intensified here and there where a car's headlights shoot out over the waves for a second, fills me with a longing to flee you.

Now, years later, how easy it is to interpret that urge as a loveless boy's fear of a perfect love that came too late, but back then it seemed (my longing to get away) almost metaphysical. In fact I said to you, as we stood on the dock, "Doesn't it ever strike you as strange to be a man rather than a woman, to be here rather than," pointing toward the crown of candles, "there, for instance? Sometimes I want to explode into a million bits, all conscious, and shoot through space and then, I don't know, rain down on everything or, well, yeah, actually catch up with the light rays that bounced off people thousands of years ago. Somewhere out there," my lifted hand was pointing straight up, "Solomon is still threatening to cut the baby in half."

You turn silent and I'm afraid, once again, that I'm boring you. Oh, now, my friend, I can see you loved my enthusiasm but didn't know what to say nor where to begin. So you looked away and I thought you were bored. The hot ingot I had become cooled and hardened.

"Shall we head back?" you asked.

"Go on," I said. "I'll stay in the beach house tonight. I want to play records very loud."

"You can do that—"

"*My* records. Anyway, I don't want to be anywhere near you tonight."

"Have I done something wrong?"

"Of course not," I said and looked you in the eye and smiled ever so brightly. I was so angry at you, but you climbed in my bedroom window and I relented.

Old friend, you studied me too closely, as though deeper scrutiny would finally reveal my mystery. But there was nothing more to learn, nothing definite in me beyond one surge of emotion after another, all alike and of the same substance, though this one broke early and fanned out timidly across the sand whereas that one broke late, right beside the reef, and shot spray up against the solicitous sky.

On the ferry the next day as we headed back toward the mainland and home, I was caught between regret for the difficult summer and anticipation of the fall. We all sat on the top deck under the sun and even the noisiest holiday-makers grew silent and breathed in the salt breeze.

Once we had docked in that surprisingly vernal inlet, the foliage to the west, where the sun had just set, was already black whereas the trees on the other side were still somberly green. Motionless up to the very moment of our arrival, the branches, once we landed, began to churn and revolve—rides in a somnolent amusement park that function only for the paying visitor. In the taxi to the train station we were jammed in with other vacationers, none of whom we knew, and I was happy to sit scrunched up beside you with one arm around your neck. But I didn't turn to look at you.

Back in the city I had more freedom than on the island, more freedom from the surveillance of your friends. You changed everything to please me. Took down the curtains, rolled up the rugs, stored furniture, painted every stick and surface white—I was in my stark, simple period. Now I've lived so long in hotels I can't imagine caring about my surroundings. They're things to accept, like people, not to change.

One night that fall I brought home a man I'd met during intermission

143

at a theater. We, you and I, had an unspoken rule not against infidelities but against adventures that were conspicuous, intrusive. But nothing pleased and frightened me so much then as to cast aside all our rules.

I set up a little campsite in the kitchen for him and me, that is, I dragged in a brass lamp (one that could be dialed down to near extinction), a scatchy radio and a Chinese red blanket. I bolted the doors and that man and I became drunk and raucous. Once, near dawn, I thought I heard you pacing the hall. Cheap music, cheap wine, fumbling sex with someone who was homely, grateful, not even very clean—what fun and anguish to defile the polished tiles of that kitchen floor beside the room where the maid slept. Just before she was due to awaken I saw my visitor out, though I prolonged the farewell by the front door, whispering and giggling. Lurching about I then restored the lamp to its proper place (my "study" as you called it), threw out the empty bottle and the cigarette ashes and cloaked myself in the red blanket. You were awake and dressed, sitting on the edge of our bed, talking and smiling but inwardly subdued and angry.

"Don't pretend with me!" I said, still drunk. "What are you really feeling?"

"Toward you?"

"Yes, of course, toward me."

You stood and looked out the window at the tree whose leaves were not coloring with autumn, just drying and curling. "This can't go on, can it?"

"What can't?" I wanted the full scene. "What can't go on?"

"I don't need to elaborate," you said and left the room.

The next day as I was walking my bicycle down the hall you stopped me at the door on your way in and invited me to dinner on the following evening. "Okay, maybe," I said casually. After all we lived together.

"Maybe?"

"All right!" I shouted. That was good, wasn't it? We needed to shout, didn't we? "Black tie? White tie? Shall I bring flowers?"

"Eight o'clock. Here." Only when I looked back did I see you watching me with the big brown eyes of a child—the child in a sailor suit you had been and whom I knew from that old photograph in the family album up at the cottage.

I had so much power over you. If I would touch you, as I did once in a while (just a touch, nothing intimate), you'd get excited. I could insist you cancel your social engagements for a week in a row and you would comply, but then that full, powerful life you led away from me would gush in through a crevice I'd neglected and inundate you and, yes, me as well. The telephone would ring, at a restaurant someone would stop by our table, people would drop in, on the street you'd be recognized and friends would draw us away.

You possessed a genius for friendship, a gift you'd refined through energy and intelligence. Your intuition was so keen that you could even sense when a shy person needed to be *ignored.* Yet there was nothing slavish about your politeness. You were cool and, among old friends at least, demanding not of favors, never favors, but of wit, if that means saying something interesting. I have not, now that you've left me, tried to imitate your style, nor could I; I'm simply carried about from place to place. When I was with you I did try to say interesting things from time to time. Not now. What I've learned is that people will get me home no matter how much I drink and pick me up no matter how little I said or offered the night before. As with possessions, I've given up conversation, but everything still goes on.

We gave a party in honor of an old musician visiting our city. The visit was only a pretext; we scarcely knew the man. Hundreds of guests came. Everyone wanted to meet him. We wanted, I suppose, to show your friends how much we loved each other all over again. I stood at the door and shook hands and told people where to put their coats. Then I passed a tray, which I liked because it gave me an excuse to keep moving. Finally I joined a group and asked our guest of honor to tell me the significance of the red thread in his lapel, and people seemed pleased by the naiveté of my question and the modesty and humor of his answer.

But I couldn't keep it up. Suddenly I was tired and even angry. I rushed to the back of the house and sat on the sooty ledge of the storage room. A few people found me in there and we had, after a while, a band of renegades among the old cans of paint and the tools and firewood. The renegades agreed parties were a terrible bore and they drank a lot and I was quite free to become silent and inch still farther out the window. To me the atmosphere seemed rebellious and one I alone had created. I was very happy until someone asked me, ever so casually, a question. She was a young woman in a black gown. She had lovely breasts and diamonds in her ear lobes, and she wasn't much taller or older than I. "What's it like," she asked, "living with him?" I could tell how much she admired you and envied me. I tore off my tie and jumped off the ledge into the alleyway and ran to the corner with a cocktail shaker in my hand—silver and engraved with your initials entwined in mine. I drank right from the frosted spigot and tossed the empty pitcher in a trash can, but only after I'd lit a match to look at those initials incised in white metal. The engraver had worked cleverly; at first glance the design seemed to be a flourish in a scroll. The letters became apparent only after—ouch! I dropped the pitcher and it made a pathetic clang against the bottom of the trash can.

I ran and ran until I reached a promontory overlooking the city and the river. There I sat on a stone and stared at the cars below as they flowed across the bridge, their lights infusing the water like the blood of an antique senator in a tub. The cool moist earth tried to talk to me but it didn't have a mouth, just something through which it exhaled. Maybe it breathed through its pores. I took off all my clothes and clasped my skinny body, shivering. At my feet lay that little puddle of garments you had brought me. At last I was free of them, the dress shirt, the shoes and socks, the coat and trousers. I studied the watch and its black Roman numerals that circuited through its round ("I," "Aye, Aye!," "eye, eye, eye," "ivy") past the ecstatic shriek "VIII" and on to the dignified "X my sign." Now it was 1:30 and the hands said "I vie," as I did with you and your light yoke, your silk shackles. I threw the watch on top of the pile and strode away, still clutching myself, into a chilling fantasy of freedom. For a moment I had the illusion I was walking through a true forest until I came to a metal grille sunk into the ground through which I could see more cars streaking down a tunnel. The warmth and odor of the exhaust filtered up around me and I stood on that grating I know not how long. Could I pry it open and drop onto the shiny roof of a car, crawl to its hood, shrink and turn silver as the ornament breasting the wind? Or slip into a window, surprising a contented family, Dad vigilant and responsible behind the wheel, Mom reading a map by the faint glow of the open glove compartment, the kids and the collie a dim, dozing heap in the back seat?

If I said nothing they might take me home to a bungalow in a development and clothe me and keep me and you would never find me. They might consign me to the back seat and I, too, could become implicated in that tangle of fur, doggy breath, cool hands and cheeks as smooth as glazed fruit, our upturned eyes seeing only the tops of buildings, then trees, then after a while the stars and our ears catching only the murmur of grownups navigating us safely to our beds.

3

The answer to the riddle—what's preserved but moves? what existed only in the past but rustles, flickers brilliantly into sunlight, then soars?—is you, your presence, thoughts of you. Higher, into the sun, as hard to see as flight in white haze, then a swooping return to pounce, sharp-clawed and weighty, on my fist and to wriggle its head into the midnight confines of the leather bonnet, the instant ruff relaxing feather by feather back into a sleek neck, blindly turning to attend that snap of branches, those laughing voices beyond the hills.

Now I forget everything, and for some time I have practiced negligence and disorder. Yet you are everywhere beside me. Talking to someone about something as we start the morning's second bottle of wine, I lean back and close my eyes, studying oblivion, but my cigarette, which I'd forgotten in my hand, singes a few hairs, and the delicate sound, like silk tearing, awakens me to a recollection of you. On a beach. Red swimsuit and there a gull above us, prehistorically huge. A scramble over rocks, past a naked man in a moon-crater he's dug out for protection against the wind—I dismiss the thought. The singed hairs fall to my sleeve.

I used to say I came here because it's the one place that meant nothing to us; my dramatic flight I kept fatuously (no, bravely) calling "the only gratuitous act of my life."

My indifference to this city was real enough, at least at first. Not knowing the language, I walked everywhere. I was afraid to take a bus; I didn't know which end to get on, or the routes, or how to pay. In all the city I had only one acquaintance, Didi. Her mother, a passionate anglophile, had made English the language of the nursery. The mother died when Didi was six. As a result she could say, "Don't dawdle," but had no words to express those obsessions collecting in her head like bad weather, turning the circles beneath her eyes ominously black and electrifying her hair.

Past the massive gates of her "palace," guarded by a man asleep behind smudged glass, into a mustard-colored atrium captioned with Latin inscriptions in relieved plaster and presided over by a rain-streaked goddess emblematic, undoubtedly, of one of the less lovely virtues (Prudence, perhaps); into the stairwell, filled if only questionably superseded by the narrow shaft of an elevator in which one person could stand, hear rattling chains and pray for ascent, as the "Virgin" might in an amateur passion play; and released into the dubious heaven of her apartment, I made my way day after day. My cheeks ached from smiling, my brain from combining and re-combining the fifty or sixty words I had learned. Next door, in her father's apartment, I'd sit beside the electric fire and watch the old man drag his body, broken at the hip and mended clumsily, from wall to wall, from the camp bed to the foul kitchen to a desk piled high with not current work but accumulated sloth; and he'd talk about Time. I have no mind for abstractions, never have. If someone speaks, as he did, of Time (in conjunction with "duration," "dimen-sionality," and "syncopation") and ends on the word *synthetic* (by which he means a process rather than a product), I sink into a swoon where Father Time hurls a slow-motion sickle out toward me, who am playing jazz on one of those featherweight pianos the Germans designed in the '30's for deluxe aerial travel. And if the discourse goes on, as the father's did, I rise from the aluminum piano stool and drift toward the concave bay window lined in bone-colored Bakelite, take a seat and, sipping Pernod, watch the massive bulk of our dirigible cast its shadow far, far below over foaming, sunstruck clouds . . .

Didi and her father quarreled like lovers. He accused her of drinking too much, sulking inconsolably, scorning her painting and sleeping away the day. His accusations were as just as hers that he drank too much, slept too little and ruminated too long on the imponderables of Time. Although a flimsy partition was all that separated their quarters, they would go weeks without speaking—and then, when they did break the silence, it would be on telephones so close to the partition that their real voices, muffled by plaster, trailed their crackling transmission: echoes through that rumorous medium, Time, which he studied and we all wasted.

His theories and their arguments I must be reconstructing out of my later knowledge (always partial) of their language. In the beginning I could only catch a phrase here and there, as though they were lunging in the dark at piñatas and I was grabbing the odd favor, its shape distinct in my hand but its function foreign to my understanding. After a spat with him she would lead me with dark glances back to her lair, to another, larger electric fire and a drafty room she had cleaned only so that it might stand in exemplary contrast to her father's squalor. At midnight (the hour *seemed* to be midnight, though it could have been considerably earlier or later; her father's poetry of Time had banished the prosaic clock), she rang the bar on the corner and soon a boy in a long apron would enter her door with two liters of white wine. When drunk again, I started mentally playing with my few words. She strode around the studio, muttering a poem she was composing, her first line inspired by a linguistic slip of mine that she had found, in her melodramatic way, "prophetic." I was trying to discover the words that would convey I was grateful for the evenings she had spent with me, but I knew I was a bore, I'd be back after I could speak with some fluency—when she stood still and whispered, "I love you."

That has always been a city of well-dressed men who stroll through formal parks, hand in jacket pocket, a silk square tumbling from the chest like a gigolo's excuse, beguiling but obviously studied. We strolled, Didi and I, past giant posters that forbade all other posters, and she offered me her arm, which I meekly took. My clothes were shabby, my hands trembling, my hair in need of a barber, my shoes large and white with rain stains, but I moved gratefully under the swaying, sequined umbrella of her protection, safe for the hour's promenade from those inquisitive male stares. I took those men so seriously—that one, rising splendidly from his sidewalk table and flinging coins with Jovian aplomb into the waiter's closing hand; or this one, gold chain glimmering under the thinnest voile shirt, glow-worm caught in a web, his black coat flipping artfully open to expose its red lining ("priest without, cardinal within")—but Didi dismisses them all as vapid exhibitionists. "Look at their tight pants. Some are fascists, some communists, but to me there is no difference. All cock and ass, cock-ass."

And this salty dismissal so perfectly expresses her sentiments that she keeps saying it over and over again, "Cock-ass, cock-ass." If a gold-haired diplomat at a dressy party chats me up, she darts a glance back and forth from his smile to my nod, my laugh to the manicured nail he raises to make a point, and I know that when he leaves she will mumble to his back flaring its muscles under the taut, English wool, "Cock-ass." Or if I introduce her to a new friend, one I have met on my own, she will look through his pile of talentless caricatures satirizing "personalities" in politics or show business, or listen to his fatuous memories of the good life of greed in Alexandria under Farouk—and stare at us in disbelief. "But he is completely stupid," she will tell me when we're alone. "You cannot spot a cock-ass, you are deceived by long lashes and ordinary good manners." She will lean over in her old

149

sports car (which is redolent of leather and gasoline) and search out my reluctant gaze in the street light. "Did you like him?"

I will nod and she'll say, in her best English, "Poor lad." She half-stands in her seat and with one abrupt gesture folds the canvas top back into the trunk. A kick of gravel spun by rear wheels lends those faded and long-neglected words of the nursery ("poor lad") a new, stinging dash.

The city revolves above me as I rest my head on the leather cushion, which is cracked by age and the elements. Like the constellations spun by a slowly turning and twisting brass projector into the faultless black planetarium dome, in the same way the glowing white façades of the city seem to stream forth from her little car, the restless, sputtering source of such slow, radiant motion. If I sat up and took notice I was reminded that only the dome's highest columns and upper stories had been cleaned and lit; the lower floors still hid behind centuries of soot and decay.

You and I picked our way through these old stones on a vacation years ago, marveling at the fact that someone had once kept peacocks here in the garden (now the portico of a church) and provided his lover, proclaimed a god, with a tepidarium lined with lapis lazuli (now only an oval pond dulled with the scum of breeding mosquitoes). We went to bed early, rose early and did our "archeology" (as you called it) seriously, zealously, books in hand. That city we toured and the one I lived in later seemed to be two different places. When we went there it must have been late spring; I recall azaleas, pink and white, hanging in pots from street lamps.

Now it was winter and on some nights cold rain lashed the palm trees, which looked like old chorus girls playing an empty house. We knew the classical city and the Christian city; this time, on my own, I've ignored monuments of every sort except as they lurch into view when Didi turns a corner and then fall backwards like toppling Goliaths stunned by the pebble the car hurls up behind us. You would disapprove, but then again disapproval is a form of concern—of intimacy. Maybe, even now you are disapproving.

When my apartment was destroyed by fire, or rather smoke, I found myself homeless in the street, face smudged with soot above, below, around my blue eyes; I must have resembled one of those peasants whom aristocrats two centuries ago would get up as Moors if a genuine black was beyond their means. I was glad to be rid of my falsely elegant quarters set down so incongruously in that folkloric district. Day after day I had sat behind sheer curtains, diaphanous in the light as love is the darkness drawn from night, where I heard rotund mothers bawl out the ancient names of their children. Imagine a fishwife screaming, "Psyche, come here. Eros, stop that!" and you will have some notion of the sounds I was attending in my dim seclusion. That was no place for a single man, a rich foreigner, a stray drone in an alien hive. I'd hear spasmodic creaking and look to see sheets and towels jerking on a line across the narrow street, or rather their shapes playing on my gauzed window— scalenes billowing into rhomboids or rectangles or twisting into broad-shouldered, narrow-waisted shadow puppets projected on my screen, tormented penitents in white robes following a pink crescent and flying a mysterious red banner split into two streamers (a pair of girl's panties and the dangling arms of a scarlet shirt). The lady from the bar down the street sent me a glass of hot milk, her remedy for inhaled smoke, and two neighbors offered me a room in their apartment. Someone said Didi had probably started the fire (until now I had not known that she owned my building).

Free of all possessions, retaining only my black face and blue eyes, I moved like a specter through that city of well-dressed men, women, children. They fell back at my approach. Students, after leaping on a passing bus, looked at my charred progress; they swayed on the open platform, dresses and shirts fluttering, books dangling on leather straps like suspended disbelief.

Peter took me in. He confessed he needed someone to "help" with the rent. In fact, he was penniless, or had only enough money to buy breakfast every morning for himself and his black dog, Anxiety. Straining on her smart leash, as soft and slender as a woman's watchband, Anxiety would pull her proud, emaciated master down the five flights into the early spring sunlight. Thick blond hair straightened and coiffed under a blower, pale body dramatized by a well-brushed blue velvet suit, his great height further exaggerated by high heels, Peter strode to the corner bar, tossed back a thimbleful of bitter coffee in a single fashionable gulp and ordered two croissants. As he nibbled one, he slipped the other to Anxiety, who ate hers with moaning zeal; then she looked up with eyes either reproachful or sorrowful and unquestionably large, avid and golden. Peter brushed crumbs off the counter with a flick of his hand, and Anxiety snapped here, there, up, down and even looked over her shoulder for a vagrant morsel before yawning and sinking to the marble floor. She placed her cool black nose between her outstretched legs—an unsuccessful attempt to regain her dignity.

I fattened them both up. The rent, I learned, was months overdue; one night the lights went out; the next day the phone was dead. I paid the bills, hired a woman to clean and cook, and bought azaleas for the terrace. The one service no one could turn off was the endless flow of water. It poured out of a rusted pipe into a stone basin on the terrace. One side of the basin was sloped and ridged into a washboard, bearded with moss. Where the water originated and who paid for it no one knew. Its flow varied. One gray morning the terrace was flooded and stray cats picked their way across it, shaking their paws dry at every step. I longed for ballerinas to learn this *pas de l'eau*: tentative placement of the toe, slow balance, suddenly a flurry of rising beats.

There are some forms of love I guard against—the form Anxiety offered, for instance. Her devotion (slavish, greedy, forgiving) must be bad for the character of its recipient: mine, in this case. Spinoza warns us against lavishing the affection on pets we should reserve for other human beings. And yet I could not hold out against her. If I paused at the front door or absentmindedly fingered her claim dangling from its hook, she lowered her head then leapt up and started her awkward spins, tearing yaps out of the air as though it were fabric she were shredding. Or once, when Peter forgot to give her food, my sleep was troubled by the weight of a succubus, no—I was the patient, the doctor was passing an alcohol-cool disk of cotton over my neck and chest, the tray of instruments rumbled up, twin streams of warmed ether blew across my cheek . . . and I awakened to find a hungry Anxiety crouched imploringly on top of me, searching my face. Barefoot and groggy, I boiled her a few grams of noodles, the only thing in the cupboard.

Didi liked the dog, too, though in a blunter way more suitable to her communist style. They were comrades and Anxiety, hypocritical and ever adaptable, toned down her bourgeois effusiveness when we went for a ride or a walk with Didi. Across a glaring gravel park the three of us struggled in silence. A white male terrier joined our party and mounted Anxiety beside the crumbling temple of Fortune. Three pelvic thrusts and it was over—except the terrier could not pull free. He whimpered, returned his front paws to the ground, Anxiety cast sheepish looks at me—and still they were stuck and in pain. Two maids in black uniforms and white, starched aprons breathlessly ran up, shouting, "Fred, Fred," adding a final vowel to the name which sounded like "Frayed, Afraid." Anxious and afraid, this two-bodied monster limped under the immensity of an imperial arch. Every pictorial indication of perspective gave depth to the scene: the mid-afternoon shadows thrown by the running maids; the texture-grading of the gravel, receding from precision to blur; the converging lines of the broad avenue beyond the arch soaring smoothly to the horizon; the cool gray vagueness of the umbrella pines on distant hills; the tensing of ciliary muscles as my pupils accommodated the paired dogs in the foreground or focused on a soundless stone harp far, far away and sharpened the detail of each marble string but simultaneously lost, lost the present . . .

I'm wandering. When we lived together I devoted my nights to fleeing you. No need to go into all that, except I'm certain you saw those nights as wonderful orgies in unfurnished student rooms—drinks, drugs, casual sex (what you considered my father's immoral influence). Every night I was lowering myself farther down the rock face. I swung in the wind on ropes payed out by you, and each time I touched the sheer wall I blindly sought with my boot for a foothold, the slightest purchase. Nothing.

Nothing.

And yet I couldn't resist demanding more line, looking farther down for that ledge or shelf I needed. Once it crossed my mind to cut the ropes and float free. Was I unworthy of the gift you'd offered? Had I summoned you with kabbala alone (the thousand readings of the letter Aleph that begins *Leviticus*) but not been ready for your coming? Now that I am ready you have hidden your face.

In those days, I was not yet the ghost I've become. Awakening in the middle of the night I would hear the squeal of tires on asphalt or the voice of a midnight drunk beseeching our windows, and I would resent your peaceful sleep, the measured rise and fall of your chest, not because it was breathing away my youth (I'd be young forever!) but because you were the living barrier between me and the danger I didn't want to digest, only devour. I pictured where my clothes were and in my imagination collected them, put them on and escaped you with the startling ease of a time-lapse film of an opening flower, its modest green petals blushing faintly, then exploding into rays of fevered scarlet.

The actual preparations took longer and produced a considerably less colorful result. I bathed my face, neck and hands in a liquid bronzer and assembled a ragamuffin costume out of moth-eaten gray slacks from a thrift shop, a see-through rayon shirt as yellow as the applied bronzer, racing shoes topped by sagging wool socks, striped in blue, and a white silk jacket embroidered with a dragon. My appearance was composed out of allusions to things or people I admired—the slacks from an old gangster movie, the shoes and socks from the athletes I'd watched at school circling the track, the jacket from a veteran whom I'd studied once during a two-hour layover in a bus terminal, the gauzy shirt from a circus barker whose masculinity had become all the more pungent through dandyism. That nothing went together or suited me I suspected no more than that these invoked male presences, sinister and glamorous, were visible to my eye alone. Only now do I see that my own beauty outshone and redeemed those clothes, any clothes, and if I speak of my beauty I do so only because I've lost it.

My life of adventure was banal, of course—a ride in a stranger's jalopy to a distant neighborhood for a "party" that, after it fizzled, left me, the sole guest, venturing at dawn down a suburban street, curving mathematically past parked automobiles as the shaded windows hurled an orange sun from pane to pane. Or the crawl from one apartment to the next as the night train of young people in a big city lurched onto a dozing siderail or shuddered into hesitant motion or was switched from one track to another, routes changing as fast as warning lights could click from red to green or zebra bars could fall or rise. Here I am, drinking and sitting on a soiled couch in an empty room, explaining you to a black-haired girl with tiny features who keeps leaning another quarter-inch closer to me and gasping to indicate she's about to say something that never gets said because a fat man whose bald pate keeps his ringleted fringe well-oiled has come to escort me to an after-hours club where I dance with a man who purports to be the mayor's younger brother and knows of a livelier spot that turns out to be his room in a run-down boarding house where I watch him dust his swollen feet with lilac-scented talcum powder and listen to him bewail the loss of a lover whose heartless opportunism is immediately evident, though only to me. The tears, gin and powder drive me back out into the night and to a party at an address I find scribbled on a corner of an envelope. The guests have gone. The host is teetering down the hall as he puts out the last of the garbage, all bottles and ashes but he asks me in for a nightcap, though night, knocked out in the final round, is dying, and as its eyes go blue, its face white, body cold, a noisy throng of spectators rushes toward the superb corpse paling in the square ring. I suddenly want you. All the way home I cry and plan what I'll say, but I get no farther than "At last I've seen the light. Blame it on my youth," and these absurd words work their rhythm into my steps. While I head home in my tatty finery I breast a tide of commuters flowing up to engulf our island. You, above it all, puttering around the kitchen, are preparing eggs and tea; my fierce avowal cools under the glint of your glasses. I say something belligerent and go to bed.

I'm awakened for dinner and submit to the kindness of your friends. As the meal moves through its many courses and the conversation varies accordingly, my restlessness grows. Behind the ropes of music and talk the unknown giant stirs, props himself up on one elbow and shakes his head. He's still groggy but ready for another round. When he looks out at us and into the glare, he smiles hideously—the rubber guard has canceled his teeth.

I wanted nothing more than to flee those assembled saints and the mild glow you shed over us all (you were always good at lighting). The giant was on his feet again; someone had drenched his head with a bucket of water. He wipes his face with a towel. He is alert. He's ready.

I left your dinner party early and rushed downtown to meet the black-haired girl with the tiny features. She had a scheme that would make us rich—all we had to do was go to this address where her girlfriend Betty would place the crucial call to a contact she had who was on the best of terms with this bouncer in touch with . . .

Peter made me handsome again. At least handsome in the selfconscious style of that city. An Australian lady washed, cut and brushed my hair into a frozen wave, breaking on an angle above the fontanelle and surging over the left temporal lobe. I, too, was encased in blue velvet and white linen. My careful ties and careless handkerchiefs matched. Unpatterned, slender shoes, as soft as chocolate bars left in the sun, hats with rakish brims, a nearly hidden gold chain long enough to suggest the chest it plumbed, silk stockings and bikini underwear, pants without pockets—when Didi saw me she said, "But now you, too, are cock-ass," and I knew I had succeeded.

Just as the most passionate cry, the most primitive outburst of sobs and shouts can be broken down into its phonemic elements and assigned to the speaker of a particular language, even a particular dialect, in the same way those nearly silent days under the orange awnings of restaurants and those revolving, spotlit nights could be categorized, if only retrospectively. For instance, the stalled, big-eyed emotional sequence that led to Didi's attempt to kill me. Or the foraging expeditions Peter and I went on after midnight: one night picking up the newsboy, a red-faced, uncircumcised peasant newly arrived from the South who was incapable of sustaining the formal *you*; another night climbing into the Mercedes of a Paraguayan we chatted with at three a.m. in the remotest section of the park; or the night after the national soccer victory seducing an excited lad without previous experience. Peter was still undressing when the trembling boy embraced me and exploded. As our guest slipped back into his underwear and lit the first of many cigarettes, he began what he called "the dialogue" by saying, pompously, "In principle it was dull." Peter had more of a taste for things of that sort than I, who retreated to another room and a jealous but exuberant Anxiety; "All is forgiven" her thumping tail signaled as she lay under the bed, concealed by the harem walls of the cotton spread. And then, at dawn, Peter joined us. He put down the half-empty bottle of vodka and told me he loved me. At noon he reached for the bottle when he awakened and we never left the house till dark. Or I could work out another sequence of the flirtations I failed to understand: Lily and her husband George, for instance, or the young baron studying Blake who confessed his love for me only when an unsuccessful film director insisted we play the "truth" game; or the sighs and unfinished sentences that the English girl favored me with when she brought the bank statements . . .

Now, I hear new versions of those stories that sometimes come clear, or threaten to. But if I am true to what I felt then and there, I must ignore gossip and avowals, since I was blind and deaf to them at the time.

To me there were comings and goings, congeries of bodies, faces floating up like thoughts out of ink. The long drive to the coast through the May fog in Didi's sputtering little car and supper in a deserted restaurant decorated with carved and painted crayfish. One party melting into another and the same opinions repeated again and again, as though conversation were being composed by the strictest serialist and, once determined, could only be inverted, transposed, or started from the middle. Another drive, this time with the Paraguayan up to a villa in the hills where an old American and his delicate Filipino lover were holding an "orgy." That night, as the Mercedes wriggled salmon-like up the curved road, I recognized that I was no longer afraid to die. Though I might draw back from a sudden threat, any prolonged one invited my indifference. We had drinks in the garden, then someone pulled me into a circle of dancers spiraling downward into the moist, hazy valley. Later I saw the Filipino in Peter's tight embrace as the two of them drunkenly rolled from one end of the room to the other. Every time the two-headed monster rolled past, the fox-trotting dancers stepped over them until finally they smacked into one wall with such force that the pier glass broke and shivered its silvery splinters to the floor. Peter and the boy were covered with odd-shaped bits of reflection—they were two continents (Europe and Asia, I suppose) wrestling under fragments of a disrupted Ocean; one piece of glass clinging to Peter's shoulder reflected my own somber eyes. After the lovers were pulled out of their dangerous rubble, they laughed—and ran up to the Princess' bedroom where a racy member of the royal family was supposed to have spent a weekend with a commoner. The Paraguayan and I climbed a tree outside the window and saw Peter raping the boy, who lay motionless and unaroused under the assault until Peter left the room for a second; then the Filipino began to masturbate energetically but with a frown, as though performing a routine yet irksome chore, or as though . . .

No more. No need to tell you that in the midst of my own adventures I would push back the body of the other man until I could see his face; for a moment I'd forgotten who he was. No need to tell you I argued with idiots about Verdi's place in the history of music. No need to tell you that one day I offered God the same prayer in eight churches.

Let me single out three images of children. The first was a French boy, no more than fifteen, who claimed he was walking to Paris on his way home from India. Certainly his feet were flat and blistered and dirty enough to lend substance to his tale. Peter and I bathed him and fed him. We took him to a movie, which he enjoyed. We bought him supper and a toothbrush. His skin was as soft and firm as yours, but his hair was different. The sun had bleached the outermost layer white but left the curls beneath a bamboo brown. That night he slept between us and called us his buddies; the next day he went down for cigarettes and never came back. The following day I threw his toothbrush away.

The second child was the six-year-old daughter of a German painter. She and her father and a group of intellectuals and I all drove in a caravan to a park of old stone monsters. While the others stayed behind at the gate under striped umbrellas and sipped Cokes and discussed political theory, the girl and I explored the grounds. Inside the mouth of a lion we sat on benches and she called out, listening for an echo that never came. As we were stepping over the weathered teeth she grabbed my hand—and I noticed that her nails were as smooth and clear as yours.

The third child I saw on an island in the South that belonged to Didi's family. For a week Didi and I stayed in her villa. Outside the windows were fat lemons on trees. The walls that followed the road to the sea were crushed under curtains of bougainvillaea. In the village we watched a woman and a band that had come over from the mainland present humorous songs in dialect under an arch of unfrosted light-bulbs. Didi and I thought we were the only foreigners on the entire island until one day we rode bicycles down to the harbor for lunch. There a yacht was moored, its teak gleaming and its mast tick-tocking like a discreet metronome. In the restaurant twenty men and women, the crew, sat at one long table. After days of seeing nothing but the dour faces and black dresses of the island women, I was blinded by these visitors from the capital with their splendid colors, coiffures, manners, jangling bracelets, loud voices. Didi muttered, "Cock-ass," but I could not stop staring at the gold filaments, silk scarves, the imperious examination of the fish stew, the charged exchange of glances after someone's insinuating remark, the whoops of laughter, the obligatory if languid political discussion. I looked up at them with wonder, like Neptune awakened by the swift keel of the *Argo*. Fools, yes. A pampered, ill-natured lot, to be sure. And yet they were as fascinating as a swarm of butterflies descending on a particular old tree, the thousands of bright wings pivoting on black bark. In their midst sat the only child, a boy in a sailor suit with eyes as large and serious as yours.

4

Gregory of Nyssa, a fourth-century rogue (and brother of St. Macrina) whose first book extolled virginity, though he himself was never able to attain to celibacy for even a single day, hoodwinked the faithful with continual exegeses of that amoral hymn to voluptuousness, *The Song of Songs*. For instance, in Solomon's verse a randy girl exclaims with thigh-rubbing delight: "While the king sitteth at his table, my spikenard sendeth forth the smell thereof. A bundle of myrrh is my well-beloved unto me; he shall lie all night betwixt my breasts." The frank lust of a teenager bored at dinner ("Will these guys never stop talking?") but intoxicated by the douse of cheap scent she has too liberally applied to her wine-warmed flesh on the naive theory that more is more and half in a swoon as she elaborates a daydream about her own present attractions and those coming, tonight's experimental romp with him ("Let *me* be on top") and the lyrical aftermath, his sleeping head nestling between her beard-rouged breasts—this passage Gregory, after privately savoring, publicly interprets in these edifying terms: "There are many different perfumes, not all equally fragrant, from which a certain harmonious and artistic blend produces a very special kind of unguent called spikenard. . . . And so when the bride says to the bridegroom, 'My spikenard sendeth forth the smell thereof,' this is the profound lesson I think she is teaching us. It is that even though one may gather from all the different meadows of virtue every perfume and every flower of fragrance, and should make his whole life fragrant with the good odor of all these virtuous actions, and become perfect in this way, even then he would not be able to look steadily upon the Word of God, no more than he could the sun."

Why do I copy out this passage for you? Not to make fun of the worthy Cappadocian who lingered over his Old Testament lovers, returning to them again and again that he might explicate a sensuality determined not to be a mystery, a languor resisting interpretation if little else. No, I simply want to anticipate your laughter at *my* method, which will be his. For I, too, will relish an amorous history, then lift a hand from the page or my pleasure and find in vivid scenes portents.

Were any of those perfumes in that "artistic" blend drawn from the flowers I lived among, knew well but cannot name? Oh, some names I know: honeysuckle on the vine at the top of the tarred drive. Once past that black intrusion into our fields, that pungent strip that boiled in summer but cracked and hardened in winter, I reach, or rather return, to blossoms, some white, others yellow, all a muted, delicious release of scent, as though the inquisitive child had cracked open, silently as possible, a drawer in his grandmother's room, one filled with the decent, sexless things of a woman age has restored to innocence, among which glimmers a white satin sachet, the plump square packet trimmed in blue silk and a tiny, crushed bow. The satin yellows, as do the flowers, but unlike them it cannot be opened. I nip the green button at the base of a picked blossom and pull out the glossy stamen whose honey I strain off with my lips. The old-fashioned charm of the vine attracts bees as dowagers madden impoverished young men.

The path a hop over the fence led downwards into a valley slimy with leaves fermenting into a ceremonial liquor, past roots swelling up and out of the ground like arms, and shoulders (biceps bulged, triceps grooved, trapezoids pumped up into thick, twisted musculature): emergent wrestlers. Downwards on a route whose turns must have been imprinted on my brain during the first year of life, so well do I follow them even now, a route ending at a brook. There it is, shuttling like a brand-new power loom bright with spindles of light, bobbins of water, working at top speed. The current is broken by a stick, but just downstream from it the parted threads rush back over each other, ply of sun over ply of shadow. Before the water glides under the bridge it calms down.

Halfway up the path my collie, Tim, has stopped. Ears up and nostrils working, he burrows into the damp soil with the fanaticism of a miser unearthing his gold. But then, like me, he pulls free of his obsession as quickly as he entered it, and comes trotting down to my side, a smile on his black lips, and a pleasant, even a vacant sense of well-being in his eyes. He glances at the water with no interest; surveying its flow is a whim of mine he respects but does not share. He sits and lifts his face into a gust of wind, squinting. Then we're off again and he's a merry Sancho Panza beside my gloomy Quixote.

Next to a crude plant that hugs the ground, its big leaves as dry and cracked as elephant hide, lies a candy wrapper. As I pick it up, its wet cardboard tray goes soft in my hand. All I'm left with is the cellophane window, spangled with rain but still serviceable as glasses. Through them the brilliant day dulls and warps—until I throw them aside and plunge deeper into the valley. We chance upon—no, not chance, since I know every inch of these sacred precincts, better to say we return, with the solemnity of pilgrims, to a clearing and the shrine it encircles: a rusted ice box.

The autumn sun steams the long grass, broken and brown and sweet to smell. Tim settles down in its coarse strands, the better to point up the silkiness of his caramel-colored flanks. His lack of reserve before the felled deity (its wooden locker doors ajar and bleached, cold chambers hot, the ice compartment itself invaded by dandelions) annoys me, and I hold his muzzle shut and catechize him, as my mother lectures me hour after hour. I'm whispering in a flossy ear adorned with a dark brown burr, the closed lotus shape of its hull outfitted with bristles hooked at the ends like crochet needles or the Pope's crook. His eyes express sincere repentance, but a moment later he's smiling again, glancing complacently around at the congregation and up to the great rose windows of the trees, their leaves suddenly still and brightened. He yawns, he sinks his head into its luxurious fur ruff, he rests his snow-white chin on a beige glove, the pose intended to convey pious concentration but in fact a disguise for daydreaming. And yet his lack of fervor does not preclude a saintly gift for loving me—not the rigid, braced, *willed* love of lesser creatures, but rather the easy knack of sleeping when I sleep, waking when I wake, pacing on hard nails across linoleum when I suffer—the knack of having love as first nature.

The frost reworked the outdoors in a new medium: diamond splinters. The maids were still in their attic rooms; the house was silent except for the sound behind closed doors of my rabbit thumping up and down the back stairs (the vigorous ascent, the tentative, fearful descent); some couturier had thrown his creations all over the downstairs, a yellow scarf of sunlight tossed on the kitchen table, a red, narrow belt stretched taut on the pantry floor, shadow-blue gowns heaped high in the dining room chairs—and Tim and I slipped out into the jeweler's workshop. There, on the lawn, was my father passed out cold in his car, black tie undone, his shirt front pulled free of its black and gold studs and buckling to reveal an arc of lean chest, frost tipping his eyebrows, rhythmical puffs of breath visible in the air as I bent down to kiss his lips, foul with last night's alcohol. His cheeks were as rosy as mine.

All through that long winter Tim and I kept to the woods. When the rabbit died we attempted to dig him a grave but the ground was too hard. Our property was an odd remnant of another era, for it was surrounded by slums; just beyond the walls were streets, cars, trolleys, unpainted shacks pressed up against each other, the children leaning out windows or spilling down stoops—all glimpsed from the recesses of our car as it headed toward opening gates. Safe again, I sat up and saw the path under snow where violets would grow again next spring; concealed behind that low-gabled house (gingerbread crumbling under too much icing) is the frozen lily pond. And over there is my mother's stable. At night the world beyond the gates would penetrate the world within, and in the valley I'd hear boys hollooing to one another—the "bad boys" as my nurse Anna called them. She herself seemed not altogether good since on Thursdays, her day off, she'd spend the afternoons dressing for a visit to the dim, dangerous city outside. I'd hang around her tiny attic room, its ceiling sloped and smelling of copper and electricity. She kept singing "Ain't Misbehavin'," which I heard and repeated as "Ain't Mr. Haven." Sprawling on her chenille bedspread, I watched her wave her hair, dangle amethysts from her ears, step behind a screen, rustle and emerge in mother's last year's shantung dress. For a treat she'd dab her perfume, an unpleasant, synthetic lily-of-the-valley, on my wrists and slip a purple, licorice-flavored pastille between my lips. Her own mouth she'd redraw in red gloss, her new upper lip larger and wetter and more curved than the one I saw six mornings out of seven pressed to the white rim of a cup below eyes the color of coffee at the moment the cream surfaces. Tim and I, wandering through the woods moments before nightfall, heard city noises from over the wall and the warm, insinuating chuckle of a man—Mr. Haven, no doubt, waiting for an Anna who, despite a song to the contrary, would be his tonight. Crashing through the woods came my mother on Jasper, foam frozen on his bit, burrs on his withers.

When my father left us, I sat in my bed, holding my knees, listening to my mother's screams. Beside me Tim lay on the floor but kept one eye trained on me. I held a marionette in my lap and tried unsuccessfully to untangle the strings. When the howling and bellowing became too loud, I locked myself in the bathroom with Tim, but he's too excited by our novel hideout to grasp the seriousness of the problem—the problem, that is, of untangling Columbine. In the morning I found all the mirrors broken, the windows in the french doors painted black, sunlight eerily orange through the still-wet brushstrokes, in the basement the stench and rubble of her burned clothes and furs, on the back steps (no longer the rabbit's lair) a hammer beside jewels, some smashed to dust, others only cracked out of their gold or silver or platinum settings, and in the stable all three horses shorn of their manes, Jasper's neck shivering and raw. In the hay lay my mother, wide awake and silent, her hands bleeding. Columbine, at last, was dancing freely, and Tim and I invited the marionette to the ice box where she took part in the service.

Because the past came first it's old, deserted, a cast-away household fixture rusting in spears of grass that are as squeaky, now it's spring again, as washed hair. Out of the wreckage of adult passion, diamonds pounded into dust; out of Mr. Haven's chuckle and the face of a stranger illuminated in match-light; out of leaf-mold and the arms and shoulders of tree roots or men—from these scatterings I fashion you.

When I left you (or you left me), I came bounding into your study with my arm around Robert—or rather with my hand reaching toward his shoulder, since he was six-four. During that long last winter with you I had kept searching for an excuse to move out. Now I'd produced one: Robert. That's not exactly true. I wanted to stay, I wanted to go, I wanted to hide curled up within your hands, I wanted to snap you in half and cast you aside. Sometimes I simply wanted a response from you, little understanding that I had it, moment by moment, though it was a tune played too softly for me to catch, so softly it irritated me.

"This must be Robert," you said, rising and shaking his hand. Robert yawned (he was nervous) and I don't think any of my descriptions of you (I could talk of nothing else to him) had prepared him for your actual presence. So much thought (not just yours but your parents' and grandparents') had gone into the way you handled an occasion that no one as simple as Robert stood a chance. I was so proud of you just then, surrounded as you were by your books and paintings and the three photographs of me in a single frame, pictures taken in this very room one afternoon. In the photographs I could see the paintings and in one of them your hand; the fingers were held as though you'd just plucked a harp string—your equivalent to a shrug. In the top photograph I was staring into the sunlight, my lips parted to speak; in the middle one I had tilted my head to one side to write something; in the bottom one I had twisted my body around and propped my chin on my fist. I was smiling in profile and the three smile lines beside my mouth were echoed in the folds falling from the shoulder of my white shirt—the lines, too, seemed to be smiling.

In his jeans and newsboy cap Robert looked absurd beside you. He had grown too tall. You invited him to join us for tea; I don't think Robert knew that "tea" could be a meal and the maid in her apron, he later told me, had seemed like a joke, something out of the movies. Clever move on your part, that tea, for I fell into my half of the ritual. I poured while you buttered things and the clattering and tinkling and stirring and passing left Robert speechless. Since I had already complained to Robert about how "grand" you could be, I was delighted to show you off at your most oppressive and even more thrilled to demonstrate my perfect familiarity with the despised formalities.

"How nice finally to meet you," you said. Robert took off his cap. In bars or on the streets everyone stared longingly after Robert; after all he did have blond hair, a brick-red face, great height and yard-wide shoulders. But here he seemed the delivery boy asked to "stay on" for a bit of cheer at Christmas time. Fortunately he had the wit or thought-lessness to grab my thigh as I walked past on my way to the kitchen for more hot water. He pulled me down beside him and kissed me. For a second I tensed (you'd never actually seen me in another man's arms) but when I glanced in your direction I saw you were contemplating your cup, and that enraged me.

"I hate to say this," I began, "but I guess I'm moving out." My words made me as giddy and fearful as those times when my mother would pull up in front of my grade school and announce that she was whisking me off somewhere halfway around the world for a vacation. My notebook and the assignment I had been worrying about turned irrelevant, like a child's savings placed beside his father's millions.

"Oh?" you said.

"Yes. I've been so torn. But well, Robert's my age and I love him and he loves me and that's . . . though we're broke and he's only got a studio . . ."

"I don't want you to be broke," you said. "Just now you think you don't want any reminder of me, least of all money, but you're used to it and after a while you'll probably want some." You paused. "Nothing spoils love so quickly as poverty. You should give yourselves a real chance."

"How kind of you," I said sarcastically. "Thanks for the offer. But you're right. I don't want a reminder."

"Unless it's coming to you," Robert, ever practical, threw in.

Sometimes, my love, I wish I had refused the money then and later; as it's turned out, you've always owned me. Fearing that Robert might dilate on the subject of my dowry, I said, "Leaving you is really hard. It's been a hard decision."

You smiled politely.

"After all you've done for me." I turned to Robert. "I told you how he saved me from my father."

"Yeah," Robert said.

"Look," you said. You were standing. "No reason to prolong this . . . interview. When will you be moving?"

"Tonight."

Placed into the heavy pages of my childhood memories are photographs, some faded, others mutilated, some shot out of focus, others blurred from the first by subjects in motion: all of men. Few of the pictures were captioned at the time and I forget names. In every case the years have mercifully airbrushed out the ludicrous styles of another era, the baggy clothes and the haircuts (a line of white scalp dividing comb-carded designs preserved in oil; lather and razor throwing the ears into pitiless relief; clippers shearing the nape of its modesty or glory) and my past is continually updated, becoming as disheveled or tidy as this year's fashions might demand.

Here's one, the first in the book: a giant in khaki takes me onto his lap and gives me a pair of gold wings from his lapel. He pierces the frail strap of my sunsuit with the grooved pin and screws the round, notched clasp in place. Would an ordinary boy have thanked him then, slid off his lap and run off to play? I remain where I am. Above me he is talking to my mother, his low voice resonating through his body and into mine, awakening a string of overtones in me, each of his words a pebble skipping over the still water I've become, up though my legs, across my pale chest, sinking deep into my mind, where the rings are still widening. As his adam's apple works, I want to touch its rise and fall. Somewhere behind me my mother is murmuring responses. For the moment she is cinched tightly into the polite form of that time and society, but if he doesn't leave soon she will explode out of her stays and grow bigger, louder, angrier. The man doesn't sense the danger. We didn't know him very well, I suppose (now I don't know him at all except in the buzzing tympanum of my stomach, the tuning fork of my clavicle, the great cracked bell of my head).

But it is his very size—beneath, beside, above me—that makes my pulse throb and my stomach sink. Let this man be the well I drown in until I can no longer hear my mother's exasperation. Falling, falling though poised motionless on his knee, I hurtle into an infernal paradise at once terrifying and calm, inverted flames dripping into crystal lights. Let him kiss me with the kisses of his mouth.

When I was a teenager—oh my love, don't fear, I won't read off a Leporello's list of infant conquests, the constant inquests of evenings, troubled nights, the wan dawns of Don Juans. I have no desire to confess what you have already forgiven. Nor will I bore you by drawing out (as some anatomical charts transform for the sake of clarity the stomach into a long, neatly labeled ribbon) a tale that lies coiled, messy but alive, in the hot hollows of memory. Take your stick and poke the steaming entrails. Read them; read me.

I'm with someone's deb daughter, a girl whose perkiness seems calculated to please adults alone and whose interest in me is as exhausted as mine in her no matter how tirelessly she flogs her attention into new spasms of smiles, questions, compliments—but then she suggests we visit a certain Tom (that wasn't his name: I forget names). Tom, she tells me, is a lonely guy, not because people shun him, heck no, anything but, he's so darned attractive—just as loner, I guess. And should we visit him?

We should.

It's a June night, midway through the short social season, and Midge (we'll call her that) and I are leaving a "theme" party, some ghastly rodeo affair. I'm wearing the costume, jeans, a checked shirt, and as my rear-view mirror reveals a few wisps of hay in my hair. How we got to Tom's house, through it and then to the pool I don't recall, but what is happening now is his step up onto the diving board, his pause, and then his slow stride and the bounce up into the night sky, where he clasps his knees, somersaults—and remains, dark pine trees all around the blazing sapphire pool. Lit from below, he hangs in the brilliance welling up to his tensed legs and to his head ducked so far down between his knees that only his black nape, water-smoothed, is visible. His throat is as bright ivory overlaid with sapphire.

Who is this who comes out of the past like pillars of smoke? A lifeguard, whose preposterous name I do happen to remember but will not give away. He is fascinated by me. At least he stares at me in nervous bursts from his lookout tower or when he descends and strolls to the water's edge, casual, lanky, but blowing imperiously on his whistle at a swimmer whose daring has over-reached his skill, or when he parades past my towel, golden hair aglow on his powerful legs. Back on his towel, nose, cheekbones and temples fierce with white war paint, he scans the beach—and stops at me. I lie like a crucifix between two swelling breasts of sand, the innocent dying between thieves. Then I prop up my chin on gritty hands and return his glance. With stealth and patience, after days of waiting, I find a moment to talk to him and something neutral to say. Surveying us are the glittering windows of my mother's seaside house.

One evening a storm blows up. The last swimmers have long since gone, including the cheerful coed whom the guard usually talks to (once, on a slow day made still slower by his embrace, the guard had lain beside her and in the bagginess of his swimsuit I detected one loose fold harden). She's gone. The guard and I are alone below mother's windows, each old pane set at a slightly different angle to reflect another segment of the darkening sky, seven hundred versions of a fractured pastoral, the trees sweating black honey, the clouds weeping nymphs and the waves tame animals grown wild.

The guard invites me into his narrow tower to escape the rain and closes the door. He's facing me. Out of the corner of my eye I see a shelf of first-aid supplies, a coil of rope, clear mosquito repellant and white sun repellant, an unstrapped watch, his painted nose and mouth, his gleaming chest, stiffening fold, intricate knees, foreshortened calves still bristling gold into the gloom, one flexed to throw his body into relief and mine into confusion; on my lips I feel a coolness concealing warmth, amber over roses, just as the fragrance of coconut oil disguises the odor of sweat, just as his arm reaches out to encircle me. Someone's outside: mother, hooded, standing in the downpour. She drags me home. Her nails press a bracelet of pain into my tan wrist. As she looks on, I gaze into the mirror and with agonizing slowness wipe away the traces of lead-white paint from my mouth.

Turn the pages, beating them back faster and faster. An Indian, on his break at last, rises from the piano and leads me out of the bar to the end of the pier. We sit on the bench. He takes my hand. With the help of my bilingual dictionary, rich in claret leather, he haltingly assembles a plan for our escape—tomorrow night, the boat expectant under a gardenia moon gone yellow, and then a plunge through parting spray to a village where his mother, at first as wooden as his devotion, then as efficient as my beauty, awaits us on the white beach, her shoulders wrapped in a pink, stirring rebozo—but the dictionary is too rudimentary to give him all the words he needs ("my devotion," "your beauty . . . dollars . . . youth"). The Bible paper whirrs and crinkles under his moistened index finger. For some reason I look around and see my father sauntering out toward us, drunkenly smiling at the tropical stars, undoubtedly search-ing for the Southern Cross. "Daddy," I say, rising with magnificent aplomb, "I'd like you to meet a friend of mine. Pablo. Yes, Pablo. This is Daddy."

"Back to bed, son. Off you go. Pablo, how about a jazz rendition of 'Smoke Gets In Your Eyes'?" My father masterfully guides the poor man back to the bar. Come, my beloved, let us go forth into the field; let us lodge in the villages. In my troubled sleep the soft tread of an opera pump shatters the gardenia. The petals fall on the rebozo which, weighted, slides away to expose the relics of a child-sized saint, all bones and brocade within the flyblown glass case.

Like Isis, I fly up and down this long river, my brother, searching for the parts of your broken body that I might piece it together again, put the heart in your chest, wrap the mangled remains in linen and fan it back into life with my wings. In three children I have found your touch, your nails, your eyes. Your sex eludes me—have the fish eaten it? And shall I copy it from memory in wax and spices or in words? My falling tears swell the river as I hide in the papyrus.

Without names or dates, without records or traditions, how can I document what happened so long ago, far upstream where the river is barely a brook and a twig suffices to disturb its current? Tim and I are playing beside the brook, now or a hundred years ago. My mother has retreated into her wing of the old, sprawling summer house. At night a man lays a fire in one room and I stretch out in front of it, my nose buried in Timmy's fur, which smells of crushed grass. The fire pops as a pocket of trapped gas hisses into a yellow flare or a pine cone vaporizes into blue, spiritual flame, hard wooden petals opening and furling back into ash. In the miniature birchbark teepee beside me a still smaller cone of pink incense threads its pine scent through the pinhole at the top. When I lift the cover there stands a sagging gray replica of the cone—which one breath disperses. This time I select green incense and watch its shiny point stubbornly resist the match's torture and then, just before my fingers are burned, the sinner smoulders, repents, exhales a whispered confession of heresies more satanic than we had dared suspect. Absolved and saved, the happy victim burns to the ground.

No one beside the man who does chores will come near us. I haven't seen mother in days. At night, now, I can hear her drag furniture from one end of her room to the other, or it could be the steamer trunk. One morning I found her black wool bathing suit flung over a couch. I lifted it, wet straps brushing my arms, and breathed in the smell.

That was a museum of other summers, of lost pastimes. Here is the Chinese checkerboard, colorful rays pocked with empty sockets—it's lost its marbles. And here the slack hunting bow that, when it was taut, only my father was strong enough to draw; beside it a leather quiver of arrows, backswept feathers dry and split though the metal tips remain lethally sharp. Up the uncarpeted cedar stairs and to the left, then to the left again, take a right: the playroom, its linoleum floor printed with a blue and green picture of the globe. I take a step toward the South Pole, change my mind and pace up Africa, stop on Italy, my shoes swiveling on its boot, amble over Asia and kneel on the apoplectic face of the East

Wind to search out a book, my favorite, the story of a spinster toad in bonnet and gingham skirt notorious for her nasty behavior toward the good-natured frogs. And here's another, a tale of a benign elephant family wise to the point of sadness, reconciled to the humiliations of a long life but gifted with a naive delight in travel—in the pranks, say, of their foreign host and friend, a monkey. The infinite sadness of the elephants in their railroad coach! They're arrayed in old-fashioned clothes and waiting with dignity at the end of the book for the beginning of yet another holiday. They have assumed an expression of mild curiosity for want of any more avid hankering after adventure. Thoroughly enlightened, detached yet compassionate, the elephants are impersonating an ordinary family, though for them the steamer trunks, the wicker hampers, the matching valises, the plush seats steeped in coal smoke, the net hammock bulging with still other impediments—all these barricades against the flames and rapids beyond have paled into mere pencil sketches on transparent rice paper through which the elephants gaze unblinkingly, gay and courageous, at the devouring fire and water of transience.

I am not resigned. Like my mother I pace through the resonant house. I'm expecting someone. Out onto the lawn I creep, small under the moon. I'm alone, the only child outdoors in a slumbering village of old houses. Bending over the artesian well I press my lips to its cold flow that jets straight up and holds a constant dome night and day, as smooth and unflawed as sherbet from the scoop. The force of its driving current burns my lips. My mouth, shocked, only now warms to the taste of the water, a suspicion of iron as faint as the trace of pears in a liqueur that seems all clear alcohol, the pears more conspicuous on the label than in the liquid.

A rust-stained canvas lawn chair, its wood arms and legs the youthful bones emerging through old skin; the burrows of black earth turned back by moles; the two half-moon bridges over the pebbled bed of the brook, their curved rails and upright stangs leprous with matte wood and weathered varnish; the unlatched door of the woodshed and the bolted door of the narrow stall that houses the gas tank; the porch with its sun-faded straw rugs and creaking swing; the frog-loud grasses and mossy stones where the brook swells just before it fans out over glassy sand into the lake; my mother's windows, curtained to contain the burning lights—this whole realm the moon articulates with the precision of the fish man boning a mullet with a black knife under a running faucet, severing the head and tail, folding back the filets, nicking the tender flesh here, there, then lifting an unbroken tree of ribs branching out from a pearly spine.

I am waiting for someone. Back in my room I dry my muddy feet in Tim's warm ruff, then slip under the sheets and pull up the spread printed with dolphins soaring out of waves. My waiting has made me tense to every sound. Are those the wheels of his Silver Cloud crunching the gravel as he glides up the drive? Does the birch outside my window tremble in the wind or under his weight? In my daydreams he hops lightly over the sill into my room and I rise to greet him. Then the hurried escape into the night, the back door left open, Tim as ready to go as I; the brake is released, the car rolls down the hill without lights or power; when we reach the gates the starter button is pushed, twin beams strafe the post office, the grocery, the penny candy store, the raised gates at the railroad crossing and the forest beyond. Only now, still in my pajamas, do I steal my first glance at him. Tim discreetly settles himself on the floor between us and pretends to doze. Our headlights catch a distant road sign that rushes toward us; just as its letters fill the windscreen I read its warning: The End.

In a book of magic I've filched from my mother's sewing room I find spells to cause death to all the fish in a pond, stir up a quarrel at table, induce courtesy, cause the appearance of little people, diagnose virginity, know a woman's initimate secrets (two methods), destroy a faithless husband. One recipe intrigues me. Pour oil from a white lily into a crystal goblet, recite the 137th Psalm over the cup, then say the name of the planetary angel of Venus, Anael, then the name of the person that you love. Anoint your eyebrows with the oil. Touch the right hand of the beloved at dawn on the Friday following the new moon. Where can I find a lily? Whose name? And his hand is beyond my grasp.

I awaken to find Tim gone. He has deserted the oval rug beside my bed. Hurrying from room to room I call his name. I stop dead center in the playroom, a colossus bestriding the Atlantic, one foot on France and the other on Canada, but not even in the most distant recesses of the house can I hear the approaching clatter of hard nails on hard wood. He's back in my room, I'm certain of it. But there I see only a tuft of white haze from his belly floating over the rug. Afraid that one of my spells might have miniaturized him, I throw back the spread of waves and dolphins, but even in the white water of my sheets he's nowhere to be found, a tiny collie paddling through that dream-tormented sea. Is he in the sewing room, paws up on the window ledge, bird-watching? No. My mother's door is half-open. When I peek in, I see everything is impeccable; the accumulation of dishes has been removed, the bed is made, the curtains flung back, the floor swept. Her long suffering is over. The maids will return; she will make me blueberry muffins in the wood-burning oven; now I can be noisy again; we'll go for swims together; we'll go to the country club Sunday suppers; in the morning she'll tie up her hair in a scarf and, after I pole the ancient Chris-Craft out of the boathouse, we'll skim the lake, waving to friends on the beach; she'll sew; grown-ups will come by for drinks; she'll smile and ask questions and invite guests to stay on for dinner; the phone will ring—but where is she? Where has she gone? I search for her and Timmy everywhere, downstairs where I expect to find her with the newspaper and cold coffee in the breakfast room, on the beach as she emerges glistening from the water, in the garage, lifting the croquet set, rusted wickets dangling from the stand beside upright mallets and pocketed balls jiggling in their sockets . . .

I've wandered so far from my subject, my dear, which is you. You are the song I wanted to sing, the god I wanted to celebrate or conjure. Before I knew you I loved you, now you've gone I find you everywhere, and for me you are my past, present and future, unchanged, equivalent only to yourself, just as in that long poem of triple rhymes, each line ending in an echo natural but ingenious, there is one single word that admits of no variation, that Dante rhymed only with itself: Christ. Somehow I've lost the design of these pages. Whereas I wanted to trace you in my past, demonstrate the ways in which experience prepared me for you, all the while skipping the things that were painful or ugly—oh, I wanted to fashion, even falsify, a lovely story for your entertainment, but that house, that woman, that summer have entranced me. I was a juggler tossing my oranges in the thick air, my little skill my only gift, but bad memories have frozen my hand and fixed my eyes and the offering—not the fruit but its flying motion—has failed. The bells will not ring. This is not you, no, rather it is gold pierced through the fabric of my infant shirt. Gold? No. A ribald song that seems to flirt with night as Mr. Haven grows more bold. Song? No. A frozen leap tucked in a fold of sapphire sky, a dive transfixed, inert. Dive? No. White kisses on my lips, which hurt as I erase the tale the mirror told. For were you gold, I'd have you in my hand. If song, your harmonies I'd still command. A dive cannot be held in bright suspense. Kiss? No. Because your touch I can't erase. Yet

I shall list for you my recompense. Gold, songs, a dive, a kiss—recall your face, perhaps, but you elude me still. I'm on your trail, but you elude me. Take my hand as with the other I open the latch to the garage door and swing it open.

The car motor is running and the garage is filled with exhaust. Coughing, frightened, I draw back, but after the fumes clear I approach the station wagon and look in—an old Town and Country, one of those station wagons with blond wood paneling on the doors. Behind the wheel is my mother, jaunty in her leopard-skin coat and matching turban and gloves. She's dead. So is Timmy beside her. I'll hang my harp on the willow.

5

Craig and I spent so much time at the theater that finally we began to live there. Moving in wasn't a decision (at least not on my part); to decide anything would have required a moment when I stood outside events or peered down at them all floodlit from the pinrail—and no moment like that came along. We brushed our teeth and washed out our underwear in a sink off the star's dressing room. For clothes we had the whole costume collection to work our way through, though Craig kept the building so warm that we could stroll around it naked. We ended up sleeping naked onstage in a hammock slung between two coconut palms, our bodies entwined like yang and yin, pang and sin.

Sunsets in the tropics are conveniently quick, a fast fade on the master dimmer, one smooth continuous descent of a shadowy hand on the rubber grip. Across the nighttime cyclorama shone as many stars as Craig had managed to pierce holes in the metal pie playes clamped to the lights.

Days and nights slipped into one another as electricity was released—or throttled to a comforting hum in the transformers. One long night we passed on the terrace of a penthouse upon cushioned wrought-iron porch furniture beside paper geraniums in papier-mâché planters. The horizon gleamed with the spires of skyscrapers Craig had stamped into a template that afternoon. The moon was a huge and incandescent old-fashioned limelight perched just behind the cheaters; the block of burning lime kept twisting and rising into the jet of ignited gas—dangerous, all terribly dangerous I'm sure, but which full moon is not?

Restless that night, I got up and went wandering backstage, down into the open dressing rooms. Beside a union notice on the bulletin board is a telegram congratulating "Fred" on an opening now ancient. A border of small bulbs outlines the communal mirror in which I can make out my own dim face but can imagine a host of brilliant fools, at once impudent and sober, staring into their gleaming reflections—Tartaglia, Scapino, Trivelino, Mescolino, Scatolino, Colafronio, Pulcinella, Burattino, Gradelino—above the still-seated Argentina, Rosetta, Columbina and Pasquella, who presses red satin circles to her cheeks, then grinds out her cigarette in a shallow, silvered disc of an ashtray. Only the ghost of a handprint, rapidly fading, distinguishes the mirror from the room. I run a finger over a leather mask on the table: bulbous nose, a wart as big if not as cool as a robin's egg, an open mouth in the horsehair beard. A box by the door sprouts ten wooden swords and a pair of stilts, one pushed deeper down than the other, their braced footrests the tentative steps toward heaven in an ascent forgotten, or in any case abandoned.

Down a long, low-ceilinged corridor I make my way, accompanied overhead by pipes hot with compressed steam that hisses, condenses and drips to the concrete floor from a loose fitting. A metal door lined with asbestos trolleys opens at my touch, a cylindrical sandbag hung from a greased pulley wire doing the work. In the storage room beyond are racks of painted flats. I can see only their borders: a Doric column against a stormy sky; the corner window of an all-night diner framing a seated customer in a trilby, his back to me but his face turned to address whom I'll never know; maroon wallpaper cut off by a cream chair rail highlighted and shadowed to appear thrown in relief; the tan brush of a lion's tail suspended in mid-flick against the distant, murderous leaves of a yucca. The whole theater, save for the rush of steam that suddenly rattles the loose joint in the hallway, is silent and I fancy myself the midnight prowler until I stand on tiptoe, lift a shade and see a pair of nyloned legs scissoring through a cold, wet, metropolitan afternoon.

I didn't like that glimpsed reminder of people in shabby street clothes victimized by weather and time, the world of errands done on lunch breaks—and I fled back to the penthouse, the starry cyclorama

173

and Craig. It was night. It was summer. We were lovers. It was night. It was summer.

Craig had a beautiful indifference to human attachments, longings, jealousies, all of which he considered "sticky." To him it was enough to exercise, eat well, build sets and plot lights. If I told him I was becoming fond of him he would go vague and polite, as an atheist does when forced to bow his head for grace at the annual family dinner. He must have sensed that my feelings were beams trained on you that had spilled over onto him, and he asked me to talk about you.

I did so reluctantly. This hesitation wasn't prompted by reticence—as you know, I'll tell anyone anything. But (surely you understand) I had tried so long and with so little success to forget you. Craig's contempt for love, or rather his dismissal of it, had struck me as modern and sensible, and I had yearned to imitate him. He would teach me; I'd be his scholar. And now, here I was, beginning our story again, an old role I knew too well and had played too long if not lately. The lines came back to me, one by one, their intonations guided by the familiar verse, the gestures and smiles perfectly timed, automatic in the delivery but once expressed recalling the emotions they will always signify.

Craig and I were sitting on a bearskin rug (dyed nutria over a thickening layer of sponge rubber) before a fire (the reflections cast by a rotating drum of crinkled aluminum foil spotlit with amber and red). Although he was intelligent so long as he was in flight, hovering around a thought, tugging at it, poking, wrestling it free, snapping it up, the moment he had to sit still to listen he began to frown and his lips parted as if, when he was grounded, he lost his talent to understand. His face was a charming compromise between the graceful girl and the hairy, aggressive boy within him, but when he tried to attend to what I was telling him the compromise broke down into its warring opposites. The girl, too timid to concentrate, gained control over his eyes, cloudless blue heavens darkened by twin lunar-eclipsed suns. And the girl also ruled his forehead, thin, taut silk worried by wind ripples—a girl one could picture being led by her parents up the staircase to the swelling din of her first dance, a moody, fragile girl lifted out of her daydreams and instructed to say clever things to adults and to expose her shoulders to tall men; or a rich protected girl glancing for the first time into a dark shack teeming with children and hungry animals—a girl, that is, being reluctantly and without preparation initiated into an active, alien world.

But the boy had his own surlier response when his angry eyebrows, black grease marks joined above the nose by a passage of gold stippling, lowered into threatening horizons above those tremulous skies or when his shaved but heavily bearded upper lip twisted into a snarl and exposed a wet canine. Then he chewed on something and, save for the frightened eyes, the entire face, bristling with male force, exposed its elaborate rigging, as though the pale skin were a topsail turned transparent. And indeed his body, tormented by my demands, seemed to strain away from me, to run before the wind I had become, the gust of my desire—oh, he was a trim ship. His high instep was a ballerina's but the hairy legs not a boy's but a man's, and the slender, smooth waist feminine but the low voice masculine, and if I compare him to a bird or a ship I do so only because he is that elegant, that fleet, and that avid of flight.

"I'm sorry," he murmured, when I interrupted myself to ask if I was annoying him. "But I don't understand you. Perhaps—" and he moved up to the footlights, which silhouetted his slim body with purple gloom and his rising, open hand—"perhaps if we staged it. Put it on somehow. Then I could see it." Now *I* could see his features again; he'd returned to my side and the revolving cylinder simulating flames.

The theater gave a performance and on that evening I hid up on a catwalk and shivered, a water-damaged velveteen robe of royal blue clothing my nakedness. The lobby and auditorium doors had been thrown open an hour before curtain to chill the house, which the crowd would all too soon reheat. A twin-bound box of programs, hurled out of a truck, was dragged up the steps by the head usher, opened, sorted.

Deep in the underground vaults below the stage, actors are beginning to make their entrances—here's a cheery hello from the *jeune premier*. He's greeting the wardrobe mistress, who tonight appears to be in truth a woman kept by a trunk, so motley is she in frayed slippers, a dirty cardigan sporting twenty straight pins for last-minute fittings, patched culottes and a brooch that may be her personal adornment but more probably is a make-do badge of office for the walk-on in Act Three.

Members of the chorus dribble, then pour in, their voices too loud and too clear, too trained. Though they arrive alone—brave, casual figures, hands deep in trench coats, a flight bag slung over one shoulder—they quickly burst into conversations about sore feet or sore throats, new union rules, upcoming auditions, one entertainer's overdose and another's obsession with a Sicilian twelve-year-old purchased for a song from the child's obliging mother. As they natter their hands dip into shoe boxes and rise hairy with caterpillars that cling to their faces as eyebrows or moustaches. A white line drawn down the bridge lends character to an anonymous nose; mascara supplies a dark flutter to a blond's lashes; lips and cheeks, pallid in the dressing-table glare, pick up color from carmined fingertips. Half-hour, and now the talk turns to the theater critic, so drunk the other night that he slept through two acts though unconsciousness did not keep him from panning Mary as Meg. Tonight's villain remarks that the critic is not the English lord he makes out to be but a Cockney—"And the *h* keeps falling off his typewriter just to spite him."

Ten minutes is called and five dancers, not on till the third act ballet, are already stretching at the barre in bulky gray sweatsuits, while a sixth shows a seventh the new combination put in yesterday: plié, changement, then this, then an attitude en pointe held for three beats. Nancy's entrance, and we're off downstage right. The curtain lowers with an electric hiss; through the fabric I can hear a solitary conscientious clarinetist practicing again and again a bass trill ending in a run up through the chalumeau. A gaffer crawls up beside me and adjusts a fresnel; I withdraw into a dark, precarious corner.

Now a trumpet essays a flourish, a second violin embarks on a dull continuo passage, the harpist strums a glissando, resets two of her seven pedals and strums again, the sixth and seventh dancers emerge from behind a wagon in the wings that is freighted with a gazebo trellised in plastic vines, wriggle their toes in a rosin box and go through the new steps on stage this time. While they're on point two stagehands carry a flat between their erect, trembling figures and deposit it behind a tormentor. The stage manager at his desk runs through the promptbook, hesitates over one cue and has a whispered consultation on the intercom with the fellow on the follow-spot. The prompter in jeans smokes a cigarette with the conductor in tails. All the instruments are warming up, and I wonder what melodic pattern will be machine-stitched out of this ragbag of bleeps, drum rolls, pizzicatti and muted hoots. "Places, places," the manager calls and the dancers scamper off as the chorus, coroneted or cowled, gather like the great dead in the subdued margin of history.

From my vantage I can see the stars below, now arrayed in a constellation of seven women, though one of the Pleiades is so small she is lost behind the heaving and glistening body of another, now extinguished to a sole giant in black velvet whose ringed hand jerks up toward me as he plucks a stone harp, and now shining as two innocent virgins in the midst of white-robed nuns holding tapers that tremble before their hymn to happiness and love; curtain, interlude, panicked dollying and flying away of one set as another creaks on and the lights dim to a nocturnal blue. Whispering sailors mourn the death of a visibly breathing hero on the raked, rocking deck of a caravel outfitted with square-rigged sails ghostly against a midnight-dark cyclorama as dry ice smoke pours from blowers held in hands just behind sight lines. The soprano in a blonde wig and muslin robe laments something from the fo'c'sle, accompanied only by a guitar and a tambourine; pirates board the vessel and the curtain descends on swordplay and a vigorous tutti. I fell asleep on my perch, like a caged parrot on a high strut dreaming of the rumorous, steamy jungle. When my outstretched green wings had carried me up the river to the thundering falls, I awakened to the final bows of a cast in coronation clothes. A snooze later and they were gone, the gazebo remained unexplained, the house was silent, a work light glimmered from a black cord below me, and Craig, nude and warm, was holding my face between his hands, kissing me as seriously as though he were a father and I the child whose fever had finally broken.

The theater bore no traces of the departed invaders save for the smell of crushed-out cigarettes and snow-soaked fur coats and the sight of discarded programs littering the floor like the paillettes ripped off the dress of a woman fleeing the ball. Craig had worked on the production as a technician and I found charming the indentations of weariness impressed on a face whose youth seldom betrayed exertion or even emotion. From his tenderness I could tell he was worried about how I had fared. His solicitude gratified me at the same moment it made me wary. We love to give help but only to those who have no need of it, or more properly to those who desperately need it but proudly or despairingly refuse to accept it. We reach toward unreachable men in distress and toward no others. Self-sufficiency may inspire admiration but not love; frank, hungry need excites pity but tranquilizes desire. Why this should be so I have no idea, but I knew my eager distress simultaneously rendered me more sympathetic to Craig and less attractive. Experience has taught me (I'm not bitter, really I'm not) something about these hydraulics of passion.

"Where would you like to sleep tonight?" Craig asks me. And I, not wanting to confess anywhere will do so long as I'm in his arms, murmur, "On the moon." We empty the stage and he covers it with two piles of

177

fiberglass rocks and a muslin dropcloth that flows down into a crater (a platform lowered a foot below the floor); on the cyclorama he projects a large, crisp earth. Beside our crater he plants the national flag and into the hole we crawl, naked, freezing, gasping for oxygen and so light that, were there air, a wind could whirl us away. The cast image of the earth becomes your familiar face, rounder and more marked with age than I had remembered it, watching me even now that I'm way beyond your gravitational pull.

Somehow I've failed to work out and Craig, a little disappointed in me, invites Thomas to live with us. Once before I'd seen Thomas at a party, unshaved and speechless, brooding in a winged armchair but thrusting cleated, orange boots out into the room. The boots were caked with mud too raw to be from this part of the country; his waist was circled by a belt made of silver medallions laced together which, if the observer squinted, fused into a luminous, turning ring; in the depths of his chair his face was pale and long, the already high cheek-bones raised higher by the cross-hatched steel engraving of his beard. The silvered waist was the zone I preferred and described to myself as "aristocratic," coming as it did between the feudal splendors of his face and the modern brutishness of his boots. But his face, despite my determination to prefer his waist, kept drawing me back. One eye was blue, the other green, the magical result of a child's chemistry experiment. Beside the green eye was drawn a curious birthmark on his temple, which I saw variously as the lair of those blushes that so often raided his cheeks or as the stinging imprint of the first hand that had slapped into breathing an infant who, though now a man, still resented delivery.

The situation at the theater quickly stabilized into a familiar and excruciating structure. Far from being the defiant and distant young man he appeared to be, Thomas had the capacity and desire to consign himself completely to us. We were the big brothers, or perhaps the parents, he'd always longed to interest, and now our interest in him was compulsive. Craig was held by Thomas's beauty and innocence; Thomas received the attention in confused but grateful silence; Craig prized and matched his silence, as though it were an original mode Thomas had invented rather than the simple, inadvertent expression of awkwardness I judged it to be; the vault of ice congealing around the lovers begged to be broken, and I did the chipping. Just as open scissors suggest snipping, an idle knife stabbing, coffee scalding, so their faces, inclined toward one another but not touching, called for the closure of the kiss, even if I had to arrange it, even if by arranging it I ensured my own suffering.

Now I loved Craig and he loved Thomas and Thomas loved Craig, but both these men could communicate only through me, as though one were the airwaves striking the eardrum and the other the fluid vibrating across the triggered hairs of the basilar membrane; for air to touch liquid it had to pass through the anvil, stirrup and hammer, and I served the function of those delicate bones.

To console me, Craig would draw me aside and assure me that Thomas was no more than an infatuation, a delightful boy from the provinces, an indoor amusement during the cold spell. And wasn't it funny the way Thomas could not finish a sentence without sinking into a mumbled "And whatever and whatever?" And had I noticed the way Thomas, embarrassed by a tarnished molar, pursed his lips unnaturally when he laughed? I had not.

The other misguided tactic Craig adopted to assure me how trivial his attachment to Thomas must be was his repeated insistence that their only bond was sexual. That their ardor might be all the more intense, Craig dressed us in wing-tipped collars and cutaways and placed us in a Victorian sitting room, me in a horsehair-stuffed rocker and them on an ottoman. A grandfather clock ticked (or rather a tape just behind the flocked flat looped around and around past a magnetic head, feeding its solemn knocking into the house speakers). A gas lamp glowed on the table beside me, its penumbra boosted by an overhead spotlight. From a distance the antimacassars under my elbows might have appeared to be lace, but up close they were clearly plastic sprayed to dull their sheen. I wore age makeup, but their faces were cosmetically young. We spoke in unnaturally loud voices in order to project to the top balcony of the empty house. Behind the frosted windows (glass sponged with Epsom salts and beer) the cyclorama darkened from sunset pinks and flamingos into the massing blues of dusk. I kept pouring an empty teapot into empty cups as we made witty small talk with such fastidious diction that the explosive p's, t's and d's sent sheets of spray flying from our mouths into the cross-lit shadowless room. After this (presumably humorous) spate of polite chatter my guests stretched conspicuously and feigned yawns and begged to retire. I led them downstage left along a path designated by tape on the floor to a bedroom that Thomas surreptitiously tugged in from the wings by pulling a thin lead of fishing tackle that had been left lying on the floor. When I asked the young men if they thought the quilt would provide sufficient warmth on such a bitterly cold night, Craig comically tugged at his collar to indicate embarrassment and Thomas, equally uncomfortable, stifled a cough in his hand. Blushes flew down from their haven, the birthmark. Once the door (flimsy plywood stained and grained to resemble massive oak) is closed into its unsteady frame, the guests collapse into each other's arms, groan with pleasure, draw apart to place a warning finger to their lips, undress with ecstatic haste, dive into the four-poster and draw its curtains shut. Just before they vanish from sight into this sea of ruffles, the high-spirited lads pop their heads out of the surf, one head above the other, and wink at the nonexistent audience.

Back in the parlor I seek distractions, first lifting a book, then discarding it in favor of a stereoscopic viewer, finally tiptoeing back to the bedroom door, to which I apply a guilty, greedy ear. Up to this point the scene is staged as farce and timing, miming, vocal tricks, double takes and innuendoes are played strictly for laughs. But now the style of the piece shifts. The character I'm representing dons a child's sailor suit and sits in the hallway outside the closed bedroom door and cries. He talks to himself. A smile flickers across his lips, only to vanish when the eyes go big and dead and the jaw drops into a sob. After starting on a high whine, the sob rumbles into the bass register and breaks off into a succession of muted yelps. The body lengthens on the floor, face down, then rolls to one side as the knees contract toward the chest.

"Okay, okay, that's enough for today," Craig says, helping me up. He has changed into jeans though he's still shirtless. A light just behind Thomas's head prevents me from reading his expression, but I can see he's pushed back the bed curtains and pulled the sheet up to his shoulders. He's smiling, the cigarette held in a tapering hand rendered longer and lighter by its subtle tremor. Craig, supporting me, leads me to a dressing room where he makes me tea with an electric coil in a mug. Much later, returning with Craig to the stage, I observe that Thomas has changed the scenery before leaving. In place of the Victorian sitting room is a misty forest, layer after layer of foliage sewn to half-lowered scrims, one dropped behind the other. The many lights are gelled blue or green and all held down to only a few points of illumination. Paper flowers are strewn across the floor and the ogival shadows of leaves play across our moving hands; the sound of our footsteps through underbrush is simulated offstage by Thomas trampling a burlap bag filled with flake glue. As we approach an old tree, thick as a giant's waist, the trunk opens to admit us to a secret bower canopied with luscious woodbine, sweet musk roses and eglantine. Craig places an animal's head over my own and sheds his clothes until he is as smooth and pale as melting candlewax at the moment it brims over its oily cup and slides down the firm taper. And indeed, in just this way, he seems to grow, burn, offer warmth and pliancy but promise, if the moment's missed, to be cold and rigid. He bends toward me and opens his mouth to kiss the snout of my mask. He gazes into my, or rather the animal's, eyes, though mine are just behind the empty holes he adores. He whispers phrases loving and passionate and they are just the words I've longed to hear but cannot, muffled as my ears are by the thickness of the costume skull. Now he rises, stands over me, and if I lift or lower my head I can scan the length of his lean body through the peepholes of my papier-mâché mask. Should I bray my praise? Lights within our bower have dawned to make him clearer, brighter, and he is still speaking. I can't decide which I want more—to hear him or to look at him, to enjoy my blissful torment or to gauge by his endearments my chances at future bliss . . . or torment. I feel that he must return, at least to some small extent, a devotion that has become my entirety.

Though I am confined in a trumpery mask and he has donned cellophane wings stretched over veins of wire, and a diligent and not very bright but repentant and frightened Thomas is running the lights, awaiting his next cue, Craig fans my bestial cheek with painted butterflies and offers a bunch of plastic grapes, outsize for visibility, to my black leather lips. Although my real mouth is compressed with chagrin and the lust of a true lover—which is metasexual, since it longs to possess the sternum, femur, cranium and the muscles and skin that bind one bone to another only if that union will further his chances of owning the *soul*—although my real mouth is a hard line of pain, I oblige him by nuzzling the fruit and batting the beast's huge lashes (I've found the exact angle at which the weighted lids close). Much as I resent the mask, the crepe flowers, the hot lights, and the small overhead branches faked out of twine, sized, wound in cloth, painted and stiffened with wire, I recognize that no lover ever presented himself with any fewer impediments, and that this setting at least has the merit of proclaiming the inevitable sense of unworthiness and artificiality.

But now Craig has become inspired and he rises ever higher above the animal at his feet; he paces around me with the tact and forbearance of a god who knows that by answering a mortal's prayer and appearing before him, the gift may blind the devotee or strike him dumb and will certainly unsuit him to the rest of his ordinary days. Yet the daring god believes that the visit must at least be memorable. If it is to bring so much loss, it should be worth losing and therefore, as the air above the altar takes on flesh, as the neck emerges out of the smoke, white wisps curling into the curve of these precise shoulders, blue haze concentrating into blue eyes, gray scarf of burned incense layering thicker and thicker into the lifting, outstretched, beckoning hand, the god cautiously steals up on his supplicant, at first a visual trick, no more than the result of the late hour, the secret ritual, the prolonged fast, the very need for some sign, an illusion to be blinked away, only later a palpable suggestion, finally an undeniable reality. He speaks to me; I cannot understand him (why did I assume I would know a god's language?). He is immense and pale as ash blown off the cold blackened log, fierce with his own strength that he prefers to veil . . . to spare me. And at every moment my mind flickers back and forth between thinking no, he is a representation, surprisingly tangible, of a power that can never be seen and yes, he is in fact here, seen and seeing. To lay to rest my doubts about his literal appearance in my room, he touches me, pushes me down, makes love to me, but too slowly, with too much control to satisfy my need. It is an act that we are engaged in, and I do not have the reserve or the fortitude to proceed, step by delicious and aching step, through an act. I stiffen at the wrong moment, gaze up into his healthy face with despair at the impersonality of his desire (no matter that the desire is for me) and the only consolation I can formulate is the thought that, since he is a god, he already knows and has forgiven my panic. The weighted lids tip shut. I need not be a good lover; he is an echo to his own shout.

When I awaken, bruised and humiliated, last night's costume disgusts me. I kick the empty head away and sidle, disgruntedly and nursing a sore right shoulder, down a corridor toward the green room. There I walk in on Craig and Thomas, both of them sprawling in canvas chairs, chewing gum and looking unpleasantly smug and idle. As Thomas listens, Craig rambles on about his own amazing muscular coordination and acute kinesthetic sensitivity, a discourse I've heard before in which he will refer with awe to Energy. Thomas is prepared to speak to me and does wink with the green eye and wave feebly in my direction (though with a cowardly hand hidden from Craig by the back of the chair) but he's taking his cues from his companion, who has apparently decided that to ask me how I slept or even to greet me would be an admission of guilt. From his loud, cheerful voice I deduce that any complaint I might make would draw from him a studied, overly polite expression of incomprehension. "Please begin again at the beginning. Now, you're *offended* about last night? Yes? You are? But *why?*" Morosely I plunge the electric coil into a dirty cup.

I knew I had to leave the theater, but before I did there was one more thing I wanted to explore.

I drew Craig aside and said I'd be going away in a few hours. He swallowed his gum, took my hand and lost his slouching, leg-swinging insolence. He attempted to dissuade me from leaving; he apologized for everything; then he agreed to help me. I told him that when we lived together you had loved me with the impious desire I had felt for the first time only last night, felt within the bole of the giant tree—a desire that I had felt for him, Craig. Of course, as I made clear, I must have loved you all along, even from the beginning, but for me the sentiment had been careless, lazy, devoid of passion, the infant's hand, translucent fingers and meaty palm, stretching into the milk-rich meshed twilight, confident of touching the mouth of its adoring mother. We are born with only one fear, the fear of falling, and that primeval anxiety now held me as I plummeted farther and farther away from your indifferent hands, which are tucked under your arms, visible (since you've turned your back) only as slightly protruding fingertips, polyps pulsing in sluggish water. No chance of stopping my fall, of being hovered back up to you by a squadron of pink and gold cherub heads outfitted with wings but not with bodies. Falling, scintillating, a diminishing star shifting, as I recede ever further, into the red band of the visible spectrum, I can only rehearse my time with you, the blue, hazy days spied through gauze curtains exhaled and slowly, thoughtfully inhaled by the open windows. You loved me as I loved Craig—with this difference, that your face was masked only by glasses always slightly askew, one pane smudged with a thumbprint and both dusty, and your love endured for years, silent and patient.

"I want to live through those days again," I tell Craig, "but with me playing his role and you mine. You look as I did then—small, blond, too young for your eighteen years."

The first moment we re-created was that time you watched me sleep.

You had first met me in Spain the year before and brought me home. Initially I had been so bewildered by your love, your friends, your celebrity that I had submitted to everything patiently and gratefully. But then I had decided I had to amount to something on my own, go to college, live by myself. That experiment ended in disaster, of course, but for one year I was a diligent student. I wouldn't make love to you—that was bad, that was a distraction, that meant I still belonged to you, not to myself. I held down two jobs, attended classes, studied, made my meals, studied some more.

Hastily Craig and I assembled that dingy student apartment as best I could recollect it and we could approximate it from among our props and flats. In one room on a narrow cot covered with an army blanket Craig lay dozing fully dressed in the button-down shirt and ironed chinos of that era. He was exhausted from the two jobs, the studies. There were ink stains on the index finger of his right hand.

I entered silently, sat beside the sleeping boy for a moment, then wandered about the other room. A study lamp on an extension arm shed the cold blue glow of lonely concentration on an open Latin book turned to a list of irregular verbs. And here is the open wardrobe, the few clothes—the other pair of chinos, two shirts on hangers, the thin winter coat. And there is the kitchen stocked with staples and lentils, the nutritious meat "substitute." Oh, my friend, so you saw me, and you later told me that you realized only then, that night when you let yourself into my apartment, that I was leading a life of my own, that I had my own ambitions, my self-imposed discipline, my integrity. You had loved me so intensely that you'd convinced yourself you had invented me. That moment while I dozed convinced you that it was not my sole purpose to torture you, that I had not moved out and refused your money to spite you. You saw that I had other interests. Latin, for instance. Ironing my chinos. Baking a lentil loaf.

Beside my bed, on the floor, was a looking glass. As I slept you lit a candle and held the mirror up and studied my reflection. Now I did so, watching the flame brighten and draw Craig's childlike face out of the shadows, then dim and float him back into darkness, just as the sun during a polar winter rises only to set.

The following summer I continued to take courses until I was so nervous and exhausted I became ill and you took me back in. For you that summer was our sweetest season together (I can scarcely recall it, forgive me). During those hot days I was always dressed in baggy white shorts and a T-shirt, I think, and I was always racing to work or school on my English bicycle (the only gift from you I'd kept). You and I slept together almost every night but I, confused and frightened by your ardor and exhausted by work and classes, had taken a vow of chastity. For me it was little more than a joke, but you took the vow terribly seriously. You were content not to make love to me so long as no one else did. We had a *marriage blanc* and you explained what that meant.

Because there was no sexual release, everything became erotic for you. Even the sound of my approaching bicycle. Or so you've said. You'd be walking along (as I was now past a backdrop of buildings) and in the airless heat of that deserted summer street you'd hear the sound of my revolving rear wheel tick-tick-ticking, slipping over the stationary gears as I coasted to a halt, one foot standing on a pedal. A block away the whirr was so faint you'd sometimes turn, a welcoming smile on your lips and greet—the empty street; you'd mistaken for my approach the accelerating wheel of your own circling thoughts spinning around the fixed idea of you, me, you, me, you and me, unity . . .

To me it was nothing, nothing at all. That bike I junked ages ago. That summer I was worried about my weight, which I had to fight to maintain by consuming whole loaves of bread, slice by gagging slice, each heavy with honey. And I hated my schedule; I was probably feeling sorry for myself. You pleased me with compliments I didn't trust and startled me with inexplicable bursts of affection. Now, as I try to understand you by impersonating you, as I seize Craig's hand and press a kiss to his dirty palm, I am more struck by his accurate portrayal of my old embarrassment than with any new understanding of why you made that demonstration there, in the middle of the street at noon. You said, "See, they've emptied the city just for us. It's ours. Everyone's gone away out of politeness," and I say those words to Craig, but he retrieves his hand and uses it to hoist the bicycle to his shoulder (time for an afternoon session with the bread). His precision in recapturing my exact response is uncanny; I haven't prompted him. If your odd kiss and whimsical words can *still* evoke the same reaction, then can I be blamed for what I did? Could I have behaved otherwise? I had to hold you off.

And the recognition that I never had a choice, yet have had to suffer the consequences of a decision I supposedly made, angers me. I've searched for you and not found you, attempted to forget you and found you everywhere, in foreign children, in my own childhood memories, in the bodies of hundreds of men I've ransacked, tearing them open as though surely this one must be concealing the contraband goods, only to throw them aside, meaningless raffia, and I've watched my own face age as I waited for your return, fearing I would no longer attract you should I ever see you again . . .

"Stop," I say to Craig. "Let's not go on." He comes back down the stairs with the bicycle and sets it on the ground, propping its weight on the kickstand, searching my face for an explanation. The curtain, lowered till now, rises swiftly and in the dark auditorium I fancy you're sitting, watching me. You're pitiless. You think that now at last the play is beginning.

6

After my mother's death I was enrolled in a boarding school and I seldom heard from my father—a Christmas greeting or a postcard from Morocco of a water-seller, gilt cups and velvet clothes, something mailed three months before I receive it. The bills and my meager spending money were handled by a lawyer, as was an absurdly large clothes allowance, hall of which was mailed directly to a local haberdasher, the remainder to a downtown tailor. These arrangements turned me into a penniless dandy. The trousers Giuseppe made for me were pocketless (the reigning fashion, as far as I could deduce from slick magazines, though no other living man I knew seemed to follow it). The other boys laughed at my cashmeres, tweeds, vests, gartered stockings, silk foulards, the houndstooth stalking cap and the velvety brown fedora (no matter how I crushed it, the fedora, like a starlet in a horror film, assumed a beguiling pose), but I wore these costumes with a mixture of chagrin and pride—they were pledges that would someday be redeemed, the accoutrements of a glamorous life I was about to lead with my father.

My school had been built on the estate of a whimsical tycoon whose taste ran to artificial lakes stocked with fat, whiskered goldfish resembling Tartar khans; he also delighted in brand-new temples constructed in ruins, the columns installed fallen, the features of statues preweathered. The Scottish gardeners outnumbered the masters; the dining hall was vaster and more gothic than Chartres. My house master, the exasperated martinet, conducted white-glove inspections of our monastically plain cells every morning at seven. At night, during the "free" half-hour before lights out, he lingered around the open stall toilets, his ginger whiskers wet with drops of whiskey. Later he would summon his favorite of the moment to his apartment and measure the boy's shivering body with a tape by way of determining his development and prospects for joining the soccer team next quarter. I was never invited, though I made many unnecessary and forbidden trips to the fountain, my bare feet tiptoeing through the band of charged light escaping through the space at the bottom of the housemaster's locked door.

In no way did I distinguish myself. Too small to play sports, too abstracted to shine in class, too fearful to make friends, I glided from dorm to chapel to classroom to the stuffy, echoing study hall as noiselessly as a cloud in trousers. I never cheated. I never won a prize or placed in a competition. I had no relatives and, during holidays, I had no place to go.

But, as best as I can recall, those days were far from bleak. The concentration I was able to apply to even the least conspicuous object (the diagonal scratch in the bottom left window pane in my room) filled my routine with menace, the subtle allusion to other windows I had seen smashed or painted black. In the first frost glinted bits of diamond; I recalled the hammer on the back stairs. The barber came at me with his clippers—Jasper's raw neck. When I strode through hundreds of daffodils down a hill I had named Rumor (since I regarded the flowers as wagging tongues), an unsuspecting collie crossed my path. We label the feelings of our childhood with the names we learn as adults and brightly, confidently, refer to that old "anguish" or "despair" or "elation." The confidence of liars. For those words meant nothing to us then; what we lacked as children was precisely the power to designate and dismiss, and when we describe the emotions of one age with the language of another, we are merely applying stickers to locked trunks, calling "fragile" or "perishable" contents that, even were we to view them again, would be unrecognizable. But come, let us jimmy the hasp and lift the lid.

The morning bell is ringing, summoning me to breakfast. My bed is rich with the warmth and odor of my own body, soup cauldron on the simmer. I ladle myself up out of those depths and look across the cold black courtyard at other boys' rooms, illuminated one by one to reveal, on the first floor, bare feet touching bare wood, and on the second a

187

pimply face gazing into his own still disappointing reflection. As I pull at clothes in the closet my hands enjoy the cold wools and the colder silks lining jackets, though I'm saddened momentarily by the hollow yelp of a hanger sliding across the metal bar. The shrilling of bells down corridors polished by rotary brushes into spirals as individual as thumb-prints; the thunder of scuffed shoes pounding and falling down carpet-less stairs and then—once outside in the courtyard, which is silent under the stars—transformed into a dry, crisp clatter; the teasing delirium of voices and the clanking of spoons against cereal bowls, a noise hope-lessly insignificant within the groined vastness of that hall, filling in now as pink light exorcises gray stone ghosts—did I *find* those winter dawns sad or do their echoes sadden me only now? Just as the haughty stars that dwarfed and mocked us had long since died, so that eager but hushed throng of boys (the crewcut wrestler with the courtly manner and cynical tongue, the science zombie who wept over sentimental records, the fatty fascist who lost weight and turned communist, lost his heart and became an esthete)—these boys wrestle, weep and strike attitudes only in my memory, however dimly they move behind the rattling panes our breath steamed white.

By the time we assembled for chapel heaven had vanished, the stars screened from view by blue sky. Our spires and battlements had burned their way clear of mist, our murmurs and footfalls had become loud enough to fill up whole rooms, and the wood organ pulsed bright and dim in cloudswept sunlight. The singing stops and the handsome, facetious face of our chaplain appears above a clerical collar he has turned into a joke, as though his vestments were no less absurd than the sacred texts he reads with raised eyebrows and a suppressed chuckle or the hymns we bawl out: "By the light of burning martyrs, we tread the bloody trail."

Snow dashed over flagstones, raced up a turret or crumbled under its own weight off a wall, cracking, sagging—and then, caught in a blast of wind, blew sky-high into flickering gestures. As these white heroics—pursuits, escapes, blinding bombardments—besieged the courtyard, the chaplain placidly made the day's announcements. Another bell, and we all hurried off to examine the new "unsat" list, which named the dunces whose grades were unsatisfactory and would be taken off the playing fields and returned to the afternoon study hall.

Neither unsat not securely seated, and certainly not athletic, I was a curious specimen: a student with his afternoons off. Had the masters ever focused on my status it would have been changed. Knowing my freedom depended upon remaining inconspicuous, I kept myself camouflaged, timing my movements with the shadows of clouds, placing my tweed jacket against the stubble of dead grass, concealing my shock of blond hair in a dart of sunlight glancing off a distant window pane. Once I was safe in my room I bolted the door, which was forbidden, and brewed coffee on a hot plate, doubly forbidden. Then I played a record of a chanteuse so softly that she sounded like the samba singer in the tub drain who comes to taunt the man home from his holiday. Outside the courtyard was as lifeless as Rio on Ash Wednesday.

From the same magazine that pictured my exotic clothes I learned that my father had attended an October in Madrid ball (held in London), had been "seen" with Zizi de la Felucca (a former Miss America), drank Sidecars before breakfast, would be hunting in Ireland, escorted some dictator's widow somewhere—and hoped to bring spats back. Since I never bothered to date my clippings and all those places (Estoril, Alexandria, Cap Ferrat) were at best vague imaginings to me, the various social events soon merged and my father became ubiquitous, less a man in time than a synchronous field of energy. When one boy laughed at a dawn-blue tie mailed to me from Charvet's, I told him, "But I'm not dressing for you. I belong to another world," exactly as though I were comparable to Samsaki Charuchinda, the exchange student recently arrived from Bangkok (already "Sam" to some) who came trailing saffron clouds, having just been released from a six-month stint at a Buddhist monastery, where he learned little of the Way but several ways to tell fortunes and cast spells. Among his titles was one that could be translated "Prince."

The letter summoning me wasn't written by my father, of course, but by the woman he lived with that summer. "Last night we were having supper with some new friends outside on a terrace, an indecently late Spanish meal that wasn't half-bad and that ended in Baked Alaska, of all things, which the Spanish for some reason think of as 'English' (does it resemble their *zuppa inglese*—or is that Italian?), when our hosts' son showed up, one of those lads in short pants who's still a child only because the Spanish haven't invented adolescence yet, I guess, and he was lots of fun, very jolly, and it was droll hearing his English (though everyone soon reverted to French to my horror, since I can't understand a word of French though I speak it fluently—is it the way the words run together, the *liaison*, which makes me think of sauce thickening or politics, no help to *me*, I can assure you) and later, back at our villa, your pop said he had a 'brat' (don't be insulted, all in good fun, you know) with much more 'class' than that boy. Fierce paternal pride! He produced a snapshot of you, hopelessly mutilated and out-of-date, even so I could see you were a delight, so we thought it would be fun for you to join us, almost instantly, specially since your father's obsessed with bullfights these days and I'm allergic to the gore and would love a playmate. I hope you're still fair. I'm a blonde and young enough to be mistaken for your sister, I trust."

The letter ended in enough X's to win two tit-tat-toe games but no signature, no directions or timetables, no money, nor any confirmation that the plan had been approved by my father. Nevertheless I wrote the lawyer who handled Dad's affairs in America and said that my father insisted I sail to Spain the day after school let out. Daddy wanted him, the lawyer, to make all the arrangements. I would also need traveling money.

Crossing an ocean presented me with a free week to sort out my past and make decisions regarding the future, and every day I would rise to that discreet knock on the cabin door. But first there was the more pressing decision about whether to shave today or wait until tomorrow, then the greater question as to whether I should sit with the Bryersons or not, that retired admiral and his wife who had so playfully and suavely drawn me into saying a pack of lies that now was quickly multiplying into several decks—the A deck where my stateroom could be found, the B deck where we swam, and a whole nether world of decks below the water line, submerged kings and queens, a diving ace, the weeping sailor, the drowned joker and the royal flush spreading across my cheeks when the Bryersons questioned closely the story I'd rattled off on the first night about my mother's refusal to drive her new roadster because she insisted it "bruised her sables." That's Mom for you, I told them, sweating and grinning. The couple exchanged a worried glance.

Once we'd landed in Spain I plunged on by train to Dad's resort. I had only my phrase book to comfort me—that and the mountain valleys opening up below me like invitations to lead other lives. There. I could switch places with that glossy-haired boy in short pants and place *my* hand on the door leading into a shuttered interior, lines of light on the whitewashed ceiling and wall, one awakening a silver flute within the brass bedstead, while he could be me, plummeting toward a palm-lined coast and a father remembered only as a drawl, the smell of Scotch and the smooth facing of a dinner jacket lapel.

Our family name made sense to Spanish ears only when pronounced in a manner as definite and assured as it was impossible for me to reproduce. I wrote it out and showed it to one taxi driver after another. The first merely shook his head (could he read?). A second excitedly drew a map in the air but just as his right index finger struggled to the top of a hill and the blessed panorama it commanded, he shrugged and jammed his hands back in his pockets. My salvation was a polyglot German jeweler who warned me I'd be arriving before the household was fully awake and dressed (it was noon); he asked me to remind my father that his hat had come back from London, this time with the *correct* initials stamped in gold on the sweatband.

How hard it is to recall anything about my first trip through that town! I guess I was so excited that the excess of emotion turned every patch of stucco glimpsed at a distance into his villa's walls, every scintilla into the flash off his monocle, every whiff of sulphur (the prevailing smell) into the odor of the hot springs where he bathed and from which he would be emerging, bare flesh ruddy and brilliantined hair a runny spectrum, oil and water iridescing into color-charged drops. Again and again each corner concealed a palace, hastily revised as we drew nearer into something small, inert but noisy until, rounding the bend, I watched the illusion vanish altogether—but just behind the next curve in the steep road a new chimera unfolded its gorgeous wings to dry in the sun: my wing, Dad's . . . Even the monotonous prattling of unseen children I could ascribe to his bastards, for surely he'd not been idle nor unfruitful. But would I appeal to his critical eye as I stood behind his other children, my hands resting on their shoulders, our faces turned toward the mild sun and the black bat of the curtained view camera flapping toward us and preparing to open its metal mouth at the instant of contact and drink away the guilt and love that pulsed within us?

The driver stopped before a gate set into a low wall, deposited my luggage on the gravel, took some of the paper money I helplessly proffered and returned coins, got back behind the wheel and, just before driving off, mimed the slow opening of the gate (his brown hand hinging at the wrist), the rapid ascent of my feet (two fingers climbing the air), hysterical hugs and liberal gulps of champagne (a thumb exploded up out of a closed fist and was then jammed between his lips as he tilted his head farther and farther back, adam's apple glugging). He disappeared, laughing and still sucking his thumb.

I stared at my first cactus and hypothesized my first lizard. Above the repeated vamping of crickets hung a silence as demanding as the spotlight on a singer too drunk to perform. But I entered that expectation bravely and called out, "Hi! Hello! Anybody here? Anyone awake?"

At the end of the path a pale curtain luffed in the breeze. Tiptoeing through the open french window and drawing back the curtain I introduced light and myself into a room clearly meant to stay dark and childless. Things were turning: a record, though the needle was resting in its cradle; and a pedestal from a showroom that was a foot high but supported nothing. Glasses of every size, filled or drained, covered every available surface, even the floor, as though put out to catch rain under a riddled ceiling. Someone had tied pink yarn bows around the necks of rubber alligators, one of which had been hanged from the mantelpiece. An ashtray overflowed with butts. In a low-ceilinged room off the kitchen I found a gloomy maid wiping dishes and depositing them on a counter gummy with party favors; she looked up and sighed.

Down a corridor strewn with sleeping people and discarded clothing and overturned bottles was an open door. I picked my way over the debris and looked in. There was a fat man, bearded and bald, his beard a confusion of black and white whiskers, asleep, one hand flung back, the other at his side, touching the blond head of a man or woman otherwise concealed in sheets. The fat man's blue eye suddenly cocks open. "Yes?" he asks on two notes through something viscous in his throat, which he hawks onto the floor. "*Ingles?*" he demands, this time his voice under control. The room, screened by silk-lined yellow curtains, glowed like the heart of an apricot, though it smelled of apple brandy and French cigarettes. An enema bag's khaki tubing described the symbol for infinity on the majolica tiles.

"Hello, Dad, it's me."

The yellowing streak in his beard fell from his lip to his chin like a tusk, old ivory, but what fascinated me were the swirls of black hair on his chest, fine aerial roots clinging to the massive, deeply scarred trunk. "Who?"

"Your son," I suggested, wondering if I, too, would someday be that hairy, wondering if he'd deny me.

His other eye opened. A meaty hand unconsciously pulled the sheet over the gold head at his side that had begun to emit tiny groans. He

192

experimented with a few gestures—one that did deny me, another that indicated confusion. The third was an embrace. As he rose he decorously wrapped a towel around his waist.

I tightened in his arms, aware that we were two strangers locked in an embarrassing social predicament, but after a moment a huge blind infant within me began to squall (Love? isn't it Love who wears a handkerchief tied over his eyes? who stays a baby?). The stuffy room dimmed like a medical amphitheater full of attention and darkness and all that remained visible was the surgeon, struggling to deliver me of this big baby.

I cried in that throbbing room, soaking his shoulder with tears, saliva and snot. He didn't push me away. I was home, even if home was a blonde woman bare-breasted above the sheets, or the dour peasant woman standing in the dark hallway staring at us, or the gathering revelers waking, kneeling and peeking out from behind the peasant's black skirts.

When the sobs stopped and the baby had been born, my father shifted me to his side and pressed his outstretched hand into my shoulder. He presented me to his bed companion, then turned me to the faces in the hallway. "My son," he said, in a voice hoarse with emotion. "My son," he repeated, and the sun brightened on cue, repainting the interior in harsher hues, bleaching out the blonde's face with titanium white, lending the black figures in the hallway marginal browns, grays and ochres and flinging off the beveled edge of a looking glass on the wall a single vertical stripe of light that transected someone's green iris, planting fire in the emerald.

My father was an immoral man. He used people as means to an end, the end his own amusement or, failing that, his temporary relief from boredom. Idle and idly curious, he would press his pudgy finger up any hole that was warm and living. He would go on long, chummy strolls with Henry, an English boy who visited us from time to time. At night he assembled the "time-wasters," as he called his companions, for long dinners on the veranda, and during those hours he showered everyone with attentions, as Jove showers Danae with his humid lust. He paced up and down the flagstones beside the glittering slab of linen between flambeaux that reeked of kerosene and, snatching dishes from the butler, handed them to the diners himself, bowing and chuckling all the while, condescending to fuss over Helene's disappointing appetite ("Here, you've neglected the spinach *véronique*. Don't you want the little white grapes at least? Try one. Permit me") or urging a tone-deaf youth with aspirations toward operetta to favor us with a zarzuela ("You know the one: 'This is his letter, he lives and loves me, what will he say, let's see, oh God, why can't I read?' My all-time favorite, adore, I adore unlettered love")—and with that he chucks lovely Linda from Texas under the chin as though in reference to her own adorable illiteracy, though he knows she can read because he watches her every afternoon in her folding chair scanning the personals in the *Herald Tribune* for coded news as to the whereabouts of her coven of witches driven out of Paris one morning after a particularly sloppy mass. Dad's insulting favors are scattered here and there until, not eating but eternally sipping, sipping, as though he were a sacred cow and the clinking ice were pewter bells tied to his neck, he charges through the crowd, turns tables on their sides, bellows rage, breaks china in a shop where nothing is sold but everything, everyone can be bought. In the sulfurous night air the little cries of fleeing guests nip at the plush hem of Satan's cape and on a distant hill a motorbike sputters up the road. The only other sounds are running feet on gravel and the ratcheting of crickets feeding a bucket down a well that, after it is drawn up, will overflow with another molten sun.

Two rented cars await our party at the foot of the stairs. Until we see them we have no idea why my father has awakened us at nine and hurried us through breakfast. Now, with all of us assembled around him, he tells us that today we're off to Granada. Linda, holding her straw hat to her head with a fragile arm lifted up out of an organdy sleeve, tilts her lips—her most enthusiastic response. Usually she remains expressionless, handing her face to us reverently, as a jeweler places his best gem before a client. The maids, obviously pleased to see us going, pack the luncheon in the trunk.

"When," someone asks once we're underway, "when was the Alhambra built?" My father undertakes to explain. He mentions the Moors, makes Othello their leader, he has Desdemona (whose name, with its double *d*, elicits his stammer) beg for a cool, hilly retreat, a request that Othello lavishly fulfills. With a final burst of daring and authority, he answers, "It was all done in the tenth century." The time-wasters gaze at him in awe.

Only on occasion does he display his knowledge, as sparing with it as Linda is with her smiles. Yet his retinue has seen him more than once before an open book, usually an illustrated volume about Byzantium. He admires Byzantine political arrangements, as complex, static and theological as those in our own household. He has of course dispensed with the airless formality of that court; Dad lets real breezes in to trouble the gold leaves and keeps us all anguished with expectation. Whom will he take to his bed tonight? Who will be the butt of his jokes? Will he be expansive and, throwing a mantilla over his bald dome, jump up and join the gypsies in a fandango, shedding clothes until he's nothing but a fat man heaving under bits of black lace, the vertical scar across his chest pink and gleaming? Or will someone's remark, either ill-intentioned or misunderstood, spoil his fun? When his fun has been spoiled he becomes violent, throws Linda off the balcony into the sulfurous pool, breaks windows, charges at guests with carving knives, brays and plays a record of "Night on Bald Mountain" at top volume. Then, spent and sulking, he huddles in a corner until those he has terrorized come one by one to beg his forgiveness.

"Just think," he says as we walk through the terraced gardens of the Alhambra, "here's the place where the Moors kept their Desd-de-demonas captive. We're shocked, of course," and at this point he puts an arm around my bony shoulders. "But that betrays our limited Christian point of view." Contained within his white suit and vest and bearing his black walking stick chased in silver, just now he does appear plausibly Christian. His beard was freshly trimmed and perfumed this morning, and his baldness is hidden by a panama hat, yellow band to match his tie; he looks respectable, years younger, a serious man willing to forgive Moorish excesses he could never commit. We are all drawn in by his reasonable, ruminating way of speaking and of planting periods at the ends of sentences by grinding the ferrule of his stick into the gravel. Christianity seems now a welcome limitation and I, too, regard the wicked Moors with tolerance. Even our little band of cardsharps, whores and layabouts grows complacent. We continue our struggle across the glaring gardens.

"If this were all mine," my father declares with quiet fervour, indicating the palace and the grounds and including in his sweeping gesture even the distant facade of the Washington Irving Hotel, "I would make you—" he turns to me, tears in his eyes, which are dilated and peaceful after this morning's dose of Veronal—"you'd be lord and master of half my domain. You'd have slaves of your own, women—a whole harem of women!" Could he be hallucinating, I wonder.

His tongue flickers over his dry, rosy lips. He blinks and frowns. A chubby finger pulls at his shirt collar. "But maybe you don't want a harem of women." His eyes swim gently toward me. "We're all worldly, you can tell us. What is your preference? The fair sex, by which I mean men, since no woman ever treated *me* fairly. Do you prefer the fair sex, son?"

The people around me are mildly curious; I can't guess what my father wants to hear. Not for a moment do I wonder what a true reply to his question might be; I only want to preserve his equanimity and our semblance of . . . normality, I suppose. Yes. Normality. I long for us to be ordinary citizens sightseeing, soudhearing, scentsmelling, the descent bourgeoisie of only the usual five senses inspecting the grounds of a national shrine. "I'm not sure," I whisper, "but I think I prefer men."

My father is immensely relieved. He pinches my cheek and smiles. The time-wasters, touched by this domestic scene, work up their own smiles. Even Linda favors us with an upward tilt of her lips. "Yes, my boy," Daddy says, taking my arm, "I thought you were unnaturally fond of me. Don't worry about it. We're all open-minded. Don't worry one bit. I can take care of enough women for both of us." The retinue nods and beams at the obvious and serene wisdom of it all.

Now I can see that my father kept his miserable little company in tow by paying out the two most common leads—money and excitement. The Lindas and Pepes were poor and too lazy or pretentious to work. He provided everything—food, shelter, drugs and finery. And they were a bored, bickering lot; he amused them by planning events. Distractions of any sort would do, a cock-fight (gory spurs and flayed wings) as well as a swim off a rented power boat or a fast drive through rain to the historic caves or a quiet evening at home with just heroin, a few records and the enema bag. His companions were incapable of devising their own amusements and relied on Dad to pick the fun and pay for it. He alone had strong preferences. They had spent so much time accommodating capricious patrons that they had ended up with no caprices of their own. Only Dad could really care to see Aranjuez by moonlight and only he would organize the outing. But as soon as we knew about the trip, then we all went into action wondering what to wear and squabbling over who would sit in the first car, who in the second, whose turn it was to provide sandwiches or mix the thermos of cocktails. So eager were we to receive his favors that no one—I least of all—stopped to consider whether they were worth winning.

Linda was the reigning mistress, and we were all required to defer to her. She presided over the table, at the formal beginning of supper if not at the riotous end. In the evening when we descended on the town, it was Linda who took Pop's arm during the *paseo* and received the bows of the local men and the women's snubs. And she had pride of place beside Dad when we went motoring. If Dad needed a pretext for evasion, he'd use her ("I can't accept your kind invitation till I've consulted the lovely Linda. She rules me in everything. A disgusting sight—the uxorious man—but what can I do?").

Yet Linda reigned rather than ruled, a figurehead with the figure if not the head for a position imperiled every week by a new rival, usually younger. "Juanita has come to stay with us for a few days," Dad would announce as he guided to the breakfasters lounging by the pool his latest discovery whose high-breasted body, tremblingly erect, and eyes, brown and shiny as burnt sugar, reminded me of no one so much as my dead mother. The court evaluated Juanita rapidly. They propped themselves up on elbows to examine her. One person rooted around in a purse for glasses and then submitted her to close inspection, another circled her to determine if she had what we called "back interest," a third scurried off to find out which room Dad had assigned the guest. After addressing her in Spanish, Pepe told Linda that Juanita was certifiably a slum child of Barcelona. Linda, tragic, superb, mounted the diving board, sliced into the water without a ripple and swam three lengths, suave as an otter.

By suppertime a change could be sensed blowing up off the bay, twisting the torch flames to light our faces and bodies from odd angles. Dad was subdued and polite beside Juanita, whispering to her as though he were just a guy on a date and the rest of us nosy strangers. Helene had listened at Juanita's door during the siesta and had informed everyone, with sympathy and malice, that Papa had "done her the honor." While we dragged a conversation in leaking buckets up the steep slope of the night, Dad and his new friend bubbled merrily like frisking kids under a rainspout. During our many pauses for breath we could hear them murmuring about—what was it now? The Spanish male. Does he make a good lover? Is he dependable marriage material? Of course Dad defended the poor, hypothetical devil, while reluctantly granting the creature is more gifted at conquest than occupation. His defense exasperated Juanita: "But the Spanish man is a child! Only you Anglo-Saxon men are real men. Only you take us seriously and make us your friends. The Spanish man wants a slave to cook his dinner and a madonna to raise his children." What could be more delicious than listening to a beautiful woman denounce her countrymen in favor of a man, a certain Anglo-Saxon man, much like oneself? Linda could not resist correcting her. "Slavery is better than neglect," she said. Juanita peeled an orange with a knife and fork and fed pungent wedges to my father. "Only vulgar people eat an orange like that," Pepe assured us. He, I suspected, knew he'd been boring Dad with his mimed re-enactments of old bullfights, his learned discussions of impotence, and the solemnity with which he approached cocaine; Pepe's only chance of staying on at "Top Boy" (the name of our villa) was by befriending Linda who, now that we'd finally left the table, played straight through "Für Elise," her one song, a recital piece from her girlhood in Corpus Christi—and then arranged herself beside me on pillows and pressed her head to mine, ear to ear. "See, Pepe, the little man and I are both so blond, we could be related. I *feel* related to you, honey," she said, ungluing herself and looking me in the eye with the humorlessness of a sheeted Baptist preparing for immersion, "and I think our souls are very, very close, you know?" She transfixed Dad with a glance; why did he court this lady before our envious eyes—and what eyes! Blue eyes red with weeping; black eyes so large they've crowded out the whites; eyes glistening like hot spills of sealing wax, still unimpressed, and my scanning eyes looking at Linda, Juanita, Linda, Juanita, father, father, my treacherous father.

And what was I feeling, you ask, as I nestled against Linda in that room while Dad did a two-step on the terrace with the Spanish beauty? Or when I stretched a match to Juanita's cigarette and Dad blew it out, then offered her the thick blue flame of his own smelly lighter? What did I feel when he and Linda fought bitterly the next afternoon by the pool? They paced around me. Linda sat on my chaise and ran an unconscious hand through my hair, as though my hair were her bright, accumulated grief. Dad chopped at the air with a hand bursting out of its fine pink glove of skin. A chair fell over, glass and blood were on the terra-cotta tiles, silences, shorter and shorter, contracted like birth pangs, a slap and a cry rang out—I begged them to stop it. Linda nursed her jaw and my father confided loudly to me, "You see, son, Linda doesn't understand the difference between commitment and attraction. I'm *committed* to Linda. I'm only *attracted* to Juanita."

For some reason Linda found the distinction consoling. She looked up through the mesh of her hat brim and asked, "Are you sure?"

"Sure I'm sure." My father rubbed his eyes and then frowned, as though, assured as he might be, he was nonetheless uncertain as to what subject they were discussing. His attention span seemed very short. Several times when he'd been winding up an angry peroration he'd lost the thread—and hurtled off into another tirade, its subject suggested by the last word he'd happened to say, its emotion dictated by the fortuitous subject. Today's drug, or combination of drugs, had sent the other inhabitants to their rooms on erring, somnambulistic feet. I'd observed Pepe cursing and mumbling as he careened from wall to wall in the corridor. Helene I found beached on the floor outside her room, awake and talking to herself but with no desire to press on toward bed. The chemical banderillas, which had felled the others, only confused my Pop, who dropped his head from its hump and trotted in circles.

On the third day of Juanita's visit her protector—no, her impresario—drew me aside and asked me to stop calling him "Dad."

"*Father?* Would that be better?"

"What?" He laughed and grew serious. "No, my boy, call me by name. We're friends as much as relatives. Besides, Juanita has such a morbid distaste for men over . . . forty. And you, my dear, are such a very *old*-looking sort of son for me to be having. Not that you look your age," he hastened to assure me. "Not a bit. You look no more than . . . *twelve*." The figure seemed to please him with its apostolic good sense. "Twelve," he repeated. "And how old are you, by the way?"

Though I was sixteen or seventeen I lied to comfort him and said, "Thirteen."

"No matter. But let's drop the 'Dad' and 'Pop' business, all right? 'Father' is no better, with its priggish sound—sounds like after church. 'Papa' is obviously too immigrant, don't you think?" He was smiling over his offhand way of dismissing all these forms of address; he was sounding like his English friend, Henry. "And 'Daddy' reeks of incest. No, best use my name. Far more twentieth-century." Our century always reminded him of science, which in turn summoned up the image of his favorite Swiss clinic where he had his blood circulated through a chrome machine once a year and "scrubbed."

When it suited him, Dad pretended he knew no Spanish. Linda or Pepe was left with the job of instructing the maids, arranging trips, dealing with visitors, answering invitations. But when he needed to he could make his wishes felt, as they were on the evening the time-wasters returned from the *paseo* to find their bags packed and lined up in the hall.

"What's this?" Pepe asked, his real eye rolling. "Are we all off on a surprise outing?"

"Not all of us," Dad answered politely.

"Where's Linda?"

"She went off in a huff," Helene said.

"Hired, no doubt," my father whispered. Pepe's live eye happened to align with the glass one and both fixed me.

Now, whenever I hear the word *humiliation* I picture the chauffeur's faultlessly white gloves lifting that pitiful, motley luggage into the trunk: Pepe's small tan valise striped in faded red, one of its clasps refusing to snap shut; Helene's shiny nothings leaking out of a paper bag; Linda's green metal trunk covered with stickers (a Moroccan *Touriste* stamp beneath two fluent Arabic squiggles rising like thin hands in prayer out of gathered sleeves—memento of a hash run to Tangier; a battered decal of the Corpus Christi "Whips," her high school football team; a red, white and blue chevron from a French liner, reminder of that crossing during which she and her favorite warlock had propitiated the sea with an eighth of a teaspoon of his semen; stickers from Hot Springs, Arkansas and Baden-Baden—a mini-history of a mini-life).

Eventually Linda appeared and eventually her tears, reproaches and threats burst forth; the crickets all around us sounded like tiny bacchantes angrily shaking hundreds of tambourines as they marched toward the light and us, thirsty for a man's blood. The chauffeur, Jorge, "helped" a spitting, clawing Linda into the car; she rolled down the window and shouted back at Dad, "Okay, you bastard, you win this round."

Dad led Juanita and me back into the dimmed, polished house. "Hate a guest who *lingers*," he said.

I expected intimacy to steal over the house now that we were alone. The time-wasters had been thinned out, I assumed, to give Juanita room to sink her roots and spread her branches. On the stage, once the chorus has exited stomping and shouting, the light concentrate to a blue spot on the lovers; I readied myself to listen to a tender duet, though I knew I'd hear it only in snatches as the couple stumbled drunkenly through the darkened house or fell silent over supper, their hands motionless while their concealed legs squirmed under the cloth. Or I knew I'd pick up a few faint notes when the grownups retired for the *second* siesta of the afternoon and set their crickets singing. I would become what their eyes, heavy with exhausted lust, rested upon across the swimming pool. I hoped I would be the innocent-appearing number superscribed above their numerals, raising them to a bewildering power.

But that didn't happen. Juanita wandered about the house alone in nervous high heels, sighing and trying her curly hair a different way in front of each mirror—a bun in the stolid rectangle framed in blackened mahogany; a seductive swoop over one eye before the silvery circle set in aquamarine tiles; spit curls in her oval vanity glass. My father grew paler and duller. When Henry, the English boy, joined us by the pool, Dad would wait only a few minutes before leading him into the house. Every day the pause before leaving us shortened. One day Dad grabbed Henry at the gate and steered him inside, angrily whispering something. Juanita snorted through her broad nose and subjected her tanning shoulders to another close look. She unhooked her bra and turned on her stomach. My job was to oil her skin, to stroke a sheen down that smooth, tense back, to feel the hot silk slide over shoulder blades and ribs as delicate as my own, to admire the nacreous hollow where her spine dove and drowned in the rising swells of her buttocks. She fell asleep cupping her breasts with her hands. As she relaxed the right hand opened and flopped to the ground.

Before long Henry was coming every morning and night, then morning, noon and night. At lunch one day Juanita was missing. My father, composed, imperturbable, explained that her native Barcelona had called her. He admitted that one's homeland so often exerted a compelling spell over the vagabond, no matter how far one might . . . and he dozed off into his soup. Jorge and I dragged his body, which seemed willfully heavy, back to his dirty, shuttered bedroom. Bits of cotton littered the floor.

Henry moved in. He brought only his cheery smile and a knapsack containing glassine envelopes. In a bazaar somewhere he'd picked up a thin white cotton shirt, which he wore constantly but never washed. Since he kept himself tan if not tidy and was very young, his dirt became something like a "look," as though a soot streak on his face, twin to the smudge on his hand, or the black crescents under his nails, even his Benedictine smell, distilled from grass, anise, clay and gin, came together into a charming new fauve style.

Henry would shrink back rather than touch another human being, he never swam or listened to records and he missed meals. Nothing interested him beyond his own straightforward rendition of "Greensleeves," which he whistled every evening at five from within his canopied chair. When he spoke it was in the outmoded dialect of Mayfair. When he meant "yes" he said "rather" with an equal stress on each syllable. He never looked at either men or women with sexual curiosity. Once I passed him in the hall as he came back from my father's bedroom. He tossed his head toward the closed door, indicating Dad, and drawled, "Oh that kid." From time to time he'd slip away for a day or two.

One night, while Henry was off on a jaunt, my father came crawling into my room. He was naked and as disoriented as a wolf that has escaped a trap only by gnawing off its paw. He rolled over on his side next to my bed and groaned. Terrified, I knelt beside him, trying not to look at his body, scarred from waist to shoulder in a diplomatic sash of puckered pink silk. I held his beard-gritty chin in my hand.

"Tragic magic," he said, his name for heroin. "Too much. I shot up too much." He tried to move. "I can't hear anything. I played the gramophone at top volume—nothing. And everything is yellow. Henry's gone to buy me more d-d-damned junk." He winced. "More! May I sleep here?"

"Yes," I said, but he couldn't hear me. I bent down until I was in his range of vision and nodded.

He slept with his huge bald head on my chest and poked one fat finger into my mouth. Although I disliked the taste of his cold, salty finger, I submitted to it superstitiously, half-believing that my saliva was keeping him alive. At last he rolled away from me and began to breathe evenly.

All along, I suppose, I had wanted this passionate, ridiculous pasha in my bed, had wanted him to hold me in his legendary arms. But now that he was here, so reduced, I loathed him. The backs of my legs behind my knees became clammy. My hands froze. My mouth was unpleasantly dry, defiled by the taste of his finger.

I dressed and left the house. Running down the winding road past walled, unlit villas, I made for town. Once there I strolled the empty streets. A gypsy boy shined my shoes under a street lamp and then, without asking permission, briskly hammered taps into the rubber heels—an "improvement" he charged me for. I paid him without a word and tap-tap-tapped my way into the shadowy botanical gardens. I sat on a bench under a banana tree and cried. Someone put a friendly arm around me. It was you at last.

7

When I came back to her, Didi was living in a palace that overlooked the ruins. Her paintings were in a new style, she'd married and divorced a husband since I'd last seen her, and her apartment was unexpectedly neat. Down below, tiny tourists labored across shimmering fields browned by the August sun but whitened in faint circles and squares by the jagged traces of temples emerging out of the ground in that way wisdom teeth erupt through the gums. A group of Orientals glided to one spot and stared obediently at a foot ruler of half-buried marble, the dog's oldest bone; once we looked at it as you read from the guidebook: "This they regarded as the dead center of the world, and from this point they measured all distances. . . ."

Didi asked me about my life. I told her where I'd been, but her attention dispersed into minute droplets that condensed into a turbulent cloud just below the figured ceiling. "No, no," came the downpour, "say something real."

I invited her to set an example and she complied by telling me about the gypsy woman who had installed herself last winter in a wagon on the streets below. Didi had taken her food and blankets and then, on a cold night, brought her up to these rooms. Now Didi was pacing across the tiles in a studio where all the canvases were turned to the wall: when she paused the air was filled with the impassioned argument of traffic. In the distance I could see the ancient amphitheater, which looked like those clumsy plasticine molds, uppers and lowers, that dentists ask you to bite into. "She insisted on sleeping in my room. I moved to the day bed. Her old dog came with her and shit everywhere, on the chairs, under the bed. My maid quit. The gypsy said she'd been a princess and . . . I don't know. Could be. Her voice—" and Didi shifted into a bass register, musical and whispering, the words as precise and irresistible as the witch's invitation to the children— "was like this. Oh, what wonderful stories she told, all lies, but . . . I liked having her here, telling me her stories. I had to wait on her; she expected it. But she frightened me. And the dog howled and whined all night, dragging its paralyzed hind legs from room to room. The princess could be so jealous. She tore the phone out of the wall when I talked to somebody too long. I found her a nursing home but she didn't like it and she came back here. I put her in a boarding house, but the landlady begged me to take her back. Finally I forced her to go away. I had to call in a policeman —I, a communist! She ended up downstairs, back in her little wagon again."

The narrow wings of Didi's apartment folded around the dark heart, her bedroom. When she stood at the door of that soundproofed chamber, she warned me, "I will not emerge from this room for twelve hours. Nothing must disturb me. In the morning the maid will make you breakfast—don't talk to her, she's a chatterbox, though I like her. But remember, I must not be awakened. I sleep a full twelve hours." She kissed me on both cheeks, inhaling sharply on the second kiss; then she shook my hand and pulled away a second too soon, closing the bedroom door behind her without a glance back.

I had keys and could go out for a walk, which I did. For a while I talked to a soldier from the South. He was standing in the entrance of a tent lit from within by a kerosene lamp. All along the boulevard were other soldiers on foot or in jeeps; they were putting up bleachers for the parade tomorrow. At the end of the thoroughfare was a glowing ruin.

When I'd lived in this city, a year or two after you left me, there were so many winter nights I walked here from my apartment, with or without Anxiety. In December the streets and squares are empty after midnight. I step out into the cold and hear the last storekeeper blocks away pulling the metal gate down over his shop front. A cat with a torn ear slinks across the street. Once I turn the corner I can hear a fountain splashing irregularly as the wind grabs the water and lets it go. Fifty paces on and the narrow street widens into a square flanked by two churches, the one on the right scrubbed, the one on the left as splendid but its doors boarded up, verdigris mottling the facade.

As I worked my way up a road curving below the exposed caves of martyrs, I kept my glance from rising to the still more impressive monument hanging above me—I would waste time and ignore monuments, those treasures of time other people have saved. My grief was luxurious, and it took the form of idleness.

How did my day go? Wake up at noon, order two coffees from the bar, which were delivered by a twelve-year-old with legs strong from soccer and a beardless face flushed from his climb to Peter's and my eyrie. As I fished for money, the boy would push his long apron aside with a grubby hand, crouch and play with Anxiety. Then he would look around disapprovingly at the unmade bed, the dishes sticky with last night's snack, the liquor bottles and (as though reproaching our disorder with his exactitude) he'd count out the change to the last worthless tiny tin coin in a voice surprisingly loud and hoarse. Peter was soaking in a sunlit but dirty tub, his head thrown back and submerged to the ears, blond hair darkened and expanding in water that had a vivacity of its own—smashing points of fire and reflected blue sky. Peter's bony knees, losing their gloss as they dried, pointed to the ceiling. I put his foaming tan coffee in its tall glass on the wet tiles beside him.

That was breakfast, followed an hour later by lunch, a three-course ordeal for which we dressed and descended. If it was warm enough we sat outside under an umbrella and picked at our squid while Anxiety hugged the pavement in the oval shadow cast by our round table. People we knew ambled past, paused to talk, joined us—and another liter of white wine was ordered. Now afternoon was hard upon us. Since the stores, banks and markets were closed for three hours we had no option but to take in a movie, where I witnessed the mouths of stars from my country open only to speak in the language of this. Restless eyes, green and immense, squinted nervously, embarrassed by the booming, cultivated tones that were being emitted. The words continued after the lips closed—and I pitied the rhetoric tumbling out of those timid, sensitive faces. During the scene in which the hero walks through a dark field the auditorium sank into dimness; a businessman beside me lifted my hand and put it under the raincoat on his lap.

Oh, but now the supper hour was approaching. Peter and I had our naps to take, a fresh set of clothes to put on, phone calls to receive, Anxiety to feed. And, after the meal, which had too many courses, too many people, too much chatter, I'd find myself alone in a great square toward dawn. A guard in uniform wavers by on his bicycle, the headlight brightening with the fall of each pedal. Dirty marble breeds a dirty cat, a second cat. The moving cars speeding beside the river begin to speak in individual voices, grunting, declaiming, objecting, all engaged in litigation.

When friends from home arrived with their sober faces and pressed, unfashionable clothes, they politely ignored my starved body and velvet suit and asked me to take them sightseeing. We climbed stone steps in the noon heat. If I stumbled they'd grab my arm and invent an excuse for me. Once inside an old building too large for human beings we'd stare at plaster swags on a ceiling or watch pilgrims struggle up wood steps on their knees. At restaurants I knew how to order food—in that way I was serviceable. Also I was good at changing money. More steps, more monuments, black, varnished masterpieces inside chapels, teeth and bones—and finally my friends would leave. They were usually your friends, your "saints," and once I felt that you were sending them not to comfort but to torment me; the contrast between their health and my illness was tormenting, as was their knack at moving so quickly, even through the summer heat, from one pile of steaming marble to another.

This time I'm here only for a few days and I'm determined to remain energetic. The moment I order a second liter and turn my unfocused gaze upon the flickering crowd, the water that bathes stone giants, the pigeons—then I'll leave. Till then I'll tick off ten items every day on my list of sights to see.

Didi drives me one night down a walled, curving road that, no matter how we turn, keeps reappearing, same tree, same convent, same crossing, as though we were on a Möbius strip—until a sudden lurch and sputter projects us down a gravel lane into such darkness that only the treetops against the sky, velvet cut-outs pasted on phantomed silk, remind me that there are qualities of darkness paling all the way to the face emerging from the shadows to greet us and invite us in. Though I had imagined we were still within the city limits, this is obviously a farm: the smell of earth, moisture dropping from leaves, a cockcrow—and now the blazing door to the barn slides open.

People who know me come up to kiss me. A languor, as pleasurable as the oiled hairs of a fur collar ticking across an exposed nape, tempts me to relax into their affection. No matter that I cannot recall a single name nor be certain where I met this tiny girl with the uneven teeth, green spectacles and baggy work pants, her spirit leaping up out of her skin with every laugh, her arms luminous as vapor lifting off a wet log, nor that obese man with the shrunken hand and a peculiar way of choosing delicate, courteous turns of phrase so at odds with the fanatical application of his finger to his nostril—nor this young woman, our hostess, whose hair, though tousled, and clothes, though paint-stained, are too well cut to admit her into easy camaraderie with her bohemian guests. A woman I met in my country emerges from the kitchen, gray hair streaming back from a face red with drink, the pungent odor of her cigar enveloping her like the greatcoat of a cavalry officer from the last century as he steps into an inn.

The vividness of these impressions drains away. We've moved to an unlit garden and I'm offered a hammock slung between two trees. Once I'm in it the stretched bowl of fabric conceals the other members of our party from my view. The man with the deformed hand discusses the

206

greatest novelist of the moment, a motherly creature who lives with ten cats in the center of the city and phones people everywhere and at all times of the night for bits of information for her epic. He had been playing Oedipus in a town in the North when she called him and asked him to find a farmer who would know exactly how you steal a pig—or, better, how a thief stole pigs during the last war. Would you use a sack? How do you silence the squeals? Tie the trotters?

My dear, since I left you I have heard so much talk, all studded with such a profusion of detail, gloves of mail slapping at my face. I picture my face as bemused, vacant, even sweet as those gloves do their work. When a life has ended and an unenthusiastic Lazarus is coaxed up out of the grave, he totters from here to there, strips of the winding-sheet still gauzing his eyes and ears, but through the cloth he can see the gloves, hear the talk and he reels before the swarm and insistence of the undead, their stories, the arrangements they keep on making.

The girl with the green glasses and leaping exhilaration whooped with laughter. I peered over the edge of the hammock and saw she was pointing up to the treetops. After a while I deduced she'd seen a bat or a flying mouse of some sort and its name in her language was the same word as *labia*—which became a general source of merriment. Food of some sort was served, though it was too dark for me to figure out what I was eating and I revised one theory after another: veal, eggplant, supreme.

But the gauntlets were moving again and new stories were told of this one who went there, said that, returned here, wanted more, accepted less until that one asked for these, traded those, lost all, recouped some. Sustained unhappiness, the sort I was entertaining, goes on too long to tolerate clarity. What it needs is the blur of fog on the side of the hill turned away from the morning sun, the composing fog that eliminates the tricky connections between objects so difficult for the painter to render (the emergence of a trunk from the ground, of a neck from the truck) and suspends in an enveloping medium only those elements grateful to the brush (the branch, the face). Drink dimmed the anxious clutter of detail, but after suppressing it ended up by shedding a lurid gleam on what remained. Best of all those agents of dilution is fiction—either the fiction of memory or fantasy—for it alone dissolves the entire scene in the cloud, brilliant or black, of desire.

The night swept in over me in soundless waves, but each breaker rustled away to reveal a jagged bit of bottle glass, an empty shell, a sand-choked carton. Now Didi and her friends, these people who appeared to know me and like me, were disputing the merits of sopranos—their diction, their phrasing, their vibrato, their range. I thought I saw the flight of a mouse from one branch to another.

Once I had moved out of your house I knew I wanted back in. Robert, the giant lover for whom I'd left you, became a fool overnight. His constant eating revolted me. He drank half a quart of milk a day and at one sitting, shoveled in mounds of potatoes, meat, bread, vegetables— and sweets. My father had told me that desserts were only for children or the senile, and I clung to his unreasonable prejudice. Even Robert's vulnerability, too like my own, annoyed me. If he loved me it was because he knew no one else; I was his only friend and he was quite content to settle in with me.

For a month I wouldn't let myself phone you. Whenever I was out walking I looked for you, but you and your friends had vanished. The bits and pieces of mail you forwarded came without comment. An attorney wrote me about the money you were giving me. That was all.

One afternoon I saw you dart out of a taxi into a shop and I followed you. A bell tinkled, the chocolates smelled so sweet, you straightened up from the counter and turned toward me—but it wasn't you, rather a quizzical stranger with a Slavic accent and a child's greedy penchant for sweets.

I knew I loved someone now, not exactly you but the freakish warm days of that winter, the reflections of traffic lights on wet pavements, the kindness of the unknown bartender who kept my glass full and wiped his hairy hands on his apron, the lyrics of songs on jukeboxes. As I wandered the city I found everyone touching and brave. Four twenty-year-olds out on a Saturday night, clustered in a corner of a bar and unsuccessfully suppressing the urge to dance, seemed heroic; they flirted with everyone who walked past them. Didn't they know (as I did) that the best thing had already happened, that their long lives, that progression from this year's hits and haircuts to next year's, from a first job to a second, a sixth, from sitting over cold coffee at dawn in a diner to sipping wine at supper on a balcony in Haiti—that this long sequence of slightly varying incidents would give them only time to see the past from every angle, as though the past were a statue they kept pacing around in ever-widening circles?

Your face swirled in a blur before my imagination, tones of color rose to greet a smudge of black, and then the focus sharpened and you were there smiling from under the funny carnival hat as you came out of the hotel and pretended surprise at seeing me. You ran toward the camera, jogging in place for a few seconds (or so it seemed) until you suddenly swarmed close, immense and dark; I froze the projector on a frame of your heavy-lidded eyes just as they went vague, a stray dazzle of sunlight in the lens casting a mysterious rainbow in the left pupil—then the film went up in flames.

After staying up all one night I stopped off at Robert's and showered, shaved and changed. In his ragged white terry cloth robe Robert looked like a large, molting bird. He opened the refrigerator and contemplated its racks of cold food for some time before asking me where I was coming from and where I was going. I told him I had to see you, that I had met someone on the pier who'd given you a dog and that we had gone to his place and made desultory love but then plunged into an orgy of talk about you.

"Are you going back to him?" Robert asked, meaning you. He yawned with embarrassment and placed a slab of strudel in the oven to warm up.

"Who know? I've got to see him. It just came over me," I said, mentally hearing one phrase over and over again: "Blame it on my youth."

The maid was glad to see me and said you'd run out on an errand but would be back soon. She seated me in the drawing room and gave me a cup of coffee. The phone kept ringing and I heard her taking your messages; obviously your social life continued to be a growth industry. Hampers of fruit and tinned things under yellow cellophane lined the butler's pantry; were you about to go on a trip? The furniture had been restored, the rugs laid, the white dining room was pale blue, paintings of a featureless but momentarily fashionable style that neither you nor I liked lined the hall and were making headway in the guest bedrooms. In your room two trunks sat, open and overflowing. The clothes in the new trunk were so small and chic; I picked up a silk shirt and held it to my chest. A perfect fit. The phone rang and rang. The doorbell rang and the maid signed for another delivery. Monogrammed towels hung in the bathroom, your initials twined around someone's. The blood leapt to my face and I slipped out silently as she raced to silence the phone again.

Didi and I left the party. Driving back down the lane, then over the winding roads into the city, passing hillside villas, swooping down on the domes of churches, sliding under triumphal arches, I felt my body becoming a reed, piping two notes, the mournful dyad. When I lived here the city was full of your absence. My longing played over everything I saw. But now even that loss has been lost, as the face of our Lord on a napkin might vanish one morning.

The next morning, before flying north, I went by the apartment I had shared with Peter. He's gone and the woman living there now has never heard of him; she was preceded by yet another tenant. As she talks my eyes stray toward the door leading out to the veranda; I half-expect to see Anxiety lying on the marble lintel, her forelegs and dozing head in shadow, her hindquarters in sunlight. But Peter, red-faced and vengeful the night I packed, swore to me that if I left him he'd put the dog out in the streets. She yapped and spun unsuspectingly when I stood at the door the last time with the Captain, who had come to rescue me and take me home. In a letter Didi mentioned Anxiety had been seen scavenging but had slinked away when Didi had tried to lure her into the car. One other time the dog, much thinner and limping, had been glimpsed from a moving bus.

That afternoon the boat enfiled the channels of the harbor, threading its way between upright clusters of pylons, asparagus in a steamer. We moved past an island and its deserted monastery. The aggressive smell of geraniums invaded the air. A grounded tanker marked the shallows. As we approached our destination more and more of the city blew across the sun-hammered tin top of the water, for the city's pastel and nougat colors had been lent to the outboards and sleepy barges drifting out to meet us, and its will to soar drove the gulls climbing the wind.

An ancient woman with blue eyes as fresh and wild as full pardon was shrieking to the helmsman in my language, "But surely you know where the Helvetius is. You must. I go across a large square—and then? And *then?* The Helvetius. Years ago I knew your language perfectly. Elveetyo? Elvaytoos? The Helvetius."

Obviously not understanding a word, the helmsman and the crew shrugged and smiled at each other and stretched out their hands and juggled invisible fruit that was large and light, since it struck the palms gently and caused only the fingertips to curl. I came to her rescue; it was evident to me alone that this woman, despite (or because of) her torn dress, laceless sneakers and tangled hair, was either a duchess or a clairvoyant.

In translating for the woman and locating her hotel, I spoke to one of the boys—the one I'd seen dashing barefoot along the gunwales, the one

I'd envied and despised for a health that made him smirk, self-satisfied, at the dirty foreign lady and then turn into the sun and shade his eyes with a raised hand that transcended self and dwarfed merely human satisfaction.

Following his directions I guided the duchess to the Helvetius. Her suitcase was no larger than a lunchbox and as light as her remaining sentence on earth. In the swarming alley outside the hotel she told me, blue eyes ecstatic and face lifted, that she had trusted God to send her an angel. She insisted on that word until my smile saddened, my lips released a scroll of gothic letters, and my shoulders broadened to support wings striped every color of the rainbow and lifted by long sheets of muscle anchored to an aching coccyx.

That evening, as the sun, frustrated with the day's painting, began to make a mess of it, I chanced upon the boy. He was in shorts, hosing down the boat. It turned out he lived with his family just across the canal from me.

Being with Sergius that long summer provided me with another life—not an alternative to my real existence, which has no character, but to every evening's round of parties and melancholy adult pleasures. At night, ablaze in a white suit, I would saunter over the bridge to a palace where I would stand, secretly bathed in sweat, and talk to women about their antique jewelry, as I had done for so many summers, and on the way I might pass Sergius, who would be too intimidated by my suit, my companions and our conversation in a language he did not know to return my nod. But in the morning I'd step out through glass doors onto a narrow balcony and look up at his window. There he'd be, tan face jutting out over a pot of geraniums, harp strings of light, bouncing up from the water, rippling on his neck. We pantomimed our plan—his descent, mine, our meeting on the bridge.

His waking hours were spent in a prison of rituals and superstitions, his "mania," as he called it. I was forbidden to pronounce the numbers three and seven; they became "two plus one" and "six plus one." He could not pass a shadow on the pavement without turning his head to one side and spitting through his teeth, more a hiss than a spit. Crossing a bridge required several false starts, retracing his path, a full turn on the second step up, four hisses. The mere mention of death sent him into a fit of twirling sibilance. His grandmother, whom he escorted every evening to the levee for a lemon ice, was the only member of his large family not too ashamed to appear with him in public. His one friend was a

211

short lad with dark circles under his eyes whose English teacher, in some zany moment, had assigned him, though he was a beginner, Whistler's *The Gentle Art of Making Enemies*; I had to translate a new passage every afternoon for this boy who accepted his nickname, "Gnome," without comment.

I was Sergius's protector. The demons would leave him alone for an hour if I was willing to take charge. "Am I your responsibility?" he'd ask me. I nodded. "Say it!" he insisted.

"You are my responsibility."

Then he'd smile.

To make me proud of him he told me about his conquests of German and Swedish and English girls, usually tourists who stayed in the small hotel next to his house. He demonstrated to me what a good swimmer he was by suddenly interrupting our walk, stripping to his underpants and plunging into the harbor beneath a gold weathervane held in the gold hand of Fortune atop the old customs house. He instructed me in the peculiarities of his dialect; its quaintness he appreciated so fully that I knew he had exposed these same trinkets to other buyers.

His one polite accomplishment was twanging a guitar and singing pop songs in my language; he had learned the lyrics by rote from a record. I was placed on a chair in a deserted storeroom the neighborhood kids had rented as their club headquarters. Sergius howled into expensive sound equipment, then asked me if I could understand the words. I couldn't. He mastered the intonations but scrambled the meaning.

We sat on grass, a unique patch of verdure in a city of stone and water, and he asked me how I could endure his mania. I told him allowances had to be made for me as well, since I liked men. He couldn't take it in. He assured me it was a scandal. He asked me if I'd tried girls and offered to secure for me the blonde in the floppy hat coming toward us. After a while he took my arm and said, as we began to stroll, "What a fine couple we are, you with your scandal, me with my mania."

I never touched him, though he took my hand once during a Kung Fu movie and whispered, "Am I your responsibility?"

"Yes."

"Say it!"

I felt again the happiness you gave me. The theater, a deconsecrated church, was squirming with amorous adolescents and raucous sub-teens, and in their midst I sat decorously, blushing with guilty pleasure, fearing that when the warrior annealed his steel fists in the fire the wizard provided, someone might have seen the boy's Midas hand in mine. A brat in pigtails kneeled in her seat and shouted over my shoulder at her accomplice whose black eyes had becomes pools of blue as the avenger flew in a magic cape and pounced on a bearded wrongdoer; I was caught in the crossfire of the kids' post-luncheon breath, but even those whiffs of garlic smelled like desire. "You are my responsibility," I said.

If I were to end with a movie, in it we would appear flying high against a backdrop of Spain. You had saved me from my father, you bought me a forged passport, you arranged our escape, you gave me a new name— yours. That name became my magic cape. In a second scene I'd show us standing by french doors looking out into a rainy garden irradiated by the blue-white sun. Schubert's *The Trout* is playing on the radio. I'm convinced I'll never be so happy again, nor was I until one midnight I gave you a dance class in a friend's studio. For once I had something to give, a skill I'd acquired during *my* brief mania for ballet after I dropped out of college. Your clumsiness I ignored (I knew how sensitive you were about your body), and when you laughed at your own mistakes I coolly announced the next combination. Admit that I handled that first class with a straightforwardness available only to the wisest lover or a perfect stranger. For an hour we centered, lifted, balanced with the curtains drawn over the mirrors. Only during the last ten minutes did I offer you the image of a man rediscovering his feet ("More turnout!") and hands ("Soften the fingers!") and shoulders ("Drop them!") and buttocks ("Tuck in!"). The excitement of one moment finds that of another, though they be years apart, and the theater full of children seething around an assumed responsibility detects its counterpart in the motionless leaves liquifying into light or the poised body of a man feeling his way back into his muscles. The instruments tune up and wait for him to begin.

Moralists say that our actions and not our intentions define us, and by that harsh rule I lose all definition. I longed away my childhood, resisted my youth, regretted the rest, and in that history appear, here and there, my protestations of good will and my pleas for redemption any serious historian knows to ignore. Nothing will come of my pleas and protestations, the outcome is in the stars, never more radiant than when they die, tyrannical novae.

213

8

Children in school uniforms sip lemonade and display a fearlessness I envy. This little boy, still flicking his head to one side between sentences though the long blond forelock that once excused the tic had been cut, boldly contradicts his father: "No, the *Empress* is the schooner, Dad." The father is unoffended by that high, clear voice and unimpressed with its mandarin accents, which are his own. And then the boy, who inherited his first name from a seventeenth-century theologian and his last from a nineteenth-century industrialist, runs off to play.

Japanese lanterns sway for the holiday over the drifting crowd; they are strung between clapboard houses in a square planted with elm and lawn. The ocean is only a block away, but the square has been laid out to exclude it, much as the manner of the summer people is calculated to ignore the water's moving plea for adventure.

My love, I write you from the island, where they're still talking about you. Dorothy sends her greetings; she speaks like you now, sniffing your ironic exhalation of a laugh through her nose, reeling off lines in conversation that could go right into a book or may have come from one, counting off points on her fingers, though she becomes confused in her organization and after A and B switches to 3. And, like you, she seasons the pedantry with a touch of irony that has worked its way through the whole dish. Still, she can be cruel, which you never were, and her irony disguises uncertainty whereas yours expressed sympathy—for my distractions, your quandary, everyone's compromises. And, unlike you, she can speak with authority to children. When they would ask you a question about anything factual (mosquitoes, say) you could answer easily and at length: "They breed on water, all two thousand varieties, and they can find it anywhere, in puddles, swamps, even in the internodes of bamboo. The females do not become fertile till they've tasted blood—it's only the females, of course, who drink blood." But should those boys or girls ask you what they should *do* (with their lives or loves), then you'd grow perplexed, find a spot on your trousers, smile, frown, search the sky for help, and finally—remember?—blurt out a sentence that began and ended with "But—." You were the apostle of the particular. If we'd be walking through the flower district at night you'd nudge me and nod toward a plate glass window: half-way back in the store, beyond a floor littered with ferns, were two bunches of tender

214

purple gladioli in vases behind black metal bars, conspicuously pad-locked. You'd whisper, "I'm sure they're innocent."

Everyone here is impersonating you. I, for one. I've mastered your way of asking the most personal questions so directly that they invariably surprise the truth out of the flattered, flustered person I'm quizzing. Bob sits as you did, one leg draped over the other, hands in the air, head cocked to one side. Little Tom, no longer so little, has eyebrows like yours that slant downwards; if they were to join above the nose they'd form the Chinese character for *humanity, people* or *man.* If read in conjunction with the open mouth, they'd mean "the members of a family." These are family members, surely, for they ask after you, if only in the sense that "after" can suggest "loosely based on" an earlier model. Henrietta asks, "Do you watch much tee*vee* these days?" and, later, "Would you like a *hot dog*?" Both times she emphasizes these words, raising her pitch and volume until I gasp at her ventriloqual art; that was your way of dealing with the twentieth century. In Henrietta's mouth, this little vocal trick is as period as an old silk pilot's scarf stuffed into a new denim jacket. One young woman tells me she saw you half a dozen times at her uncle's parties when she was a child; everyone came to life when you entered the room, she says, though she thought you were nothing special. Your remarks were circulated, even a puzzling one, like a new but possibly edible fruit passed from one monkey's paw to another's. Because you drank too much, she says, you turned a whole generation alcoholic.

You'd be amused how many adults of both sexes claim to have been your lover. I'm lost in the crowd, my one distinction obscured by all these smoking torches. Belle—who stayed with us only that one sum-mer, right?—remembers the visit as a year and has letters to prove it, or at least lend credence to her version of things. Let her have her year; it alone makes her interesting to young people. Oddly enough, her husband has staked a claim over another year, though we scarcely knew him. Strangest of all, the Captain, ordinarily so careful about his "standing in the community," won't deny rumors that he once shared your bed, and this grotesque possibility is discussed in front of his grandchildren, the infamy of the deed, I guess, redeemed by the glory of its perpetrator. Dody, of course, has written her book about you and lives off the spiritual if not the material royalties. The Baganda of Africa judged a man's health by the length of his shadow; you must be thriving.

If there were no teenagers here I'd feel easier. At least I'd still be the youngest one among your friends, who would still oblige me by clucking over my nutty ideas. Remember the summer I had us sitting on tatami mats and filled the house with plants you ended up having to water? An old porch swing hung on chains was all I'd permit in the drawing room; after it fell under the Captain's weight, pulling down half the plaster with it, I declared the devastation "interesting" and preserved it: two patches of exposed insulation above, one the shape of China, the other of France, joined by a sagging seam that represented the mysterious affinity between those two countries. I'm sure everyone pitied you for having to live with a mad boy. Now I'm sane and long since an adult. At dusk and from a distance I'm still mistaken for seventeen, though every step toward me adds a month, a year—until, at ten paces, three decades descend on me and I'm an adorable gnome. My looks don't bother me except in one or two respects. I relied on them for so long to draw people to me that now I have no way to start a conversation. And the innocence of my face used to forgive my nasty teasing; now I've had to put kindness into my voice and words.

Experience has taught me you were kind but powerless and that my struggle to make you punish me, save me, stop me, teach me was misguided. You do not hang over the storm, firm hands in a sunlit study grasping a glass ball black with turbulence. Minute electrical charges craze the swirling clouds, but the cool glass sphere silences the thunderclaps, which are translated to your fingertips only in the way tremors are felt in a spoon by someone stirring a demitasse in Switzerland when the earthquake erupts in Tibet. Last night you were the Dalai Lama again and we were standing in a train together, swaying on metal straps. A mother and daughter sit looking up at us. I want them to see that you love me (they've recognized you), and just before you get off at your stop you do touch my shoulder. We speed on above turning, screaming prayer wheels, sutras on paper slips fluttering from the spokes—

"Are you all right?" someone, perhaps, yes, Belle asks as she leads me from the dance floor. A crowd parts for us, their lips compressed, eyes averted; once again I'm the mad boy! I press the glass of lemonade to my forehead and go through the motions of pretending to recover from a dizzy spell. My clothes, I notice, are fine, the trousers clean, shirt dry, shoes on, and when I lower my hand from my face I'm relieved to see it's not smeared with grease or blood.

Back in my rented bed I read this passage from a letter by a Renaissance writer whose contemporaries called him "Divine": "As for

216

myself, my eyes fill with tears when I remember how affectionately, in church and in the streets, the dear, sweet, lovely little Countess Madrina used to kiss me. The mischance through which I fell asleep beside her when I found her ill is now a stock scene of comedy . . . Alas, all these things are resolved into the air that carries away the sound of voices."

Picture the scene as you lie beside me in this single bed so lightly your side of the pillow isn't even dented. My father, though long since dead, is in the next room playing billiards with another man who holds the cue stick and watches twin serpents of cigarette smoke curl up the caduceus. As they stand back and contemplate the colored balls under the tent of scorching light, their faces are suspended in shadow, only the lining of their upper lips gleaming with an emerald-green plundered from the baize table. My father is one of those gloomy statues who guard the entrances of churches but when he bends down to make a shot, he changes from portal knight to gaudy dey, a ring on every finger and his bald dome shiny and veined.

I can hear families tiptoeing home through the night fog. An ice machine hums on the porch and from time to time the freezer ejects another shower of cubes. The yellow mosquito light outside above my door is snapped off; the darkness permits me to peek safely through the blinds at the patriotic bunting sopping up the fog. Another family, armed with a flashlight, glides past, the child in a yellow hood and raincoat. In the distance the Japanese lanterns still sway above the deserted square. A neighbor turns on a radio that blares news for no more than a minute.

Mother has always believed that travel is broadening, at least in the prospect, and for her now, deep in the folds of her tent hung with extinguished lamps and carpeted with a rug stitched in stylized elements from an oasis (a palm frond, a pomegranate, a fountain), the prospect has narrowed to the sliver of night seen through the parted flaps. She props her white cheek on a gemmed hand that smells of lanolin and rosewater and she sucks the mouthpiece of an unlit hookah; its water chamber bubbles and she tastes cold ash. In her imagination she turns over the miniatures of memory, then scatters them, so that each one overlaps and partially conceals the next.

I scatter mine, and see you climbing into my window after we fought, your spirit outstripping your clumsy body. Though I had resolved to be asleep, or, if awake, angry at you, I was awake and afraid for you. What else could I do but help you over the ledge? And here you are propped up in bed, reading, dawn leaking in through the curtains, your ashtray piled

217

high with cigarettes, each a new anxiety you'd selected, tasted, discarded, all of them bitter, a few still smouldering. When you said, "This can't go on, can it?" all I could think about were the records. Who would get the records? Now I loved your records as much as mine. I could deduce from your face that you thought I was laughing at you. Or maybe you were disgusted that I considered my only loss would be musical—but the mind, at least, threads its way like lace from knot to knot and the open eyelets *are* the pattern. The sun has bleached out most of the pictures at the beginning and the end of the album. Only those packed in the center are still vivid, and they are the ones in which the sultan sits in white robes with his beloved under a white arch against a night sky on which a scimitar moon has been painted in heavy gold leaf. Fruits, trees, and fountains in the garden beyond do not diminish in perspective. Rather, they remain large and distinct, crowding toward the viewer.

A billiard ball strikes another with a smart tap and the second rushes to its destination, sinks and rumbles through the subterranean workings of the table. In her tent a woman gathers pictures and returns them to a sturdy box lined with salmon-colored silk. In the fog two dogs call back and forth from one yard to another, Tim and Anxiety howling through the years, each filling the night with short, imperious yaps that test the depth, sound for echoes and, hearing none, hearing nothing but the antiphonal voice of the other animal, bark and bark and bark as though time were a burglar who could be frightened away.

I saw you many times after I left you, and you have to admit that we had some good evenings together. We'd talk about your new love or mine, and I think I was able to give you some excellent advice, though you never took it. I stayed over at your house a few nights and that meant a lot to me but not much to you, so I stopped doing it.

So many great men destroy the lives of those around them—lovers, wives. The wife imitates his extravagant vices at night but does not rise at dawn to pick her way through the party rubble to the study. She, too, consults the spirit world, winters in Greece, keeps odd hours, experiments with drugs, has a theory about evolution, hates Poulenc, listens to too much talk—but for her nothing comes of it. She becomes haggard and opinionated, while he stays pink-cheeked, curious, industrious. Eventually her enthusiasms narrow to macramé and vodka. Have I become your monster? Am I the ruined wife?

I was in Florida when Belle reached me at last. A man I'd just met had come home with me to the rented beach house. We had been engaged in violent sex (the violence was all in the things he whispered to me), and I debated whether to answer the insistent phone. I did. Belle asked me if I was sitting down. She asked me that twice.

"No, Belle," I laughed, "what does that matter?"

"Sit down," she repeated. I did. She told me that you had been ill for two weeks with bronchitis, which turned into pneumonia. Since you were very old you hadn't been able to fight it off. And you had died. And been buried. Then she told me at length and with real animosity all she had gone through in trying to locate me.

I thanked her and hung up. When I returned to the high, glassed-in room overlooking the beach the stranger asked me what had happened. He was very understanding and sweet—you would have liked him. He took me into the shower and bathed me and washed my hair, embracing me again and again. I cried so long I could hardly stand up under the assault of hot water. Then I poured us drinks and we talked for hours. Finally we made love after all; he was just as violent, even more violent than before, as though nothing had intervened; for some reason I was grateful.

After he left I put on shorts and walked along the beach and looked at the palms curving away from the ocean. My old adolescent feeling that it was odd to be a man rather than a woman, to live here rather than there, now rather than then, struck me again. I wanted to hurtle through space and time.

Satan stoops to make his opening shot in clouds of sulfur smoke; the cue ball, white as the sun, speeds across a green void and cracks open a firmament of colored, numbered spheres that roll to fill all the space we can ever know. The mother, sultana in a black felt tent, stoops to read the patterns woven into the carpet. She pictures lovers in that garden saying, each to each, "Happy are we within our sacred grove, two forms, perhaps, but one soul, one love. The dervish birds whirling within the trees wail songs conferring immortality. But bigger birds in paradise devour themselves with envy of that endless hour when we met and love, will laugh, have lost track of where we were, are—heaven? Iraq?"

I step out on the porch in bare feet. Gusts of fog hold me gently. I'm hungry but there's no place on the whole island still open at this hour, whatever the hour might be. It could be dawn already, but I can't tell—the weather will hide the light for hours. Everyone's asleep, tucked away in historic houses under heirloom quilts, a whole community whose only aberration was you. Perhaps Belle or the Captain is dreaming of you or me, and I glide through this fog as I might through their brains. When you slept you rubbed your hand over your eyes and nose in one precise half-circle—like a cat washing itself.

I'm sure I must be a wraith in someone's head right now; so many people looked at me oddly this afternoon when I walked up from the ferry landing to the square, bag in hand. Of course I'd forgotten it was a holiday, though one glance at the bunting and lanterns, the band-stand and the glasses of lemonade, reminded me.

I danced with Belle, and as we twirled another fat face dawned above a dark shoulder, then one drew out of shadows into the lantern light, and yet another person, in heavy age drag, gave herself away by her laugh. Not the sound (she was too far away for me to hear her) but her manner of throwing her head back with abandon while her precise, businesslike hands fussed and tugged at her cardigan to keep it from sliding off her shoulders. They all came over to me, our ancient rivalries abandoned, the difference between my age and theirs no longer significant or (in the eyes of the children) even noticeable. We were just glad to see one another. Whenever we gathered together in twos or threes you put in a star appearance—at least it felt that way. Everything was done in remembrance of you. It was so strange playing out this little piece before indifferent young eyes, as though we were members of a secret fellowship, now dissolved, introducing bits of ritual into casual conversation, each word or gesture thrilling the initiated.

I can picture you standing in our midst, drinking, deferential, modestly listening to someone's shapeless story flung out before you—and then you say something cutting, shears snipping so many yards into a pattern.

The saddest thing, the thing that makes me groan and step off the hotel porch into the night, is remembering how *modern* we all thought we were way back then. Old money, old names, these old houses were the legacy we ignored. For us there was only the figure in the foreground, standing so casually and confidently, yours, peering out into the night with a dreaming calm, then snapping your focus back onto Belle or the Captain. What would you say next? All of history—the panes in the windows with their violet tints and trapped air bubbles—was just a nice place to visit, but the old law was being lifted by you, word by word, the prohibitions broken, and some festivals dropped from the calendar. From a high place, belfry or minaret, I can see the garden and the strolling sultan and the beloved, wearing green hoods, the color of paradise. They are small but perfect.

The fog dematerializes the harbor and the boats, each gemmed with one ruby and one emerald, then floats the image up again from the bottom of the developing pan, and I sit down on a stone step, my left knee creaking. The creak startles me into thinking how arbitrary it is to be locked into this century, this language, this skin, and I stare out at myself with the humiliated dignity of a Civil War soldier, his blue eyes eerily white, looking at the camera as though to say, "Here I am, nineteen years old, a bit hungry, trying to remember the name of an old school chum I haven't seen for years, my toes cramped in my left boot; I'm not afraid of the bee circling the photographer's hooded head, though it would be funny to see him jump up, stunned, toppling the tripod—oh, God, you out there, take pity on me, on my left sideburn fractionally longer than the right, on my strong hand upon the saber hilt, and on my last joke resolved into the air that carries away all sound of voices."

And just as Tim and Anxiety bark at each other through the fog, so I call out to that soldier: "But I have no pity to offer, since I, too, am dying, and someone saw fit to play the same prank on me, imprisoning me within an antiquated tot's body, lacing me into a straitjacket that holds my arms folded in resignation before the maddening vision of a man or god who has died, gone away or never existed save in the tense, opaque presences of those things and people who, by virtue of claiming attention but denying the understanding, of demanding love at the cost of rewarding sympathy, must be addressed as "You." And indeed, after I have risen from the stone step that left its icy wet imprint on my skin and have resumed my prowl, the fronts of some houses congenially proclaim they are on my side, open to inspection, tolerant of what they see—they are all "I's" that speak to my experience, whereas other houses—incomprehensible, disturbing, yet brimming over with mysterious invitations to happiness or pain—they must be called "You." And the rest of the buildings on the island, that is most of them, are uncharged, and they are houses that want no pronouns.

Coming here on the ferry today I studied all the other people on the deck. The floor beneath my shoes pounded with the beat of the old engine and the air was pure with salt when it flowed but foul with gasoline and fish whenever we idled. The sea, an actress who'd had too much to drink, was everywhere at once, splashy, a swirl of ruffles.

The motor made so much noise no one could speak. We were silent and contemplative, seated or standing bodies, unmoving though the wind did its best to create the illusion of apparent motion by rippling our hair and clothes and placing us against a capricious, sluicing background. All to no avail, since the wind, like the confusion of angels around the throne of heaven, only emphasized the solidity of what does not move. As I looked at the other passengers, I could easily pick out those expressionless, intriguing beauties I address as *you*, those same faces, dark or fair, brooding or elated, whom I'd always believed I could love, even if I'd seen them only for a moment on a train or a bus or passing me on the street as I headed away from your dinner table, your saints, into the noisy, quickening night, its shouts muted by the containing glass sphere that you, or I, the magus, hold though it roll across a billiard table as green as the paradisal hoods of the sultan and his beloved within their garden, its pomegranate, palm and fountain besieged by mist and the howls of two lost dogs.

Picador

☐	**Burning Leaves**	Don Bannister	£2.50p
☐	**Making Love: The Picador Book of Erotic Verse**	edited by Alan Bold	£1.95p
☐	**The Tokyo-Montana Express**	Richard Brautigan	£2.50p
☐	**Bury My Heart at Wounded Knee**	Dee Brown	£3.95p
☐	**Cities of the Red Night**	William Burroughs	£2.50p
☐	**The Road to Oxiana**	Robert Byron	£2.50p
☐	**If on a Winter's Night a Traveller**	Italo Calvino	£2.50p
☐	**Auto Da Fé**	Elias Canetti	£3.95p
☐	**Exotic Pleasures**	Peter Carey	£1.95p
☐	**Chandler Collection Vol. 1**	Raymond Chandler	£2.95p
☐	**In Patagonia**	Bruce Chatwin	£2.50p
☐	**Sweet Freedom**	Anna Coote and Beatrix Campbell	£1.95p
☐	**Crown Jewel**	Ralph de Boissiere	£2.75p
☐	**Letters from Africa**	Isak Dinesen (Karen Blixen)	£3.95p
☐	**The Book of Daniel**	E. L. Doctorow	£2.50p
☐	**Debts of Honour**	Michael Foot	£2.50p
☐	**One Hundred Years of Solitude**	Gabriel García Márquez	£2.95p
☐	**Nothing, Doting, Blindness**	Henry Green	£2.95p
☐	**The Obstacle Race**	Germaine Greer	£5.95p
☐	**Meetings with Remarkable Men**	Gurdjieff	£2.95p
☐	**Roots**	Alex Haley	£3.50p
☐	**The Four Great Novels**	Dashiel Hammett	£3.95p
☐	**Growth of the Soil**	Knut Hamsun	£2.95p
☐	**When the Tree Sings**	Stratis Haviaras	£1.95p
☐	**Dispatches**	Michael Herr	£2.50p
☐	**Riddley Walker**	Russell Hoban	£2.50p
☐	**Stories**	Desmond Hogan	£2.50p
☐	**Three Trapped Tigers**	C. Cabrera Infante	£2.95p
☐	**Unreliable Memoirs**	Clive James	£1.95p
☐	**Man and His Symbols**	Carl Jung	£3.95p
☐	**China Men**	Maxine Hong Kingston	£2.50p
☐	**Janus: A Summing Up**	Arthur Koestler	£3.50p
☐	**Memoirs of a Survivor**	Doris Lessing	£2.50p
☐	**Albert Camus**	Herbert Lottman	£3.95p
☐	**The Road to Xanadu**	John Livingston Lowes	£1.95p
☐	**Zany Afternoons**	Bruce McCall	£4.95p
☐	**The Cement Garden**	Ian McEwan	£1.95p
☐	**The Serial**	Cyra McFadden	£1.75p
☐	**McCarthy's List**	Mary Mackey	£1.95p
☐	**Psychoanalysis: The Impossible Profession**	Janet Malcolm	£1.95p
☐	**Daddyji/Mamaji**	Ved Mehta	£2.95p
☐	**Slowly Down the Ganges**	Eric Newby	£2.95p
☐	**The Snow Leopard**	Peter Matthiessen	£2.95p

☐	**History of Rock and Roll**	ed. Jim Miller	£4.95p
☐	**Lectures on Literature**	Vladimir Nabokov	£3.95p
☐	**The Best of Myles**	Flann O' Brien	£2.95p
☐	**Autobiography**	John Cowper Powys	£3.50p
☐	**Hadrian the Seventh**	Fr. Rolfe (Baron Corvo)	£1.25p
☐	**On Broadway**	Damon Runyon	£3.50p
☐	**Midnight's Children**	Salman Rushdie	£3.50p
☐	**Snowblind**	Robert Sabbag	£1.95p
☐	**Awakenings**	Oliver Sacks	£3.95p
☐	**The Fate of the Earth**	Jonathan Schell	£1.95p
☐	**Street of Crocodiles**	Bruno Schultz	£1.25p
☐	**Poets in their Youth**	Eileen Simpson	£2.95p
☐	**Miss Silver's Past**	Josef Skvorecky	£2.50p
☐	**A Flag for Sunrise**	Robert Stone	£2.50p
☐	**Visitants**	Randolph Stow	£2.50p
☐	**Alice Fell**	Emma Tennant	£1.95p
☐	**The Flute-Player**	D. M. Thomas	£2.25p
☐	**The Great Shark Hunt**	Hunter S. Thompson	£3.50p
☐	**The Longest War**	Jacob Timerman	£2.50p
☐	**Aunt Julia and the Scriptwriter**	Mario Vargas Llosa	£2.95p
☐	**Female Friends**	Fay Weldon	£2.50p
☐	**No Particular Place To Go**	Hugo Williams	£1.95p
☐	**The Outsider**	Colin Wilson	£2.50p
☐	**Kandy-Kolored Tangerine-Flake Streamline Baby**	Tom Wolfe	£2.25p
☐	**Mars**	Fritz Zorn	£1.95p

All these books are available at your local bookshop or newsagent, or can be ordered direct from the publisher. Indicate the number of copies required and fill in the form below   11

....

Name_____
(Block letters please)

Address_____

_____

Send to CS Department, Pan Books Ltd, PO Box 40, Basingstoke, Hants
Please enclose remittance to the value of the cover price plus:
35p for the first book plus 15p per copy for each additional book ordered
to a maximum charge of £1.25 to cover postage and packing
Applicable only in the UK

While every effort is made to keep prices low, it is sometimes
necessary to increase prices at short notice. Pan Books reserve
the right to show on covers and charge new retail prices which
may differ from those advertised in the text or elsewhere